BLENHEIM ORCHARD

BLENHEIM ORCHARD

Tim Pears

BLOOMSBURY

First published 2007

Copyright © 2007 by Tim Pears

The moral right of the author has been asserted

Bloomsbury Publishing Plc, 36 Soho Square, London W1D 3QY

www.bloomsbury.com

A CIP catalogue record for this book is available from the British Library

Hardback ISBN 978 0 7475 8695 1
10 9 8 7 6 5 4 3 2 1

Export paperback ISBN 978 0 7475 8887 0
10 9 8 7 6 5 4 3 2 1

Typeset by Hewer Text UK Ltd, Edinburgh
Printed in Great Britain by Clays Ltd. St Ives plc

Bloomsbury Publishing, London, New York and Berlin

The paper this book is printed on is certified by the © 1996 Forest
Stewardship Council A.C. (FSC). It is ancient-forest friendly.
The printer holds FSC chain of custody SGS-COC-2061

FSC
Mixed Sources
Product group from well-managed
forests and other controlled sources

Cert no. SGS-COC-2061
www.fsc.org
© 1996 Forest Stewardship Council

For my mother, Jill

Part One

1

A Family in the Morning

Thursday 19 June 2003

Children interfere with their parents. Siblings mess with each other's minds. Wives intrude upon their husbands' dreams.

Ezra Pepin realised that he must have moved in his sleep, must have inched across the king-size bed. Sheena had drawn him towards her, that's what she'd done. Sleep-swollen, warm-blooded limbs brushed and rubbed against his. Was he still asleep? An aquatic detachment, limbs underwater.

His wife murmured in his ear, tugging him to her. He eased his naked body over the mattress.

What time was it? Ezra allowed his eyelids droopily to open, then close, enough to expose a grainy impression of the wall beyond. Four connecting lines of light, a rectangular frame in the gloom. The morning was trying to push in, to impose itself through cracks around the monochromatic curtains. No sound of children. How long did they have?

Sheena's warm leg between his legs, drawing him to her. Was she awake? Her hot, sleep-filled breath, murmuring non-word sounds – desire, encouragement – in his ear.

'Is it safe?' Ezra whispered.

His phallus in her hand. She took it into her. Ezra's breath

3

caught with gratitude; he relished unmuzzled sensation, the yielding, enveloping welcome.

'Are we safe?'

She murmured her assurance and pushed against him. He reciprocated. He didn't need to look to know that Sheena's eyes were closed, too. He pressed his right thigh against her; wondered whether Sheena wanted to be stimulated any further into wakefulness, even with pleasure, or whether she preferred to remain half-asleep, moving the way they were. Undulating in the dark. Deep underwater creatures, making somnambulistic love.

When it was over Ezra lay, breathing hard against her. He turned on to his back. Sheena rested on his chest.

Ezra opened his eyes. The sun had forced a little more light into the room. 'Tea?' he whispered.

Ezra tied the belt of his white towelling robe as he descended the stairs. A mug of good strong tea: the least he could fetch her in return for an unwarranted, first thing in the morning gift. Sheena knew how much her husband loved it then, the way an orgasm flushed the synapses of his brain and sent him out into the waking world with clarified perception and intent. Ezra tried to remember what it was he'd ever done to deserve such a mate; was unable to come up with anything beyond his habit of taking her tea in bed in the mornings. It didn't seem enough, somehow.

Judging by its weight, the kettle was sufficiently full. Ezra lowered it back on to its base and switched it on. Instantly there issued from it a low growl. He reached to the cupboard above for mugs, registering as he did so two things – a pair of connected facts – simultaneously: one, the kettle was already hot; two, there was someone in the walk-through sitting-room. He could only see her hand, on top of the back of the white sofa.

'What are you doing?' Ezra asked.

There was no reply. Ezra parked the mugs on the kitchen surface. Maybe she'd gone back to sleep. The kettle was boiling. He took teabags from the caddy, poured water.

4

'Waiting,' Blaise answered. She pulled herself up, the top half of her head appearing above the back of the sofa, a scowling puppet.

'What for?'

Blaise gazed at her father. 'I don't know,' she said, then lowered herself back out of sight.

'You want a cup of tea, darling?' Ezra asked. 'The kettle boiled. Maybe that's what you were waiting for.'

Another long pause. Using one of their fan-shaped sugar spoons that seemed to have been invented for the purpose Ezra squeezed the teabag from Sheena's china mug, lifted the red lid of the old nappy bucket they used as a compost bin, and dropped it in. He added semi-skimmed milk to the tea.

'No,' Blaise said.

Taking a route to the stairs via the sitting-room, Ezra paused beside the sofa. He laid his free hand on the back of Blaise's. She was wearing floral cotton pyjamas. She looked up at him, non-committal, her brown-eyed gaze uncannily like her mother's even though Sheena's irises were blue.

'Back in a sec,' he said.

Sheena was surely asleep. Her lips were slightly open: she looked stunned in that way in which a person awake never does. Ezra didn't want to say her name, to tell her that her mug of tea was here, in case he woke her. But if she was only dozing then he ought to let her know, otherwise she might not hear him, might carry on lying there longing for that first delicious sip, be severely disappointed to find the mug on her bedside table in ten minutes' time, cold, a creamy skin on its surface. He whispered her name. She didn't stir.

'Your tea's here,' he said a fraction louder. Nothing. He placed the mug on the table with a measured audible thump, and left the room.

Sunlight poured into the house through every east-facing window. Entering the living-room Ezra said, 'It's crazy you waking so early at your age. You know you'll . . .'

The white sofa cushions held only the impression of Blaise's sturdy form. Looking around, Ezra discovered her in the kitchen, standing in front of the open fridge, one hand on the door handle, staring at whatever was inside. The cool, bright contents. Maybe, Ezra thought, Blaise wasn't awake either. She was kind of sleep-walking, like her mother. Teenage girls did that, didn't they? Moved their bodies around the house in their sleep. Or was it objects they moved?

Blaise closed the fridge door with a sigh, which could have come from the hinge. She turned towards her father. The room was full of light.

'What shall we have for breakfast?' he asked.

'I was wondering . . .' she began.

'Hey!' Ezra said. 'How about a fry-up?'

Blaise winced. 'Are you kidding, Daddy?'

'A slap-up mixed grill. Sausages and bacon.' Ezra strode over. 'Plenty of eggs. Scrambled. Fried. Whatever.'

'I don't think so, Dad.'

'Black pudding, Admiral. Haggis.'

'Gross.'

'Hash browns. Baked beans.' Ezra looked in cupboards, checked the fridge, frowning.

'That is so unhealthy, Daddy.'

Ezra shook his head. 'We have not a single one of these items in the canteen. Anyway, you're right.' He screwed up his face. 'How did people eat all that meat and grease for breakfast and *do* anything afterwards? Will we ever know such pleasure again?'

Blaise shrugged.

'I'll tell you. Forget breakfast, Admiral. Brunch. Saturday. We'll go for a family jog, all of us, what do you say? Stagger back sweating, gasping. And starving!'

Blaise stared at her father. Then a grin broke on her blank face. 'Permission to speak, Flight Lieutenant?'

'Permission granted, Admiral.'

'It's a spiffing wheeze.'

'Why, thank you, sir. Of course we'll have strictly segregated

6

duties, absolutely no blurring of rank. If you do the eggs, Admiral, that's your job, do you understand me?

'Yes, Flight Lieutenant.'

'No one else touches the eggs. No one! You can overdo them, underdo them, scramble them to a sorry pulp. That is your job, your responsibility, and no one else's. Are we clear?'

'Clear as mud.'

'Will that be all, sir?'

Blaise looked very solemn. She frowned, and nodded. 'It will, Flight Lieutenant. Thank you for your help.'

'You're welcome, Admiral. At ease.'

Blaise helped herself to a glass of milk. Ezra watched. It was a quarter to seven in the morning and Blaise had forgotten for a moment that she was an adolescent, enmeshed in the disaccord of puberty, had allowed herself to act like a nine-year-old. She even gave him a milky kiss as she left the room. He called to her before she got into the hallway. Blaise turned.

'Don't go back to sleep now,' he said.

Blaise smiled, and departed. Ezra sat at the kitchen table, sipping his tea. It seemed to him, now that he thought about it, that he'd been demoted. Didn't he use to be a Wing Commander? Or maybe that was the rank they'd allocated Sheena, who didn't actively participate in the game but would frequently be referred to by the others. He did recall that Hector was the Brigadier; when they first began Hector would say, 'I'm the Biggie Dear.' Yes, Ezra admitted, it was some time since they'd last played.

The sound of footsteps on the stairs. Identifiable at once, each member of the family's particular weight upon the carpet. The length of the pause between each tread. These footsteps reached the ground, approached the kitchen. They paused outside. A three-year-old boy hid, plotting.

His father began singing. 'Everyone is sleeping in my house.' An improvised ditty. 'I'm all on my own, quiet as a mouse.'

Louie jumped into the kitchen doorway. 'Boo!'

Ezra acted out a major heart attack, from which he barely recovered. His son was pleased beyond reason; pleased with

7

himself, with his father's performance, with the tickling, vengeful hug Ezra gave him.

Scrutinised by his younger son, Ezra Pepin stretched up above the fitted cabinets in the kitchen, clapped cereal packets together, and brought them two at a time to the table. Weetabix and Cheerios. Cornflakes and Shredded Wheat. Extending his long arms, reaping Oaty Bites and Shreddies, Golden Grahams and Bran Flakes.

On top of the wall cabinets was the only place in their kitchen to store them. Sheena, on tiptoe, would complain, 'I can't . . . *reach*, damn it. Why do you *put* them up there, Ez?'

It was her tall husband to whom the conducting of breakfast customarily fell. Sugar Puffs and Frosties. Special K and All Bran. Louie Pepin didn't take his eyes off his father for a second. He observed proceedings with a three-year-old tyrant's beady vigilance: the boy had established as a point of principle that not a single grain of cereal be allowed into his bowl, never mind past his lips, until the entire phalanx of packets had been lined up on the kitchen table in front of him.

'There you go, Peanut, that's the lot. Louie?' Ezra looked wildly around the kitchen. 'Peanut. Where on earth are you? Help.'

Louie slid a box of Rice Krispies sideways to reveal his grinning face.

'Thank God,' his father gasped. 'I thought you'd disappeared. What a relief. Now, which one do you fancy?'

'Wait,' Louie ordered, suddenly serious again, transferring his attention to his cereal bowl: glazed on the outside with the black and white hexagons of a football, a pitch was marked out on the inside. Louie shifted it around, making minute adjustments, until the pitch was at a precise horizontal to him. When he was satisfied with this geometry, he surveyed the panoply of cereals.

'Take your time,' his father yawned. 'No hurry, old bean,' he said, closing his eyes, snoring.

'Cheerios!' Louie announced. Ezra woke and poured: airy morsels of sugared wheat tumbled into Louie's bowl with an insubstantial patter. Milk followed. Louie lifted a heaped spoon, emptied the contents into his mouth and chewed, staring at the wall ahead with the glassy gaze of a ruminant.

Ezra made two rounds of toast, spread one with raspberry jam and one with acacia honey, and carried the plate and a second cup of tea upstairs. The curtains were still drawn: it took some moments for Ezra's eyes to adjust to the semi-dark. Pillows stacked up behind her, Sheena was sitting up in bed, with her eyes closed. She opened one of them as Ezra placed the tea and toast on her bedside table, as if studying him through a telescope. He picked up the empty mug, leaned over, and kissed her. She murmured thanks as he did so.

Life before the invention of mirrors was hard to imagine. It was a relief to Blaise Pepin that her parents had chosen to send her to a school where, within wide and tolerable bounds, she could wear what she wanted. Neither was she sorry not to be a Townie or a Goth, dressed in a uniform of their own every day of their lives. No, not at all. It was just this moment of a morning that was a bore. This moment of revision. Oh, Blaise could decide what to wear. She could take a look at her wardrobe as she had just now, grab knickers and bra, put on these combats, vest, shirt. It wasn't that. That wasn't a problem. No, the only problem was that, once attired, she always seemed to change her mind. Looking in this mirror, here in front of her, she realised she appeared too short. Too fat. Too pale. Too spotty. She'd have to start again; this is what took the time.

Louie swallowed another spoonful of Weetabix Banana Crisp Minis. Beside him, his father listened out for the snap and thud of his newspaper's arrival on the doormat. Ezra gazed at the wall clock with drowsy eyes. Half-past seven. That lazy paper-boy was late again. As if reading were a habit he needed to feed Ezra perused the cereal boxes surrounding his younger son. There were two identifiably different kinds. The colourful cartons which Ezra bought – and Louie chose to eat from: these contained *complex carbohydrates to help kids concentrate*, they were *great sources of bran fibre*, they could *kick start your day*. They had free gifts inside, masks to cut out, coupons to send off along with a trifling sum of money for exciting monsters, robots, cars.

Then there were dull, neglected packets of cereal Sheena had bought, which were organic, or *biologique*. Wheat free, gluten free. Vegetarian, vegan. No sugar, no dairy, no soya, no GM, no hydrogenated fats. No free gifts. Reasons to eat organic: *Treat your body like a temple. Create balanced ecological communities. Blossom the planet.*

It was awfully odd. Ezra could imagine the marketing gang at work falling on such a brief. 'Sell organic to children? A breeze, Ez!' Or was he missing something? Was there some moral nuance he simply couldn't see? Some ethical incompatibility between natural product and product marketing? More plausibly: maybe the manufacturers weren't geared up to cope with great demand. Maybe those companies didn't *want* to grow. Awfully strange, really.

'Weetabix!' Louie requested.

'I don't know how anyone can eat that,' mused a quiet voice.

Startled, Ezra looked up and saw that they'd been joined at the other end of the table by his elder son. All Hector's life he'd been giving his father these jolts, with his ability to transmigrate from one spot in the house to another without making a sound. Hector was gazing now out of the window.

'Have you had your toast?' Ezra asked.

Hector turned his thin head slowly, though when his eyes came to rest on his father it seemed to Ezra to take his son a further few fractions of a second to focus. The boy carried with him his own time delay, his own faint blur, as if eleven years had not been long enough for Hector to quite get used to having a body. He looked back to the window before answering, softly, 'No.'

'Don't you think you should?'

'Not really, Daddy,' Hector answered vaguely, his attention apparently focused on some spectacle outside. Then, as if a gaggle

10

of maidens in school uniform were passing through their back garden and made the thought occur to him, Hector said, 'It's girls who need a big breakfast.'

'Excuse me?' Ezra said, and yawned.

'In performance tests,' Hector murmured, 'boys do best when they're hungry.'

'What are you on about?'

'It's true,' Hector said, nodding as if to himself. 'Girls do better when they're fully fed. Porridge. Toast and honey.'

'You need to eat, Hec.'

Hector scratched his dry scalp through his thin brown hair. 'Mood is also a factor.'

'Hector.'

'It says so in the paper. A new study. Go ahead, Daddy. Read it.'

Hector slid the *Independent* across the table, towards the log jam of cereals.

Ezra felt his teeth clench. 'I wish you wouldn't *do* that. It's *my* paper, for God's sake.' It looked as if the boy had taken the newspaper apart to make firelighters, then changed his mind and crumpled the pages more or less back together. 'This was not in the contract,' Ezra lamented.

'Blaise reads it too, Daddy.'

'She doesn't mutilate a newspaper when she reads it,' Ezra pointed out. 'I mean, why do you have to destroy it?'

Hector smiled. 'You sound like Arthur Conan Doyle, Daddy. If someone else got to the freshly delivered copy of *The Times* before him, he'd refuse to read it and sulk just like you.'

'I'm not sulking, my boy. I'm reprimanding you.'

'Oaty Bites!' Louie yelled.

Ezra shook his head. As he poured Oaty Bites into Louie's bowl, the cereal packet offered Ezra Pepin helpful wisdom. *Try to avoid worry and anger. Thinking positively about life and anticipating good solutions can help your well-being.*

'By the way, it's the first day of summer,' Hector informed his father and brother.

'Today?'

11

Hector frowned. 'Well, actually tomorrow,' he said, 'if you want to split hairs, Daddy.'

Ezra followed his son's gaze through glass towards the sheer, unconflicted blue sky. The day lay out there, hours of benevolent light upon this island, a day calling out for human participation. When Ezra looked back, Hector was gone from the table.

In the almost dark Sheena Pepin lay on her curled side, beneath the white cotton sheet, in a state of perfect happy rest. Even though she'd given Ezra sex and been to the bathroom, put on pyjamas, drunk the tea that Ezra had brought her and eaten toast, she'd still been able to slip back into this dozy bliss. Her limbs were heavy, too heavy to lift, though as long as she let them rest on the mattress she had, rather, a sensation of weightlessness. It was as if the bed were floating in space. Exactly the right height of pillows was under her head; no neck or shoulder muscle ached. Sheena lay in a foetal position, and she had only to scrunch up a little tighter, or stretch out minutely, and her body's pleasure became magically exaggerated; the whole of her skin luxuriated in warm-blooded languor.

Dozing on a Thursday morning. It seemed to Sheena that she was nothing but a fraud. The drive which, in her opinion, set her apart from others was a sham; left to her own devices she'd like nothing better than to languish here till noon. Today and every other day. Nothing but a lazy sensualist, heedless of her burdens and her duties.

Tonight, Sheena knew, she and Blaise should go to bed as early as Louie, since they had to be up well before dawn tomorrow. Maybe that foreknowledge contributed to her stupor now. She reached out a reluctant arm, pressed the button on her clock to illuminate its digital figures. Seven forty-five. It really was time to get up. Then, as if to mock the disparity between such resolution and her true desire, she felt a familiar body crawl into bed behind her. Sheena rolled over. He nestled against her.

'Mummy?'

'Yes, Hector?'

'Nothing.' He buried his head in her arm.

'What is it, Hec?'

After a while Hector said, 'I don't think Ed likes me.'

'Ed?' Sheena inhaled the dry smell of Hector's hair. 'Ed Carlyle?'

'Yes.'

'What's the problem, sweetheart? Does it matter if your friend's brother likes you or not?'

'I like him.'

Sheena caressed the back of Hector's neck. 'What does Jack say?'

'I don't know.'

'I love you,' she whispered. She kissed his forehead, squeezed his bony body to her. 'Everybody loves you, Hec. Come on. Time to get up, both of us.'

The dishwasher bothered Ezra Pepin. The way you had to rinse bowls before you put them in, otherwise they'd come out with flecks of cereal stuck fast. If you rinsed them under the tap for a further two seconds they'd be clean anyway. But Sheena claimed that when Ezra washed up by hand he failed to rinse properly: you could taste the washing-up liquid.

It was probably his fault, Ezra reflected: no doubt he'd bought a cheap, special-offer model, when everyone knew the thing to do was to consult a consumer magazine and purchase what they recommended, some exorbitant Bosch or Siemens that did the damn job properly and didn't annoy you every day with its ineptitude.

'Daddy,' Blaise wailed as she came into the kitchen. 'Have you seen my jacket?'

'Which one?'

'You know. The brown denim one.'

Ezra dried his hands on a tea towel. 'No idea, darling.'

Blaise groaned. The upper half of her body crumpled. It was fortunate her legs remained firm.

'Ask Mum.' It occurred to Ezra that he'd read somewhere that women tended to possess a sense of where each family member's possessions were around the house, refiguring the shifting map from moment to moment. 'She's meant to know that kind of –'

'She said to ask you.'

Ezra frowned. 'When did you last wear it?'

'When I came home from school.'

'What did you do when you came home from school?'

Blaise stared at the kitchen tiles, then up at her father. 'Played football with Lou.'

'I did win!' was proclaimed from the table.

Ezra nodded. 'You left it outside. It's draped over the low branch of the apple tree.'

Blaise confirmed the claim with her own eyes and, half-smiling, said to her father, 'Well done, Daddy.'

'It's a gift,' he said.

Some had been up for hours; others dashed pell-mell downstairs, half-dressed, hair askew. It didn't matter: all five members of the Pepin family endeavoured to leave the house at the same moment. The hallway was the location for a rugby scrum in which no one could find the ball. Hector trudged towards the door weighed down by a bulging rucksack.

'You'll need remedial osteopathy by the time you're a teenager,' Ezra lamented. 'Do you not have a locker?'

'They're not cool,' Hector said. He shrugged, perhaps to indicate to his father that hauling all his textbooks to and from school didn't make much sense to him either; this happened just to be the way things were.

Sheena was tying the laces of Louie's new trainers, cursing Ezra for not having bought ones with Velcro straps.

'What about Blaise?' Ezra asked. 'She never seems to bring anything home.'

'She's not so punctilious about her homework,' Sheena said. 'You got Lou's bike helmet? And she doesn't care what other people say is cool. Do you, Bee?'

'Depends who's saying it,' Blaise said. 'I'm off.'

'You see, boy?' Ezra said. He attached bicycle clips to his ankles. 'Who cares what's cool?'

Hector looked crossly at the carpet. 'People don't bother her,' he

14

said, before stumbling out of the door in his sister's footsteps, closely followed by the rest of his family, who, apart from Peanut Louie in the child-seat on the back of his father's bicycle, dispersed in a multiplicity of directions.

2

The Dustbin-lid Hunt

Friday 20 June

Overhead lighting along the low ceiling. The windowless corridor appeared overexposed. There was a throbbing, a dull pulsation behind his eyes. Ezra leaned forward, resting his elbows on his knees and clasping his hands as if in prayer. He gazed at his black brogues on the grey dusty floor. The intricately patterned perforations and decorative stitching impressed him. It must have been done by an automaton, he realised. Although when he thought about it he seemed to remember seeing the word *hand-stitched* somewhere – and considering the price he'd paid for them, at that shoe shop next to Walters in Turl Street, it was possible. It was likely.

It occurred to Ezra Pepin, as he stared at the zigzag edge of a seam, that the idea of a machine doing such laborious work was preferable to a human being. But then he corrected himself: it was terrible, actually, that shoemakers around the world, skilled artisans, had been and were continuing to be made redundant by automation. It was tragic. Although, on the other hand, the truth was that he didn't really feel comfortable with the notion that a faraway cobbler, knuckles arthritic and swollen, was losing his sight in a squalid factory just so that an Englishman could wear these beautiful leather shoes.

Ezra studied the left brogue. At the front a host of tiny perforations swirled around a triangle of larger ones. He pictured the awl of a machine dancing across flat cuts of leather as it punched the holes. He could visualise the dance clearly, and hear it, too: in his mind a staccato rhythm became alloyed with melody. There was something sublime, Ezra figured, in this mechanical choreography, these ballet-dancing needles. Yes, indeed. A mechanical sublime.

All of a sudden his shoes were cast into shade.

'Mr Pepin? Would you come this way, please.'

He looked up. A uniformed policewoman was standing in front of him. She'd made an unsmiling request. She was a little older than the others. Close-cropped hair, faintly Asiatic eyes and cheekbones; a little racial colour. Satisfied she'd got his attention, she turned and walked away. A hefty, solemn, authoritative figure. Ezra followed her around a corner, along another corridor, to a door through whose small window she invited him to peer.

'Is this your daughter?'

The glass in the door was grubby, as if too many people had leaned too close in order to look through. Smeared with grease from the skin of their foreheads. More likely, though, when you thought about it, was that the smudges were on the other side, incarcerated sinners pressing their noses to the glass, praying for help. Or maybe, receiving no answer, they'd spat at the glass in protest. It was interesting, really quite intriguing. It surely revealed, whatever else, something about cutbacks among cleaners in municipal employment.

'Mr Pepin?'

Actually, Ezra spotted when he looked closer, there was something *inside* the glass: strips of wire were embedded within it. To strengthen it, presumably. Or make it shatterproof? So there could be no splinters with which suspects could inflict harm upon themselves? Both, perhaps.

'Mr Pepin. I said, *Is that your daughter?*'

Ezra's perspective altered abruptly, as if someone else had wrenched the focus of his vision. Hunched on the seat of a moulded plastic chair, a chubby girl hugged her folded legs. Her face was

17

hidden between her knees. She looked too small, Ezra thought, to be thirteen, almost fourteen years old; had curled up tight and created an optical illusion, that of a much younger self. The ground beneath his leather shoes began to move, as if St Aldate's police station had been built too close to the river.

'Mr Pepin?'

Ezra pressed a steadying hand against the door surround. 'What?'

'Is that your daughter?'

'My daughter?' He gazed at the coiled form. 'Yes. There she is. That's her.' He took a deep breath.

'She wouldn't tell us her name.'

'Why not? I mean, she wouldn't?'

'Refused to say a single word. Even to make a request.'

Ezra gazed at his girl. Her feet, her muddy Doc Martens, up off the ground, gathered against her haunches, as if there'd been something dangerous scuttling across the floor. 'A request? What for?'

'A lawyer? A phone call?' He registered the slight shrug of the policewoman's shoulders beside him. 'A glass of water.'

Her head was close to Ezra's, as they each gazed through the rectangle of glass. He detected a sourness in her breath. I must act well now, he told himself. I have nothing but humility, and contrition, to offer. Perhaps this woman has authority to let Blaise go.

Ezra stared through the greasy window at his daughter. Behind him, indistinct voices murmured along the corridor. A throb in his forehead; and tiny pieces of grit behind his eyelids. There was nowhere to hide. Light shone everywhere.

He'd barely got in to work an hour earlier that Friday morning, having seen Hector off to Cherwell with Jack Carlyle and cycled Louie to the Montessori Nursery in Wolvercote, when his mobile rang. He saw the number, then heard the open-air ambience of a crowd.

'Minty? What's up?'

18

'I'm outside the Wasteland, Ezra.'

'What's happening?'

'I can't see. They're keeping us on this side of the bridge.'

'Can't you tell whether work's started?'

'I don't know. It's all quiet over there. But Ezra, it's Blaise. There's been an accident. An ambulance arrived, siren wailing.'

'Oh, God.'

'No, no. Blaise is all right. She was taken away in a police car. Right in front of me.'

'A police car?'

'That's all I know.'

'Family crisis,' Ezra told Chrissie Barwell, snapping his bicycle clips back around his ankles. 'Cover for me, can you? I'll call you.'

He pedalled his hybrid bike along Oxpens Road directly towards St Aldate's police station, Louie's child-seat rattling behind him. It seemed plausible that he might reach there before the car, waylay the arresting officers, relieve them of their underage nuisance before they began a hard-to-rewind process of paperwork. He cycled fast past the College of Further Education and the ice-rink, that marooned galleon beached on the grass.

'I'll look into it, sir,' the male officer at the otherwise empty Reception told him through a glass partition. 'Take a seat, please.'

Ezra realised it was quite possible that they weren't even bringing Blaise to this station. 'I just want to know –'

'Yes, sir. I'll look into it. Please take a seat.'

Ezra Pepin sat down. He got up again, went to the door, stared at the indifferent traffic crawling in and out of the centre of Oxford over Folly Bridge. He regretted having put on a vest this hot morning: he could feel it stuck to his back. He watched policemen and women entering and exiting the station through a gate to the side, by car and bike, on foot. The older generation of policemen – his age, in other words – were hulks. Young ones tended to be shorter and slighter than their senior colleagues, in some strange policing reversal of the general trend.

'If I was dictator for a day,' Sheena had once declared to Ezra,

19

soon after they met, 'the first thing I'd abolish would be uniforms.' Odd, specific moments embedded in one's memory.

He returned to the bench running around two walls of the Reception area, gazed at a poster that asked whether he was making life too easy for criminals. Probably, Ezra admitted. He was dumb enough. How stupid could a man be? It had not occurred to him that Blaise might be arrested. Sheena, sure, many times, though she'd never been so much as cautioned. Or maybe it had occurred to him, if he were honest, a possibility bobbing into consciousness that, because it was unwelcome, he'd shunted off to a margin of his mind. He'd have to have it out with Sheena; he'd give her what for, that's what he'd do.

Silence. Had planes vacated the sky? Voices were hushed, banging doors muffled. All was quiet. Had cars stopped whining past? Blaise listened hard. She could hear something: blood pummelling her ears. Her heartbeat walloping her ribs.

She stared through her knees, between her feet, at a spot on the dirty floor. She could make out fluff, a human hair, the texture of the hard ground, but she kept on gazing until such details ceased to make sense. There was something wrong with the light. Sunlight shone through the small window. On this spot upon which she focused, sunshine met evidence of the malfunctioning ceiling bulb. Flickering in the dust and grit: a painting whose colours were alive. Blaise gawped at shimmering fluctuations of white and yellow light, and it was as if there were a place in her brain to which the image was filtered directly. A kind of correspondence was set up between the vision and nerve cells in her grey matter, and there they played together, like musical notes of yellow, like sparkling tastes of light, her anxiety dissipating as she gawked, blank-brained, mesmerised.

'Would you come through, sir?'

The Reception officer buzzed open the door, and met Ezra on the other side. 'Take a seat there, please. Someone will be with you in a moment.'

Over there was the desk sergeant; activity familiar from TV. Once you got through the door from the municipal Reception you were admitted to, implicated in, a recognisably forbidding process. Here were the police, plain-clothed and uniformed. And two or three shifty-looking individuals: suspects. Undercover detectives, maybe. Lawyers, even. Ezra had no idea who they were. He felt bereft of knowledge and power, aware on his daughter's behalf of the fundamental threat that made even the most innocent among us guilty in the presence of police: the threat of incarceration. She was in custody, he had to get her out. But how? He had no authority here. Of course: he should get a lawyer. He should ring Dan, one of his tennis quartet, a solicitor.

He had gazed down at his shoes, and become lost in thought. A shadow had come over him. Ezra had looked up. A uniformed policewoman, Asiatic, with bruised eyes, was standing in front of him. 'Mr Pepin? Would you come this way, please.'

And now here he was, peering through the grilled window at Blaise, hunched up on a plastic chair. 'She's refused to say a word.' The policewoman's head was close to Ezra's. Her breath smelled old.

'I'm sure,' Ezra said, 'whatever she's done –'

'She attacked a security guard.'

'Attack? That's not possible. My daughter wouldn't –'

'She hit him in the face.'

'No. I'm sorry,' Ezra said, shaking his head vigorously. 'I believe someone must have made a mistake.'

Ezra turned aside from the window. He found the policewoman waiting, and he glanced away from her interrogative gaze, off down the empty corridor. It was as if whatever nonsensical act Blaise was accused of was merely a set-up, a deceipt, to ensnare her father. Ezra was actually the one under suspicion here. He wiped his forehead with the back of his hand.

'Might school,' the policewoman said, 'not be a more appropriate place for a girl than a violent political protest?'

'Yes, yes. Thank you, officer,' Ezra said. It was intolerably hot in

21

here. 'I appreciate your advice. Shall I take my daughter home now?'

The policewoman studied Ezra's face, as if she were remembering a mugshot from some previous, unprosecuted crime. 'This is an extremely serious matter, Mr Pepin.'

'Of course it is.' He mustn't argue. He needed to agree, to keep calm.

'We've heard from the security guard in question. His express wish, apparently, is that no charge is brought. He says it was an accident.'

Ezra bit his lip to keep from smiling. 'I'm sure it was.'

'His colleagues are prepared to support him by claiming to have seen nothing. And we assume that your daughter's comrades will prove to be similarly blind.'

'No doubt it was a minor –'

'He's up at A and E now. She broke the man's nose.'

Ezra shook his head.

'Fractured his left cheekbone.'

Ezra was unable to match the words to imaginable action. Blaise break someone's nose? The words described some cartoonish parallel to reality. 'I'm sorry . . .'

'Be grateful she's your daughter, that's all, not your son. And there's a man out there with an outdated sense of shame.'

Ezra sensed the unwavering gaze upon him. He struggled, failed, to meet it and hold it for more than a testing moment. 'I am,' he said quietly.

'I'd advise you to keep an eye on her, Mr Pepin. There's a Family Support Network in Oxford. They offer counselling. Individual. Group.' She sighed. 'It can help families through a difficult patch.'

Ezra accepted the leaflet the policewoman passed to him, and saw her fingers move towards the door. 'I'll call them,' he said.

The policewoman's hand faltered, and less reached than came to weary rest on the door handle. 'No, you won't,' she said.

'Excuse me?'

'You people never do.'

22

Ezra lifted his gaze, and met the woman's frank stare. 'You people?' he asked.

'Middle class. Professional.'

'Not so professional.'

'Educated. Your children slip off the rails, you let them, you know they'll reclaim their advantage in due course.'

'I don't know. I mean, I hope so.'

'Oh, you worry about their grades, and CVs, when they make mistakes in full view of the world. Then, what?'

Ezra had the feeling he was hearing a speech its maker had been rehearsing for years. What parental inadequacy had she perceived in him, to bring it out of her here, now?

She turned the door handle. Ezra followed her into the room. It smelled of sweat and dust and stale smoke.

'Your father's here,' the policewoman said.

The figure in the chair remained as still as she had been all the while, but stiffened, sinews tensing.

'He's come to take you home.'

Ezra stepped out from behind the policewoman, and began to nod his head gravely, although his daughter could not yet see him. He had to stop himself from rushing over, hugging her. Who knew what game the police could play? After what seemed like a long time there was a twitch of movement around Blaise's knees; her plaited brown hair fluttered; she raised her head slowly, and turned towards her father. There was a puffiness around her red-rimmed eyes.

'I'm here, Blaise,' Ezra intoned. 'Let's go.'

Neither of them spoke as they left the police station, crossed the road, walked up St Aldates. Ezra hailed a taxi. It veered to the kerb. They climbed in; sat side by side. There was only one thing Ezra wanted to do, and that was to wrap his arms around his daughter and hug her tight to him. But he hesitated: there was a distance between them, and he sensed it was Blaise's privilege no less than her obligation to bridge it.

It wasn't just the horror of what he'd heard her falsely accused

23

of. Blaise's birth, the first of their children, had been the mystic event of Ezra Pepin's life. He'd been lifted bodily from a terminus at the end of evolution: placed instead within its abundant procession. Watching Blaise grow up was a daily reiteration of this genetic truth. She presented her father with both himself reproduced beyond his lifespan and an improvement upon him. The boys, coming after, were remarkable events in themselves, simply. Ezra was glad the children had arrived in that order, that it was a female, a yin to his yang in nature's reproductive division, who'd delivered revelation.

At this moment, however, as they sat in the taxi with a sliver of space between his left arm and her right, Ezra understood he'd been deceiving himself. It was no more than a commonplace, the bond between father and daughter: the man responds primarily to the child's reiteration not of himself but of his mate; and if he sees himself in her as well what is that but narcissism?

Ezra gazed at Christ Church College, through the open gate to the great quad. The traffic was barely moving. Ezra didn't mind. He stole discreet glances at Blaise: there was a residue of camouflage paint on her face, flakes of it dried in her hair. He figured he'd accomplished a noble deed, rescuing his daughter from a police procedural labyrinth. He tried to picture a bloody scene among the trees at the Wasteland, but he could only visualise Blaise as a potential victim of violence, not its perpetrator; the scene fragmented in his mind, echoing the chaos which he assumed had caused Blaise to be arrested for something she had nothing to do with.

Blaise's view, out of the window on her side, was of the shops beyond Pembroke Street. The taxi shuffled forward behind a convoy of buses, the sun glaring off their windows: each of them stopped across from the Town Hall to disgorge a horde of park-and-ride shoppers, whom Blaise observed marching along the pavement, striding towards the centre. They looked like they'd woken from hibernation with a tremendous hunger, and come rushing into the city.

Blaise thought of the Wasteland. Once an industrial tip, it was closed forty years ago and covered with a layer of topsoil. Nature reclaimed it. The seeds of trees, shrubs, weeds found their own wind- or bird-dropped way there. Roots grew, fingering in amongst brick, glass bottles, rusting tubular metal. Plants anchored themselves, with their subliminal persistence, in layers of rubble and mud. The surface of the Wasteland sank and buckled.

The Pepins picked blackberries there every autumn, a family ritual, followed by evenings of steaming jam jars and bubbling pans as one or other of her parents made bramble jelly that would last all year. The Wasteland was Louie's jungle, Hector's Sherwood Forest. Blaise recalled the dusk five years earlier that Sheena and Minty took her and Ed to listen to a nightingale on the far side, by the railway line.

She looked back at the shoppers. They were all in a hurry. It was amazing how many of their faces were set in expressions of great determination. Whatever it was they wanted was vital; nothing and no one was going to get in their way. The taxi crawled around the corner past Queen Street and Cornmarket. What if the streets were empty? Blaise wondered. The shops still and silent. Lights blinking off. People gone. Buildings ageing, decaying, crumbling. How long would this urban growth take to become a wasteland? Coltsfoot breaking through the tarmac. Ivy throttling the ruins.

Her father's voice interrupted her thoughts. 'Tell me,' he said. 'What happened, Blaise? It's not true, is it? That you hit a security guard. What really happened?'

Blaise kept her attention on a line of tired, sated consumers, waiting for a bus to take them and their shopping bags back home.

'What went on there?' Ezra asked.

People are greedy, Blaise knew that. We all are, in one way or another. The difference was in what you were greedy *for*. Why they gobbled up whatever scraps were thrown at them, that's what was so sad.

'Blaise? You didn't talk to the police, darling. You can talk to me.'

Blaise turned to her father. It wasn't that she didn't want to answer, it was just that there was something swelling in her throat, and if she opened her mouth it would come shaking out of her. Eyes shut, she swallowed it back down.

'What happened?'

'I didn't mean to, Daddy,' Blaise said, snuffling and taking deep breaths in between. 'I didn't mean to.' She shook her head, mumbled something to the window. She was sniffing hungrily, as if drawing sustenance from a fragrance in the air.

Ezra put a hand on her shoulder. 'Come here,' he said, pulling her to him. 'It's okay. Come here.'

Blaise's warm breath smelled sweet, as if she'd been eating satsumas. She let her father hug her, turning towards and into his embrace. It occurred to Ezra, as he felt his chin, on top of her head, forced up a little, that she was taller than the last time he'd hugged her. At some point where their bodies almost touched, not quite his skin to her skin but through clothing somewhere, he could feel her pulse. Her body began to relax into his. He concentrated his attention upon the soft, reassuring beat of Blaise's heart; it felt more intimate to him than his own.

'I just tried to stop him, Daddy,' she said, trembling. 'He was dragging Bobby across the ground by his hair, Bobby was screaming.'

'There, there, darling,' Ezra whispered.

'I had this spanner,' Blaise stuttered. 'I just wanted to hit his body. But then he turned . . .'

'It's all right.' Ezra hugged his daughter. 'I'm here.'

So that's what happened, Ezra thought. An accident. In which case, he reckoned, some of the blame should be laid at his door. Or rather on his small lawn; not to mention St Barnabas Church of England Primary School playing field; or the wide inviting vistas of University Parks. Yes, a definite measure of culpability resided in the patient hours of a doting father tossing a tennis ball to his daughter; in the endless retrieval of wild misses and glancing mishits with bat, stick, racket. Encouraging her eye for a ball, the hunter's acuity, augmenting it with efficient pectorals and flexible elbows. Make contact with firm forearm. Add that last-second injection of velocity with a flick of the wrist.

Blaise's sobbing subsided, in her father's embrace. In a freak accident she'd hit at the man's body with a spanner, but it had struck him in the face. Blaise didn't swing like a girl – not like the girls of Ezra's generation – she swung from the shoulder, she put her back into the swing, and she swung up from her feet planted on and springing off the earth. What puppy fat she had left was less a hindrance than, in movement, graceful weight. When Blaise hit a rounders ball she bounced up off the planet to do so: she hit the ball with the whole of her chunky body, she gave it all she had, and for that Ezra had to take some of the blame. He drew a clean white handkerchief from his pocket. 'Use this, darling.'

Blaise took the handkerchief and blew her nose.

The taxi stopped at red lights halfway down the high street. Blaise opened the door and jumped out. A cyclist was gliding down the nearside of the vehicles: the door, swung open, abruptly blocked his path and he mounted the pavement, swerving between pedestrians who'd just crossed the road, his brakes squealing. People flinched and staggered. Blaise ran through them, along the short precinct between St Mary's Church and All Soul's, towards the Radcliffe Camera.

Ezra stared after her.

'You want to keep an eye on her, mate.'

Ezra watched Blaise put distance between himself and her. He had about two seconds in which to choose to stuff a note into the taxi driver's maw and dash after her. Instead he slumped back in his seat, telling himself that neither he nor Blaise wanted him to chase her. You had, he believed, to respect what people told or showed you they wanted. You had to trust your children.

'Turn the car round, please,' Ezra asked him. 'Take me to the police station.'

Bicycling back along Oxpens to work the light was clear, and the air still. Crisis had come and, though hardly resolved, moved on like a brief phenomenon of the weather. A memory came back to Ezra Pepin. From when Blaise was two years old and needed a daily expedition out of their rented flat on Walton Street into open air, and what Ezra would always remember as the time of the Dustbin-lid Hunt.

As he cycled, Ezra recalled how all through one windy autumn he became a man possessed by a simple quest: where do the lids of black bins go? They get blown off. Or the dustmen don't bother to put them back: you come home on dustbin day and the lid's on the ground. Another time it's some yards away, blown up against the neighbours' fence. Put it back but that's not good enough, is it, as well you know: one day it'll be gone for good. But where?

Ezra strolled the terraced streets of Jericho with his toddler in her buggy. Everywhere they looked they saw topless black plastic bins. Looking after a child, your mind has hours in which to spin fanciful webs: Ezra attuned himself to the shifting atmospheric pressure, the microcosmic climate, in Jericho's grid of streets. Mini anticyclones and depressions. Westerlies driven in from subtropical highs up on Walton Street; trade winds sweeping towards the canal; a warm sirocco blown up Richmond Road between the synagogue and the Lebanese restaurant.

Airflow patterns along the terraces and avenues. Fluctuating pressure gradients. Where were dustbin lids blown? As Ezra pushed Blaise's buggy he conjured arcane forces, purposeful tornadoes stealing them, a kleptomania of nature. Or scurrilous squalls, argumentative gales, buffeting each other at T-junctions and cross-sections, with innocent dustbin lids caught in the cross-flow and whisked away.

Walking your child around the neighbourhood: there was only so much, after all, for a redundant anthropologist to see. There was only a universe. One day they searched the graveyard behind Lucy's Ironworks and had to go back there for days for Blaise to watch the alchemical men welding and smelting through the huge grubby windows. They went down to the canal where in the absence of black shields floating on the mucky water they threw stale bread to smug mallards. And they invariably went via Walton Lane, so that Blaise could hiccup with laughter as they bubbled along the cobbles.

Father and daughter took circuitous routes to the playground in the corner of St Barnabas School's playing field, thick with leaves from the plane trees and sycamores. There, Blaise tottered and stumbled. Whenever she – or any other of the sprites in their jumpsuits and wellies – started to fall over, they seemed to then accelerate towards the ground. As if the earth were greedy for infants.

They poked around the garages behind St Barnabas Church. They peered into the courtyard of the almshouses on Great Clarendon Street. They peeked through gates left open in case some deranged pensioner, under cover of gusting weather, was hoarding them in his backyard.

Until one November morning came when the air had the jitters. Crisp packets, chocolate wrappers, swirled about them. An empty Coke can skittered across tarmac. Ezra and Blaise were just crossing Walton Street, at the corner by the health centre, when they glimpsed a dustbin lid being blown around at the bottom of Cranham Street! Blaise chuckled, as Ezra ran the pushchair down the pavement. The black lid whirled and spun so that their view of it alternated, between full circular display and the mere edge of it flung like a frisbee and merging here with the council flats behind, and then reappearing there, a hovering ellipsoid.

Blaise jiggled in the pushchair, and Ezra drew breath from his folly. Chasing after a dustbin lid, he could see admitting to Sheena, was not quite sufficient justification for spilling their daughter on to concrete. He paused to secure her in the straps, and clicked the fastenings. A big mistake. When he looked up the lid was nowhere to be seen. Crossing Cranham Terrace, and then Allam Street, he scampered down to the bottom and, breathing hard, looked this way and that along Canal Street. Nothing. He felt strangely alone, standing at the junction. Then a sheet of newspaper careered around the corner, veering south, and they were up and running again, Blaise screeching, Ezra's lungs gusting with fresh hope. He was sure now they would come to some hitherto hidden cul-de-sac, some as yet unrevealed yard, at the end of which there'd be a blizzard of lids, swirling and circling in the wind like ravens.

There was none. Ezra trotted, walked, wound down, with no further sighting of their lid or any other. Blaise grew restless. Ezra persisted into the boatyard. Blaise moaned for the swings. So he relented, he gave up, and let the mystery remain one. A magic trick, an urban phenomenon still unexplained. Where do dustbin lids fly to?

Minty Carlyle fulfilled a provisional arrangement to collect Louie from his childminder. Her son Jack was Hector's best friend, and came back from school to the Pepins' house. Minty phoned Ezra and told him that Blaise was safely home. He assumed, as he cycled swiftly home himself that early evening along the road whose name changed every half mile – Walton Street, Kingston Road, Hayfield Road, indicating the area's continual piecemeal development – that since she hadn't gone with Blaise to the police station Sheena would still be involved in the action at the Wasteland. As he crossed Farndon Road, where Hayfield became Bainton Road, a glance to his left snatched a glimpse of a good-sized crowd, and their murmur, too, which within moments was lost in the air behind him. A minute later he glided into Blenheim Orchard.

Ezra pushed his bike past the Saab and the Golf – parked in their allotted spaces in front of the house – and down the paving-slab path at the side. He put it in the shed, and entered home through the kitchen door. The table bore the aftermath of a half-eaten meal – pizza crust, the naked white flesh of fish fingers. Boiled broccoli florets. Abandoned carrot. Empty chairs were pushed back un-tidily. The only sound above the hum of the fridge was the digital squeaking of a computer game: Ezra looked through to the open-plan living-room, where Hector and Jack lay side by side on the carpet, leaning on their elbows like sunbathers, playing chess on the flatscreen TV.

Hector had bought the game with his pocket money the weekend before, and as soon as he'd scanned the moves had taken his father through them with the authority of a grand master.

'The rooks only shoot their laser cannons in straight lines,' he

30

explained, miming the trajectory to help his ageing pop understand this modern operation. 'But the queen' (a superheroine in shiny chainmail), 'she can do flying kicks in *every* direction. See?'

Ezra watched Jack and Hector: a pair of docile gawks at the mayhem their fretful fingers concocted. Bishops flourished daggers from beneath their cassocks and hurled them in arrowed diagonals at infantry pawns, who bleeped to death. Knights approached an opponent and vanished, then reappeared again in a surprising position, from where they struck with scimitars.

It was impossible to tell whether or not the boys were actually enjoying themselves. It appeared to Ezra as if the game were an irksome nuisance, which, having entered, they could only escape from by seeing through to the end, an action-packed contest that made Ezra mourn the tedium of real chess. Originating in India – or was it China? – fifteen hundred years ago, each slow game, played between two minds deep in concentration, invoked a history of civilisation. And in a generation it was simply slipping away, becoming a relic, a curio. Chess sets sifting down the chain through charity shops, car boot sales, internet selling, to a last resting place in the dusty corners of eccentric museums.

Ezra shook his head at the memory of how much he'd loved chess as a boy, of how many hours of his life he'd wasted in the exasperating depths of its polyphonic repetitions. An only child with few friends, his mother had taught him; he was able, at about the age Hector was now, to beat her easily, and from then on found one or two other oddbods amongst his acquaintances with whom to collaborate in mental combat.

As the years after university went by, however, the pool of possible partners dwindled. Even now, Ezra admitted, if he were asked for his favourite hobbies he'd list chess, when he'd not actually played in years. Working out as many moves ahead in the dizzying infinity as you were able: there was no longer room for such speculation, was there, in the quickening pulse of our leisure time?

*   *   *

Without disturbing the players, Ezra made his way upstairs. Louie was in the bath. Minty was kneeling on the floor, leaning against the tub.

'Hey,' Ezra said, stooping to kiss Minty. She extended her neck, offered one cheek, then the other, pressing each cheek against his as she did so. He would have kissed his son as well, except that the boy had a grey plastic helmet on his head. Louie lifted the visor.

'Daddy, I'm is a knight in armour.'

'I'd never have guessed, darling.'

'I'm is swimming.'

'My, my, this water is cold.'

'First he wouldn't get in the bath,' Minty explained. 'Now he won't get out.'

'You've got one minute, Peanut.' Ezra lowered the loo seat lid and sat down. 'No news?'

'Simon rang just a minute ago. He's been thrown out, he thinks they've just about cut through the last one. Guess who she is?'

'I can't imagine,' Ezra said, raising his eyebrows in a gesture that he trusted was not too disloyal. He had to confront Sheena this evening; it was her irresponsibility that he'd been pondering on and off all day at work.

'I really appreciate this, Minty,' he said. 'You get back home, now.' He wondered whether or not Minty knew what had happened to Blaise. 'Have you spoken with Blaise?'

'Just "Hello". "Hello." You know?' Minty pulled herself up. 'We'll see you on Sunday, Ezra.'

'What?'

'Supper. Here, right?'

'Oh, of course. See you guys then. Come on, Peanut, here's your towel. Pull that plug out.'

Louie was in bed in time to receive his full two book quota. Ezra picked his way across a rug strewn with cars, trains, farm animals and medieval warriors in a gruesome, time-travelling pile-up, to read one book about a fox thwarted from eating chicks by a lazy dog and another about a somewhat dysfunctional but basically loving family of hedgehogs. He used to be repelled by this anthro-pomorphism, but Sheena borrowed a neverending shuttle of such books from the library, the children enjoyed them, and now only a stubborn residue of his resistance remained.

Ezra hugged tight his son's willing little body. Louie informed his father of subjects of which he intended to dream: horses. Princes. Cars. Not cars, motorbikes. 'Right,' Ezra acknowledged. 'Fine,' as he retreated out of the room. Knights. Helicopters. Castles.

Hector stood on the landing in his pyjamas. Without his spectacles on he looked a little lost. Ezra approached him from the side.

'You off to bed, soldier?'

Hector jumped like a startled deer, as if he was not an urban boy standing in his own house but some rural child, disturbed on a hillside. Once he'd collected himself Hector said, into the stairwell, 'I'm not a soldier, Daddy.'

'I know, Hec.'

'I'd watch some telly but it's trash. I'll read. Actually, I'll re-read.'

'What already?'

'*The Amber Spyglass*. Dad? Wake me up if Mummy doesn't come home.'

'How will I know when she hasn't come home, Hector?'

Hector stared. His father would do this: utter these sentences whose clarity was disturbed by humour, like a drop of milk in water.

'You'll know,' he said, finally, nodding. 'Of course you will.'

Then Hector let his father give him a rare kiss goodnight, before stepping silently into his room.

Blaise was in the kitchen, chewing peanut-buttered toast. She'd long since bathed and washed her hair, and was back in her beads and sweats and flared jeans. Watching her from the doorway, Ezra found himself assailed by the memory of being thumped by another boy at school. They must have been twelve or thirteen – Stephen Winter was the boy's name. It was the last physical fight Ezra had ever had. He could recall scrutinising his reflection in the mirror over the following days: a bruise, changing colour around his eye

33

and his cheek, which he'd borne with a confusion of shame and pride. He shook his head and stepped into the kitchen.

'You didn't eat with the others?' Ezra asked.

Blaise looked up at her father as she chewed, slowly, before swallowing. She shook her head.

'Is that enough?' he asked. 'Shall I cook you something?'

Blaise shook her head again, and looked down at the table.

Ezra nodded. He was about to ask her something, he wasn't sure what, when the back door swung suddenly open and in burst Sheena. She brought with her a pungent cloud, rank with marsh and sweat, and a still trembling elation, an insanity, corroborated by her wild black hair, muddy face and wide grin. She dumped a bag on the tiled floor.

'We did it,' she told Ezra, looking up, and only then did she see their daughter, obscured behind Ezra. 'Blaise!' Sheena said. 'Blaise.' Sheena pulled Blaise up into a hug in which, with a wide open arm, she then included Ezra. She spoke into Blaise's hair. 'You can't *believe* how proud of you I am.'

The three of them squeezed each other in a smelly, eager scrum. Blaise was weeping.

'Isn't our girl incredible?' Sheena said. Her eyes were closed.

Ezra eased out of the trio. Sheena and Blaise closed the gap he left, their limbs tightening together. Blaise sobbed. Sheena murmured, 'You're amazing.'

'But, Mum, the man,' Blaise mumbled.

'I know, sweetheart,' Sheena soothed. 'I know. And I know how proud we all are of what you did.'

At length Sheena withdrew her left arm from around Blaise's shoulder and took a step back, opening the shell of their embrace. They stood facing Ezra, Blaise an inch or two the shorter, her left arm around her mother's waist. Her damp, sad eyes shone. Sheena had on someone else's T-shirt, too short and too wide, over a black catsuit. She looked like she'd taken part in a filthy yoga session. Ezra needed to talk to Sheena alone. As if in complicit telepathy, Blaise wiped her eyes, and said, 'Do you want me to run you a bath, Mum?'

'Oh, sweetheart, would you? I'd love one. Will you tell me all about it while I'm soaking?'

Blaise nodded, and walked away through the living-room.

Sheena turned to Ezra. She looked exhausted. Ezra passed her a glass of red wine. 'I'm glad you're back,' he said. 'But I'm very angry, Sheena.'

'Cheers,' Sheena said, chinking Ezra's glass. 'They so didn't expect it, Ez. All *day* we stopped them. All right. It's only one last day. They'll start tomorrow.'

'Sheena.' Ezra unwound the cork from the corkscrew.

'We've done everything we could. It feels good.'

Ezra threw the cork into the open bin. 'I want to know what she did,' he said.

'She was brilliant, Ez.' Sheena lifted the glass to her lips and drained it, swallowing with a murmur of satisfaction. 'This lout was beating up Bobby Sewell – you know, one of the guys who came down from the north, the ones who've really befriended Blaise – and she tried to stop him. She was so brave.'

'Did you see it?'

Sheena looked at Ezra and frowned. Then she looked away again. 'Yes. Of course. She was just trying to stop him, but he slipped, and kind of fell towards her. It was unfortunate.'

'Unfortunate? You know what happened to the guy?' Ezra raised his hands in a pleading gesture. 'You were supposed to be looking out for her. She's thirteen years old, for Christ's sake.'

'Yes,' Sheena nodded. 'I was underneath a truck. But Jed Wilson went with her to the police station.'

'He wasn't there when I got there.'

'Someone rang you at work, Ez. They were told you were already on your way.'

Ezra perched against the edge of the kitchen table, and took a sip of wine. 'You should have seen her,' he said quietly. 'Curled up in a plastic chair.' He shook his head.

Sheena smiled. 'We knew she'd be released without charge.' She went over to the sink, turned on the tap and filled a glass with water. She drank it down in one long gulping swallow.

'You did, did you?' Ezra said. 'I didn't get that impression at all. It was a fluke that she's not facing a charge.'

'There's no need to mollycoddle her,' Sheena said, breathless. 'You don't do her any favours.'

A band of heat flared across Ezra's chest. 'Mollycoddle?' he responded. 'Damn it, Sheena, I let you have her take part in all this without a word of caution. Don't throw my leniency back in my face. And I was the one who had to take care of it. They wouldn't release her until one of us went to get her, would they?' Ezra took an irritated sip of his wine. It left an aftertaste of vinegar. 'She wouldn't even tell them who she was,' he murmured.

'Good for her.'

'No! Not good for her, Sheena.' The events had seemed clear to Ezra, rumbling through his mind during the course of the day. Sheena was supposed to be apologetic. She would be upset when he described the scene in the police station. It hadn't occurred to him that he'd need ammunition for his argument. 'She's a child. It's our job to protect her,' he said. 'I mean, are you oblivious?'

A grimace tightened Sheena's countenance. 'Well, look, Ez,' she said, 'it's over now.'

The anger had migrated to Ezra's head, a ball of heat moving around his upper body. 'It's not over for this guy in the hospital.'

Sheena stared at him. 'A vicious thug,' she said, incredulous.

'A human being, for Christ's sake.'

She shrugged, and something about the gesture made him realise something that should have been obvious. He said, 'She's only trying to copy you, after all.'

'Oh, come on,' Sheena frowned.

'She's only trying to impress you.'

'Do you think so?' Sheena shook her head. She put her empty wine glass on the sideboard. 'I think that bath'll be run by now,' she said, and left the room.

Ezra set pasta to boil, and made a pesto in the food processor, robotically adding ingredients. Their mutual incomprehension had floored him. Was it simply because he wasn't there? If he'd taken part in the protest, would he have been able to see that Blaise's act of violence was admirable? Or that Sheena's irresponsible example was actually an inspiration? He ripped up green leaves for salad with trembling fingers. He could hear the water from Sheena's bath running down the pipes as he halved and juiced a lemon for the dressing. Perhaps they were living in a Wonderland, where you could flip a coin and good became bad, right became wrong.

'Blaise says goodnight,' Sheena told him when she came back into the kitchen, dressed in clean jeans and T-shirt. She had a white towel around her drying hair, wrapped up on her head like a turban.

Ezra served the pasta and salad. Sheena ate greedily. 'That was delicious,' she said, her lips shiny with olive oil. 'I'd better get back to the vigil. They'll have a bonfire lit.'

'You have got to be kidding.'

'I should. They're expecting me. I mean, it's nearly over now.' Sheena leaned over to Ezra, squeezing his arm, drawing his averted eyes back towards hers. 'You know how much I appreciate your support, Ez. I know I couldn't have done this without you. But you do believe in what we're doing, don't you?'

What an unfair question. The non-combatant asked if he supported the war. 'Of course. I guess.'

Sheena smiled, and kissed him. 'I'll grab an apple,' she said, taking a couple from the fruit bowl. 'See you later, Ezra.'

After washing up, and tidying the sitting-room of Louie's toys, and gathering newspapers for the recycling bin, Ezra Pepin traipsed upstairs. He undressed, performed ablutions in the bathroom, and lay in bed, yawning. On Monday he was due to lead a presentation to the Board: Ezra checked he'd put his Pocket Memo on the bedside table to record any ideas that might occur to him, but he fervently hoped that he wouldn't wake yet again. He was due just one night sleeping straight through, that's all it would take to replenish his energy; it was just that he couldn't remember the last time he'd had one.

The house was quiet. The carnival of family life in abeyance, for a moment, in which he might even be able to collect his thoughts. Sheena was out, the children were sleeping. Except, he sensed, that one of them wasn't. How or why Ezra figured this he didn't know. Because of some noise, he assumed, but as he listened now he could hear nothing, beyond the barely audible sound of their almost new house muttering to itself: a sigh in the pipes, a squeak from a ceiling beam. Down in the kitchen the dishwasher swished, hurling hot water at dirty plates and mugs; into the plastic cage of cutlery. The washing machine heaved and spun a soapy load. Cotton under-wear – tiny Y-fronts, boxer shorts, knickers – tumbled in the dryer. Lifting the summer duvet and leaning to his left, Ezra let gravity lever him out of bed. He walked through the open doorway of his and Sheena's bedroom out into the hall. Louie was fast asleep. He looked in on Blaise: she slept soundly. He closed the door and stepped across to Hector's room.

Hector turned on to his side as Ezra entered. 'Are you still awake?' his father whispered.

Hector sighed. 'I can't sleep.'

Ezra sat on the edge of Hector's bed. 'Let's get something straight,' he said. 'I'm the insomniac in this family. You're a little young to take over, don't you think?'

'It's not my fault.'

Hector had put his glasses back on. It took his father a moment, in the near dark, to register that they were sunglasses.

'I thought they'd help me sleep,' Hector explained. 'I don't think they do,' he said, and took them off.

Ezra stroked the hair from his son's forehead. 'Don't brood, Hec,' he said. 'We've spoken about this.'

'I can't help it, Daddy,' Hector complained. 'To be conscious is an illness.'

'It is, is it?'

'That's what Dostoyevsky said. A real thorough-going illness.'

As more objects in the gloom became visible to Ezra, he identi-fied his own Penguin copy of *Notes from Underground* lying on the floor – his son must have filched it from his bookshelves in the spare room. It was impossible to predict what would catch

Hector's imagination. It was clear already that he was clever – he'd been doing well in his first year at comprehensive – but in a quite arbitrary way. His interests were whimsical. His every report through primary school had contained the comment, *Could pay more attention in class*, because no teacher seemed able to engage him. Instead, he'd announce a new interest – geometry at school last term, his guitar at home – in an offhand way, and then become absorbed in it to an alarming degree. Hector immersed himself, and that was how he read books: their son's body went into a zombified slump on a sofa and his spirit was sucked out. When it returned, it took a while for his family to be convinced that some part of him had not been left behind.

'Daddy,' Hector breathed now. 'Tell me a story.'

'Okay,' Ezra whispered. 'Sure. How about, let me see, do you remember *Last of the Mohicans*?'

'No, I mean one of *your* stories, Daddy. From the jungle.'

'Oh, okay,' Ezra nodded. 'Fine. Let me think.'

'Dad?'

'What, Hector?'

'Have you ever felt like you didn't belong?'

'Where?'

Hector looked puzzled. 'Anywhere.'

Ezra put his hand on his bony boy's arm. 'You feel out of place?'

Hector looked affronted. 'No,' he said.

'I know: Hec. Listen. I'll tell you about when I was first there. Okay?'

'Yes.'

'Okay,' Ezra said. He took a deep breath, exhaled slowly. As he did so he repositioned himself on Hector's bed, as if physical readiness were necessary; for the start of a story he'd told, over the years, many times, he needed to prepare himself.

'I'd been in the village for some weeks,' Ezra began. 'A couple of months, learning the Indians' language, and the most rudimentary, easily observable things about them. There were thirty people in this village. I'd been told by the brothers at the Jesuit mission downriver – who were the only people from the outside who'd had contact with them – of the Achia's flippant attitude to children. Mothers, they told me, slipped away from the hut to give birth alone, through a hole in their hammocks, expelling the baby on to earth below.

'If a baby is malformed, the Brothers said, the mother discards it at once. If a child cries too much, if it's a nuisance to her, the mother kills it. If an infant son falls sick and dies, the father will kill a daughter. If the father has been killed by an enemy, or is sick and cannot hunt, the mother calculates the chore of feeding her children on a dwindling supply of banana and plantain, and fish that must be caught, and she might kill one or two of them.'

'That's awful, Daddy,' Hector murmured.

'This is what I was told. Achia children who died were then forgotten, as if conjured out of people's minds and memory, into nothingness.'

'Oblivion,' Hector breathed.

'Birth, the Jesuits explained to me, appeared to be easy. Childbirth, they claimed, becomes more difficult the more a culture comes to value the individual. As if the value of an individual soul can be measured by the pain a mother goes through to bring forth a human being into his or her existence.'

'Is that true?' Hector asked, prodding forward the story he half remembered from a previous telling.

Ezra frowned. His children asked to hear the stories that he'd never finished writing: a curious validation. 'One night,' he continued, 'I was awoken by Pakani, the best hunter in the tribe, whispering in my ear, "A child comes."'

'"Now? Your baby?" I asked him.'

'"My child will come. I go."'

'Pakani fled into the forest, its night-time dangers apparently less forbidding than those posed in the village were he to stay.

'I found Tikangi, his wife, close to her hut. She was squatting on a bed of ferns, beside a crackling fire. Three or four people crouched around her in silence. Her brother, Patawi, knelt back on his heels, knees planted apart, in front of and facing away from her: Tikangi grasped hold of her brother's shoulders, which offered

40

her the stability she needed in order to be able to undulate her belly backwards and forwards with her contractions.

'I didn't know how long this scene had been going on. But all of a sudden a tiny figure appeared on the ferns. The child had fallen. Tikangi hadn't uttered a sound.

'One of the others around her picked up the baby, but neither he nor anyone else said a word. Nor did they smile. I would say they almost, I don't know, Hector, *ignored* this baby that had come among them. It was very strange, and it would take me the rest of my time there to understand that their silence was very deliberate. For the helpless newborn baby (a girl, who would be called Kabuchi) was in grave danger, and they – her grandmother, two uncles, and two guardians whom we might call her godparents – were responsible for protecting her.'

'Protecting her from what, Daddy?' Hector whispered, in a sleepy but attentive voice.

'The baby was in danger from the dead,' Ezra said. 'From the souls of those Indians who had died cut off from the tribe, out hunting. Their bodies had never been found, so they were not sent to the Invisible Forest with proper ritual and company. They hovered outside the village at night, on the lookout for someone to take with them on their journey. They could smother the weakest among the living, and they needed no more than a word, laughter, a mother's gasp in labour, to know: if one of the dead found out that a girl had just been born, she would be as good as dead.'

Hector's head seemed to sink a little into his pillow.

'The baby's godfather cut the umbilical cord with a bamboo splinter and tied it. He then bathed the baby with cold water from a bamboo and beeswax container, washing away the blood. When the trembling baby was clean the godmother took her, held her in the crook of her arm, and massaged warmth back into her body.

'She administered a forceful massage to the baby's head, her palm pressed on and around her skull. After a while she passed the baby to the grandmother, who continued to massage her head. I, clothed, shivered in the night, but the naked Indians paid the cold no heed, concentrating their solemn attention on the baby.

41

'Tikangi, meanwhile, had delivered the placenta.'

'It's so messy, Daddy,' Hector said in a sleepy voice. 'All that blood and stuff.'

'One of her brothers gathered the ferns on which the afterbirth had fallen and took the bundle away to be buried.

'The grandmother passed Kabuchi to her uncle. He massaged for a while and then, to my surprise and embarrassment, passed her to me.'

'What did you do, Daddy?' Hector asked, yawning.

'How could I refuse? Your Dad – a young Oxford graduate student, brought up in a country town in the south of England – took the newborn baby in his hesitant fingers and massaged her tiny head. When the time felt right, I passed her to the person closest to me, her godmother. She then passed Kabuchi back to Tikangi, who put her baby in her sling and walked slowly back to her hut. The other Indians separated without a word and went each to their own huts.'

Ezra stopped speaking. He could see that Hector's eyes were closed. His boy was slipping into sleep.

'Soon,' Ezra whispered, 'everyone was asleep. Campfires crackled, the wind blew in the trees. Out in the jungle jaguars prowled; the white men – woodcutters, clearance farmers, road-builders – toiled without respite; and the restless spirits of the dead remained each alone. The tribe had a new member.'

Ezra Pepin kissed his son on his dry forehead, and retired to his and Sheena's bedroom. What seemed like a long, long time ago he'd woken with her absent, and now the day was finally ending, but she was gone again. He pulled the duvet over his shoulders, lay on his right side, and waited for sleep.

Some yards away, Blaise was curled up in a foetal position. She'd slept this afternoon; had only been pretending to be asleep just now. Trying to make sense of the day, her mind kept returning to the moment she ran from under the vehicle, yelling, and flew towards the men.

Blaise had been crouching beneath a huge-wheeled yellow digger. More than half of the others had clamped themselves to machinery. No one had got a lock to her: she clasped a connecting rod above her head to which she was not otherwise attached. The security goons were picking up any floppy bodies they could and hauling them away.

Blaise could see her mother. Or rather she saw her feet, sticking out from the undercarriage of an enormous dump truck, just in front of one of its huge vulcanised wheels, whose scale rendered Sheena's feet doll-like. Mad, Blaise thought. They might not even notice her under there, and drive the vehicle off, crushing her mother like a toy. Blaise's mother was brave and insane: she had no idea what danger she'd put herself in. She always assumed she and everyone else would get out of any trouble.

The foreground of Blaise's frame of vision was breached abruptly, by a heavy-set security guard dragging something. A body. It was Bobby, being pulled by his dreadlocks. His hands were tied behind his back.

'Come on, mop 'ead,' the guard grunted as he pulled Bobby, who alternated between floppiness of his limbs and – snorting with pain as the roots of his hair were tugged from his scalp – kicking his heels into the ground, and quickstepping backwards. Which only made the security guard's job easier, so that after a few shuffling feet Bobby once more went limp, and then grimaced with the resultant pain. The guard didn't appear to mind which way Bobby wanted to travel. 'Fuckin' moppet I've got,' he called to his colleagues.

Bobby gasped. A white-toothed rictus distressed his painted face. His eyes squinted shut.

'We can turn 'im upside down and mop the cabin.' Guttural laughter in the trees.

Blaise wasn't sure whether the heat that flared through her own head, threading capillaries of blood across her eyes, was her rage or Bobby's pain echoed in her scalp. Her fingers scrabbled in amongst the undercarriage above her head. Blind they found a box, and lifted its lid, and withdrew a heavy metal tool. She broke from beneath the digger, and ate up the ground. 'No!' she shouted, grasping the solid monkey wrench in both tight hands. She drew it back behind her shoulder, and as she swung it the security guard looked her way. Alerted by her yell, he turned and dipped his big-boned face towards her.

The heavy end of the wrench connected with a thud: soft on his flesh and hard on bone. Then everything stopped. The man lay down, groaning. Blood oozed from between fingers held over his face. Blaise stopped, the wrench fell from her hands. There was no more aggression after that: the shouting ceased, the chaos in the clearing stilled. Everyone acted warily, properly, the act of violence bringing about a strange decorum. Blaise let herself be led away. An ambulance came; police cars.

His face twisting towards her, into the flailing arc of the head of the heavy spanner.

3

Fudge Making

Saturday 21 June

When Sheena woke she knew it was late, from the silence in the house and from the sun that sudden dazzled as she drew the curtains open. Her head was silted with the memory of beer; her tongue, the walls of her mouth, were coated with resin from spliffs she'd shared. Eleven fifteen, the clock confirmed. The night came back to her, sat around the camp fire outside the Wasteland: no one said anything for hours, drunk and doped into a beaten silence. Guitars strummed, a drum beat, more defiant drone than song, the trancelike summons of a rite. Mole beside her, hours floating by.

She shook her head away from the clock, brusquely, as if chronology were something it offered but which Sheena chose to refuse, along with all futile regret for the night before.

By the time she had let a long hot shower purge and rinse and vivify her, and come back into the bedroom with white towels wrapped around her body and her hair, Sheena could accept sounds from outside, and was able now to look out of the window without the sunlight assaulting her: Ezra had cat's cradled washing line to and fro across their modest lawn; he was hanging up a second or a third load, pegging clothes of wondrously assorted size. Beyond, white sheets hung, still in the breezeless morning. Blaise was chasing Louie in amongst them, floundering after him. Her little brother then took his turn to pursue Blaise, shooting at her with a clothes peg gun; the report it produced from his lips reached Sheena's ears. Blaise ducked behind linen as he popped her, and died dramatically, clutching a sheet in front of her, her weight pulling it from the line as she fell. In unconscious homage, it struck Sheena, to some Czech or Polish film Ezra had once taken her to. Its climax a similar scene, with the blood of the hero betraying his mortally wounded presence as it spread across a hanging sheet. What a shame, Sheena could remember thinking, that the film was in black and white. How much better it would have worked in colour, the blood red on white.

As she dried her hair Sheena wondered to what extent Ezra was and would be making the same mistake with all his children that he'd made with her: that evangelism with which he'd shared his favourite films, books, music. 'Listen to this tape, babe,' making her sit down in his room under the eaves in the old flat on Walton Street. 'I didn't know I still had it.' And it could be anything, that was the joke; Ezra lacked a systematic approach to music, culture, life in general. It could be Patti Smith, Roland Kirk, Joseph Haydn. Rumillajta, Philip Glass, Mercedes Sosa. Some indigenous tribal music.

'I'm sorry,' Ezra would protest, 'if I lack a classificatory gene. The unifying factor, darling, is that of beauty, not genre.'

The unifying factor, Sheena regretted, was each item's random arrival at a particular ripe moment in Ezra's life such as to place it within his subjective canon. 'Come with me, I'm going to show you something,' he'd said once, dragging her through the middle of Oxford to the back entrance to Christ Church and into the picture gallery. Striding past fine but apparently irrelevant paintings to a small sculpture on a shelf at the end. *Dancer*, by Henri Gaudier-Brezska. 'Will you just look at the energy in this figure?' Ezra said, shaking his head in wonder. 'Can't you feel it?'

'Actually, no,' Sheena didn't quite muster the honesty to say. 'Fantastic, sweetheart,' she probably did concur, and he'd have nodded. Relieved. Glad. Justified.

And the films. She moved in with him, above a shop across the road from the best cinema in Oxford, which had converted its one screen to two that just enough students, in those early days of video, still patronised to keep open. There were early-afternoon showings of classics when the two of them had the small auditorium all to themselves: sprawled like movie producers in a studio screening room, calling up to the projectionist to 'start the film, boy', a private joke Sheena enjoyed more than the soporific Pasolini, Bergman, Tarkovsky that so transfixed Ezra he rarely noticed her dozing.

Of course, Sheena conceded now as she dressed, the truth was that Ezra was her cultural mentor, the male lover who opened her eyes to an aesthetic realm. Her medical Yorkshire parents who took the family to a Christmas choral service, sent their children to piano lessons and visited the Playhouse maybe twice a year, were, Sheena understood, irredeemably provincial. Ezra's maddening advocacy might have put her off his particular choices, but he made her aware of a feast available.

Sheena came to perceive culture less like Ezra in terms of time, as a historical procession bearing gifts to the present, than of geography: she a British beneficiary of multicultural appetites. So that when she ventured laterally from Ezra's narrow inroads and discovered her own tastes, for kitsch Spanish films, for cajun and salsa, for thrillers with female detectives, honesty obliged Sheena to acknowledge Ezra's influence – one which he then strenuously denied.

As he pegged the washing to the line, Ezra Pepin screwed up his eyes against the sun, pleased with how much housework he'd accomplished already, while his wife slept on. He wasn't sure what time she came home, but it must have been late. She'd slid into bed without waking Ezra some time after sleep had eventually admitted him, and a couple of hours later he'd woken and lain there, watching her, the thin duvet thrown back from her warm body curled away from him. Now he kept hoping that she'd not appear until he'd finished just one more task. Pictured his naked wife slumbering on, gaining replenishment.

Sheena was a year younger than Ezra, three or four inches shorter. Her figure was barely changed from that of the woman he'd met at twenty-four, and if her white flesh was a little looser when he massaged it, and settled a little lower on her hips, this remained less present decline than presentiment of a distant future.

There was a full-length mirror in their bedroom in which after a shower Sheena would give her nude body frank appraisal.

'You're looking gorgeous, darling.' Ezra would lob some honest compliment her way. 'I mean, my God, your breasts.'

'Yes,' Sheena would reply without vanity. 'Because I swam so much as a girl, I told you, built up my pecs. That's why they've stayed this firm.'

'I'm sincerely grateful to Leeds municipal swimming pools.'

'After breast-feeding three children, you should be. You should see some of the women at Esporta.'

'I don't need to hear about your drooping friends, honestly.'

'No, I mean the ones who've had implants. When we lie on the floor at the end of a class. Wind-down time.' Sheena let out a squawk of laughter. 'Their boobs pointing at the ceiling.'

Sheena weighed herself on the bathroom scales once a day, but it was the visual rather than numerical evidence, as she twisted and gazed over her shoulder at the reflection of her arse and thighs, that would prompt her to lay off butter, chocolate, cream for a week or two. Count the laps when she went swimming with Hector. That was all it took, until she'd nod at the reflection of what as far as Ezra could see was the same athletic body he was already wedded to a fortnight earlier; he assumed the variations were merely cyclical.

'Good grief, you're in fine shape, woman,' Ezra would declare, unable to refuse the temptation of squeezing his wife's bottom as he passed.

'I'm just lucky,' Sheena shrugged modestly, and she meant it. She took little personal credit for her good fortune. She had jet black hair, odd strands of which Ezra would occasionally notice before she did had turned white overnight; they, too, seemed not so much evidence of what was happening now as discreet intimations of

48

what would eventually come. He'd seen one this morning as he lay beside her. In the next day or two Sheena would spot it too and tug it out with a matter-of-fact grimace, less out of vanity than of irritation.

Sheena's lustrous black hair was anomalous above blue eyes, pale skin, a snub nose and thin, mobile lips. Inky and gothic, it was like none of her relations' since a great-grandmother who possessed either Jewish, Spanish, gypsy or Indian blood, depending upon which aunt or uncle in her extensive family had been whispering their prejudices into her ear. Sheena was proud of her hair, whatever genes had bequeathed it, and she kept it long and wore it in any of many styles according to her mood of the morning and how much of a hurry she was in: plaited, pony-tailed, braided, bee-hived. Tied up, tied round, tied back. Pinned, plumed, her black tresses pliant but distinctive, the ever changing, always striking feature around her plain and open English face.

As for Sheena's clothes, Ezra thought as he pegged up the last of them on the washing-line, he wasn't sure she'd ever changed her style. She wore either blue jeans or stretchy sports apparel, with pale-brown working boots. Layers above: T-shirts, tracksuit tops, armless fleeces, cardigans. The no-nonsense working clothes of a woman with no need to impress anyone; a small-business employer and mother who rolled up her sleeves and mucked in with whatever needed doing. Maybe the colours had changed, Ezra conceded. Maybe the fabrics had evolved.

On special occasions, notably those social functions connected with Ezra's work to which partners were invited and, with each modest promotion, increasingly expected to come, Sheena put on what she referred to as fancy dress. It was true that she drew upon herself Saratoga's finer lingerie, sheer hosiery, flowing dresses from Whistles or Jigsaw, high heels and jewellery, with more girlish pantomime than sensual womanly relish. And when they got home after such evenings it never occurred to Sheena to dally and vamp over a nightcap with her husband, to seduce him as the elegant woman of the night such attire allowed her to be; she simply discarded it on her way to bed, while Ezra paid the babysitter and

49

locked up. Shoes on the landing. Jewellery beside the basin. Tights and panties on the bathroom floor. It wasn't a trail laid for a hunter to follow, and Ezra had to move fast if he wanted her to let him undress her. Her dress draped across a chair, bra on the carpet, and Sheena tucked up naked in bed, where she may or may not feel like sex, her mood in the matter having little to do with the clothes she'd worn or the evening out. If she lacked the appetite for it, Ezra had learned there was little point in hoping to coax it from her; while if she was desirous, then he could take as much pleasure as he wished in doing her bidding.

Sheena pulled on a pair of blue jeans and a white T-shirt and went downstairs. Sunshine poured into the house: summer began when you could walk barefoot on the kitchen tiles without the stone chilling your soles. Flies buzzed against the window panes behind the sink. Hector had the *Oxford Times* opened and spread out across the kitchen table in front of him: stooped and squinting through his glasses at the broadsheet, he looked like a small old man. Sheena leaned in between Hector's bent spine and the back of his chair and hugged him, looping one arm under, the other over, his shoulders. His floppy brown hair smelled dry and musty as she nuzzled it. She raised herself up, stroking his face with her rising hand and tousling his hair with the other. Hector ducked and bobbed away.

'Oh, Hector, sweetheart, don't you go all teeny on me,' Sheena moaned. 'Let me enjoy you while you're still scrumptious.'

'Did you read this?' Hector asked. 'Yesterday's *Oxford Times*.'

'I just got up.'

Sheena moved to the sideboard and put the kettle on, while Hector read to her. Plucked a teabag from the tin, cut bread for toast.

'*Girl, fifteen, hurt in hammer attack,*' Hector intoned quietly. '*A teenage schoolgirl and a male friend were attacked with a hammer as they walked near Oxford city centre. The pair were set upon by a gang of white, black and Asian youths as they walked by the underpass near the Westgate Centre last Wednesday.*'

The door opened and the others came in, Blaise carrying the red plastic washing basket filled with airy, folded sheets. Ezra bore a wounded soldier over his shoulder.

'I'm is all right now, Daddy,' Louie gasped. Ezra let him down, and he ran through to the sitting-room. Blaise took the washing upstairs.

Hector carried on reading. He spoke softly, and precisely, head bowed. It appeared that he was uttering the words aloud as an aid to his own reading rather than a wish to convey information to others. '*The fifteen-year-old girl, who was wearing her school uniform, suffered injuries to her hands and head when she tried to intervene to stop the attack on her companion.*'

Ezra kissed Sheena. 'Morning,' he said. 'You get some sleep?'

'Sleep?' Toast popped up. Sheena put the two slices on a plate and spread butter. 'Sure.'

'I rang the hospital,' Ezra said.

'What?'

'To see if the guy's all right.'

Sheena turned slowly towards Ezra. A thin line of honey drooled from her knife on to the kitchen surface, a few inches from her plate. 'Why?'

'He checked out.'

'Good.' Sheena shook her head. 'That means he's okay. It wasn't as bad as you imagined it to be. Can we forget about him now?' She spread jam on the second slice.

'What are we doing today?' Ezra asked.

Sheena took a bite of toast. 'Meeting Jill at the office, remember? Make up for not working the last two days.'

'You're kidding.'

'I'm washed out after yesterday, Ezra.' She took another muffled crunch. 'I'd much rather hang out here with you lot.'

Louie was readying a convoy of Thomas the Tank Engine, Catwoman and a comic monster from a Shreddies packet for a perilous trek from the skirting board out behind the TV into the interior of the sitting-room.

Hector didn't raise his voice, but read on, with a gloomy

determination. *'The man, aged twenty-one, suffered severe swelling and bruising during the Castle Street assault, which took place at around 2.40 p.m. Another girl who had been walking with them ran for help. The injured pair were both treated at the John Radcliffe Hospital, Oxford, but were discharged later that day. Their injuries were described as serious.'*

Through in the living area, sitting cross-legged on the big pouffe, Blaise had switched on the TV, and using the remote was hopping between music channels, with the sound mute. She was checking the moves of the dance routines, Ezra guessed. She chewed a pencil. Maybe she was analysing editing technique for her media studies class: all music videos were cut with a rapidity that, to Ezra's aged eyes, obscured rather than displayed the dance; disguised how bad it was, suggested a slickness that wasn't there. Music videos seemed to him to be travesties, dance routines defaced by an ersatz choreography of cuts and camera moves, when dance cried out for a cameraman and editor prepared to allow the dance to reveal itself. He made a mental note to rent a DVD of *Blood Wedding*, sit Blaise down and see what she made of it.

Or maybe she was just embarrassed for her parents to hear the music she liked. They might like it too.

'The man seen to use the weapon was described as being around twenty, black, of slim build and five feet ten inches tall, clean shaven, and wearing a cream-coloured hooded Nike top, Rockport shoes, and a black baseball cap. The rest of the gang were described as being white and mostly Asian, and in their teens and early twenties.'

Louie took a break from his godlike manipulation of his toys' destiny across the carpet, to come back to the kitchen table and drink some milk. He saw what Sheena was eating and said, 'I want toast.'

'You won't like this jam, sweetheart,' Sheena told him.

'I do want it,' Louie said.

She held it out towards his mouth. 'It's rhubarb,' she said, as he bit off a greedy piece. Sheena waited. After a second or two she could see the jam's tartness express itself in her boy's grimace. She held her hand out in front of his mouth, and Ezra watched Louie regurgitate the claggy morsel into her palm. From nowhere there materialised in Sheena's other hand a tissue, with which when he was finished she wiped Louie's mouth. 'Drink more milk,' she said, 'to take the taste away,' as she used the tissue to wipe the mess off her hand and into the bin.

Ezra was impressed by his wife's conjuring efficiency, ever unfazed, unsqueamish with this daily earthy parenting. He made her a second cup of tea. She went through and reclined on the white sofa, her eyelids lazily open, her lips sleepily parted, smiling at her mate and offspring as if slipping peacefully away from them.

'You look like that actress, darling,' Ezra told her. 'What's her name? In that film.'

Sheena blinked in slow motion and gazed up at him. 'Are you saying I look like Greta Garbo in *Lady of the Camelias*?'

Sheena was psychic. She could read Ezra's mind. He passed her tea. Blaise, her back to them, thrust her face forward into the hands on her lap. Then, withdrawing it from that posture of incredulity, said as if to the TV, 'No, Mum. Sorry. He meant Kim Basinger in *8 Mile*.'

Hector wandered through from the kitchen. 'Actually,' he ventured, 'I think Dad was alluding to Anna Karenina. She looked just like Mummy when I read it.'

Blaise turned round. Her expression suggested she found it beyond comprehension how an intelligent young woman like her came to be surrounded by fools.

'He said *film*, Hec. Did he say *book*? No! He said *film*.'

Hector looked up, into the vacant air above his head, his tongue pressing against the side of his mouth in a thoughtful way. 'Yes, true,' he agreed, standing his ground, gently. 'But he might have *meant* book. You know what Daddy's like.'

By the time he thought about which actress his wife resembled, Ezra Pepin had forgotten who he did mean. If indeed he'd meant any particular person or film at all. Perhaps he'd just meant that his lovely consumptive spouse looked like an old-fashioned movie star from the silver screen.

'Don't be silly, you two,' he said. 'Your mum's spot on. I meant that she looks like Greta Garbo.'

'Never heard of her,' Blaise shrugged. She sucked on her pencil, then took it out of her mouth and tapped it against the tiny jewelled stud in her right nostril, before turning back to her silent music on the TV.

Sheena smiled, though whether at the validation of her intuitive powers and knowledge of cinema or at the comparison of her face with that of one of the two or three iconic beauties of the twentieth century, Ezra wasn't sure. Rather than enquire, he kissed her instead; her neck, and ear. Blaise stole a distasteful glance over her shoulder. Louie abandoned his plastic pilgrims and clambered on to the sofa, forcing himself in between his parents.

Blaise blanked the TV off and turned, frowning. 'Did you two make out on your first date? If you can remember that far back. It's about time we were told, don't you think, Hec?'

'Blaise,' Ezra said. 'There are three impressionable people in this room. I should know. I'm one of them.'

'Your Dad?' Sheena smiled. 'He was so slow I thought he had to be gay. He gave not the slightest hint of being attracted to me.'

'Are you joking?' Ezra said.

'He was cute, but he had no idea how to make a move.'

Blaise chuckled. Louie asked, 'What move?'

'How can you *say* that?' Ezra protested. 'Don't say that. Not to them.'

'I kept going round to his flat. One night a storm broke. Pelting it down. I got ready to leave, to bike back to the Cowley Road, and he said, "You don't want to go out in this. Stay the night."

'*At last*, I thought. "We've got a lilo," he said. He stumbled over to a cupboard, yanked it out and started blowing it up. There were about five blokes, his fellow tenants, various graduates and other layabouts slumped on the sofa watching TV, smoking dope and drinking beer. I thought, Well, this is romantic.'

'What was romantic about it?' Hector asked.

'Get up to speed, squirt!' Blaise told him, laughing.

'Your father clearly wanted to keep me in the sitting-room at all costs. He tried to blow up the lilo, and the nozzle kept, I don't know, *jumping* out of his mouth. And he kind of chased it with his lips and tried to find it again. He had trouble finding it.'

'Don't tell us,' said Blaise. 'You had to do it for him.'

Sheena nodded. 'I volunteered. But I also took the opportunity to whisper in his ear that I could hardly sleep in here with everyone watching telly.

' "I'll turn it off," he said. "Look at the lazy slugs." '

' "No," I hissed. "Wouldn't it be simpler if I slept on your floor?" '

'Your Dad nodded very solemnly, like he'd not thought of this, and said he'd go upstairs and put covers on the spare pillow and duvet. And off he stumbled. You have to remember, your Dad's got a light head. Half a can of lager.'

Blaise frowned and nodded knowingly.

Ezra shrugged in a *don't blame me, how was I to know what was going on?* way.

'So he went upstairs and he was gone five minutes. Ten minutes. I'd blown up the lilo. The TV was droning on. I dragged the lilo upstairs.'

'What is lilo?' asked Louie.

'He was asleep?' Hector conjectured.

'Worse,' Sheena said. Then she turned to Ezra. And so his children turned to him. 'You tell them.' Four kind, expectant, mocking faces. It was the worst kind of show trial: Ezra Pepin left to deliver the final damning evidence for his own prosecution.

'All right,' he said. 'Okay.' He was pretty certain the anecdote had only a hazy connection to truth. 'It had taken me fifteen minutes of wrestling around to get the duvet inside what I thought was the duvet cover.'

'Yes?' Sheena prompted. 'And?'

A comic story that through familial repetition became fact. The sacrifice demanded by humour! 'It was only when I moved on to the pillow and found I was putting it in a duvet cover . . .'

'That you realised you'd put a pillowcase on the duvet?' Blaise turned to Hector. 'He'd spent twenty minutes stuffing a duvet into a pillowcase.'

'Poor Dad,' said Hector, grinning.

'Poor Daddy,' Louie agreed. 'Dat id funny,' he decided, solemnly, and reurned to his caravanserai.

Sheena and Blaise exchanged expressions of amused sympathy. *You see what I married?* one seemed to ask, shaking her head.

Yes, but you notice who I have for a father? asked the other, nodding. *Who's given me his genes? At least he didn't give you any of his genes. Be grateful for that.*

Green-helmeted, Sheena Pepin cycled along Kingston Road. She rode the same men's racing bike she'd bought from Walton Street Cycles the week she moved to Oxford seventeen years earlier – the only addition, when Blaise was two years old, a tiny child's saddle on the crossbar. Sheena felt her daughter safer within her embrace than in a child's seat invisible behind her, and in an accident she'd rather Blaise fell surrounded by her body. Ezra was infuriated by this delusion.

'If a collision occurs,' he told her, 'your grip on the handlebars will break, the kid will be thrown loose. I won't allow it.'

He was right: a seat above the back wheel, child belted in, was the safest option on a busy road, in amongst the dead jostling metal. Cars were out to get you, silent assassins: stealthy vehicles prowled the streets looking for victims.

Conscientious parents turned themselves into rickshaw drivers of the Western world, children on trailers and add-ons, distracting mothers and fathers with their yackety-yak, overloading and unbalancing them; Sheena was glad to be relieved of the humility. She walked with the children henceforth, or took a bus. She liked the emblematic value of a saddle on her crossbar, though, and kept it there: for the image it conveyed, of a mother of children who was now cycling to work.

She passed the cinema, and opposite it that very flat they used to live in. Funny, the parts of stories we tell, she considered, to spin the family myth. It was true, though, Ezra was charming in a diffident way: he'd neither resisted her advances – accepting them with the insouciance of a more confident man – nor made many of

56

his own. She'd had to stay calm. He was not long back from South America when they met. Most days, after a lazy breakfast he wandered over to the Department of Social and Cultural Anthropology and spent the day there, or in the Bod, reading and writing. He'd come back, take his turn to cook a stew, and then he'd join his co-habiting fellows in a dopey slump on dead beat furniture, cramping the TV. The smell of cannabis was sweet and safe, though Sheena only ever smoked it once back then: she found herself trapped in a catatonic body with a brain that had forgotten how to think. It was like being in a car whose wheels were locked and went round and round in a slow, hopeless circle; whenever you thought, oh, well, it'll run out of petrol eventually, you'd look at the fuel gauge and see that it was full, and fear of whoever had refilled it mocked your paralysed being.

Whenever after Sheena heard the phrase *out of body experience*, she thought, Sounds like fun to me, because I once had the opposite. She'd only learned to smoke marijuana recently, at the age of thirty-eight, with younger fellow Wasteland campaigners, discovering that without tobacco it had a quite different and benign effect.

Perhaps Ezra and his flatmates' intellectual endeavours wore them out and they couldn't help but sink in the evenings; maybe Sheena wasn't challenged enough in her junior research fellowship at the lab. But the furthest she could drag Ezra from the TV den was up to his bedroom under the eaves, where she taught him how to make love to her. Here. There. Slower. Faster. Not now. Wait. Don't wait. Do this. That's good. Yes. No. No. Yes. Yes.

Though a little bemused by the revelation of his ineptitude ('I thought I was satisfactory at least,' he pleaded. 'I mean, I didn't have formal complaints before,') Ezra took it on the chin. He appeared less threatened than amused by instruction, and applied himself to the demands of pleasuring her.

Ezra was different from the men Sheena had gone out with before. She'd been drawn to silent men. She'd conceived the idea as a child – years before experience of it – that sex was a kind of naked combat between a woman and a man, in which each tried to lose;

to make the other win; and which women were naturally better at. Whether she'd grasped precociously a universal truth, or whether a childish misconception had perverted her later experience, Sheena couldn't tell; but this was indeed how sex seemed to her, and she was attracted to taciturn non-talkers, to relationships that were straightforward barters of carnality. Men were easier to understand that way. The odd thing about Ezra was that although he talked, and was funny and kind, and shy but convivial, he was also just as self-reliant as her previous boyfriends. He demanded little of her: his struggles were with himself; his energy channelled into the thesis on a remote tribe of Indians; self-worth and self-doubt co-existed deep inside him. She didn't know whether she'd fallen in love, but one day she realised he'd fitted into her life as if her body and her mind had recognised the shape of him, and gladly enveloped it.

She'd known right away, Sheena recalled as she rode across St Giles and into the Broad, that Ezra would be a good father. She turned right into Turl Street. Maybe it was as simple as that: she'd snagged the first man whose paternal capabilities were apparent. Reaching the High, Sheena dismounted from her bike, and at the pelican crossing she pushed it over the road. The office was a walk-up down one of the alleys off the High. *Home Holidays 2nd Floor* was one of three name plates by the door. They didn't attract much casual passing trade, nor did they intend to, though a Far Eastern couple had trudged up the lino-covered stairs a few days earlier to ask, 'We see the buildings, we see the university. Yes, now we like look in homes of people. You book for us, please.'

Sheena was just in time for inclusion in a Starbucks order. The entire workforce were in position this Saturday afternoon.

'One tea for Sheena, chocolate for Jill,' said Luigi when he returned, passing round the biodegradable mugs. 'Frappuccino for Colin. That leaves Stella, raspberry tea coming through, and a plain espresso for me, Luigi.'

Luigi had heavy brown eyes, a boxer's nose and crooked lips, and Jill owned what Sheena called a maternal crush on him, unsteady as he brushed past and stepped through to the converted

58

cupboard he shared with Stella. His ripped clothes were particularly scruffy today, Sheena thought.

'You look like a yob,' she told him.

'She's English,' Jill apologised, 'she knows nothing about style.'

Luigi smiled indulgently, misaligning for a moment the thin sideboards and goatee inscribed with a razor blade on his olive skin.

'Is only incredible, Jill,' he said quietly, 'that you do.'

'Aaaaah!' Stella squawked. 'You bloody creep, Luigi. Get your head out of people's bottoms, mate, and into this website.'

Stella was taking a money-earning interlude during her world tour; it was her job to open the post, answer the phone, process emails.

The three young flexitimers tended to stroll into the office around midday, and then worked Saturdays, often Sundays too. The weekend as a distinct category of the week was irrelevant to them, anachronistic as Sheena's grandmother's insistence on Friday for eating fish, Monday for washing.

Colin was an Oxford history dropout, and he was in charge of the database for Home Holidays. He often arrived at the office as Sheena was leaving, to work through the night and be glued to the screen when she came back in the next morning. In truth it was a bit cramped in here now, and she and Jill huddled together at Jill's desk to go through their research on Cheltenham.

In Blenheim Orchard Ezra lay sprawled on the sofa in the sitting-room, plodding his way through sections of the Saturday paper. Politics. Sport. Culture. Money. You really had to dedicate the best part of a day. TV. Property. Travel. Ezra soaked it up, the vital ephemera connecting a citizen to the world around him. After the slump during the war in Iraq, travel companies report that holiday sales have picked up, but that families prepared to be flexible in their choice of destination can still discover late bargains. The new Leader of the Commons, Peter Hain, is reprimanded by the Prime Minister and the Chancellor for suggesting that the wealthy should pay more income tax. A male babysitter in Scotland is jailed for abusing a boy and trading images of him with other paedophiles over the internet. The disestablishment of the Ba'athist party in Iraq has made redundant the vast majority of civil servants, judges, engineers and others, who'd joined the party out of expediency. Electricity, clean water, cooking gas and fuel for cars and machinery remain scarce. Disbanding the military has put hundreds of thousands of angry young men on the streets.

Articles dissolved in the dry dust of Ezra's insomniac's brain, leaving behind a residue of discontent. When he ought, he castigated himself, to be preparing for the meeting on Monday.

Sheena rarely read a newspaper; watched or listened to the news. She possessed trenchant opinions on political issues, but it was a mystery how she formed them. Through titbits of information gleaned from conversation with fellow Friends of the Wasteland, perhaps. Her outlook on the world, though, was constant, unflinching. Not principles, exactly, more a matter of character applied to current affairs, and it was lucid as ideology. Ezra envied Sheena her outlook that allowed for little nuance, none of the wishy-washy tolerance that sentenced him to see all sides, to take none. Although he never said as much to her, he harboured the suspicion that it might have had a physical cause: Sheena had been told by a homeopath she visited that her intestines were too long, cramped into the space inside her.

'You have the colon of a much taller person,' Ezra told her. 'You'd be much better off with a semi-colon,' he joked, but he appreciated that it was no laughing matter to struggle practically every day of your life with indigestion, cramps, constipation. The daily procession of matter inching its arduous way along the winding, twisting, passages inside you. Peristalsis sluggishly shunting food. Such a person, Ezra figured, would have little patience with subtleties of argument that only coagulated action. They'd met when he was reeling from his experience in the jungle, and he'd fallen in love with her certainty, the way she strode forward through life. Somehow – he didn't know how – he'd helped her see what she wanted. It wasn't science: she derived no satisfaction from lab research, which was something she'd drifted into as a kind of feeble sop to her parents in the general direction of medicine; no, what Sheena had wanted, then, was a family.

Ezra set aside a finished section of the paper, already yellowed by the sun glaring through the window. His eyes ached, and he closed them. After some minutes he fancied that the sofa was suspended above the floor. He began to float into sleep.

A voice startled him.

Ezra opened his eyes. Blaise was standing between the sofas, gazing down at the scattered debris of newsprint.

'Excuse me?'

Blaise frowned. 'I said I don't read the papers any more, Daddy.'

'You don't?'

'They make me sad. Their editors don't send the reporters out to tell us what's happening in the world, they send them out to find bad news.'

'Really?'

Blaise nodded. 'We did it in media studies.'

Ezra wondered whether he'd been asleep a minute or an hour. His body felt light; his eyes were sore. 'Is that wrong?' he asked, squinting towards her.

'If the reporters say they can't find bad news, the editor says, "Look harder. I don't want you back here unless you've got some."'

Blaise stopped talking and gazed into the middle distance. She ran her tongue around her lips. She looked older than her thirteen years should have allowed her to; someone who'd heard too much already of famine and war. 'I suppose,' she said, 'I don't understand it, Daddy. All the things that are wrong and no one *does* anything.' She shrugged. 'Maybe I'm just not clever enough. I mean, I know I'm not as clever as Hector.'

'No, no, Blaise, don't be stupid,' Ezra assured her. 'Intelligence is about a lot more than just IQ, you know.'

'It's not fair but it's all right,' she said. 'Just because he's my younger brother. I mean, however much philosophers try to interpret the world, it's not enough, is it? Mum's right, isn't she? The point is to change it.'

61

Ezra raised his head from the cushion, and nodded. 'Your mum and Marx both.'

'Are we supposed to make the world a better place,' Blaise asked, 'or just enjoy ourselves?'

She sat down on the pink sofa across from Ezra and then, before he could give her any answer, as if remembering something she should have done earlier, Blaise took her mobile out of her pocket: Ezra watched her observing her thumb articulate messages, like an autonomous digit separate from her. No one does anything? Ezra wondered. Isn't quite enough done, though, really? Isn't there more than enough intervention?

'What's funny, Daddy?'

'Nothing, darling.'

Blaise returned to her texting. When he was her age Ezra read voraciously, drawn to tales of remote, mysterious regions. Odd pockets of Europe, beyond the mountains, in countries of steep-wooded ravines, whose people remained untouched by great events, and lived by customs the restless scrabble of progress had rendered anachronistic. The Khazars of the eastern steppe. Albanians with their blood feuds. Lapps. Woodsmen of the Black Forest. Tribes there and further afield who possessed a magical, a fetishistic energy, retaining nature's secrets – secrets of man's nature – forgotten in the industrialising rush. As a boy Ezra was fascinated, drawn to the exotic, the naked, the strange.

He spent his pocket money on historical atlases, pored over maps of Europe that showed boundaries shifting with every turn of the page, in the endless quarrelling of history, its squabbles and devastations. The migration of nations. The periodic formation and dissolution of empires, in whose margins tribes established themselves for a few generations, then vanished. The Scythians, fierce warriors, who left magnificent gold ornaments, and buried horses, in the graves of their chieftains. Illyria. The March of Verona. The Teutonic Knights. Wallachia. Bessarabia. He browsed in second-hand shops for books containing picture and description of peoples of the world. The multiplicity of custom precluded all certainty about our own, and Ezra found that insight as liberating as it was unsettling.

Did he expect Blaise to see the world in that way? Today? It was no longer possible for her generation. Once hidden tribes were now indigenous people. They were cheap labour who trekked from their remote villages to free-trade zones, for cash wages. Consumers of products in the globalised marketplace. Their identity changed to the flavour, the inflection, in their particular take on hip-hop; in their physiognomies that might lend originality to an advertising campaign; in the bright paintings of eye-catching naivety. It happened to every tribe that modern man made contact with, studied, befriended.

Ezra looked across at Blaise, sprawled on the pink sofa. She was retreating from him just as fast as she could, hiding from her father behind a pierced belly button and a studded nostril, the micro tattoo of an Oriental snake on her hip. Behind baggy blue jeans flared and frayed, bright fishnet, hair spiked and patchily, tuftily, coloured. A kaleidoscope of fashion, or anti-fashion. One or the other.

'What do you call yourself again?' he asked.

'Blaise is a grunger,' explained an invisible voice. Father and sister both started. Hector was perched on the windowsill.

'Don't be dumb, boffin boy,' Blaise said.

'When did you come in?' Ezra asked him.

'She's a mosher, Dad,' Hector said, slipping off the sill and dawdling over.

Screwing up her face, Blaise appealed to some invisible presence between her father and her brother. 'Do I look like someone who likes nu-metal?'

'What are you, then? She is, Dad.'

'You know nothing, you little hippie pre-teen,' Blaise declared, jumping up and grabbing Hector, who let himself roll on to the sofa and be tickled by his mock irate sister. Ezra couldn't tell whether the pleasure Hector took from this punishment was purely masochistic, or if there was a claim of superiority in riling his sister to such response. When she was satisfied with her victory, Blaise

63

rose and marched towards the kitchen. 'I'm going to do some cooking,' she said.

Ezra accorded his children what he reckoned to be their rightful autonomy, allowing them without intrusion their own interior world. Yet it irked him, somehow, the way that Blaise had begun to remove herself physically, to concrete arenas, retreating behind the clatter and racket of skateboards, the pounding resentment of rap, the indistinctly mumbled argot of urban tribes.

Actually, hip-hop grew on him each time he clapped the ear-phones of Blaise's Walkman to his head when he found it lying around, and used it to help him polish shoes or do the washing-up. Though he was just as likely to find jazz on her mini-disc, or heavy metal, or funky techno, so eclectic were his daughter's tastes. He recalled how doctrinaire were the fine gradations marking the boundaries of musical sectarianism when he was a lad. He even found himself eavesdropping on the same punk bands that he, at thirteen, fourteen, had fiercely championed. The Ramones, The Clash, Stiff Little Fingers would pound Ezra's ears with a raucous nostalgia.

Blaise measured out two hundred millilitres of condensed milk in the glass jug; she weighed four hundred and fifty grams of granulated sugar on her mother's retro scales; fifty grams of butter, twenty five of cocoa.

'It's chemistry,' Sheena had told her. 'Cooks have reached conclusions by trial and error. There's a history.' It was her one vital lesson in the kitchen. 'If you don't follow the recipe, when things fall apart don't blame anyone but yourself.'

Blaise added four teaspoons of water and two tablespoons of runny honey to the mixture in the saucepan, and began to stir it with a wooden spoon. The low gas flame was invisible in the sunlight, its hiss audible only if she leaned close to it, but the sugar dissolved and the chocolate and the butter melted. The forms in which each substance existed obeyed the heat, melting from solid separateness into one sweet liquidity.

In between checking the recipe every two minutes to reassure herself there was nothing unexpected awaiting, Blaise grabbed her father's measuring tape from the dresser in the hallway in order to select a cake tin as close to eighteen centimetres square as she could find. She greased it with a dab of butter, which she spread around the tin with the waxed paper the butter had been wrapped in, as she'd seen her mother do.

The mixture heated up slowly. It wouldn't reach boiling point until fourteen degrees hotter than water. A few bubbles at the side indicated its simmering. The cloying smell made Blaise's mouth water. She wouldn't repeat the mistake she once had, though, of testing a little at this stage off the wooden spoon: her tongue was scalded. She'd not regained her sense of taste for days.

The brown mixture boiled, not frenetically like water but slowly, bubbles easing up through the surface, which became covered with tiny eruptions. Blaise watched for many minutes. It was hypnotic. It roiled and seethed in a way that indicated a transformation going on inside its conjoining molecules, whose echo Blaise seemed to sense fermenting inside her.

Blaise poured a small plastic bowl of water from the cold tap. It was too warm, so she added a couple of ice cubes, then dropped a little of the mixture off the wooden spoon into it. When she dipped her fingers in the bowl and tried to pick it up the morsel broke up, so she tried again, and again, another smidgin every thirty seconds or so because a particular moment was about to come and she wasn't sure how long it would last.

After a dozen tries, a gobbet in the water bowl suddenly adhered to itself, a tiny ball. Blaise turned off the heat. The mixture continued to seethe: it had been created and was now alive, and it didn't need the heat but carried on bubbling away. Tilting the saucepan by its handle with her left hand, Blaise began to beat the mixture with a wooden spoon. This part of the performance was a chore. It helped to concentrate on technique: you couldn't just whirl the spoon around the pan, or zigzag it through the creamy liquid; you had to assist in the blending process, whisking the mixture by lifting spoonfuls, and folding it back on itself. The task was a laborious one, but if you concentrated, after a while you could lose yourself in it. Beating the mixture, in the way she copied Sheena doing, felt to Blaise as if she was folding a story back into itself, increasing the complexity of the storytelling, though this was a narrative told at a molecular level, not with words but chemical elements. The rearrangement of a subatomic alphabet.

The strain of the repetitive motion told in her wrist, and in her lower arm. A discomfort which intensified, into two specific spots deep in the bundles of nerve and ligament which burned and hurt. Blaise resolved not to stop what she was doing, though, even for a second. She carried on whisking with a steady action. The pain grew even hotter, but instead of pretending it wasn't there she focused on it and it became smaller as well, refining itself into a pair of intense but tiny needle points: withstanding her suffering altered the meaning of the sensation, from pain to one of self-mastering triumph.

In due course Blaise felt the material beneath her spoon undergoing another transformation: the smooth liquid was thickening; it was also altering its substance in another way, becoming granular.

Over in the sitting-room area the smell of fudge treacled the invisible air. Hector was unable, eventually, to resist it. 'I suppose I'd better go and help Blaise clean the bowl,' he told his father.

Blaise was pouring the fudge from the saucepan into the greased tin when Hector strolled into the kitchen. He watched the mixture spread, finding its level. He moved a little closer as Blaise used the wooden spoon to slide as much as she could from the pan.

'Shall I give you a hand?' Hector asked.

Blaise would put the tin in the fridge to cool, and when the fudge had set she'd cut it into squares. She could hardly wait, though; she'd planned to put the pieces into a plastic box in time for when Sheena got home, but looking at it now, brown and sweet and buttery, she thought she might just abduct the tin to her room and eat all the fudge herself, spoon by hot, sickly spoonful.

'Oh, Hec,' she replied, 'do you think you could possibly scrape the pan?'

He shrugged. 'Well, if you *want* me to, I don't mind.'

Hector gazed at the sugary chocolate stuck to the bottom and sides of the satisfyingly large saucepan. Blaise took the tin over to the fridge.

'I hope it's not too hard, like last time,' Hector said. 'It was like toffee. I almost cracked a tooth.'

'Make sure you clean everything and clear away,' Blaise told him.

Hector took a dessert spoon from the cutlery drawer. 'You should never overcook fudge,' he murmured, and began to scrape.

Blaise's footsteps up the stairs dissolved into Louie's scampering down. He ran to the window and, standing on tiptoe, said, 'Daddy! Daddy! Look!'

Ezra tumbled off the sofa and ambled over. A thin man was cycling along Wellington Drive. He was bent forward and pedalling furiously, but his progress was slow and precarious, for he carried under his right arm a stiff length of rolled-up carpet. He looked like a scrawny looter, Ezra thought, who'd stolen someone's old rug. He appeared almost acrobatic in a faltering way.

Ezra spotted a muddied spade sticking out of a pannier, just as Louie asked, 'What dat man id doing?'

'I reckon he's taking that carpet to his allotment, Peanut,' Ezra guessed.

'Why?'

'It's an old carpet, he's going to use it for mulching.'

'Why?'

'He'll put it on the ground to stop weeds growing where he wants to grow vegetables.'

'Why?'

'We can't eat weeds.'

'Why not?'

When the boy got into *Why?* mode you had to pause him, point his brain towards an obstacle. 'I'll let you try some weeds for tea and you can see for yourself.'

That seemed to do the trick: Louie pondered. They gazed out together, at the bright and empty street. Then from Nelson Avenue

67

came an elderly lady on a rickety, black sit-up-and-beg bicycle. As they watched her pass Louie said, 'Daddy, why dat lady not got carpet?'

'Damn good question, Peanut,' Ezra said. 'I don't know. I really don't know.'

'I will do drawing, Daddy,' Louie said, with sudden zeal. 'I will do a cowboy on a horse.'

'Good idea.'

'I will show it to you.'

'Thank you.'

Staring at the ceiling, Ezra could hear Hector practising his guitar. Blaise was around at the weekend more often than she used to be. 'We're going to the Village,' she used to inform him on a Saturday morning, catching the bus with a couple of friends to trawl through the mall outside Bicester, partaking of England's passagiatta round the shops.

How pleasant it was when all the children were at home in the sagging middle of a weekend day: each doing their own thing for a while, then getting itchy for company and a change of scene; they'd visit each other, or come down like Louie now, who carried paper and crayons and without a word to his father proceeded to kneel on the floorboards and draw.

With his eyes closed Ezra pictured the slow, migratory flow of his children around the house in the tedium of a Saturday afternoon. There was Monday's meeting to be prepared for, a decent bottle of wine to be bought for Sunday night, and Hector needed a new pair of swimming trunks for the morning. But there on the sofa Ezra lay through the afternoon, a paterfamilias visited by his children for no other reason than to reaffirm each other's existence.

Eight years earlier Sheena Pepin had herded her family home from an enervating summer fortnight in drought-stricken Provence like some bedraggled platoon retreating. The children were bad-tempered, the drive was a slow haul back up through France in an overheating car, and there was a long delay at the docks before they could board the ferry back across the Channel to Poole.

Sheena's friend Jill McTear's package holiday to Greece, meanwhile, had been cancelled when the operator went bust. Finding themselves at home for two weeks with no obligations, no one aware of their presence, Jill and her husband and two daughters pretended their house was a villa they'd rented in a strange city. They toured Oxford in an open-top bus, spent a morning in the Ashmolean, another in the Pitt Rivers. They took in the exhibition of Willy Ronis photographs at MOMA, saw *A Midsummer Night's Dream* in Wadham College Garden and *Free Willy 2* at the MGM in Magdalen Street. They played LaserQuest at Gloucester Green, went swimming at the leisure centre in Abingdon, and gambled away a fortune of pound coins at the dogs in Blackbird Leys. Tarried in Freud's on Walton Street to write postcards. *Wish you were here. Actually, you are.* Walked around with craned necks and a copy of John Blackwood's book, studying the secret gargoyles of Oxford.

'It's true,' Sheena responded. 'We never do these things. We're too busy.'

The only person the McTears told that they were home was their babysitter, so that Jill and Ted were able to go out to eat at Gees, Al-Shami, Aziz on Cowley Road. Jack Gibbons played Gershwin in Holywell Music Room. They revitalised their relationship with the city, and at night they slept in their own beds. The fortnight ended too soon on the most relaxed and enjoyable holiday the McTear family had ever had, and thus was born in the two women's kitchen conversations – each looking to get into some new, part-time line of work, both Jill's younger girl and Hector starting playgroup – the idea of a travel company that would offer itineraries for people in the Oxford area to have a holiday without the cost or discomfort or stress of check-in deadlines and flight delays, sickness and sunburn, lost luggage, the misunderstandings that arise from foreigners' inadequate English, hard beds, soft beds, hostile insects and bad drivers.

The selling point of Home Holidays, what made it more than

a xenophobic gimmick, or an indulgent hobby – an increasingly profitable business, indeed – was that it was an ethical enterprise, one that afforded its clients a sense of virtue and relief: their vacations were kind to the planet. No aeroplane fuel fouled the benighted atmosphere; no gallons of petroleum burned out on the autobahns of Europe – or even motorways to the English coast.

Stay Home. Stay Calm. Respect the Earth.
Home Holidays

Sheena threw herself into the business. For twelve months she and Jill performed research: they visited medieval churches with extant doom paintings, followed the journey sewerage takes out of the city, produced maps of picnic spots in wildflower meadows and cycle routes around town. With their husbands suddenly babysitting every evening Jill and Sheena checked out live music, at Catweazle and the Bullingdon as well as the Sheldonian, and they started up their company with a simple brochure.

Tell Your Friends You've Gone Away
Then Stay.
Home Holidays

Home Holidays was supposed to be halfway between a hobby and a business for two women with young children, but Sheena found that she not only enjoyed meetings with the bank manager, a PR consultant, prospective advertising clients; she was also very good at them. Efficient, straightforward, authoritative. The business grew and after two years working out of Jill's spare bedroom they rented the same inaccessible office in the centre of town in which they were now, seven years later, reviewing the data for their eighth town or city: Cheltenham.

'We're looking at reenactment of the Regency atmosphere,' Sheena conjectured. 'It was a spa and a summer resort. Its inhabitants would stay to be pampered, wouldn't they?'

70

'The population was less than seventy two thousand as recently as 1960,' Jill noted.

Sheena pondered as she spun slowly round in her chair. 'We need to emphasise the post-modern mix of flavours that money buys.'

Jill pored over their notes. 'Over fifty per cent of wards in Cheltenham have a greater than average proportion of pensioners living alone, compared to the rest of England.'

For Sheena, Jill was an ideal business partner, a large, affable woman with whom she'd been friends since they met in a health visitor's clinic at a doctors' surgery on Beaumont Street, two tired women with tiny first-born babies.

There was no doubt, Ezra reckoned, that Sheena was drawn to stolid, diffident people, as they were drawn to her, and she and Jill developed the company with a gradual but insistent annual increase in turnover.

'Jill does the paperwork,' Ezra once explained to Simon and Minty Carlyle, 'Sheena makes the decisions,' which wasn't true at all, he admitted – in response to Sheena's outrage at the imputation of both bossiness and laziness – 'except fundamentally.' In fact Sheena worked hard, and Jill laid out the pros and cons of where to publicise or with which entertainments agency to sign a contract, but Jill needed Sheena to rubberstamp the most trivial decisions with the imprimatur of her assertiveness, and her instinct for how the company should grow.

'Latvia,' Hector broadcast from the blue glow of the computer screen. 'Albania, Daddy. I don't like it. You're surrounding us.'

'Get off that thing, damn you, boy,' Ezra ordered from the floor, where he was constructing a train track with Louie. 'We pay BT by the minute. It's costing your mother and I a fortune.'

'That's why it's so slow. You should get broadband, Daddy. Belarus,' Hector sighed.

'You heard your father,' said Blaise, coming into the room. 'Log off, Hec.'

Hector peered at the screen. 'Guess who's expecting a call,' he said. 'Why don't you use your mobile?'

'Mind your own business,' Blaise said. 'Daddy. Lou. Anyone want a piece of fudge?'

The Pepin family moved house in 1998, after the Blenheim Orchard estate was built on a trapezium-shaped plot north east of the Wasteland between the canal and Woodstock Road. Hemmed in between houses on one side and hedges on another, behind the sports pavilion of the college which owned it, the site was, when opened up, much bigger than Ezra Pepin – who'd cycled by each week on his way to tennis in Summertown – could have imagined. Especially after the neglected, unpruned fruit trees, their twisted branches grown in amongst each other like the hair of some tribe of wild women, had been cut down. A hundred apple, pear and damson trees were cleared, but their existence commemorated for ever in the name of the estate they'd made way for.

Ezra was promoted across to Operations at the same time as it became clear to Sheena that, barring catastrophe, Home Holidays and homeholidays.com would soon pay for a higher mortgage. The Pepins visited the show home at Blenheim Orchard. It had a Victorian revival exterior, high spec finish interior, *classic and contemporary in perfect harmony*, and it looked pleased with itself, a sprightly younger sibling of the old houses across Woodstock Road. Ezra and Sheena put a deposit on one of the five-bedroomed town houses, with two parking spaces each, on Wellington Drive. It was only later, on the day they moved in, that they realised each room in the show home had been stocked with three-quarter-size furniture. But the move meant a room for each of the two children, a spare bedroom, and a study for Ezra.

'You'll finish your thesis once and for all,' Sheena promised.

It was about a week later that Sheena announced her third, entirely unplanned, pregnancy, the product of a night they took a chance on dates and cycles: Louie duly joined the family, and before he knew it Ezra's office was back in the spare room.

While his children played and squabbled around him on this first hot day of 2003 Ezra recalled the Pepins' last family holiday abroad, that sweltering fortnight in Provence in which they shared

72

gîtes with other families of Sheena's tribe. Blaise and Hector had trotted off each morning to join their cousins, and somehow Ezra and Sheena found themselves alone together for large chunks of each day for the first time since before Blaise was born. It was too hot to move, they spent afternoon siestas and nights sweating, uncovered, sleepless, and Sheena turned on as Ezra had never known her. Heat and fatigue seemed to remove them from their bodies, which they watched with interest crawl towards each other. They wanted to make love all the time, more than they ever had, even when they'd first got together; almost as much as they wanted to sleep: after sex they slid into sticky unconsciousness.

In between bouts of sleep they answered the craving of their bodies with more sex, greedy flesh slipping and slithering against sweating flesh. How great their last real holiday had been, Ezra remembered. Back home, Sheena started the company, and they'd not been abroad again.

'Macedonia,' Hector said. 'A new office opened in Skopje. Wonder how they get on with the one in Thessalonika, Daddy?'

'Hector,' Ezra implored. 'Please.'

Hector gazed at his father, then rose from the chair and drifted away. Blaise leaned forward, steered the mouse and clicked to get offline. As she did so the telephone rang. Hector plucked the cordless receiver off the table.

'Pepin residence,' he intoned solemnly. 'Hector Pepin here. How may we help you? Certainly, Akhmed, she's right . . .'

Blaise took the receiver off her brother. 'It's me,' she said, and listened. She collected a few strands of hair in her fingers. 'I'm not sure,' she murmured. 'I'm studying.' She fed the hair she'd gathered into her mouth, and chewed it as she listened some more. Then she opened her mouth and let her hair fall out. A few strands remained, stuck to her lips with saliva. She blew them away. 'I suppose so,' she said. Then Blaise looked up. Her eyes registered that her father and both her brothers were idly watching. 'Hang on,' she said into the receiver. Holding it to her chest, she exited the room and trotted upstairs.

Hector picked his way across the toy-strewn floor. Standing above his father, he gazed out of the window.

'Turkey, Daddy. Ismit. Now that you're part of this corporation.'

'I've explained,' Ezra said. 'Isis Water has been taken over by a large German company, called DeutscheWasser. We're only owned by them. We're still a separate little outfit in Oxford.'

'It's not just bottles, Daddy. You provide tap water now. Waste water. Pipes. Sewerage plants. You're huge. You're spreading to the edge of Europe. Beyond.'

'I am not Isis Water, Hector. I'm a lowly nobody in Operations. You know that.'

Hector frowned. Unconvinced. 'You're going global, Daddy.'

Ezra gazed at his son. So serious, always had been. Ezra had already accumulated more tickling, wrestling, rough and tumble hours on the carpet with Peanut Louie than he had in eleven years with Hector. His older boy had the curiosity of a pessimist who needs to know exactly what it is that's likely to spring upon him. He'd got a bee in his bonnet and already he knew more about the structure of the sprawling company that employed his father than Ezra did. The sun through the window behind Hector haloed his fine-boned, delicate face. His hostage to adolescence, as Sheena called it.

'What's your point?' Ezra asked him.

'I worry they'll send you overseas,' Hector said, frowning. 'To one of those places. Far away.'

Ezra smiled. 'Don't worry, my darling. Your father has no exportable skills whatsoever.'

Blaise's voice came through from the hall. 'I'm going out,' she yelled. 'See you later.'

'When?' Ezra called back.

'Whenever. It's Saturday, remember?'

With that Blaise clearly considered the exchange over: Ezra heard the front door close. He stood up and walked through to the kitchen, where he pulled the three-quarters-full black bag from the swing-bin. He twirled plaits out of opposite sides and tied them together, and carried the bag through the house. He walked out of the front door, between the cars and round to the dustbin under its lean-to. Only having dropped the bag in and replaced the lid, the whole process accomplished with swift efficiency, did Ezra Pepin look up. There at the end of Wellington Drive he saw Blaise walk the last few yards towards a boy of similar age. Dark skinned. Asian. Sleek black hair. The boy made no move towards Blaise, but waited for her on the pavement. As she reached him he turned with her, and they began to round the corner into Churchill Avenue side by side. And for just a moment before they disappeared Ezra saw, or thought he saw, his hand join hers.

4

Swimming

Sunday 22 June

There was silence in the kitchen. Padding feet could be heard descending the stairs. Sheena slouched in, dressed in Ezra's white cotton towelling dressing-gown, eyes closed, groping like a blind woman. 'Morning,' she greeted people. 'Thanks for the bathroom-door slam, Louie. On a blinking Sunday.'

Louie grinned. 'Dat wad funny.'

'No, that wasn't funny,' Ezra admonished him.

Unable yet to summon the strength to raise her eyelids, Sheena emptied the remains of a bottle of orange juice into a glass by touch alone. 'You know what I hate?' she asked. 'That the council won't take plastic in our recycling box.' She held the empty bottle out towards the swing-bin, as if a servant might pop up to take it from her. But she must have been focusing what energy she had, because all of a sudden her hand jerked from the wrist and the bottle spun, glanced off the top of the bin and fell to the tiles with a hopeful, hollow clatter. 'I hate we have to put plastic in the bin.'

'Or try to, anyway,' said Ezra. 'Stay there. I'll do you some toast.'

Even if she hadn't attended another campfire vigil at the Wasteland the night before, Sheena Pepin would have woken slowly. Emerging from sleep, she required a period of decompression

76

before entering the atmospheric pressure of her day. Breakfast had to be taken in stages, her metabolism and digestion eased into action. She took a sip of orange to prime the pump. 'Where's Blaise?' she asked.

Louie shrugged. 'Don't know.'

'Asleep,' said Ezra. He placed a plate of toast with jam in front of Sheena, and a large mug of tea.

'Where's Hector?'

Before either of the others could betray him, Hector gave himself away with a twitch and rustle of newspaper.

'What on earth do you think you're doing up there?' Sheena demanded.

Hector kept his reader's head bowed. 'Nothing,' he said quietly.

'Did you *know* he was up there?' she asked Ezra. 'Those cupboards are not designed to take your weight, for God's sake, Hector. Don't act like an idiot, because you're certainly not.'

Hector up in the shadows began turning red in stages. The boy blushed one zone at a time. It began with his neck and rose, creeping up over his chin and along his jaw.

'If that corner cupboard falls off the wall,' Sheena told him, 'not only will you be injured, but there'll also be one heck of a mess.'

A crimson rash spread across Hector's skin, suffusing his cheeks, reddening his forehead, making his pale ears glow in the gloom.

'I can't believe you knew he was up there, Ezra.'

Hector did his best to keep a low profile, to drift beneath the parental radar. But he was drawn to the tops of things. He climbed chests of drawers and wardrobes and hid his days there reading, or watching what went on below from up above the lights. When he was younger he'd monkey around rooms from one piece of furniture to another without touching the ground: take hours reconnoitring the sitting room, planning his route with the pernicketiness of a mountaineer, adjusting an elaborate circuit with a shift of an armchair an inch this way or that for a precise increase of difficulty.

'In dangerous situations, Daddy,' Hector would explain, 'what we climbers do is eliminate risk.'

Ezra admired his son's shy, scientific eccentricity. Hector now clambered down first to the work surface – Sheena was quite right, Ezra admitted: Hector looked far too big for such a stunt – then to the floor, and took his silent place at the table. There he spread pieces of toast with careful layers: one with marmalade and tomato ketchup, the other with Marmite, peanut butter and honey. Ezra tried not to watch Hector chomp his disgusting breakfast, doing so in a dutiful manner that gave no hint of pleasure. Sheena chewed hers with drowsy jaws. Louie crunched a dry Weetabix. Ezra drank his second mug of tea – already, after cereal, less pleasant-tasting than the first one of the day.

By the time Blaise appeared, the others were rising. Her lips were puffy, her eyes swollen, with sleep.

'Want to eat, better hurry,' Sheena said.

Blaise surveyed the wreckage of breakfast strewn across the table: soiled crockery and cutlery, small puddles of sugar-brown milk, bloody globules of raspberry jam, crust-crumb shrapnel.

'Gross.' Blaise made for the fridge. 'I'll just have juice.' She was wearing Sheena's white bathrobe, having recently outgrown her own, a pink one with a picture of Buffy the Vampire Slayer on the pocket.

'Mummy did dink juice,' Louie chuckled. Blaise continued to the fridge, where she saw confirmed her brother's blab. 'Mummy did do dat.'

'Mum?' Blaise demanded, aghast.

'First come, first served, sweetheart,' Sheena shrugged, getting up from her seat. 'Second rule of family life.'

'You *know* that's all I have.'

Louie turned to Ezra with a serious frown and said, 'Blaise do like cereal *some* times.'

'*Most* days that's all I have. You *know* that, Mum.' Blaise made for the door.

'I'm sorry, sweetheart,' Sheena said, doing the same.

The kitchen was cramped with table, chairs and bodies, obstacles to Blaise's attempt to overtake her mother and reach the door first.

'Come on, Bee,' Sheena said. 'Give me a hug.'

'No,' Blaise said, heading for a gap that Sheena was closing rapidly.

'Go on. I said I'm sorry.'

They met in the doorway. Blaise's options were to accept Sheena's apology or try to wrestle her out of the way. She chose the latter, to Ezra's dismay, and the two of them grasped at each other in combat holds. Only for what he saw to reorder itself, in a blink of his eye, the image or his perception of it clarifying as mother and daughter, in their matching white bathrobes, embraced. And then they ambled upstairs together. 'Just don't think I'm going swimming, that's all,' he could hear Blaise say, in a good-natured tone of voice.

Silence fell. Ezra met the gaze of his two sons. What could he tell them? He shrugged in a way which he trusted to convey both the insoluble mystery of female behaviour and the boys' need for tolerance. Patience. 'Impossible to explain,' he said. 'A different juju.'

'Juju,' Louie laughed. 'Dat id funny.'

'Yes, that is funny,' Ezra agreed. 'Now you two get on upstairs, battle it out for the bathroom.'

Louie looked up at Hector. 'Chase me!' he said.

Hector peered down at his brother. 'One,' he said. 'Two.'

Louie ran chuckling for the stairs.

'Dad?' Hector said. 'Mum said what the second rule of family life is. What's the first?'

Ezra fed two dirty bowls to the dishwasher. He frowned. 'What do you reckon?' he asked.

Hector screwed up his eyes, and scratched his ear. 'Mum and Dad are always right?'

Ezra clicked a finger at him. 'Spot on, soldier,' he said. 'Very funny.'

Hector nodded gravely, and turned to the door. 'Three!' he yelled. 'Coming!' And ran from the room.

They rode in convoy along Oakthorpe Road, and over Banbury Road at the crossing and down through the car park, Ezra first with Louie in the child seat behind him, then Hector, and Sheena bringing up the rear. At Ferry Sports Centre Hector led the way into the Men's changing room.

'Come on, you two,' Hector exhorted. 'Let's beat Mummy.' He yanked T-shirt, shorts and pants off in a cartoonish flurry of skinny limbs; pulled on swimming trunks. 'Oh, hurry up, Dad,' he moaned, as his father sat on the bench and began untying his shoe laces.

'You go ahead,' Ezra said.

Hector shovelled his clobber into a locker and pattered off, scratched goggles swinging from his hand.

Louie extricated himself from his clothes item by item, then folded each one neatly. He pulled his diminutive trunks up to his paunchy torso. By the time he and his father entered the green shimmering light of the cavernous swimming hall, Sheena was already ploughing her lonely furrow, an early one of the forty Olympian lengths of the main pool that she would complete. Hector, two or three lanes away from her, conducted an energetically ineffective backstroke, his goggles lending him a lunatic seriousness.

The high ceiling of the hall amplified the yells and splashes of the swimmers, an echoey resonance that gave a sense of excited anticipation. Ezra and Louie walked hand in hand across the wet, slippery tiles to the learner pool. Some people liked to plunge into chilly water. Let them, if that's what they wanted: Ezra was happy to return to the womb, to loll in warm liquid while Louie splashed around, to feel his joints yield and his limbs stretch. Watching the other top-heavy dads, ludicrous in their near-nakedness, failed experiments of nature. A tattooed father from the Cutteslowe estate; a couple of north Oxford professionals; a visiting academic or two from distant cloisters of the earth. Ezra found himself surrounded by a multicultural apology for manhood with narrow shoulders, thin legs, gross bellies which could only be excused, surely, if they were food stores, like camels', ready to sustain their carriers on some long swim, some cross-Channel loll to come.

Toddlers in one-piece swimsuits, lined with compartments holding precious white ingots of polystyrene, floated like jellyfish. Five-year-olds with orange armbands splashed a turbulent doggy-paddle with which they made no discernible progress, while others who'd been granted the secret of buoyancy slithered through the water like eels.

Ezra towed Louie around the pool. 'Kick, Louie! Kick your feet.' He watched the women too, their shapes as unlikely as the men's. This fat young matriarch, that one coming in now with splendid legs, alarming low bosom. There a skinny waif in a bikini whose children had left no trace of their occupancy, except for stretch marks etched on her flat abdomen. Here a woman gracefully lowering her chunky body into the pool. Ezra was surprised by the urge to bite them. He floated in the too-warm water and imagined gliding from one to another and sinking his teeth into some sweet part of their anatomy – until a part of his anatomy made its presence felt, and he looked away. At the barefoot young lifesavers in their yellow polo shirts and red shorts, observing like umpires from their high chairs.

Ezra caught occasional glimpses of regular swimmers walking from the changing room to the cold, big pool. Some of those women were sleek, healthy animals. Were they more or less sexy than these tired mothers? They churned up and down in the cold, chlorinated water; after a certain number of lengths they climbed out and strode back across the tiles. Regimented exercise, joyless, a frigid kind of thing to do. No wonder Sheena, just emerging over there, wearing the white bathing cap, practised it. It was weird, really: him, this lazy sensualist, and her, marching back towards the changing rooms. No, Ezra preferred to float here with the other indolent Dads, in this water, warm as the Mediterranean he and his family no longer swam in.

Sheena and Hector were out and showered, dressed and half-way home by the time Ezra coaxed Louie from the pool, their fingers wrinkled, only by reminding him of the sweets machine out in the corridor. In the shower room they peeled off their trunks and stood naked at the urinal, father and son, thirty-nine and three, the warm water having loosened Ezra's muscles and ducts, and peed together. Louie bent his knees, leaned back and craned forward, so that he could watch himself grasping his little penis with both hands, and direct the proud flow before him.

'Come on, boychick,' Ezra said. 'Ready for the shower?'

'Look at this.' Jed Wilson urged Blaise over. 'This is what it said.' He had the tousled hair and pinched eyes of someone who'd only just, this Sunday noon, awoken.

Blaise studied a newspaper photograph of the outside of the house in which she now stood, torn from the Property section of the *Oxford Times*. In case she was blind, Jed read out for her the words below. '*Sunnymead. Large property located in this most sought-after area of Oxford.*'

Bobby Sewell sat on the floor. He'd phoned to invite Blaise round. 'My little saviour,' he called her. Using the corkscrew of a Swiss army knife he was opening the bottle of her father's wine which Blaise had brought. 'In this most conveniently situated side road,' he added to Jed's description of their abode, using a strangled voice he imagined appropriate for estate agent speak. 'In this most attractive avenue.'

'*With outline planning consent for demolition,*' Jed continued, '*and the construction of three luxury town houses.*' He turned to Blaise. 'You know, like, mate, what the fuck is that?'

'It's fill-in development,' said a third man, quietly, whom Blaise had not met before.

'We call it in-fill, Zack,' said Bobby. To Blaise he said, 'It was decent of the estate agents to draw our attention to it.'

'I'll tell you what it is,' Jed said. 'It's vandalism, that's what it is. There's nothing wrong with this house. It's a beauty.'

'Bit new for my taste,' Bobby said.

'New?' Blaise asked. 'How old is it?'

After a pause, in which neither of the other two answered, Zack said, '1922. It's written above the front door.'

'Go on,' said Jed. 'Have a look around. It's bigger than you'd think.'

'Go ahead,' said Bobby, proudly.

Blaise explored the empty rooms alone. The upstairs had a strong smell, more powerful than any house she'd been in before, as if a family's furniture, clothes, belongings neutralised a building's personality, which had now been liberated and could express itself, for the first time in eighty years. This one smelled mustily organic, she thought. Of dried or drying plants.

There were four bedrooms, three of which the men had commandeered, the unbrushed wooden floors scattered with a debris of clothes, sleeping bags, thin foam mattresses. What exactly was she doing here, Blaise wondered. What did she want from Jed or Bobby? Why hadn't she gone swimming with the rest of her family? She enjoyed swimming. The musty smell of the house was not, she decided, unpleasant. Old wood, and tobacco. A suggestion of greenhouses. Bonfires. The house was fixed in autumn. What had happened to her friends? They were cordial enough at school; didn't she want to see them at the weekend? Well, apart from Akhmed, her mobile wasn't exactly stacked up with requests for her company.

Blaise went back downstairs. What did she think, or hope, that Jed or Bobby might want from her? Bobby was in what was probably the sitting-room, at the front of the house. There was a picture rail running around the dirty white walls; she could see where paintings had once hung. Bobby had a pot of purple paint, and was daubing a sentence around the room. So far the large, uneven letters spelled out, *FORESTS PRECEED CIVILIZATIONS, DESERTS FOLL . . .*

Blaise went through to the back room, where Jed and Zack drank red wine from mugs.

'What do you reckon?' Jed asked. 'Not bad, eh?'

'How long do you think you'll be able to stay?' Blaise wondered.

Jed shrugged. 'We've got a couple more mates hitching down from up north tomorrow.'

Blaise sat cross-legged on the hard floor. She glanced towards Zack, to find him studying her. His face was unshaven around a blond moustache. He looked down, at the scuffed knees of his jeans. 'Are you the girl who got arrested?' he asked, before glancing back up at her.

Blaise nodded. She wondered what they'd told him; what he thought.

'She's one spunky kid,' Jed said. 'Bobby was in trouble.'

'I hope it helped the cause,' Zack said softly. His long, thin limbs were folded at the joints like tent stretchers.

'Don't start,' Jed said curtly.

Suddenly, Blaise wanted to tell this Zack she wasn't sure how proud she was of what she'd done. That since it happened she kept seeing the man's bloodied face, and hearing his disbelieving groan. But Jed and Bobby thought, just like Sheena, that she'd done something wonderful, and it was easier to take shelter in their good opinion than to brave a cheerless search for her own.

'All I'm saying,' Zack murmured, 'is people need somewhere to live.'

Bobby came into the room, his dreads flecked with purple paint, just as Jed said, 'Yeh, well, maybe they should do what we're doing.'

'He's not starting again, is he?' Bobby asked. He had the paintbrush in his hand, and as he passed through towards the kitchen he leaned deftly towards Zack and splodged his nose bright purple. Zack ducked away too late. Without a word he lifted his T-shirt, and wiped the paint off his nose with it, as best he could without a mirror. Blaise saw the thin skin of his belly creased into narrow folds. A line of brown hairs rose from his jeans to his belly button.

Bobby washed the brush in the kitchen sink.

'Running water,' Jed told Blaise. 'What more could we ask for?'

She turned to Zack. 'Do you do anything?' she asked.

'Yeh,' said Jed. 'He's got an allotment.'

Bobby came back, wiping his wet hands on his unwashed combat trousers. 'He's going to spend the summer growing vegetables, aren't you, Zackie?'

'Who for?' Blaise asked.

'Tell her, Zack,' Jed demanded. 'We all want to know: who for?'

'I just believe you have to start with yourself,' Zack said quietly.

'There's your answer,' Jed laughed. 'That's how to change the world. Start with yourself.'

'Fiddle while the earth burns,' said Bobby, lighting a cigarette and coughing with laughter. 'Any of that wine left for the workers?'

Zack sat with his head bowed, his shoulders hunched. Blaise realised that she was laughing, too.

'Zack's going to lead the vegetables in the revolution!' Jed announced. Bobby high-fived him.

Blaise chuckled. It occurred to her that they were making fun of Zack for being apolitical, just as kids at school made fun of her for her political involvement. But then she heard herself say quietly, as if against her own will, yet still loud enough for everyone to hear, 'Zack's Zucchinis!'

And Bobby, gulping her father's wine, turned to high-five Blaise, too.

At seven-thirty that evening Simon and Minty Carlyle strolled around the side of the Pepins' house, tapped on the glass pane of the kitchen door and let themselves in. Sheena was testing a dish for flavour.

'Hello there,' they cooed. 'Hi.'

'Hi.'

'Come in,' Ezra sang. He was opening a bottle of Chianti: the corkscrew's wings lifted like ears at the approach of thirsty guests. 'Come in.'

'Sorry,' said Sheena, 'running a bit late here.' She stepped aside from the stove to greet Simon and Minty holding her arms out to the sides, a spatula in one hand and a pepper pot in the other.

'You look like a seventeenth-century painting,' Simon told her. '*Allegory of Gluttony*. Be far better nude, of course.'

'Oh, get away, you!' Sheena told him in mock indignation.

The two couples exchanged kisses to each pair of cheeks. Minty pressed for a little more than the others, putting one arm around first Ezra's back, then Sheena's, and pushing her upper body against theirs in a meaningful semblance of an embrace. It said, Of course if we didn't see each other practically every day, at yours, at ours, at school, you blokes on the tennis court each Friday morning there doesn't happen to be the last stand of the Friends of the Wasteland, then we'd enjoy a great big bear hug because we're so close. In the meantime here's an indication, at least, of the fullness of that friendship.

'Take a look at this wine,' Ezra invited Simon. 'Adrian had, what, a dozen bin-end bottles? I bought six. Less than a fiver each, it's laughable.'

'Good, is it? "Castello di Fonterutoli".'

'The Mazzei family. Reckoned to be the best Chianti vineyards.'

' "2000." Good year, was it?'

'That I'm not sure, Simon. The best year, wasn't it? Or was that 2001?'

'One or the other, surely,' Simon frowned. 'I wouldn't like to stake my reputation on which.'

'Of course, I may be thinking of France.'

Either Sheena or Minty might have recalled a little more about the vintage of recent Italian wines, but each of them knew better by now than to interrupt. Whether Ezra believed he and Simon were modest connoisseurs, or whether he was merely burlesquing the role, Sheena was never quite certain. She meant to ask him after guests had gone, and always forgot.

Soon they were seated around the table and tucking in to pasta.

'Oh, Sheena,' Minty exclaimed, 'what is it? You have to tell us.'

Sheena's mouth was full. 'It's fresh fusilli,' Ezra said.

'Literally, *little spindles*,' said Simon.

'From that place in the covered market,' Ezra continued.

'Well, sure, sport. I didn't mean the pasta.'

'Tuna,' Sheena said.

'No, but there's something else, isn't there?'

'Lemon.'

'Of course there's lemon, Ezra, we can all taste the lemon. But what is it? Oh, it's delicious, Sheena.'

'Yes, yes, indeed,' Simon felt obliged to mumble.

'Pine nuts, obviously. Garlic. Parsley.'

'Right, Minty.'

'Anchovies?' Ezra enquired.

'Anchovy?' Sheena demanded. 'Are you serious? You think there's anchovy in here?' Her mouth had assumed the shape of a smile, but Ezra suspected this was misleading. 'I've been cooking meals for you for fifteen years and you think this tastes of anchovy?'

'Ah. Capers,' said Minty, rolling one against the roof of her mouth with her tongue.

'Yes,' Sheena smiled.

'I got it!' Minty declared.

'But what else?'

'More? Great. Don't tell us! Let me guess again.'

After salad, and fruit, they took coffee and the chocolates the Carlyles had brought through to the sitting-room area, Ezra following Simon's dishevelled figure, trying hard to shift focus from Simon's bald spot shining out, under the halogen lights, from his lanky grey hair. A spray of fine dandruff was scattered across the shoulders of his blue silk shirt.

'But you have to admit,' Simon was telling him, in his high-pitched voice, which made him sound like a much younger man. 'I mean, not wishing to blow my own trumpet or anything, but there can't be too many domestic architects who've taken part in protest at a housing development.'

'Blaise upstairs?' Minty asked Sheena.

'She ate with Hector and Louie,' Sheena nodded. 'She's torn between joining the grown-ups and the tedium of our conversation.'

'Hey, I didn't tell you, darling,' Ezra cut across. 'Blaise had this call yesterday.' He told her – and their friends – about the boy with whom Blaise may or may not have held hands.

'Well, that was probably Akhmed, wasn't it?' Minty asked.

Ezra and Sheena stared blankly at her.

'I'm sure Ed told me.' Minty arched an eyebrow. 'Aren't they a bit of an item?'

'An *item?*' Ezra demanded. 'Who is he?'

'He's in the class above Ed and Blaise.'

'He didn't look any older than her,' Ezra shrugged.

'His father owns that restaurant on Walton Street,' said Minty. 'The Raj Cuisine.'

'You're kidding,' said Sheena. 'That was our favourite, Ezra, wasn't it?'

'An item,' Ezra frowned. 'She's not mentioned him.'

'She's thirteen, Ez,' Sheena said.

'Welcome to the world of teenagers' anxious parents.'

'Do put a sock in it, Simon,' Ezra objected. 'Two boys. You know it's different for us.'

'True enough,' Simon admitted. ' "The sooner a boy loses his virginity, the better for all the women he's going to sleep with," as Colette – wasn't it, Minty? – put it.'

'Oh, please,' said Sheena. 'That is so sexist, and offensive in every way. So, what, have you had poor Ed deflowered, or whatever it might be called for boys?'

'You must be joking!' Minty said, chuckling on the sofa into which she'd shrunk, so that her knees were higher than her behind and her skirt sliding by degrees down her black tights. Poor Minty, thought Ezra, with her dark hair cut short and gelled back, with her bright-red lipstick on full lips. Her long nose, her large brown eyes. Always trying so hard. He was glad she wasn't his kind of woman: it kept their friendship relaxed. She had good legs, though, he had to admit, tucked up under her like that, shifting position. He had to make an effort to keep his gaze from wandering to her calves, her knees, her thighs. He was grateful she had no breasts; that she was just a bit too bony for his taste. And no wonder, the way after praising it to the skies – a clever ruse – Minty left half her food uneaten on the plate, before stepping outside for a cigarette. As if smoking filled her stomach, not her rib-engirdled lungs.

'Ed? You have to be kidding,' Minty laughed. 'Ed is such an innocent. I suspect he'll be like one of those actors who play schoolboys into their twenties. It's genetic, of course. Simon was like that when we met.'

'Did you take his virginity, Minty?' Sheena asked. 'I don't believe we knew that.'

'I say, that's not really true, is it?' Simon objected.

'His father had already hauled him off to some brothel on a trip to Paris. Hadn't he, sport?'

'Marvellous bloody thing to do,' Simon said in his unbroken voice. 'The madam dealt with me herself. Fifty if she was a day.' Simon sighed. 'Gave me the most tender and beautiful experience of my life.' He shook his head with nostalgia. Then, as abruptly as if he'd received radio controlled orders to change the subject, Simon said, 'I say, did either of you see the news just now? They've almost got him.'

Sheena frowned at Simon. 'Yes?' she wondered. After a few seconds without explication she asked, 'Who got who?'

'The Yanks,' Simon said. 'Saddam. A secret military unit: Grey Fox. Part of their Intelligence Support Activity. Manhunters.'

'Assassins,' Minty murmured.

'Deep penetration agents,' Simon said. 'Part of the Pentagon's black world of undercover operations.' His wine-flushed face grew more roseate as he spoke. Beads of perspiration appeared on his forehead. 'Their signal interception aircraft flying in low passes over the Sunni Triangle, scanning the airwaves for Ba'athist communications. Unmanned drones. Photo reconnaissance aircraft.'

Minty shook her head. 'War games,' she said.

'The war's over,' Sheena pointed out.

'Because Bush put on a uniform?' Minty responded sharply. 'Stood on an aircraft carrier, and declared victory?'

'The Yanks are right,' Simon said. 'Once they've got Saddam, the violence will die down, and disappear. Grey Fox will find him one night.' Simon narrowed his eyes. 'Early one morning. They'll blow the doors on some dusty compound. Men in chunky camouflage gear – carrying their automatic weapons in that odd way they do, pointed at the ground – will pour in.'

Minty was shaking her head. She took a breath, like someone

about to dive underwater. Before she could begin, Sheena said, 'You know, he's talked like this around the fire at the Wasteland. You could see our young comrades, they have no idea how to take him. Who is this ageing warrior? You can watch them trying to work out what they think.'

'I thought you'd be there last night, actually, Sheena,' Simon said. 'That Mole character, too.'

'I was,' Sheena stated. 'I didn't see you either, Simon. Must have been after you left.'

'But –'

'Ezra,' said Minty. 'You haven't said anything in ages. You've been gazing glumly at that wall over there.'

'Have I?' Ezra said, blinking. 'I'm sorry.'

'No. Don't be. I mean, are you okay? It's not like you, that's all. Are you depressed about something?'

'Depressed? Of course not. You don't, do you? As you get older. Life kind of evens itself out, doesn't it?'

'Well, you shouldn't be, you know,' Simon said, his voice deepening in tone. 'I mean, you're a hero, old chap, honestly, you are. I was just thinking about you the other day. You've done that shitty job to support your family, you've gone to that ugly place every day to give your children this.' He opened wide his arms, indicated with his eyes and nods of his head the house around them; all it contained, and all it conveyed.

'Excuse me,' Sheena said. 'If he hadn't got that promotion last year, I'll have you know, and if Jill and I didn't leave more than we probably need to for reinvestment, I'd already earn more than he does. And next year I certainly will.'

'Yes, you've been looking after kids, Sheena, and you've been building up your business,' Simon nodded. 'But still, what Ezra's been doing is actually, in my opinion, heroic. I don't think it's generally acknowledged, that's all I'm saying, and maybe it is a burden shared by you and other women now, but this supporting your family doing work you don't value or enjoy, for year upon year.'

'What about you?' Ezra demanded.

90

'Me? No, no,' Simon objected, modestly. 'I'm not a real man. Because I happen to love what I do, you see, there's something fraudulent about that. I meet clients, I draw, I discuss problems that happen to fascinate me with engineers and builders. And the money appears as if by magic to pay for Ed's piano tuition, to support Minty's writing, to pay for whatever we want, really. I'm just very lucky. No, Ezra, you're the real man, you're the hero.'

'Very true,' Minty nodded. 'He's right, sport. You are. You shouldn't be depressed.'

'I'm not depressed.'

'What do you call it, then?' Sheena asked. 'You've made a great sacrifice, apparently. What do you call the price you pay?'

'Look, it's not me,' Ezra objected. He realised that his body had lowered itself into the sofa in an after-dinner slump. Pressing his fists into the cushions, he raised himself up. 'Of course, my experience is one thing. It's not important. It's important to me, personally, but I'm fine. Don't worry about me. How can anybody not be depressed?' Ezra spread his arms in a sweep that made it clear he meant something, somewhere in the world beyond their four walls. 'Sure, your boys should catch him, Simon. You honestly think it will end then?'

'Whether it ends this month or next year, that's not the point,' Minty claimed. 'The point is, it was illegal.'

Sheena raised her eyebrows. She'd managed to change the subject once, and here it was back on the agenda. The one political subject in all the years of their friendship that Minty got excited about.

'We've been over this,' Simon said, with an air of tired forbearance. 'Resolution 1411 clearly states –'

'And the other point,' Minty interrupted, 'is that Blair lied. I mean, he kept saying, "Believe me. I have access to secret intelligence whose sources I cannot divulge. Trust me."'

'Of course you can't put informers at risk,' Sheena said.

'The only intelligence I had was from reading a newspaper,' Minty continued. 'I don't believe Iraq had links to al-Qa'ida. Or weapons of mass destruction, deployable in forty-five *days*, never mind minutes.'

'The search is not over,' Simon said. 'There are more sites to be investigated. The Iraq Survey Group are –'

'Are you pretending,' Sheena said, 'to be more naïve than you really are?'

Minty blinked. 'Excuse me?'

'"*He lied to us.*" He's not our Daddy, Minty, he's a politician.'

Minty clutched a disposable lighter in the fist of her right hand, Ezra noticed. She was alternately squeezing and relaxing her grip. 'He knew Britain was going to war, since his visit to George Bush's ranch last year.'

'So?' Sheena asked. 'Yes. Okay.'

'Doesn't that bother you?'

'Does it bother the people of Iraq? No. They've been liberated from abject fear and cruelty, from the rule of an evil dictator.'

'A sovereign nation invaded,' Minty said. She clenched her body as she spoke: her shoulders swallowed her neck; elbows hugged the sides of her torso. 'Against the wishes of the vast majority of countries of the world. Undermining a consensus that's taken generations to build up.'

'Yes, and I'm proud of that,' Sheena said. 'We're in the vanguard of humanitarian progress.'

'"We"?' Minty echoed. 'What is this "we"? I mean, I hate the use of this "we". Our Prime Minister, our troops, our weapons. No thank you.'

'No, of course, sorry, I forgot,' Sheena said, mock-apologetic sarcasm colouring her voice. '*Not in My Name*, right? Of course not.'

Sheena referred, as all four of them knew, to the anti-war demo before Christmas, a march through town from Cowley Road to Broad Street, a photo of which featuring Minty Carlyle holding one pole of a banner had appeared in the *Oxford Mail*. Words could be like insects thrown into the air between them. Two couples, old friends, who knew each other too well; for whom it was difficult to discuss great events without boring each other with familiar views, or else veering into over-personal aggression.

Minty looked at her hands. She was scraping the wheel of the lighter over its flint. She turned abruptly to Ezra. 'Why don't *you* say anything?' she asked. There was anger in her voice. As if they had some pact to support each other in such a dispute. 'You've gone silent again.'

Ezra leaned forward, took his glass and drained it of the last of his wine. What could you say when your past implicated you? When you had interfered, how could you discuss another interference? There was only one way: by pretending you were innocent as anyone else in such a sitting room, such a conversation, as this. You never know, you might even fool yourself. Dan, a member of their tennis quartet, a solicitor, had once told him that most guilty accused genuinely convince themselves of their innocence by the time their case comes to court.

'When they,' Ezra said. 'When "we,"' he corrected himself, for amusement's sake, 'were bombing Baghdad, I thought about those human shields. You know? Those peaceniks who went and camped by dams. Archaeological sites. Museums. I just thought, it's all wrong. It's the wrong way round. It should be the advocates of war, the ones prepared to accept a little collateral damage, who should have gone over there. And lived with families in residential neighbourhoods. Hung out in the marketplace. You know?'

It dawned on Ezra too late that what he'd just said could be taken by Sheena as a direct – and, if perceived as being prompted by Minty, disloyal – challenge to her. He hadn't meant that at all. He risked an anxious glance in her direction. Sheena wore a very particular expression: a dilation of panic in her eyes. Ezra recognised it with relief. It expressed a momentary floundering, when her certainty was questioned, a greying of the black and white rendering of the world that she required.

'That's a wonderful point, Ezra, old fellow,' said Simon. His complexion that had become more florid over the years reddened further through the course of an evening, as if the red wine were working its way direct to capillaries in the skin of his face. 'Which has absolutely nothing to do with anything.'

They all laughed.

'You're right about the "we", though, Minty,' Sheena conceded.

'We, us, have nothing to do with it. We are so powerless. We really are.' She got up and fetched a bottle of sambuca and four small glasses. Ezra went to the bottom of the stairs and, directing his attention upwards, listened. Silence. When Blaise and Hector were small, Ezra and Sheena's nights had been littered with booby-traps: cries, kicks, shrieks. They could detonate their parents out of deep sleep two or three times each. Louie was a good sleeper, by far the best of the three.

Simon turned the lights down even lower at the dimmer switch. Minty came back inside from a visit to the garden, the stale reek of a cigarette on her breath.

'What about our children?' Ezra wondered, once they'd resumed their positions. 'I mean, really, Blaise surreptitiously meeting some strange boy at the end of our street. Waiting for our girl to walk to him. Was he supposed to turn before she reached him? Was she supposed to stride haughtily past him, or walk obediently in his wake? You know what I mean? They have to discover everything for themselves. Have to work it all out with no help from us. We can hardly blame peer pressure for being such a powerful influence on them. It fills a vacuum.'

'It is kind of pathetic,' Minty agreed.

'There's no structure,' Sheena said. 'And we're surprised when they stumble into drugs and alcohol and STDs. When all they want is to consume. To fill the emptiness.'

The quartet were silent. It was late. Ezra thought about his week ahead, the meeting tomorrow he ought to prepare for. It was time for the Carlyles to go home. He took a sip of liqueur, and swallowed it.

'Did I ever tell you two,' he asked, 'about this one time with the Achia? I'd returned to the village from a trek downriver to the Mission, restocked with supplies: rudimentary medicine, sweets, basic tools. They were all I had to offer. Within moments of getting back I was surrounded by children, as usual. I learnt their language painfully slowly, and the children had more patience with me than the adults. They were also my informants, sharing gossip as they sucked on the sweets that I gave them. Anyway, that day I'd been back an hour or so when Tokoti, a boy of ten or eleven, told me, with a certain amount of envy, "They are getting ready to cut Wekoni."

' "Wekoni will be cut?" ' I asked him.

' "They will cut him. He asked his father to be cut." '

'Cut?' Simon asked with a grimace. 'Good God. How cut?'

'Listen,' Minty admonished. 'We might find out, even.'

'Now, Wekoni,' Ezra continued, 'was an older brother of Kabuchi; he was then aged twelve or thirteen. He was entering puberty and growing lustful for the girls and the women of the village, but until he had been cut he remained a boy. Sex was out of the question.'

'Ah,' said Simon, nodding, and raising an eyebrow at Sheena. 'It gets interesting.'

'His father, Pakani, ordered Wekoni from the village. His mother, Tikangi, held on to him, weeping, imploring her son to stay. The boy seemed unnerved, his body boneless, easily pulled by her. So Pakani strode over and struck his wife.'

'Bastard,' said Sheena. 'And don't give me any of your cultural relativism,' she said defiantly, to no one in particular. 'A wife beater is a wife beater.'

'Tikangi fell,' Ezra continued, 'and let go of her son, who stumbled off after his godfather –'

'The man,' Minty interrupted, 'who would have lifted him from the ferns where he'd fallen as a newborn baby.'

'Right,' Ezra nodded. 'Have I told you that story? Well remembered, Minty. Thank you. Impressive.'

'I was listening.'

'His godfather, Chimuni, stood waiting for Wekoni at the edge of the clearing. His mother's lamentations rang in his ears, "*Don't go, my son. My son, stay with me.*" Which clashed with his father's harsh injunction, "*Go. Leave us, boy. Leave us and go.*" '

'They sound like actors,' said Simon.

'Well, they were. I mean, great acting is not *pretending* to be someone else. It's *being* someone else. Look at Mark Rylance. Or Ben Kingsley. Such performers are rare, that's why they're so powerful. Those two Achia were superb. Anyway, Chimuni took Wekoni into the forest to spend the night: an act of great courage for both man and boy, because at night jaguars prowl, and so do the spirits of the dead. And on the eve of his initiation a boy is particularly vulnerable. It'll be the first time that he's ever spent a night outside the camp.

'After a sleepless night in a tree Chimuni and Wekoni returned, but only to a clearing a little distance from the village. Here they spent that day and then another wordless night. Neither of them ate anything. They sipped only a little water brought by Wekoni's godmother.'

A dislocation now occurred in Ezra Pepin's perception: he spoke, but also saw himself speaking. The sight gratified him. His father's generation had had a war to fight or at least live through; he had this experience to draw on, authentic, exotic and brutal, that he may not have been able to finish writing about but by God at least he'd lived it and he could talk of it to his friends, and be rewarded by their receptive faces. His own minuscule amount of knowledge, or even wisdom, earned in the jungles of Paraguay.

'At noon on the third day,' Ezra continued, 'Chimuni brought Wekoni back into the village. His father, Pakani, was standing outside their hut. People were pretending to ignore proceedings, but everyone was up and about the camp. No one wanted to miss a thing. At his son's approach Pakani knelt down in front of his hut. Without a word Chimuni raised his heavy bow and struck Pakani on the back of the head, at the hairline.'

'Just deserts,' said Sheena.

Ezra ignored his wife's comment, but a glance in her direction recorded a yawn. Well, Ezra thought: it's after eleven, she's had late nights, and what's more Sheena was bound to have heard this story before. A price you pay for enduring marriage. Sheena was entitled to a discreet yawn.

'Pakani barely flinched,' he continued, 'as blood spurted from the gash on his head.'

'Why the father?' Simon asked, tiredly.

'The scar would ennoble him,' Ezra explained. 'Though it would

also show that Pakani, the great hunter, was from this moment on
– and he was in his mid thirties, I suppose – an *old* hunter.

'Chimuni turned and led the meek boy back to their clearing.
And now various men emerged and followed. In the clearing they
knelt on all fours, forming a kind of bench or table, upon which the
boy lay on his back.

'Taking up a bamboo knife, Chimuni cut into the boy's torso. He
cut thin lines, in a pattern that was symbolic of Wekoni's double –
the animal which he had been named after by his mother. Wekoni's
was the spider monkey, and Chimuni carved a number of crude
images emblematic of it; a bundle of lines resembling its skeleton.'

The sitting-room was almost dark. Minty must have dimmed the
lights further the last time she came back in from a smoke, and it
had had the effect of making people lower their voices. They were
speaking in virtual whispers. Ezra was feeling almost reassured. He
felt, at this moment, almost at ease with himself. They were
amazing things he, Ezra Pepin, had once seen, after all. Almost
the first outsider, the first European, certainly, to have encountered
this tribe. But it was now getting late for a Sunday evening, and
that was why Simon was trying desperately, his jawline trembling,
to stifle a yawn. Simon, in fact, his eyes glazing over, looked as if he
was slipping into a quiet antechamber of sleep.

'Wekoni gritted his teeth,' Ezra continued, speaking a little
faster, 'and undertook the rite without a murmur. He knew that
when they'd healed, the cicatrices would beautify him, make him
attractive to and worthy of women.'

'Yikes,' said Minty.

At least Minty was fully awake and attentive. Ezra was grateful
for that. He had the weird feeling that something was trying to
break into his brain, some thought, some insight or memory. But he
would not let it. 'A few years later,' he continued, 'when Wekoni
was ready for marriage, he would be cut again. On the back this
time, gouged with a stone that would leave long, wide, ridged scars.
For now the boy gritted his teeth. When Chimuni had finished,
Wekoni was covered in blood. Chimuni was covered in blood.
Blood trickled over the patient bent bodies of the men beneath.'

97

Simon slowly shook his sleepy head. Sheena leaned forward and began to hook the small liqueur glasses off the coffee table with her fingers.

'My God,' said Minty. 'Well, you're right, Ezra. We really don't have anything like that for our young people, do we?' She was gazing at him with wide, admiring eyes. 'You're so right.'

A connection occurred in Ezra's brain, and understanding flowed through. It filled his head with rage. At himself. At Minty, too, a shameful hatred, because she was trying so hard, God bless her, shaking her head in wonderment. Trying just too damned hard. As he understood with merciless certainty that he'd told this story, to these same three people – his wife and their two best friends – on another Sunday evening more recent and futile than he could bear to contemplate.

5

A New Water Bottle

Monday 23 June

Isis Water's headquarters in Station Square was a huge and perfect rectangle, built of sandstone and glass, with a flat roof. When it rained, excess water drained off at the sides through the mouths of gargoyles carved in the likeness of Rowan Atkinson and Richard Branson, Olive Gibbs and Richard Dawkins. The roof was so perfectly level, however, that a fine shallow slick remained on the surface.

Oxford had been designated the epicentre of England's Diamond Region of science and innovation enterprises: the city's universities offered new businesses precious intellectual synergies. 'Simple problems have complex solutions,' Ezra Pepin, Assistant Head of Operations, would tell clients. 'Complex problems have simple solutions.'

The Oxford Transport Survey was designed to discourage commuters and shoppers from coming into town in their cars, and encourage them to use other means instead. Speed-reducing humps appeared like blisters on the tarmac, traffic lights multiplied; there was a reduction of car parks in the centre of town and an increase in park-and-ride buses, with special lanes for buses and bicycles. The scheme was an apparent success: drivers were deterred, the roads became emptier. The speed of what little traffic there now was increased, with the result that cars flew back into the city centre in greater numbers than ever before, until the traffic backed up once more along all the arterial routes into town in exhaustive, growling, bad-tempered jams.

Other than the scheme's failure, however, it proved to be a great success. New research showed that quiet, civilised towns lost their mercantile energy and declined towards financial entropy – the city of dreaming spires had been in danger of falling asleep – and traffic jams were identified as one method of adding dynamism to an urban environment. Station Square was redesigned for the Millennium, as Oxford's commercial showpiece, not as a pedestrian precinct, as had been expected, but around a vast intersection of cars, lorries, buses and bikes.

With traffic gridlocked outside Isis Water for hours at a time, petrol fumes turned the shallow puddle on the flat roof into chemical rainbows. Airborne pollutants settled on the building, and more rain fell as if into a child's bubble bath, the roof fussing and frothing.

At a microscopic level – its molecules' partially negative oxygen and hydrogen atoms – the water was seething, an arousal of incessant vibration, susceptible to the insidious invitation of gravity. 'Come down,' whispered the centre of the earth. 'Come to me.'

Rainwater seeped through the roof of the headquarters of Isis Water. It infiltrated the resinous, rendered surface, confounded and short-circuited electrical mechanisms, and dropped to the sealed lead below. Gradually, undeterred, black and viscous with tar it drooled down from the ceiling, forming tiny puddles on the floor of the boardroom.

Algal blooms flourished on the ceiling of the Chief Executive's office. Acid rain dripped on to his teak desk, and burned through the veneer.

'Whose idea was it,' Klaus Kuuzik, the new CEO, asked Ezra Pepin during the last storm of that spring, which had coincided with his first day at work, 'to site the offices of the senior people in the company up on the most vulnerable floor of the building?'

The roof, designed for multiple use – al fresco lunches, sports, outdoor meetings – was certainly popular. It was used all the time: by men in overalls and waterproofs retarring the surface, replacing blown fuses, drying out the substructure, soaking up puddles with industrial sponges, and sweeping water off to the sides with wide metal brooms.

For the moment, at least, the summer had come, the sun risen without impediment on a blue-sky Monday morning, and the roof was drying out.

Sheena loosened the white towel around her body and let it swoon to the carpet. Ezra opened a drowsy eye. He watched her peer between her breasts in order to fasten her black sports bra, then twist it halfway around her, put her arms through the shoulder straps, pull it up and secure her bosom. It was Monday morning and he didn't want to get out of bed again, ever: after a lazy weekend spent ignoring it, he'd found himself awake at 3 a.m. worrying about this morning's meeting. He guessed he'd got back to sleep about five minutes before the alarm went off.

Sheena stepped into a pair of high-cut black panties and pulled them over her crotch. Ezra wasn't sure he could move the rest of his lifeless body, but he felt the tip of his penis tingle, and swell. Muscular legs were eased into a pair of tight leggings. As Sheena pulled them up her thighs, they tightened along her calves; Lycra yielded and stretched across her bottom, her belly.

'Watching you get dressed,' Ezra murmured, 'makes me want to take your clothes off.'

He reached over and scooped her waist and pulled Sheena to him. She fell backwards on the bed and he leaned over and kissed her, wriggling the rest of his limbs across her as he did so.

'Let's make love,' he said.

'It's late.'

Ezra Pepin fondled his wife. 'Let me ravish you, woman.'

Sheena laughed. 'Look at the time, Ezra.' She let him grope and snog her a moment more. Then Ezra leaned back and rolled aside, allowing Sheena up.

'Later,' she whispered, and left the room.

'Later!'

Ezra lay on the bed, his full penis the yearning centre of his mineral being. He wondered whether he had time enough to bring himself off. He looked at his watch: he should have left the house five minutes ago.

Ezra swung out of bed and stumbled to the en suite. As he brushed his teeth his heart retrieved supplies from zones of engorgement and returned them to the main arteries. He rubbed shaving oil into his skin. It was difficult to imagine other men masturbating. There was something sad about other people doing it. But they were, weren't they? At any moment there were hundreds of men and women around town, all over the city, jerking off. Set aside from the hubbub, the traffic, stilled, silent and gasping, solitary men and women in bedrooms and bathrooms in countless houses, whacking off. It was a wonder that there wasn't some fierce imperceptible tremble, a flutter, in the background of the urban roar.

Ezra Pepin cycled to work along the canal towpath, in his shirt-sleeves at eight-fifteen, glad the sun was drying out the potholes that sprayed mud on the trousers of any middle manager foolish enough to commute to his office this way. He bicycled past the Wasteland, from whose depths he could hear the grind and roar of heavy machinery churning up the ground. On under Aristotle Bridge, past Lucy's Ironworks and the backs of the two-up, two-down, quarter-of-a-million-pound, flood-prone pea-pods of Jericho. From the low boats strung along the canal came the sweet smell of wood smoke. Poplar, was it? As if living that bit less protected from nature's whims made the boaties wary of giving full assent to summer just yet.

Young drunks heading home that way late at night would sometimes be struck by comic inspiration, and unfasten the canal boats' moorings. If they managed not to betray themselves chortling at their originality they could release half a dozen long boats, which would drift south through the night with their snoozing occupants, who'd wake to find themselves in a log jam down by Upper Fisher Row.

Ezra forked right at the lock and cycled through Rewley Park estate, reaching Isis Water round the back of the building, where he locked his bike to one of the hoop racks.

'Okay, fellows,' Ezra Pepin addressed them. 'Are you kitted out? Chrissie, you have the prototypes?'

'On the trolley, Ez.'

'Rodge, you have your figures?'

'All here in my head.'

'Gideon, images?'

'On disc, Ez.'

'Our designer's here, right?'

'He's relaxing with a herbal on the mezzanine.'

'Good, good,' Ezra smiled. 'Now, all I want to say to you is this: you're the best we've got. Do yourselves proud. And let's enjoy ourselves. I don't want us to have any regrets. Are we up for this?'

'Yes.'

'Are we ready, team?'

'We're ready.'

'Let's go.'

The men and women wore dark suits, and white or light-blue shirts. There was a faint sour trace of coffee in the atmosphere that the air conditioning had not quite removed. The men wore ties whose colours ranged through the red section of the spectrum: rusty, or wine-coloured; roseate or crimson. Except for the Chief Executive, Klaus Kuuzik, who wasn't wearing a tie at all, but sat awaiting the presentation, the top button of his shirt undone.

'A little background, ladies and gentlemen,' Ezra said, to the seven members of the Board and the four other Heads of Department brought in to the meeting. 'Here we have our instant classic Isis Spa Water bottle. Ivy green. Glass. Instantly recognisable by seventy three point five per cent of AB consumers.'

'It's that kind of product recognition that will remain our benchmark,' said red-haired Roger Slocock, of Marketing.

'Last year,' Chrissie Barwell took over, 'we supplemented the

Spa with Isis Mineral Water, in cobalt-blue, thank you, Gideon, and Isis Spring Water – both sparkling and still – in clear glass.'

'Sales have been more than encouraging,' Gideon Juffkin said.

'We now have over a dozen boreholes across the Chilterns,' Chrissie resumed. 'Feeding plants set up to supply minutely filtrated and oxonated water in quantities far in excess of our current needs. We're ready, in short, to enter the mass market, without forfeiting one iota of our reputation for quality, class and style.'

'May I introduce Kevin Banfield?' said Ezra Pepin. 'The acclaimed futuristic designer. We commissioned Kevin to invent an asymmetrical plastic bottle devised specifically to evoke the fluidity of water.'

Kevin Banfield sat quite still in a Paul Smith suit and polo-neck pullover, silver-haired, with a goatee beard. When he spoke he did so precisely, his thin lips barely moving.

'I'm inspired by nature at its most elemental,' he said. 'Fire, water, air. By fossils. Bones. Bleached and seaworn wood. Ideal forms that nature with its arsenal of creative weaponry contrives. I've been called an organic essentialist. Also: an organic minimalist. But this is 2003. What inspires me as much as nature are new materials, processes, technologies – in this case injection moulding – that allow industrially created yet truly biomimetic forms.'

Chrissie and Roger passed around copies of Kevin Banfield's prototype Isis Spring Water plastic bottle.

'I've tried to realise the Isis vision,' Banfield continued, 'by capturing the liquescence and the optical purity of Spring Water, inside a three-dimensional form that reflects the joy and the sensual beauty of nature itself.'

'The ripple-effect packaging,' Roger Slocock pointed out, 'refracts both the light and the colour of its surroundings.'

'And here,' Chrissie Barwell continued, 'are Kevin's blue Mineral Water, and his green Spa Water, versions.'

'We're impressed and delighted,' Ezra said, 'by the way that Kevin has innovatively expanded on the aesthetic attributes of our original, while managing to adhere to the rigorous practical realities of the blow-moulding production process.'

'My hand-picked team of sales operatives,' Gideon Juffkin took over, 'are on standby, ready to fan out from Oxford with suitcases of these prototypes. South along the Thames Valley, north across the Cotswolds. Into the West. Wales. Scotland. Across the country, and beyond.'

The boardroom table was an accumulation of geometric shapes of Canadian maple, which could be taken apart and put back together in a wide variety of patterns. Ezra had heard it said that Klaus Kuuzik began meetings by having his executives push and pull the rectangles and trapezoids, the semi-circles and squares, into a specified shape. This morning they were seated around the outside of a wide horseshoe.

As Gideon Juffkin spoke, Chrissie dimmed the lights and Roger switched on the projector. 'These fabulous plastic bottles,' Gideon continued, 'will take us into new trade sectors.' Bright computer-generated images of stacks and shelves of Kevin Banfield's bottles in various settings dissolved one into another under Gideon's voiceover. 'We're talking not just supermarkets and off-licences, but on-premise outlets: the impulse sector, sandwich bars, major multiples.' Ezra admired Gideon's convincing illustrations; they seemed to present a foregone conclusion, were pictures called back from a triumphant future. 'Petrol station forecourt shops,' Gideon continued. 'Grocery independents. High street vendors, style bars, retail outlets of every kind. There's no doubt in our mind: this is where Isis Water moves to the top of the UK bottled-water sales table.'

'Which is precisely where we all want to be,' the Chairman's voice broadcast as the lights came up, before he led the Board's round of applause.

'An exemplary presentation,' Ezra heard accountant Alan Blozenfeld mutter to the Head of Operations, Jim Gould.

Then Klaus Kuuzik asked, 'And what about the water?'

Remaining murmurs of approval, and the echoes of handclaps, died away. The room became quiet. Ezra swallowed, and opened his mouth to speak. It was his place, as team leader, to answer this question. The only trouble was that his mouth was empty. His brain was blank. It was most odd: he felt calm, relaxed, ready to explain in outline and in detail, using clarity, statistics and wit, anything and everything Mr Kuuzik and the Board members and the Heads of Department might want to know about the water. It was just that he had nothing to say.

The light in the room seemed to change, to become brighter; perhaps the sun was coming out from behind a cloud. Eleven people looped around the oxbow table were watching him, waiting for Ezra to say something in reply to the Chief Executive's simple question. What about the water? Ezra didn't mind. His tongue wouldn't work, that was all. It occurred to him how similar this interrogational moment was to those in the Viva he'd have to take when he finally finished his PhD. Yet how different. Then he would have to defend the complexity of his work; here he had only to justify its simplicity. Its ability to make money. A hero? Was that what Simon had called him? What nonsense. All he had to do was to perform. Well, he surely would. In just a moment or two, something would come to him. In the meantime, Ezra felt tranquil, at peace with himself and the world around him. His calm was pierced by the sound of a human voice.

'Our job, Mr Kuuzik,' he heard Chrissie Barwell say, 'is to give our client not what she wants, no, but what she didn't know she wanted. Only when she receives it does she realise, Yes! *This* is the one thing I have always desired.'

Ezra nodded, and spoke. 'What Chrissie is saying,' he elaborated, 'is that we might recall the recent example of children's milk sold in schools in this country. It cost thirty pence a glass. When the same volume was put into plastic bottles, and the price was doubled, kids bought four times as much milk as before.'

'Their health improved considerably,' said Gideon.

'A healthy consumer is a happy consumer,' said Chrissie.

'And all of us, when we consume, are children,' Roger Slocock said.

'What we should never forget,' Ezra finalised, 'is this: that our customers don't buy the water. They buy the bottle.'

106

At which everyone looked again at the artefacts Kevin Banfield had created, and the room filled once more with applause.

The trolley was wheeled smoothly out of the boardroom. Along the carpeted corridor of the sixth floor ambled the four members of the team; shoulders back, they entered the lift in silence, and ignored each other, avoided the gaze that would give them away, until the lift had slid into motion and passed the floor below. Gideon Juffkin started hammering the aluminium panelling with his fists. Ezra closed his eyes and dropped his head back on his neck, relishing the adrenaline alive in him. Chrissie let out a long shriek, and Roger growled, 'We are beautiful,' and they cared not who might have stopped and stared as the lift descended through four more storeys to the ground.

When they got back to Operations, Ezra said, 'Let's postmortem this before you chaps disappear.' But no one cold sit still around his desk, so they walked out across the open-plan floor towards the stairs.

'We own this building!' said Gideon.

'We're the Four Musketeers,' said Roger Slocock.

'I'm D'Artagnan,' said Chrissie Barwell.

'I'm the old one, I guess,' said Ezra. 'Who was that? Athos?'

'Hey, Ez, don't you know?' said Chrissie, punching his shoulder. 'Old is the new young.'

Ezra laughed. 'You can mock, girl,' he said. 'But as long as my quick IQ speeds remain better than yours, may your jibes turn to ashes in your mouth.'

'Yeh, Chris,' said Roger. 'Leave da boss alone.'

'Come on,' Ezra said. 'Let's have lunch together.' He led his team to the canteen, feeling a little like a popular teacher, which really was somewhat ironic.

Sheena Boycott had met Ezra Pepin not long after his return from the South American rainforest at the age of twenty-four with his notes and his records of consanguinity, marriage taboos, trade relations; of hunting rituals, shamanistic practice, intoxicants. His task was contained, all he had to do was collate the material he'd gathered and write it up, and although Sheena had the sense that something of his experience in Paraguay haunted him, he wouldn't admit to it.

Anthropology, Ezra explained to his girlfriend, had taken fifty years to become an established and respected academic discipline. Then it started breaking apart. Study of the Other as an objective act was implicitly flawed: power relations between academic and primitive; anthropology as a continuance of colonialism; the subjective nature of observation which purported to be objective. These and other objections began to rupture the surface of the subject, Ezra explained drily, as if to assure Sheena he was giving her information about his academic discipline, and certainly not about himself. He'd always been intrigued, he said, by different cultures' attitudes to childhood and youth. When an opportunity to visit a Jesuit mission in a remote region of South America landed in his lap, he made his one and only trip abroad for fieldwork.

'Mopping up the last of the primitives, are we, Pepin?' his supervisor, so Ezra told Sheena, had mocked him. He spent a year with a small tribe who'd had no contact with the outside world. When he came back he told his colleagues in Cultural Anthropology next to nothing of what he'd found, other than the working title of his PhD – *Rebel Energy Quelled: teenage ritual as a strategy of tradition among the Achia of Paraguay*.

'You'll be the first to read it,' he'd say to anyone who asked.

Sheena moved into the flat on Walton Street. One after another of Ezra's fellow tenants moved out, the last shortly after Sheena confirmed she was pregnant. Ezra laboured at his thesis. His grant was running out, but he was able to pick up a little teaching. Sheena worked extra shifts as a lab assistant. The rent on the flat was cheap, and she even managed to put some money by.

All Sheena or Ezra would remember of the months following their daughter's birth was sprawling in bed or lounging in the sitting-room, the three of them. It was like being put under house arrest, Ezra reckoned, except that you'd passed the sentence yourself. Imprisonment with company you'd chosen. Blaise seemed to him the exemplar of what a one-month, a three-month, a six-month-old baby should be. Evolution had finally reached its goal. A ridiculous delusion, *created* by evolution, of course, he knew that. Which in this case just happened to be true.

Ezra began teaching undergraduates, and came home grouchy. Preoccupied, despondent.

'What's wrong?' Sheena asked.

'How can I teach what I don't *know*?' he wondered.

'Teach what you *do* know.'

'But what I *don't* know is much greater than what I *do* know,' Ezra worried. 'I fear it always will be.'

'But then no one would ever teach anything, would they, and then where would we be?' Sheena demanded.

'We'd be, I don't know, cave dwellers? Maybe we'd still be amphibians. I'm not against teaching, obviously. I'd just rather not do it myself.'

'Would you rather other people who know *less* than you do did the teaching? Where's the logic, Ezra?'

Ezra found he felt better getting his hands dirty; doing odd jobs. He discovered some measure of calm in combining thinking and doing. The chief drawback was that he had no skills. There was even more he didn't know about physical work than what he didn't know about his own academic discipline, so he could only find the most menial labour, for minimal pay. But at least he felt fine about taking it.

'I'm not pretending,' he told Sheena. 'I'm an unskilled manual worker. I don't claim to be anything else. You know, by the way, that shamans in tribal cultures often do manual work?'

So he helped a chap along Kingston Road with a Transit move furniture when he needed a hand; he assisted a gardener clearing undergrowth and mowing lawns; and he painted the flats and houses of acquaintances who didn't want to do it themselves but couldn't afford a professional decorator. The paint left over from these jobs Ezra brought home and stacked in the brick outhouse across the yard from the flat. Half-filled tins of gloss with which he painted the doors of the flat different colours. Emulsion that periodically he'd mix in a large bucket – remnants of magnolia and apple-green, lilac and sunset-pink, stirred to a lugubrious beige – and redecorate a room. Instead of spring cleaning, he spring painted.

'Wait a minute, Ezra,' Sheena said. 'Are you saying you think you're some kind of shaman?'

'No, Sheena. I mean that in tribal culture shamans are the individuals with the freedom of time and thought to engage in spiritual, or artistic, activity; they represent intellectual life, the whole stratum of those who work with their minds, who transform not matter but perception. Artists, teachers, academics.'

'Ezra, you're weird. And that colour is dire.'

They'd gone into parenthood with high ideals, inspired by Ezra's accounts of tribal societies where children spent their first years attached to the mother or father or member of the extended family. But Ezra's only relative was his father, while members of Sheena's tribe swooped down from Yorkshire in small swarms to coo briefly at the kid, then sit back to be fed and entertained before leaving.

Blaise, Sheena suspected, was one of the more demanding babies born in the Western world in 1989. It was as if she'd eavesdropped from the womb on Ezra's promises. At night she cried to be fed every two hours. For months Sheena was unable to use the toilet without Blaise hanging in an awkward sling at her side. She discovered that there was no one she'd rather be with than her slowly growing baby sprawled in the bouncer chair gurgling up at her, kicking her little frog legs. For about ten minutes. After that, Sheena admitted to Ezra, it was impossible to spend time along with a baby without infantilising yourself. He explained that tribal parents ignored their babies much of the time, they just got on with what they had to do with limpets on their backs.

From that moment on Sheena threw herself into local campaigns. Handing out leaflets and reaping signatures on petitions for the Rainforest Action Group; taking part in Earth First?'s occupation of Timbmet timber yard, up on Cumnor Hill, in protest at the importation of timber from tropical rainforests, with Blaise in a buggy and the six-month-old Hector in a sling. Sheena's activism began as much as somewhere to go with her children as a response to political conviction.

Ezra published in time three essays, derived from his thesis in progress, in academic journals, but his reputation in the university faded, from that of a scholar of intriguing promise to a familiar case of prevarication. Sheena got odd jobs too, and, with child-welfare benefits, they scraped along in a more or less contented hand to mouth.

Hector had arrived just as Blaise was starting at a crèche in Warnborough Road, and the Pepins bought their first house, a two-up, two-down artisan's Victorian terraced cottage, the smallest house on Kingston Road, an hour or two before the property boom reached its peak and started slipping backwards. Sheena saw the job advert in the *Oxford Times* for *Graduates who don't want to teach? Become free-thinking executives of the future*, in the company who'd just bought out Walton Well Water, Oxford's family-owned mineral-water company. She told Ezra he ought to apply, and she helped him prepare for the job interview.

'What,' Sheena asked, 'are you hoping for from this employment, Mr Pepin?'

'Er, wages?'

'Wrong, Ezra.'

'Friendship?'

'No, no.'

'Paid holidays for the first time in my life?'

'Don't be ridiculous. You look straight at the most senior person there, and say, "I want your job."'

This Monday lunchtime, eleven years later, Sheena decided to consume alone her hummus-and-avocado-salad ciabatta, apple, and carrot juice. She left work and walked along Merton Lane, took the path beside Merton College and sat on the warm grass out in Christ Church Meadow. She thought of that joke every so often.

'I want your job.' The humour was in the idea of Ezra possessing such ambition. They never discussed his work at home. It was an unwritten rule of their marriage – she understood the work must be unbearably dull; it was a badge of honour between them. They'd soon stopped referring to Isis Water at all, as each year it kept Ezra from his true path in life and increased the guilt that silted silently in Sheena's stomach. Ignoring it was the only practical solution.

But Simon had brought up Ezra's sacrifice last night after dinner, in that blithe way of his, and today Sheena found herself unable to ignore it. Incredible, she thought, looking back: how come Ezra didn't volunteer to be the full-time childminder when Blaise was a baby? Did she ever ask him to be a hero? No, that's not what she wanted. Why on earth didn't he let Sheena go out to work, when it turned out she both enjoyed and was good at running her own business? The sun was hot on her neck, so Sheena wriggled around so that she was facing the other way. Only to find the sun stabbing at her eyes. She put her carrot juice down on the grass, and shielded her eyes with her hand. The plastic bottle tipped over, spilling orange liquid into the earth before she could grab it upright.

What Sheena felt was more than irritation. Yes, her feelings seemed to have changed. The silt was stirring. The guilt was giving way to something else. It felt like anger. Could that be true? If so, was it not authentic emotion welling up from deep inside? Which honesty compelled her to allow to rise?

What an impossible situation she was in: unless she could help Ezra out of this rut, that also loaded her with a burden she in no way deserved. What did he want, really? Surely between them they could work out what Ezra wanted, and needed, to fulfil him.

On Monday afternoon Jim Gould asked Ezra Pepin to join him for a little privacy in one of the think-tanks off the open-plan office floor. He brought along a tray with two cups of tea, and accoutrements: tiny sealed tubs of semi-skimmed milk, sachets of brown and of white sugar, plastic twizzlers, napkins. Minuscule packets of bite-sized biscuits. A reassuring profligacy.

'Excellent presentation.' Jim frowned, swirling the teabag around the cup with his twizzler, impatient for the tea to brew.

'Thanks,' Ezra nodded. The energy of the morning had dissipated. He felt tired again. 'It's easy when the product's good.'

'It helps.'

'There's no need to bullshit.'

Jim pointed the twizzler at Ezra, as if to wag it in admonishment. 'You're a one-off, Ezra,' he said. 'Now, listen. Tell me. Who owns Isis Water?'

'What do you mean?' Ezra asked. 'DeutscheWasser just bought us.'

'Of course. And that's it?' Jim put the white twizzler in his mouth, left it between his lips like a toothpick, and broke open a tub of milk.

'There's more?'

'DeutscheWasser's a subsidiary of VBD.'

'I see. VBD? Okay.'

'Which is owned by the American Hamahachi Hollywood Corporation.'

'Really? I didn't know that.'

'Which is part of the Bundesgeld empire of Berlin. Sugar?'

'I see,' said Ezra. 'How come you know all this, Jim?'

Jim shook his head. He lifted the tray off the table and poured the packets of accessories, used and unused, into a wastepaper bin off to one side. He clapped his hands to clear them of crumbs of biscuit and sugar. 'None of it need concern us, Ezra,' he said. 'You understand? This is what I want you to know: that there is nothing sinister about what I'm telling you. DeutscheWasser have made clear: they do not intend to change a thing in the working practice of what is a thriving company.'

'Right. The only evidence of any change in ownership that we're aware of is that Mr Kuuzik has been made Chief Executive.'

'Exactly, Ezra. And it's Mr Kuuzik who's asked me to have someone in Operations do a little blue-sky thinking. Take time out to contemplate the future of bottled water.'

'The future? Is that all?'

113

'Sure,' Jim said, unsmiling. 'The industry in general. Isis Water in particular, obviously. Naturally, I thought of you. No desperate hurry. At your own pace. But quietly.'

'Quietly?'

'Keep your thoughts to yourself, I would.'

'I will.'

'I'll leave it with you, Ezra.' Jim took a gulp of tea, snapped the lid on to the cup, dropped it into the bin as he stood up, and walked away.

Blaise flushed the toilet, and washed and dried her hands. She opened the bathroom door, stepped out, and closed it quietly behind her. She stood in dimly lit gloom. There was a hole, she realised, a slash, in the net curtain hanging in the small window at the far end of the landing. A bladed beam of sunlight cut through what the light revealed to be a subaquatic atmosphere, slow and turgid, in which thick motes of dust floated like krill. Blaise watched them. Their movement suggested that they possessed an enigmatic amount of autonomy. The thin blade of sunlight reached all the way through the ocean air to a dreary rug; illuminated with precision a threadbare patch. A criss-cross of brown backing cord.

There were three doors along the landing. Were Akhmed or his mother tracking her movements above them? Blaise looked down the stairs: the ground floor of the house was subdivided into a front room and a back room; the hallway ran from the front door to the half-size kitchen pegged on, with a bathroom above, to the rear of the house. Akhmed and his mother were down there, in those snug rooms.

There must be three rooms upstairs, Blaise worked out, in the same space as the two rooms below. She took a deep breath. With one step she reached the first door, turned the handle, pushed it gradually open. Its hinges creaked with separate, teasing squeaks. It might have been a device calibrated to warn an occupant of an intruder – there was someone inside the room! Don't be a fool, she told herself. Don't be an idiot. It's four o'clock in the afternoon.

The hinge squeaks were not as loud as the sound of Blaise's heartbeat, anyhow, which pounded in her ears and surely out of them, like the beat from cheap headphones, into the open air.

Blaise peered inside. There was an empty bed along the wall opposite; cupboards above; boxes underneath. She extended her neck around the door. Running along the next wall, head to toe with the first bed, was another. She stretched in a little further. There was a third bed against the wall behind the door. A man lay in it, his head on the pillow. His mouth was open. And so, Blaise realised, were his eyes. She gaped in horrified silence. Her loud heart had stopped pounding altogether: it hovered, between one beat and the next, as the man stared at her, with sly, half-open eyes. He had a black beard, made of tight curls of hair. The whites of his eyes were flecked with brown.

She had done wrong, and she had been found out. Now, rigid with fright, she awaited her dire punishment. The prospect filled her with dread. Although the dread, she sensed, promised pleasure, too, in taking what she deserved.

The silence was breached by a sound issuing from the man's mouth. For a second Blaise assumed it was speech, an accusatory utterance. Except it gurgled too much for words in any language, and it came from deep in his throat. After a few seconds of further silence it came again, as the man inhaled, and she realised with an air-gulping breath of her own that he was snoring. Trembling, Blaise began to retreat from the room, pulling the door quietly closed.

Akhmed had walked out of school in step with her. They'd crossed Banbury Road, and walked along Beechcroft Road.

'What do you want to do?' he asked. He was already going out of his way, heading in the direction of Blaise's home.

'Nothing,' she said.

'Yeh,' he said. 'Let's do nothing. I'm not bothered.'

He didn't look at Blaise when he spoke to her, or when she spoke to him, but in between she could sense his eyes upon her.

'I'll be happy on my own today,' she said.

Akhmed watched his trainers land pigeon-toed on the pavement. He glanced across at her, and away. 'You want me to help you with maths again?' He shrugged. 'I don't mind. It's the same stuff we did.' He put his hands out to the sides, palms up in modest solidarity. 'I didn't like it, either.'

They paused, while on the pavement ahead of them a driver manoeuvred her red car, in sideways instalments, into a tight parking space in front of a house. Half the inhabitants of the road had converted what had been tiny front gardens; their cars sheltered against the walls.

'I think I'll just go home,' Blaise said.

'I know there's nowhere to go,' Akhmed said. 'We could go to Alexandra Park, I suppose. That bench by the tennis courts.'

Blaise turned to him. Akhmed seemed to be studying the final precise movements of the crablike red car. It was a mystery, why he followed her around with quite such persistence. Why he demanded her company. Once they were together he had little to say. No, that wasn't quite right: they chatted easily enough. It was more like she had the constant feeling that there was something else he wanted to say, and was about to. But never managed to. Even now, pretending to look at the car that had been blocking their way, there was something in his bearing which suggested that any moment now he'd turn to her and say it; tell Blaise the thing that had been, that was always, on his mind. She knew plain enough what it was. What Akhmed wanted was to reprise the long, dry kiss they'd shared three weeks before, leaning against the trunk of the weeping beech in University Parks.

'Did you tongue?' had come into her mind at the time, heard from the mouths of other girls. 'Did he tongue you?' So Blaise had poked her tongue tentatively through Akhmed's closed lips, only to wonder what she was supposed to do with it once it got there. Taste his gums? Slide it over his teeth? Then she felt the tip of his tongue, and wondered whether that was a mistake, and withdrew. Blaise had little appetite to repeat the experience. She suspected that Akhmed did.

'I know!' she said, suddenly. 'Let's go to your house.'

'Yeh, right,' Akhmed said, with a colluding chuckle.

116

'No, really,' Blaise said. 'Take me to your house for tea.'

Akhmed frowned. 'No way,' he said, looking down the street.

Blaise waited. After a while, Akhmed glanced at her, for just long enough for her to spot the anxiety in his eyes.

'Okay,' Blaise said, and she resumed walking.

'We can't,' he called after her.

'Fine,' she called back, shrugging her shoulders. 'I'm going home.'

'You've no idea,' Akhmed complained, as much to himself as to her. 'Wait,' he said quietly. Blaise was twenty yards off now, and walking further away from him with every step. 'Hang on,' he pleaded. He only wanted time to think, but she wasn't even giving him that. Still, he had long enough, he realised, in which to wonder why it was that the sight of her strolling away from him actually made the hunger he had to be with her, to see her, more intense. That wasn't right at all. The craving sharpened and swelled inside him, in a yawning gap somewhere near his heart and his lungs that needed to be filled, and could only be filled by one particular person on this planet. Blaise Pepin, who'd appeared two years earlier in the class below him. Had he asked her to?

'Okay,' Akhmed yelled. He scurried after Blaise, and caught up with her along the wooden fence outside the Baptist church. 'Come on, then,' he said. They turned the corner, heading south, Akhmed shaking his head. 'You don't know what you've asked,' he said, as if the course of action upon which they'd now embarked were an immutable compass bearing, that neither he nor Blaise could dream of changing now.

'What on earth is the matter?' Blaise wondered. 'Don't you think your dad'd like me or something?'

'Dad?' Akhmed asked. 'Dad?' He squinted at her as if she were unbelievably stupid. 'Dad wouldn't mind,' he said, in a tone that suggested anyone in Oxford would know that. He kicked a pebble into the road. 'This is so not a good idea.'

'Take your shoes off,' Akhmed hissed, as they entered the house. He closed the door and glanced nervously along the hallway, and up the stairs. 'Quick,' he said. 'In there.'

The air smelled of onion. Cumin. The hallway led to the kitchen, through whose half-open door Blaise caught a glimpse of a brown-clad figure. Coriander.

'Go on,' Akhmed urged. 'In the sitting-room. Sit down. I'll be back.'

Blaise sat on the sofa of a sky-blue three-piece suite, which had a fringe of gold tassels brushing the carpet. On the coffee table in front of her was a gold-patterned plastic box, containing a cardboard box of pink tissues.

Akhmed came back into the room. He peered at Blaise with a suspicious frown, as if worried she might steal something.

'Where's the bathroom?' she asked.

'What?' Akhmed replied, his face contorting with incredulity.

'I need to use the toilet?' Blaise said, turning the statement into a question with a sarcastic lilt.

Akhmed directed her upstairs. 'Do you actually want a cup of tea?' he asked her in the hallway. His tone hinted at how much he'd prefer her to say no.

Blaise smiled. 'Sure,' she said.

Akhmed sniffed. 'Milk and sugar and stuff?'

By the time Blaise returned to the sitting-room, her heartbeat had slowed, and quietened. Akhmed came in, looked at her with distrust, and said, 'I hope you didn't wake Yusuf.'

Blaise felt a quick surge of panic. 'I couldn't help needing to . . .' she began, but trailed off as Akhmed left the room again. She heard voices in the kitchen, hushed and indistinct. There was a glass cabinet behind one of the chairs. Blaise could see glasses and cups and crockery. She heard the front door open and close: someone entering or leaving. So many people in one house, with three tiny bedrooms. On top of the widescreen TV – it seemed bigger than her family's television, though this was a smaller room, so perhaps it was an illusion – stood a model of a building. A church. It could have been Italian, Blaise thought. Or Iranian. Or Spanish. Actually, she acknowledged, she had no idea; was too ignorant even to make it worth hazarding a guess.

It had a dark-roofed, bulbous dome, which seemed to have been painted with a different –

'Don't touch that.'

Blaise jumped. She turned round. Akhmed's elder sister, Taslima, stood in the doorway.

'I was just looking,' Blaise said. 'I didn't know –'

'It's the Al-Aqsa Mosque,' Taslima said. 'In Jerusalem.' She wore a headscarf. Blaise had seen Taslima often enough at school, never in hijab: Akhmed told her his sister put it on or took it off at the end of their street. Blaise hadn't quite believed him. Taslima looked slightly insane, as if afraid on this hot summer's day of non-existent rain.

'It gives the azan,' Taslima said. 'The call to prayer.'

Blaise stared blankly at her.

'Five times a day,' Taslima said. She waited long enough for the first glimmer of understanding to break across Blaise's face, then left the room.

After a minute or two Akhmed came in carrying a blue plastic tray with a teapot, two cups and saucers and teaspoons, a small jug of milk, a bowl of white sugar.

Taslima came back in after him. 'Speak Bangla to Amma, you little toerag,' she said.

The tray banged on the table, china teacups rattling against their saucers. Akhmed knelt on the floor, his face tightening with anger. 'Don't you disrespect me,' he told his sister, without looking up at her.

Blaise realised that a woman was now hovering in the doorway. She was staring at Blaise. Their mother, she assumed, although a brief glance told her that she looked nothing like either Akhmed or Taslima: her facial features and her body, clothed in a loose brown tunic and trousers, were much broader than the others' fine-boned slenderness. She spoke, in brief, emphatic sentences. Taslima answered her. Akhmed knelt on the carpet, bent over the table, waiting for the tea to brew. Blaise kept her head down, too. She could feel when the women were looking at her from the direction of their voices. When they spoke, the syllables sounded solid in their mouths, morsels of plain, sticky rice they rolled on their tongues.

'I won't hear the last of this,' Akhmed whispered, as he poured the milk.

Taslima addressed him. 'You are so full of it, you.' She left the room, and Blaise heard her footsteps on the stairs. Their mother hovered still, a few inches further back from the doorway, into the hall.

'I know!' Blaise said.

Akhmed was shaking his head. His hand trembled as he poured tea into the two cups.

'Ask your Mum if white girls are allowed to go to the mosque school.'

Akhmed flinched, as if he'd scalded his hand. He lifted his head a little. Blaise could see his eyes dart right towards her, and left towards his mother.

'The madrassah?' he said, and frowned. 'You shouldn't make fun of our religion, Blaise,' he complained.

'I mean it,' Blaise said. 'I'm serious. Go on. Ask your mother.'

'I'm in deep enough,' Akhmed said, in a petulant tone of voice, before shaking his head. 'I'm so stupid,' he admonished himself.

Her father's voice had come to Blaise. A sentence of his, spoken to her inner ear with the clarity of a bell: *You can't understand people from outside their culture.*

'How else are people like me supposed to learn?' she demanded of Akhmed. 'Ask her.'

Akhmed watched Blaise with that suspicious expression: she really was about to steal something. Then he turned to his mother, and spoke to her in Bengali. As she listened to what her son said, she looked at Blaise. Her eyes lit up; eyebrows knitted together in a mimicry of Akhmed's frown; eyes darkened. It was as if, without words, she was trying to communicate to this impudent girl what was going through her mind. She ended up smiling, briefly, then nodding in solemn acknowledgement of whatever Akhmed had told her, before disappearing back down the hallway towards the kitchen.

Blaise took the mug of tea from Akhmed, and leaned back on the sofa. Her dad, she thought, would be proud of her. She drank the sweet tea in small gulps; felt it going down her gullet and into her stomach in warm and pleasant draughts.

6

Ping-pong

Tuesday 24 June

On Tuesday morning Sheena Pepin's family left the house before her: Ezra was going to drop Louie off at the nursery and ride back down the canal towpath to work; Hector had gone round to the Carlyles', was going to cycle to school with Jack. Blaise, Sheena thought, had left too. She was in the hallway, making to leave, when she heard the door of Blaise's room open. Blaise rattled down the stairs and headed for the front door.

'Where are you going, sweetheart?'

'Out, Mum,' Blaise replied, opening the door. She wore her new indigo top, and jeans whose frayed hem almost disguised the fact that she'd grown an inch since buying them a fortnight earlier.

'Me, too. You want to look in at the Wasteland?'

Blaise's hand rested on the door handle. 'To cheer the bulldozers, Mum?' She turned round. 'Yeh, okay.'

'I know, Bee,' Sheena said, nodding. 'You're right. A bit futile now. No, but just in case there's someone on the vigil at the gate.' Sheena zipped shut the compartments of her rucksack. Something she'd forgotten snagged at her mind.

'I mean it,' Blaise shrugged. 'I will cheer them.'

'You will?'

'They're doing the right thing.'

'The right . . . ?' Was Blaise feeling off-colour this morning? her mother wondered. 'What do you mean, sweetheart?' Sheena asked. 'What about our action?'

Blaise shook her head at the ground. 'The action was stupid,' she said. She smiled indulgently. 'The whole campaign was stupid. I can't believe I took part.' Blaise turned and walked out into the sun.

'Hey, hang on there a moment, young lady,' Sheena demanded from the porch. 'What are you talking about? We've spent the last two years working together, you and I, with a hundred other people, to protect the Wasteland. You've been amazing, Blaise.'

'Oh, I've been an idiot,' Blaise told the sky. She'd reached the back bumpers of the cars, and she remained looking up at the blue sky, as if in the wispy strands of white cloud high up there were words she might, with a good deal of concentration, decipher. She turned round, and stared at her mother. 'Why did you get me involved, Mum?' she asked.

Sheena was too surprised to think of what to say. 'Well,' she tried. 'I don't know. I mean . . .'

'No,' Blaise said, shaking her head. 'No, Mum. I'm not blaming you. It's my fault.'

'It's nobody's *fault*,' Sheena attempted.

'How come it didn't occur to me,' Blaise asked herself, 'who those flats and houses are going to be for?'

'We know the arguments,' Sheena mustered. She put a hand out to her side, as if to indicate some list pinned up by the telephone. 'We have heard them about a thousand times.'

'Yes, Mum, but was I listening?' Blaise wondered. 'Social housing. Affordable homes. Like, poor people who can't afford the prices people like us can, can have somewhere to live, maybe? What was I, deaf?'

Sheena could feel a kind of prickling sensation in her stomach; tolerance of Blaise's attitude turning to irritation. 'But it's not the issue, Blaise,' she said. 'You know that.'

Blaise looked away, down the street of near identical sand-coloured brick houses, as if pondering them, and their outrageous value, anew. 'I think it *is* the issue, Mum,' she said quietly. 'The only issue. I mean, it's not you, don't worry,' Blaise added, abruptly. 'It's just me,' she said, planting her left hand on her chest. 'But all the rest is disguising the issue. It's hiding a rich hippie NIMBYism behind all that nature bullshit.'

Sheena gasped. It felt as if she'd received an underhand punch to the stomach. 'Who's a hippie?' she blustered. 'NIMBYs? Us?' Sheena paused, took a conscious swallow of air, and breathed out. 'Bullshit?' She stepped forward, facing her daughter along the tunnel between the Saab and the Golf. Blaise kept saying she wasn't criticising her mother, so how come Sheena could feel her blood thumping around her veins, a bulging behind her eyes? 'For God's sake, Blaise,' she said, more harshly than she meant to. 'Be serious. There are fifty brownfield sites in Oxford marked for housing development. They can build anywhere. The Wasteland is – it was – a precious wildlife reserve.'

Blaise shrugged, and smiled sweetly. 'But Mum, since when was I so interested in green woodpeckers? Blaise Pepin the Twitcher. Yeh, right. How often did I take my binoculars to look at reed warblers? Oh! Just since the council tried to build some dwellings for poorer people across the canal from us. Wow. What a hypo-critical coincidence, eh?'

Sheena realised she was confused herself. She couldn't work out whether or not to agree with her daughter or to defend herself from disguised assault. 'Well, sweetheart,' she said. 'I'm awfully sorry I ever got you involved.'

Blaise produced a grin so full of irony it might have choked her. 'Don't be silly, Mum. Parents are supposed to try and brainwash their children, aren't they?'

Sheena tried to control herself, but her raised voice bounced towards Blaise off the shiny glass of the car windows. 'How dare you!' she spluttered.

Blaise made a grimace of comic indignation. 'I'm joking, Mum,' she said. 'I'm only kidding.'

Before Sheena could say anything more, Blaise turned and strolled away – in the opposite direction, Sheena was relieved to see, from the canal. She stared after her daughter as she walked along Wellington Drive, and long after she disappeared into Spencer Street. Sheena's heartbeat settled. Why did that ungrateful girl say those things? What on earth was going through her brain: was she being insidious and cleverly critical as Sheena's heart told her she'd been, or actually as innocent as she was making out? This day of all days. Today was Blaise's birthday. Sheena's breathing slowed. It struck her suddenly that she was standing outside. That she had yelled at Blaise not behind the privacy of double-glazed sash windows but in the open air. Sheena became aware of her surroundings: there was silence so absolute in the immediate vicinity that all she could hear was the whine of cars on the distant ring-road. It was as if their neighbours, having been forced to listen to an ill-tempered mother, were now lurking behind their windows with a kind of horrified tact.

Sheena rushed back inside, and closed the door firmly behind her. With the back of her hand she wiped perspiration off her forehead, and her upper lip. She regretted that she hadn't responded to Blaise's disguised attack with some subtlety of her own. Sheena pushed herself away from the door, and made for the kitchen. She cleared the table, filled the dishwasher, wiped surfaces, regaining her equilibrium. The truth was that whatever game Blaise was playing, it was her adolescence, no one else's. Her turmoil, her hormonal volatility. All parents could do was to stand steadfast in their position at the helm of the family; it was more important to remain there, offering stability and leadership, than to try and get inside her mind.

Sheena fetched her bicycle from the lean-to behind the house. She pressed the back tyre of Blaise's bike: almost flat, the front one, too, confirming her guess that Blaise had stopped using her bike many months before. She walked or bussed everywhere. Maybe it wasn't cool to ride a bicycle any more – apart from those tiny stunt bikes a couple of boys had visited Blaise on a few months ago. Sheena pictured them riding away, jumping their bikes on and off the pavement, standing on the pedals like jockeys, their lean youths' arses high up in the air. Rare visitors.

Sheena tried to jounce her hybrid on and off the kerb, but the bike mocked her attempt at girlishness, and only bounced itself back at her.

Over the canal bridge the vigil, at the high new steel-mesh gates to the Wasteland, was unmanned. Which meant that it did not exist. Sheena wasn't surprised: it had been a spontaneous afterthought to the final action of the campaign, there was no rota organised, and it was too late now to change anything. The dead embers of the campfire at the side of the towpath looked like the aftermath of some unhappy picnic. Mourning a small wildlife site had not sustained the vigil beyond the weekend, and why should it? Maybe, if Sheena were honest, Blaise was right. The roar of the contractors, flashes of yellow metal moving through the branches of the willows, the crackle and groan of trees falling. Maybe they *should* be cheered. Maybe that's what you did, you fought with all you had for what you believed in and then, if your adversaries won, you shook hands and cheered them on their way – through a door to the future. The future was theirs, and it was only yours too if you followed them. Nature reserve or social housing, after all: weren't both desirable projects? Just because a developer would make a lot of money out of one did not, as some of Sheena's more fundamentalist fellow activists chose to believe, render it immoral.

Sheena cycled on, into the glare of the morning sun, annoyed she'd not brought her sunglasses. That was what she'd been trying to remember when Blaise thumped downstairs. It was bright and hot as August already, this glassy Tuesday morning in June.

A little further along the canal Sheena came up off the towpath and cycled west along Aristotle Lane, between the recreation ground and the Canal Walk Development. At the corner of Waterside estate, one path, which always smelled of dogshit, led to the bridge over the railway, and on to Port Meadow. The other ran here, all around the outside of the fresh wooden fence of the new Phil and Jim primary school site.

Sheena leaned her bike against a metal stanchion and locked it. She pushed through the swing gate and looked up and down the railway line. To her left she could see Oxford Station, and a congregation of carriages and platforms and red lights; to her right the three tracks curved off out of sight a couple of hundred metres away. There was nothing coming from either direction, so she crossed on wooden boards laid between the rails. Through another metal gate, crudely weighted to swing shut behind her with an ugly clang, Sheena entered the Aristotle Lane allotments. Beneath her rucksack, her T-shirt stuck to her back.

From double-dug, deep-weeded, manured and seeded plots green shoots sprouted. Large versions of the beansprouts Hector had grown on the kitchen windowsill for school; of Ezra's pots of basil planted at weekly intervals. Jill McTear had always preached the grow-your-own gospel.

'Look at the size of our garden,' Sheena complained.

'Get an allotment,' Jill invariably suggested. 'The taste when you've grown vegetables yourself: there's no comparison.'

Sheena walked between the plots. Here and there short old men pottered between shed and bed of their allotments. Gathered sticks or bricks or buckets. They erected delicate structures out of bamboo poles and willow switches, with the patience of visionaries. Experimental skeletal frames for buildings that would grow organically.

None of them, as far as she could see, was actually digging in their carefully laid-out plots: it was as if they were less gardeners than retired observers of a collaboration between seeds and soil.

A tall, thin young man with a blond moustache, who nodded hello, was digging a long trench. Sheena also passed one or two women, thirtyish, with small children playing in a section of the plot like a sand pit. The mothers plunged spades into black soil, stamped them further in, heaved each clod up; bent over to tug weeds loose.

In the far corner of the allotments was an overgrown area of scrub and bramble. Sheena negotiated a path around thorns and between nettles, lifted her feet over wild roots. Bent branches and stooped beneath them. The place was another, tiny piece of wasteland. A satellite to the Wasteland.

Sheena picked her way into a small clearing. In the middle,

invisible from outside, was a low bender, covered with drab canvas. Mole was sitting cross-legged staring at a Butagaz burner, its flame a haze. A small kettle was heating up. Mole raised his gaze to Sheena, and nodded. She sat across from him, swinging her rucksack off her shoulder to the ground, and pulled out wrapped items of food. Mole swapped the kettle for a small frying pan and cut a knob of butter into it, even before Sheena unwrapped and passed him two sausages from Feller's Organic Butcher's. The pan accepted them with a sizzle. Unsurprised by her arrival, now he seemed to know exactly what she'd brought him: he took her gifts of eggs, bread, tomatoes, mushrooms, teabags and milk, nodding at each item as if she'd merely delivered his order. He was truly psychic, she thought. Or was it that wherever Mole pitched his tent people took it upon themselves to bring him alms? And what they gave was entirely predictable.

Who knows? It wasn't something Sheena was going to ask him. Mole said so little he deterred her from talking. He made her hear the redundancy of her words; the fatuity of her voice. Its imposition upon the silent air.

Mole wore army-surplus clothes. He was squat and stocky, with a black mop of curly hair and a full beard. His cooking style, with the one pan on a single hob, was deliberate, methodical: when the sausages were fried he took them out and put them on a plate to one side; melted more butter, cut carefully up and fried mushrooms and spitting tomatoes. Cut bread. Buttered bread.

Sheena Pepin had first seen Mole when she was up a ladder, tying a banner between willow branches on which were brightly daubed the words: THE SKY IS HELD UP BY THE TREES. Looking down she'd seen a man walking slowly, bent over, deep in concentration. When she reached the ground she saw that beneath a Neanderthal beard and grime was a youthful face, and that, hovering between his thick, filthy fingers, two thin and delicate dowsing rods twitched and swung.

'What do you reckon?' Sheena had asked the young diviner. 'Are there force fields here? Occult energy. Do ley lines converge below us?'

He took his time before gazing back at her, with black eyes that Sheena felt burrow into her. Then, solemnly and shyly, Mole had nodded his head of matted hair.

Last Friday, shortly after dawn, Sheena had waded through the rank water of the reedbeds. Mole followed her, four more in their group behind, crouched down in the boggy water, groping slow and muted in the light and smoky morning. Reptilian in their wetsuits and drysuits, they slid through the swampy breeding habitat of water voles, stirring up with their movement fetid odours. Up ahead, Sheena spotted a guard standing on the canal path: he was facing away, east towards the back gardens of the houses on Hayfield Road and south along the towpath. She turned and made a gesture of silence with a finger to her lips. Mud squelched in her footsteps underwater. Willow branches above their heads squeaked against each other.

A little further on they hauled themselves out, and squatted on a dry spur amongst the high reeds. Sheena turned, to find Mole already passing her the pencil-thin periscope she'd just decided she was ready to employ. She nodded in acknowledgement, smiling to herself at the way his taciturnity infected others: you soon imagined you were communicating as psychically as he did. She peered through the reeds at a fluoro-jacketed man with a tripod and theodolite. Another with a red-and-white-striped totemic stick, moving together through the Wasteland.

Drivers had turned off the engines of their bulldozers and stood smoking, awaiting their masters' orders like the beaters of some country-house shoot. Checking her watch, Sheena turned and nodded to Mole and the others crouching behind him. And at ten minutes to eight precisely, on the last Friday morning of the spring of 2003, out of the reedbed the skinsuited waders had risen and run.

Mole did everything with cautious intent. He moved with an anthropoidal lumber that drew attention to his physical strength, and also suggested that he could spring into action any time he wanted. He'd appeared at the Wasteland just after it was registered

129

as a Town Green, as if to join in the celebration. In retrospect it was as if he knew the celebrations to be illusory, and the campaign would need fresh impetus in the months to come.

Sheena watched him. 'How old are you, Mole?' she asked. She thought he might be anything between twenty-five and thirty-five, or even older, behind that beard and tanned, weatherbeaten skin. She didn't expect him to answer the question. As if her inability to guess were due to some purposeful evasion on his part, a measure of intentional disguise.

Mole broke one egg, and then another, into the pan. The gelatinous liquid solidified, and whitened. He scooped tiny spoonfuls of hot butter on top of the intact yolks. 'Twenty-four,' he said.

Sheena watched him eat, this young man who lived with so little. He nodded to her occasionally with a certain grave gratitude. She felt no flutter in the stomach, no exciting uncertainty; no, nor trepidation either, coming here again, the fourth or was it the fifth time, even though she realised plain enough that people knew this stranger was here, and were watching. Allotment holders, forever having the fruit of their labours nicked, and being undermined by bottle-diggers, were snoops from necessity. Sheena had become a recognisable local figure, too, and surely there were people who knew people she knew. Yet she allowed herself to act with a careless, numb bravado.

They drank tea as the sun rose higher. It beat down upon them and also upon the earth, warming it up, drawing the vegetation that grew inside the soil out and up towards its life-affirming heat. Mole rolled himself a cigarette. They sat in silence. Sheena closed her eyes. Her blood moved thin and easy around her body. Without sight, her other senses became keener: she could hear the air vibrating around her, could feel it on her skin, could smell the ground coming to life around her. She sensed the potential of all the slumbering life in the earth's crust as it warmed towards the sun. Stirring. Realising its opportunity.

When she opened her eyes it was to find Mole looking at her. He put down his enamel mug. Without rising to his full height he turned and crawled into the bender. Sheena followed. They lay on

130

groundsheets and blankets people had given Mole. The smells of woodsmoke and patchouli oil that came off his clothes were stronger inside the tent and so, as she removed them, was the aroma of his body. She kissed and caressed him, his beard a both unpleasant and arousing novelty to her, like the stale tobacco taste of his mouth. Sheena could feel herself moisten well before, for all the sensual exploration of her caresses, Mole hardened. When eventually she felt his erection firm in her grasp she took him into her.

She didn't need him to touch her with his fingers or his tongue. All she wanted him to do was to move back and forth, back and forth, and that is what he did, with a slow deliberation. The longer he thrust at her the more Mole perspired in the warm bender, and the more the smell of his sour sweat was infused with the scent of patchouli, and a yeasty tang of beer.

'Yes,' Sheena exhorted him. 'Keep going. Yes, don't stop. Just keep going like this.' The sun beat down on the canvas, and into the heat of their exertions.

With every move they made Mole gave a deep grunt. In his gradually quickening breath the smell of dope emerged from his lungs. His libido, slow to rise, promised to be as obtuse as his speech, reptilian, unimaginative, resolute, and it was all Sheena wanted.

'People are still asking what women want,' Simon had said at some point the previous Sunday. 'Six hundred years after the Wife of Bath. No, Ezra, I say, what do you think? Tell me, Sheena. Would a woman want a man who gave her orgasms, but never asked her for one of his own? Would she like that?'

Simon leaned back. Sheena and Ezra and Minty waited out what was only a rhetorical pause, knowing not to interrupt their friend when he was about to bestow upon them the answer to his own question.

'Well, of course she would,' he'd said, leaning forward. 'And of course she wouldn't. That's the point, isn't it? Men and women appear to be equally complex, unpredictable, infuriating creatures. Who both, oddly enough, like to screw.'

131

Simon spoke such nonsense, he really did, but he made Sheena laugh; there weren't many who did that. Poor Ezra, who tried so hard for her. Who wanted so much to do the right thing for his partner, her every orgasm something they toiled for, an effort, a labour, each session a clumsy foray into her erogenous zones, a blind search for her clitoris or G spot, an attempt to bring something new – a different angle, a different rhythm – and invariably the falling back to tried and trusted old routes to a well-worn satisfaction.

What did she do for him, though? Well, something: he usually got it up for her. Though it occurred to her he'd not asked for a blow-job in years. The truth was, Sheena admitted, she'd been in love with Ezra, once, without his ever having really turned her on. Her own sensuality remained as much of a mystery to Sheena as it ever was. Each of her small children had been edible – to gaze at their bodies could literally make her salivate; a common maternal response. With Hector this hunger continued, was as powerful now, as he moved to the brink of puberty and began to withdraw from her physical affection. Hector seemed so gorgeous to Sheena: when she was still allowed to cuddle him it wasn't hard to imagine taking their caresses further, into full-blown seduction.

It was for the children, Sheena told herself, that they stayed together this long. She and Ezra were friends, companionable shapes of wood bobbing in water, and each had come to an accommodation with his or her own need. Ezra surely knew of her cursory liaisons, opportunities that had presented themselves from time to transient time. But something had to give. If there were only Blaise and Hector they could float as free from each other as they wished once Hec was sixteen or so – except that now there was Louie, their accidental gift; their beautiful punishment for one lazy, late-night gamble.

'Yes, yes, go on . . . God,' she moaned at the muscular bearded troll who was burrowing into her, thrusting deeper. 'Don't stop. Keep going.' This was sex: Sheena could feel deep inside, at the liquid edge of sensation, a distant wave. It was slowly approaching. She knew that beyond it there'd be another, and another, just as long as this animal in his stifling lair was able to keep fucking her, overpowering her amongst the smells of canvas, dope and sweat, which mingled in the tent with the juicy, sweet-smelling hunger emanating from herself.

Blaise and Ezra Pepin whacked the ball at each other with an eager aggression. Ezra threw himself around, relishing despite his fatigue the thirst of his lungs and sweat on his skin. The Ferry Sports Centre hall smelled of sour old rubber, and the overhead lights filled the arena with a stark and hostile luminosity designed to render human beings wan, pallid, overly realistic. But neither father nor daughter, alone at a table-tennis table this Tuesday lunchtime, paid heed to anything other than their contest.

Blaise got her body behind every shot, and swung the bat with the whole of her right arm. She moved with a surprising and supple fluidity, easing back on to her toes between strokes, while her father made his shots with a flick of the wrist and moved jerkily, snappily, in an effective but awkward manner that appeared old-fashioned, as if it had developed for the way that ping-pong used to be played, but was being rendered extinct by evolving technique.

Their rallies were conversations between them, each serve the proposal of some notion intended to inspire quick-witted repartee.

Here, what do you think of this?

Interesting, but had you considered: Crack!

Fine. Yes. And how about: Crack!

Ah, but on the other hand: Crack!

Fascinating point you raise, but then: Crack!

Blaise had put on weight around the age of seven or eight, and carried it as a temporary accompaniment. She moved with the grace of the lean child she'd once been, and the woman she'd started to become, her body morphing, elongating, in front of her father's eyes.

'Shot!' Ezra conceded, as the white plastic bubble flashed past him, a note of pride in his voice which suggested, had anyone been there to hear it, that since it was his offspring who'd made the shot then he deserved some measure of credit.

133

Ezra had to remind himself that there was more time, always more time, than you thought. Blaise's bat struck the ball with such a loud bony thwack that even if the projectile was not actually a blur in your vision then the terror that sound invoked could make it so. But only for a millisecond. Then the blur resolved itself into this light and airy globe which, if Ezra stepped back away from the table, slowed down and drifted towards him, allowing him time to position himself, to freeze in a stance of readiness for a split second of his own. Before striking with a whip of his wrist, to stun the ball with a fatal blow. Ping-pong as martial art.

They stood well back from the table, then, both father and daughter, neither forced to by the other's excellence, in truth, so much as opting each to do so because it was from that position that they could play long rallies of spectacular smacks and whacks. Of leaping defensive lobs, and last-gasp retrievals.

'The champion's *soaking* it up!' Ezra commentated on himself, his trainers squeaking on the lacquered wooden floor, lunging grunts echoing in the high roof. Blaise's white polo shirt clung wet with perspiration.

Although it was from that position that they had the most fun, Ezra kept an unfair advantage in reserve. As Blaise went ahead, 3–2 in their best of seven games, so Ezra inched closer to the table, hitting the ball back earlier, forgoing the pleasure of open rallies for a cramped, competitive effectiveness. From a crabbed hunch he chopped and sliced the ball, making sly drop shots and acute angles, forcing his daughter to scramble after shots she couldn't quite reach.

'It's not *fair*, Daddy,' Blaise shrieked, her face flushed, as she saw victory slip from her grasp, again, and he had to concede that it wasn't. One day Blaise would beat him, Ezra accepted. But not yet, not this day, even if it was her birthday – a fact to which neither had made reference – and if he could put off that day as long as possible it was, he trusted, as many fathers surely had before him, as much for her as for himself.

*   *   *

It was the custom in the Pepin family, initiated by Ezra from witnessing its like amongst the Indians he'd studied, to make no acknowledgement of someone's birthday until the evening.

'Give a person time alone to come to terms with being a year older,' he'd say. 'To consider where they are in their lives, and what it means. Don't overwhelm them with the noisy gifts of celebration before giving them this precious one. It's a matter of discretion.'

So that supper, to be eaten all together at six o'clock, was approached by each member of the family with a sense of anticipation that had been brewing all day.

Before going to work at noon Sheena had come back home and made a chocolate cake in the shape of a hedgehog, whose chocolate icing she covered in chocolate buttons, halved and sticking up like spikes, with a glacé-cherry nose and coffee beans for eyes. Louie was now helping his mother lance fourteen candle holders between the buttons, through the icing to the sponge.

Ezra came through the door breathing hard. 'I'm not late, am I?' He kissed Sheena and Louie. 'Well done, you two, that hedgehog looks well and truly spiked. Do I have time for a shower?'

'I'm not sure about this,' Sheena said. 'We had a terrific row this morning. Sort of.'

'Sort of?'

'Well, it wasn't a row, exactly.'

'We played ping-pong. She didn't mention a row.'

'I don't know what it was. We've not spoken since.'

'What was it about?'

'Nothing. I don't know. She accused me of having brainwashed her into joining the campaign. How glad she was they're building houses on the Wasteland.'

Ezra stepped towards his wife. 'You look tired, darling.'

Sheena stepped back, pushing him away. 'Well, actually, you, for that matter, look exhausted. I'm fine, Ezra. This is not about me.'

'Blaise is probably ambivalent about being another year older. Fourteen. It's a difficult time in anyone's life.'

'Yes, well, it wasn't very nice. Don't blame me if she sulks all the way through supper.'

'Where is she?'

'Upstairs. And no, you don't have time for a shower. Louie, can you go and tell Blaise and Hector it's time to eat.'

Ezra dropped his briefcase and jacket on one of the living-area sofas.

'Can you hide this?' Sheena asked, handing him the cake.

'Sure. Oh, and I put a bottle of Prosecco in the fridge this morning.'

Toad-in-the-hole was Blaise's favourite, and the only vegetables she'd always eaten, right through from infancy to the present, were roast potatoes and Bird's Eye frozen peas, and as these were arranged before her she responded with a smile that to Ezra seemed to wipe all the pressure and distortion of adolescence right off her countenance.

'Oh, Mum,' Blaise beamed. 'My favourite. And gravy too.'

'Meat?' Hector queried, as if he'd never seen a tray of sausages embedded in batter before.

'Don't fret,' said Sheena. 'Can't you see those two veggie ones for you?'

'And me!' Louie chimed.

'No, Peanut,' Ezra told him. 'You like the chipolatas from Feller's? Those are the ones you like.'

Ezra opened the wine, condensation on the green bottle, and he poured a glass for Blaise with the bow of an obsequious waiter, a tea towel draped over his forearm.

'Would the señorita care to try the wine?'

'No, thanks, Daddy.'

'You like I justa pour?'

'I don't want wine, thanks.'

'Oh. You sure?' Ezra straightened up. 'I thought you might like a little on your birthday.' He moved around the table.

'I'll have some,' Hector volunteered.

'Sure.'

'Ezra,' said Sheena. 'He's eleven years old, remember.'

'Almost twelve!'

'If it's Blaise's birthday,' Sheena pointed out, 'you must be eleven and three-quarters exactly, Hector.'

'You might as well say almost ten,' said Blaise.

'Let me see,' Hector said to his sister. 'Is eleven and three-quarters as close to ten as it is to twelve?'

'Yeh, all right,' Blaise conceded.

'I mean, that is quite a three-pipe problem, Watson,' Hector persisted.

'That's enough,' Sheena told him. 'Let's remember it's someone's birthday.'

'He can have half a glass, then,' Ezra suggested.

'It's a school day tomorrow,' Sheena told her husband. 'That's all I'm saying.'

Hector's eyes widened above a thin-lipped smile as his father poured. The bubbles frothed a brief foam in the champagne flute.

'Actually, I don't like alcohol, really,' said Blaise.

'All the more for us,' Ezra smiled weakly, pouring some for Sheena.

'I'm not even sure why people drink it.'

'You'll probably learn in time,' Ezra told her.

Blaise shrugged, like it was all the same to her what other people did. 'That intoxication. Why do people want it? Isn't the perception that nature's given us good enough? I don't understand, that's all, Daddy. I wish I did.'

'It's a treat, darling,' Ezra laughed.

'Yes, but you and Mum have it every day.'

'I beg your pardon?' said Sheena.

Ezra put his elbow on the table and scratched his forehead. 'Surely not.'

Blaise tucked into her food. 'This is so yummy,' she said.

'Well, cheers,' Sheena said, raising her glass, which Blaise saluted with water, Louie with apple juice.

'Chin-chin,' said Ezra, clinking glasses with Hector.

Blaise wasn't challenging them, Ezra accepted as he ate: she genuinely didn't understand why people drank alcohol, and it wasn't her fault that her enquiry made her father feel a little louche.

The bubbles in his Prosecco less tickled than irritated the top of his mouth.

'I'm surprised,' Hector said, looking across at his sister, 'that you eat these sausages, actually.'

'Hector,' Sheena groaned, 'don't bring this up again. Didn't we agree to live and let live?'

'It's not halal, is it?' Hector persisted.

'We eat meat,' Sheena said. 'Once or twice a week. We buy free range, we buy organic. You know that, Hector. That's our deal. Your father agrees.'

'Who, me? Absolutely.'

'You don't have to, Hec. That's fine. Leave Blaise alone. She can make her choice too.'

Blaise stared at her brother with narrowed eyes.

Hector turned to Sheena and said, 'Okay, Mum. Shall we get our presents now?'

'Yes!' said Louie. 'And me!'

'Happy Birthday to You,' they sang as Ezra and Louie came in from the hall bearing the hedgehog cake.

Blaise let Louie help her blow out fourteen yellow flames, which they accomplished impressively, only for the candles to reignite with a magical impudence. And though they'd used such candles many times before they all acted amazed, for Louie's sake and for their own. Blaise and Louie blew them out again, and again the flames burst up. Sheena shrieked, Ezra cheered, Hector accorded the company his indulgent crooked smile.

'Shall I carve?' Ezra volunteered. 'Wait: I don't suppose you'll want any hedgehog meat, Hector, will you?'

They ate the chocolate cake with a pot of tea. Blaise licked her fingers one by one, then opened her presents. From Sheena and Ezra an amethyst necklace from Port Meadow Designs, and a £50 voucher for a clothes shop on George Street. 'Thanks, Mummy,' Blaise said. 'Thanks, Daddy,' and she kissed and hugged them politely.

From Hector a CD by Television, a seventies band apparently

enjoying a revival. Ezra suspected he'd once owned an album of theirs himself – this very one, possibly; it might even still be in a cardboard box of vinyl, in his old room in his father's Wiltshire cottage.

Sheena said she'd never heard of the band. Ezra didn't believe her.

'You know The Ramones, though, right?' he demanded. 'I must have played you loads of their songs.'

Hector leaned towards his father in a confiding manner, with a serious expression on his face. 'I like them, Daddy,' he said gravely. 'They're very good, actually.'

Sheena made a face that signalled her complete disinterest. 'Never,' she said. She sat back, observing: an idea, she realised as she watched her family, was forming itself.

'Thanks, twerp,' Blaise said, and she and Hector gave each other a kind of emblematic hug that reminded Ezra of Minty Carlyle's, except that the same degree of contact implied opposite intent: hers of greater intimacy, theirs of a mutual restraint from siblings' enforced familiarity.

From Louie a tube of tennis balls, and in return, kind of, there was a present for him from everyone, a new hexagon-patterned plastic football; and for Hector a new pair of swimming goggles, which he promptly put on, and wore for the rest of the evening. Birthdays were occasions of joint celebration in the Pepin household.

As Sheena watched one and then the other of her husband and children, she seemed to see them as being both individuals and members of a family with a clarity that was entirely new. They were of the same flesh and blood, living in a web of symbiotic relationships – yet each one was also an autonomous individual, with needs entirely separate from the others. 'Well, of course,' Sheena said to herself, but still, this truism shone in her mind with the lucidity of a revelation, and it gave her the answer to Ezra's needs. As they sat there around the kitchen table, watching Blaise open her presents, a proposition came to Sheena: just as his family had – as Simon perceived – made Ezra a heroic prisoner, so it could provide him with the escape. Yes. He could take them with him.

There were more presents for Blaise: from her godmother, Jill, and godfather, Ian, a joint present, a digital video camera; various gifts from maternal grandparents, from uncles and aunts and cousins. And a Jiffy bag with the spidery handwriting and the Devizes postmark of Grandpa Clive Pepin.

'Wonder what's in *there*,' said Hector, as he left to test his goggles in a deep bath, tottering a little tipsily towards the stairs.

'What *could* it be?' Blaise agreed, tearing the bag and then a small package open, to reveal (along with a characterless birthday card. A deteriorating scrawl across it, *To Blaise, with love from Grandpa*) a box of After Eight mints, which Ezra's father gave each of the children every birthday; and which Blaise now ritualistically handed over to her parents, in exchange for its cash value, rounded up to a five-pound note.

7

The Best Idea You Ever Heard

Tuesday 24 June

Sheena was right, Ezra conceded as he yawned through Louie's bedtime read: he was dog-tired. Between his eyes and the inside of his eyelids he could feel minuscule granules of grit. Insomnia and the outlay of energy involved in the presentation yesterday had drained him. Today was a restless snarl of phone calls, faxes, emails to get the prototype bottle into production as soon as possible. Word had come down from on high early this morning: plant capable of such a process needed to be in place by the end of the summer. What kind of quantities, and in which location, did not appear to have been decided, so that Ezra and Chrissie Barwell had an impossible task: to put together variable speculative tenders and offer them to appropriate companies for provisional costings. It had been an unreasonable and exhilarating day's work – sandwiched in the middle of which was a seven-game ping-pong thriller, on his daughter's birthday.

'What will you dream of?' Ezra asked his son.

Louie lay in bed, embracing his new football. His eyes wandered the room. 'It's a secret,' he decided.

'Sleep tight.'

'Don't let bed bugs bite.'

'Night, darling.'

Ezra repaired to his desk in the spare room to plan a schedule for the following day. He'd taken the unusual step of emailing home various documents to deal with in peace. But Sheena was using the internet on the computer downstairs, and it would break their unspoken pact if he insisted upon the need to use it for his work, would in an instant elevate his job to a position of preposterous importance. And Sheena, to be fair, never used the home computer for Home Holidays business.

When he'd done as much as he was able to, Ezra looked out and saw the sun had gone down. From the window by his desk he could glimpse, beyond the chimneys and aerials of Blenheim Orchard and Waterways, a patch of Wytham Wood on the horizon: between the black of treetops and the blue-black of sky was a single thin streak of burnt orange. Ezra gently pressed the light switch off, lest a loud click should wake anyone.

He looked in on Hector – he and Louie dissimilar asleep as awake. Floppy brown hair in place, mouth cagily closed, he lay on his back, unnervingly still. It was Sheena's opinion that Hector had been a sentry in a past life, on some frontier of civilisation: he'd fallen asleep when the barbarians came. As if he weren't really sleeping now, Hector took a deep breath into his eleven-year-old chest and held it, listening out for evidence of threat. Sleeping still alert, still holding his breath, Hector's respiratory system working in some mystically anxious way.

Peanut Louie in his room had already started to scuff and strain beneath his duvet, torment scrawled in his three-year-old features, on the very brink, it seemed, of waking, in tears. This was how Louie spent his nights, thrashing about, grinding his teeth, tossing his wild mop of blond hair.

Each morning, though, Louie woke cleanly, and with one slow blink of his eyes wiped away the entire night, a mere blip of neurotic unconsciousness of which he retained no memory, yet which had replenished him fully. Then Louie would jump out of bed and begin rearranging his train track, sleep a brief pause in the vital, self-important labours, never completed, only repeated and refined, dismantled and begun again, of a three-year-old at play.

While Hector would wake in the same position he'd dropped off in, and gaze at the ceiling, before rising slowly, in the regretful resurrection of a tomb effigy. For sleep's blank intermission had done nothing to alter the world or himself in it.

Ezra kissed Hector's still forehead. His hair smelled like straw.

Light leaked from the bottom of Blaise's bedroom door. Ezra knocked lightly.

'Who is it?'

Ezra opened the door. Blaise was lying in bed, reading: whatever book or magazine it was she slid under the duvet.

'How are you?' he asked.

'Okay, Daddy.'

Ezra picked his way through the junk and detritus across Blaise's carpet. Clothes were strewn across bed, chair, floor. A being from outer space might have searched for meaning in such chaos, he thought: evidence of passion, a psychological condition, natural disaster? He was the alien, and the meaning eluded him. In recent months Blaise seemed to have threaded her way through a crazed succession of different styles – goth to skateboard hip-hop to retro grunge – trying on masks of tribal youth. Nowadays she tended, as far as he could tell, to mix everything up, in an eclectic rag-bag of her own devising. Ezra hoped that his daughter possessed the self-confidence not to need to belong to any one group; rather that than the gauche aloofness of a misfit. He thought he should mention the violence from the Wasteland. There was surely more to say. But perhaps not on this day.

Ezra reached the bed and sat down. 'Happy birthday, darling,' he said.

'Thanks, Daddy.'

'Does it feel good to be fourteen?'

Blaise shrugged. 'Good? Bad? I don't know. Not much I can do about it, is there?'

'I guess not.'

'I can't turn the clock back, or wind it forward, can I?'

'Would you want to?'

143

Blaise frowned at her father. 'Daddy. Why do you ask questions that don't have answers? You always do. I suppose you always have, all my life.'

Ezra was delighted that Blaise appreciated his enquiring consideration of the complexities of existence. It was a vindication.

'You ask, I don't know,' she said. Attempting to express what she meant, she tilted her head and screwed up her eyes, as if the words might be hiding along her hairline. She glimpsed them: 'You ask unnecessary questions,' Blaise told her father.

Yes, Ezra thought. That's right. That's what he did. Perhaps that was as good a definition of civilisation as any. The asking of unnecessary questions.

Blaise said, 'I should think it drives Mum mad.'

'Mum?' Ezra asked, disconcerted. 'You had a fight today, right?' he continued, as if by reminding Blaise of it he might tip the balance back in his favour.

'No,' said Blaise. But then, Ezra's eyes upon her, she lowered her head. 'Kind of.'

'What was it about?'

'Nothing.'

Ezra sandwiched his daughter's right hand between his. 'Blaise, I know Mum jumps off the deep end. And I know she doesn't always listen. But if you could just bite your lip sometimes.'

'I know, Daddy.'

'You need to be tolerant. That's what I've learned. Your mother sees the world in black and white, Blaise. She's a passionate person. At any one moment we're a hero or a villain. Then it changes.' Ezra rubbed the back of Blaise's hand. 'She loves you very much, you know.'

Blaise nodded, her head still lowered.

'She doesn't mean what she says when she yells.'

'She didn't yell.'

'It's not nice, I know that. Just give her a little room. It's not difficult to do. Tiptoe a little around her. She's the most wonderful person in the world. She really is.'

'I know.'

144

'I'm just telling you this, darling. I mean, you're fourteen. You're not a child. I don't know.' Now it was Ezra's turn to shrug, his hand on the back of Blaise's rising into the air and opening out its palm towards her in a gesture of self-effacing generosity. 'It might be helpful.'

Blaise raised her head. She had an odd expression on her face: bemused; indignant. 'I don't know, either, Daddy,' she said. 'Mum thinks if we do the right thing, the world will be a better place. And she's right.' She looked up at Ezra. 'But what's at stake, Daddy? Nothing.'

'Isn't it?'

'It's easy to have principles when you can afford them.'

Ezra shook his head and squeezed his daughter's hand. At that moment a yawn overcame him. Mouth agape, eyes closed, he bobbed up and then down with it as if on the swell of a wave. 'Sorry, darling, I'm a bit exhausted. Look, let's you and me agree to do our best.'

'Listen, Daddy,' Blaise said, just as another yawn assailed her father.

'I'm off to bed before I fall asleep on yours,' he murmured. 'Give me a birthday hug.' He leaned towards her, Blaise leaned forward from the pillows, and they embraced. She smelled of oranges. He could feel her ribs close to her spine with one hand, the bones of her shoulder with the other.

'Daddy,' her voice said behind him.

'What, darling?' he asked, as they pulled apart.

'Can't you say something to Grandpa? I mean, *you* don't even like *After Eights*.'

'Blaise, I've told him about a hundred times. Your Grandpa doesn't listen. Or he doesn't remember, as he insists. I think we're stuck with that custom.'

Downstairs, Sheena was still at the computer in the sitting-room. 'Don't look!' she exclaimed as Ezra approached.

'What's going on?' he demanded. 'The women in my house are all hiding things from me.'

'Keep away,' Sheena commanded, covering the screen with her arms. 'You'll find out in a minute.'

'Find out what?'

'It's a surprise. I've got something to tell you. Now go away.'

'I'm going,' Ezra obeyed, backing away towards the hall. 'Look, I'm in reverse.'

'Five minutes, then I'll tell you everything,' Sheena promised.

'I'm going to take my shower.'

There was a great temptation, Ezra found when he was tired, to prolong the evening. To put off the one thing you needed – sleep – and luxuriate instead in the languorous sensuality with which fatigue imbued, in this case, a shower. Eyes closed, allowing his consciousness to sink and dip towards sleep, while hot water thrummed on his shoulders and coursed over his body. The sensation of water became unspecified. It wasn't just this element falling on that part: water, warmth, skin merged into a tactile melt. It was trippy. It reminded him of how after a party, high on whatever, he loved the aftermath almost as much as the night itself; the next day's voluptuous calm.

Ezra brushed his teeth, smeared some moisturising cream into the lines on his face and swayed from en suite into bedroom just as Sheena entered by the main door. They met between the end of the bed and the built-in wardrobe, and remembering that sex too could be great when you were exhausted, as long as you could stay awake, Ezra swam into Sheena's path and embraced her.

'I've got to have a shower myself,' Sheena said. 'I won't be a minute.'

'Don't torment me,' Ezra said, squeezing a buttock through her leggings. 'You don't need a shower. I don't mind.'

'I do, Ezra,' Sheena said, pulling free from him.

'I even like it, darling, your sweat and your . . .'

But she'd disappeared into the bathroom.

Ezra sat down on the end of the bed. He had a white towel wrapped around his waist. How wonderful it is, he thought, surrendering to the impulse to let go, to fall back on to the bed, his legs still dangling over the end. How wonderful it is to have central heating, and then for summer to arrive, and never have to wear pyjamas again.

Lips he saw first. Full, crimson painted lips, pouting then pulling back to reveal heavily applied mascara and powder. On a man's face. Pouting at him, winking, running his tongue around his lips, flicking it in and out, lewd, crudely suggestive. But wait, the face was also presenting itself to a mirror to be made up. A pout for the application of lipstick; a long wink to coat the eyelashes.

It was himself, Ezra understood, at whom he was staring. He didn't look quite like how he thought he looked in real life – his features were broader – but of course it wasn't so easy to tell beneath the face paint.

He also realised that he was being turned on. Was he turning himself on? It seemed kind of ludicrous, yet something was undeniably happening. The face in the mirror, too, was becoming increasingly animated; it expressed a commensurate, a symmetrical, arousal, was less gesturing now than writhing. Ezra wondered whether the face really was a mirror image, unreal, real only in glass. He longed for it to be not a reflection but a person, for in this dream he wanted, needed desperately to have contact with human flesh, even his own. Yet something was happening. There was contact, wasn't there?

Ezra Pepin woke up. He opened his eyes and leaned forward, to find that some kind of monster covered with wet black hair was consuming him. This startling moment of horror gave way to the realisation that Sheena was kneeling on the carpet at the foot of the bed and fellating his erect penis.

Ezra lay back again on the white duvet and closed his eyes. The image of a weird sea monster bobbing aboard him had shocked his brain awake: he urged it to return to the drowsy margins of sleep; to the delicious and troubling confusion of his dream. But it was impossible. Dreams could never be re-entered. So he tried to empty his mind, and let it fill with awareness of the sensation engendered

147

by the sea monster, no, no, not that image, empty your mind of that image. Let your mind's eye be fed by sexual stimulae alone. Let what colours, shapes, textures fold and unfold there as they will. Give yourself over. Let Sheena sink you into a drowsy, subliminal bliss.

It wouldn't work. Despite the fact that Sheena toiled hard for him, bobbing up and down, the acute liquidity of arousal began to fade. She couldn't do it on her own. Unless Ezra did something pretty soon his erection would start to diminish. He summoned up images one after another, an array of women, from movie stars doing his bidding to girls at the office in pornographic scenarios to the children's schoolfriends' mothers naked, to find one that might snag, a rapid succession, from early girlfriends to his first crush, an older girl in primary school. Deborah Mitchell was her name. She was much older than seven-year-old Ezra Pepin; she was a majestic and beautiful nine- or ten-year-old. Impossibly mature and out of reach, except for the day she ambushed him. Amused or irritated, presumably, by the little kid who trailed her home along the short cut through the abandoned warehouses. Deborah appeared out of nowhere and grabbed him. Restrained, he went limp in her embrace.

'Fight,' Deborah said. 'Fight back.' But Ezra had been too awed by her presence enveloping him to obey her command. So she tickled him, and that forced a reaction, and they tussled. She held him to her but she also tickled him to make him struggle to get away, to make him squirm in her grasp; he began to understand that she, her body, seemed to be acting as if he was tickling her, which he wasn't, she was squirming of her own free will, she was rubbing herself against him in a mysterious way. With a kind of inexplicable inefficiency.

They struggled on in this way for a long, dispiriting time, until Ezra found it unbearable the way he wasn't there any more, the regal girl was alone with herself and there was only his useless body left. He wriggled it loose and ran away.

But what if Deborah Mitchell had known about fellatio already and was prepared to inflict it upon a boy stalking her, upon his juvenile erection? What an initiation that would have been; my God, what a thrill. The thought of it throbbed intense feeling back into his penis. Ezra Pepin at thirty-nine lay on his marital bed while his wife applied commendable effort to his pleasure, but he was really seven-year-old Ezra being beautifully, rhythmically interfered with by an older woman, the delectable and expert ten-year-old Deborah Mitchell, the princess, the Helen, of St Peter's Primary School in Devizes, bringing him off with a worldly, naive, intuitive precocity.

Because the truth was, Ezra reflected as he lay gasping and spent and Sheena scurried to and from the bathroom with tissue paper to wipe semen from the duvet cover; the truth was that Sheena wasn't very good at it. It was either that or there was something odd about his penis, because she assured Ezra she'd performed the act for men before him who'd been incontrovertibly grateful.

'Men love having their cocks sucked,' Sheena had informed him in that matter-of-fact way of hers. She'd done it to other men and they apparently enjoyed it, had given Sheena the self-assurance of a competent craftswoman. Maybe Ezra had less sensation in his penis than other men; or more; or in different areas of it than them. Maybe the precise location of erogenous zones was far more subtle than was generally held; more shifting, perhaps. He didn't think so. He found it easy enough to give himself a hand-job, and Sheena, now that he thought about it – now that he recalled – was perfectly fine at that too. But fellatio required a more sensual, warm rhythm of lips and tongue, a subtle receptivity to the minutiae of response. Like the swimmer she was, Sheena could plough grimly up and down the shaft of his lonely manhood for as many lengths as it took; a woman in one of those Tantric paintings of lovers in conjugal union but with their minds on higher things. Sheena, Ezra thought, could give a blow-job while compiling a shopping list.

Of course he'd tried to guide her, he remembered, as he sat up and wondered where Sheena had disappeared to. 'A little slower, that's it, that's nice. A little higher up, yes, no, don't come off, further down now, good, good, no, that's where you were before, and you're speeding up again . . .'

149

Sheena had become irritated, tried too hard, bad-temperedly. Ezra lost erections. There's not much a woman can do with a limp prick in her mouth. Because the problem is, Ezra thought, as Sheena reappeared in the bedroom wrapped in her white cotton dressing-gown with two mugs of herbal tea, that although you needed to tell your partner how to please you, discussing the mechanics of the act while committing it were two activities not always easy to reconcile.

And so he, they, had given up. Ezra claimed not to enjoy fellatio; even if he didn't believe it, he didn't mind admitting to his wife that he was weird. 'People are, darling. Sure. Me too.' And Sheena didn't exactly demand with grievous threats he let her give it to him. They got by. They made it, like just now, when whatever it was that possessed her to assault his sleeping body, she'd got into a groove and persisted with it, and he'd come up with the necessary additional ingredient.

'Come on, Ezra,' Sheena said, 'get into bed. I want to tell you this thing. Come on.'

Ezra crabbed backwards, rucked the duvet up under his arse and over his legs.

'Here,' Sheena said, passing him a mug of mint tea. 'Listen. It came to me. Today. Just now. At supper.'

'What came to you?'

'A revelation. Of something so obvious.'

'A revelation of what?'

'That's what I'm going to tell you. Listen.'

Ezra leaned obediently back into his white pillows against the beech headboard. He could feel a stickiness where his penis nestled against his thigh. He blew on the herbal tea, and sipped it patiently. There was an aching weight, a pressure, upon his eyes, and he wondered why he was so stupid as not to have been sound asleep for at least the last three hours.

'I was watching you,' Sheena said. 'You and the children. And it just struck me all at once. My husband is thirty-nine years old. He works in a crappy job in a stupid company which he joined yesterday, except that yesterday turned into twelve years. Look

150

at him. He's exhausted. And this is the man I was drawn to? The young academic just back from the Amazon –'

'Actually, south of the Amazon –'

'Who when he presented his first informal lecture drew over fifty colleagues and undergrads to that seminar room in the Anthropology Department.'

'Was it really fifty?'

'Turned out they were still interested in aboriginal tribes. The next lecture they had to relocate – people were coming from different disciplines.'

'Surely not, darling.'

'Don't you remember? The buzz. One line in the *Gazette* and word of mouth. Something special was expected from that man. Who had interest in publishing his thesis when he'd hardly started writing it from two, three presses?'

Ezra nodded. 'Four. The chap at Columbia.'

'What happened to that young man?'

'I suppose –'

'I'll tell you what happened, Ezra. Nothing. That's what. You're still there. Waiting, biding your time. That's what's so crazy. All these years. That's what I realised.

'No, don't say anything. And don't yawn. Listen. We had an agreement, you'd pay the rent, well, the mortgage, okay, bad timing but whose fault was that? No one's. Neither of us had much of a clue then. We had no interest in interest rates. And the agreement was it was meant to be temporary. But the years went by and I let them just slip past, and it's a bit like . . . I don't know, like your dad's birthday presents. After-dinner mints for young children; it's so stupid, but no one told him, or he didn't get the message, and three times a year another one comes.'

'How does that compare?'

'I'm trying to tell you, don't you see? We've let the years go by. No, I did. A sideline business with Jill, another child. And you? You just carried on in your quiet way, your – as Simon put it – heroic way. I'm so stupid I never saw what other people obviously

151

did – this poor fellow supporting his silly wife and her regular output of mouths to feed. I can see the statue: *Ezra Pepin mounted on his bicycle*. Heroic mode. Monumental.'

'Very funny.'

'It's not funny, Ezra. I've been sleeping. I've woken up.'

'Fine. But, Sheena –'

'No, wait, Ezra. I asked you not to interrupt me because this is important and I've nearly got there.'

Sheena's wide eyes. Her emphatic gestures, her vehement enthusiasm, made it hard for her to follow, to catch, the fleeing news she wished to give Ezra. And if it occurred to him that she was not addressing him alone, that he was a mirror in which to address herself; and that somehow she reminded him of no one so much as little Deborah Mitchell all those years, all those minutes, ago, trying so hard and awkwardly to please herself with him, then it was not because he thought Sheena was acting. No. Of that he was certain. Whatever it was she was trying to communicate, and was hopefully about to because Ezra didn't think that he could possibly keep himself awake for much longer, whatever else it was, it was sincere. Sheena meant what she said.

'Oh, look, Ezra,' she said. 'There's so much to say, and you look so tired, so I'll tell you what it's all about. We move to Brazil.'

Sheena smiled. She beamed at her husband. 'Well?' she asked.

Ezra didn't know what to say. He wasn't sure whether he still possessed the power of speech. Where the hell did that come from? It was like when he visited his dad and they'd be standing outside the front of the cottage, and a low-flying fighter jet boomed over from the Downs behind the back of the house. It stopped your heart: you couldn't help but duck. 'Move to Brazil.' What on earth? It came out of nowhere. Ezra was flummoxed. One thing that had never once occurred to him, in fifteen years together, was the possibility of his wife having some kind of mental breakdown. Move to Brazil? Her eyes shone with insane conviction. Though he noticed, now, a certain tremor, a flickering uncertainty around her lips.

'Well,' he attempted. 'It's an incredible –'

'The point is,' she interrupted, 'we go for two years. This is the plan. The business is up and running: Jill can steer it, I already asked her, we've got a good team, and I can input from Brazil. I can still make executive decisions.'

'From Brazil?'

'And something too you know we, I mean the Friends of the Wasteland, made a link with the Landless Rural Workers Movement of São Paulo? Exchanged information and ideas for actions and moral support. We twinned, on the net. We've lost our Wasteland but they're still fighting, squatting unused land, I could help them, you know I need to be involved in something, Ezra, but it's like you said the other night with the Carlyles, in England there's nothing at stake, a bit of grass here, a house there, it's civilised and dreary, thank God, really, let's be honest, but there's no passion.'

'Wait a minute,' Ezra said. 'Slow down, darling. I hear what you're saying, but what about the children?'

'That's the beauty of doing it now! It's like we can redeem your long postponement, because Blaise can do her GCSEs there. Not actually her GCSEs, we've always hated that specialisation at sixteen, heading for A levels, haven't we? She can work towards the international baccalaureate.'

'In Brazil.'

'Don't worry. I've looked it up. And when we get back she can enrol at one of the private schools in Oxford that do the baccalaureate.'

'Are you joking?'

'I've got the whole thing planned. Don't you think it would be a wonderful education in itself for Hector? I mean doesn't it make you cringe to see the way he's becoming a drippy, thin-lipped Englishman?'

'Hector?' Ezra wondered, pursing his own thin lips. 'Oh, I don't know.'

'That crap Simon was saying about arranging your son's sexual initiation. Please! But maybe in a more general way you *should*. If we could give our son the opportunity of salsa, capoeira, carnival just as he enters his teenage years. Loosen up those English hips.'

'Hey, wait a minute.'

'Yes, you too! You and me could do salsa classes together.'

No wonder Sheena had a manic look in her eyes, Ezra realised: her pupils were dilated.

'And Louie: you're always telling me his football skills are precocious: how about two years for Louie playing on the beach? I watch the World Cup, don't forget. I know how the Brazilians play. You told me yourself: English boys don't love the ball. You see? The timing. You see?'

'Okay. Wow. You really are working this through.' Already tired, Ezra felt himself being drained by Sheena's zeal.

'And the best thing is, Ezra, the whole point is, you can throw that bloody job back in their faces, you can walk out of that ugly prison for ever, and go back to the natives you've always wanted to, so you can finish your thesis. We'll be right there! Well, I mean a long way away, of course, we won't come with you, unless you want us to visit. Who knows, maybe your tribe's having to deal with land issues? Maybe I could even help them.'

The unease Ezra had been sensing began to reveal itself, its physical existence, now. Each word Sheena spoke with her sincere enthusiasm seemed to correspond to, awaken, a spidery word insect in the pit of Ezra's stomach, which began crawling around there, disturbing buried anxiety, stirring up acid. That's what it was. Fear.

'Darling.' He managed to move his tongue. 'It's a magnificent idea. But the Achia I lived with were a thousand miles from Rio, as the crow flies, I'm not sure you realise the distances –'

'Not Rio, Ezra. São Paulo. There's a superb American school there, and Rio?' She shook her head solemnly. 'It's extremely unsafe nowadays.'

'Rio, São Paulo, okay, eight hundred miles across the Paraguayan border. But you can't just fly in and out –'

'Oh, please, Ezra,' Sheena admonished, her face a frown of frustration. 'I should have known you'd pour cold water on this.'

'Hey, darling, no way. Not at all. I'm completely excited by it, I'm just trying not to get carried away, that's all. I'm playing devil's advocate. For example: I can't quite see the money. Take away my salary.'

'We rent this house out. The rent covers the mortgage, with a good deal left over, about enough to rent a house in Brazil. My money pays our expenses, school fees, flights. Don't worry, Ezra. I've done the sums.'

Ezra had to keep calm. He had to play for time. He felt like he was slipping, as if the acid in his stomach was eating into his foundations. But he had to keep smiling, that was the most important thing, he had to keep focused on right now, to make Sheena believe he was knocked out, blown away, enthralled by her plan. And the odd thing was that despite his bowels churning and his exhausted mind becoming aware of a looming darkness around it, he knew he could manage. Experience had prepared him for just such a crisis. He'd been acting his whole damned life! Was he going to stop now, when he most needed to continue? Hardly!

'You're incredible,' he told Sheena, returning her bright gaze with an appreciative adoration of his own.

'And what can we possibly lose?' she continued. 'If the whole thing falls apart we jump on a plane and come home, carrying the experience with us. If nothing else, Ezra, we'll have got you out of that stupid job, right?'

'You're just amazing, darling,' Ezra smiled. Yes, he was acting, every fibre of his being was bent on duplicity. What a sorrowful contrast with his wife, incapable of the slightest guile. One-dimensional? Yes, maybe, that's right in a way, but there was everything in that one dimension, a noble human being. Sheena had more *substance* than any two or three mercurial women he could think of. And maybe she was right! Maybe this ridiculous idea was a good one! What the hell? It was true: it didn't matter if it didn't work out, they had a house, her business, they weren't going to starve, so why not take a chance? He was almost forty years old, for Christ's sake. Didn't Ezra Pepin *deserve* the opportunity to throw it away?

155

'It's *fucking* absurd,' Sheena said, the rare curse spitting from her mouth. 'I feel *guilty*, Ezra. I don't have to feel this. Why should I? Enough.'

'Enough,' he agreed. 'No more. Come here.' Ezra shifted across, leaned above Sheena, and kissed her. Her lips, her mouth accepted his with a melting readiness, her blood-filled expressive flesh merging with his.

'I can't believe,' Sheena said quietly, when they broke apart, 'how selfish I've been.'

'Don't be silly,' Ezra murmured, grazing her jawbone, her ear, her neck with kisses.

'No, I know it's not just me. You as well, I know, you wanted children too and there's a price to pay. But isn't this making up for it? Isn't this the best idea you ever heard? Am I not one clever woman, sweetheart?'

Clever, yes. Clever was the least of it. Ezra's fingers confirmed how aroused Sheena was, how ready her body was to accomodate his; her flesh impressed by her mind's guileless machinations. She really was incredible: he might have been acting when he said it, but actually now he thought about it Ezra realised that he also meant it. It was true. Sheena *was* amazing. And maybe, he managed to at least suggest to himself, she was turned on too by the prospect of his potential. He *was* so different after all from the young man she'd met: he couldn't return to the Achia, of course, but there had to be somewhere he could go, something he could muster in a continent of options, and then it wouldn't be too late to become the middle-aged man he could be. A maverick academic – an authority on the universal awkwardness of adolescence, let's say – admired in a world that he, a lower-middle-class boy from Wiltshire, had once crept into, and then slunk away from.

Maybe this was the man that was turning Sheena on, a courteous intellectual, a man of dignity, integrity, stature; a man such as this could command her respect. For the first time in he had no idea how long Ezra Pepin made love to his woman with assurance and conviction. He wasn't acting. It was Sheena the whole time whom he brought to a gorgeous, shuddering fulfilment. And it was he and no one else who revived, and seemed to levitate from his bodily exhaustion as if shedding a skin, Ezra Pepin, sinewy, leonine, present in his desire and in his intention.

Part Two

8

The Allotments

Wednesday 25 June and the Days Following

Is there any greater pleasure to be found in this life, Ezra Pepin wondered, than in contemplation of a scheme designed to reap its architects future happiness? A time such as this we'll look back on all our lives.

The calendar would move on into July, the world turn, great events close by and far off take place. Ezra had little more than a blurred impression of the differentiation or succession of days. Apart, that is, from the first one, the day after Blaise's birthday, and Sheena's proposition. On another bright morning, Ezra cycled out of Blenheim Orchard with the air of a man freewheeling from his home towards fresh destiny. The tarmac along Kingston Road was pocked and scarred from trenches dug for gas, electric, water. Broadband, highband, cable. His bike was jiggled, his bones were shaken, and he didn't mind. He took the traffic-calming ramps along Walton Street with the verve of some veteran skateboarder. What a beautiful impediment they were!

Ezra Pepin's good humour might have dissipated from here on if he'd let it, but he was able that sunny morning to stall and man-oeuvre, ignore beeped horns, scoot his bicycle between the jam-packed cars looping round to Hythe Bridge Street with the aloof insouciance of a man soon to escape this snarling confinement.

161

Having locked up his bike Ezra strolled across the wide plaza in front of Isis Water and in through the glass doors to the spacious reception area. Looming above it, all the way to the roof of the building, was a dizzying cavernous vestibule. Hanging there a transparent Perspex cube the size of a lorry container, swaying like a censer in some great cathedral of commerce.

An artist lived inside the cube. Ezra could see her now, performing stretching exercises like an astronaut. She was halfway through a six-week installation. All the furniture in her floating room was made of Perspex. Clothes, kitchen hardware, electrical equipment, were formed as far as possible from transparent material. The artist slept, cooked, ate, bathed, urinated and defecated on twenty-four-hour public display. Her fruit-peelings, vegetable and other food leftovers, and personal excreta, accumulated in a Perspex bowl: visitors could watch the waste being broken down over the period of the installation, turning before their eyes from raw sewerage to friable compost.

Garbage, the piece was called, and Ezra reckoned it an insipid follow-up to Isis Water's previous cultural sponsorship campaign, which Operations had run in collaboration with Marketing: images on the theme of *Thirst* had been commissioned from young artists and photographers. The results were reproduced on large billboards that appeared illegally in set-aside fields beside the motorways of England. Before they could be removed by county council officials, however, the images were attacked by vandals and spray-painted by hip-hop graffiti artists; figures were defaced, pictures slashed and scarred. Or subtly doodled over. Paint was hurled across the boards. Slogans materialised. The words *Isis Water* appeared for the first time, like a curse.

Who was targeting the company? Why? The desecration seemed both specific – *isis water underground* – and arbitrary: *drink the rain*. Threads of grainy night footage began to appear on the internet, of masked persons unknown assaulting the billboards. Footage that began to work its way on to terrestrial television news. Footage which, at the culmination of the campaign, was exhibited in major art galleries in New York and Beijing.

My God, thought Ezra Pepin, won't it be a little sad to leave this nonsense behind? To find again some authenticity in what he did. What kind of work was it, to move from one ephemeral, stimulating project to another? Schemes of such variety and disconnection.

Today was the start of something different, and he walked across the ground floor smiling and nodding to everyone he passed. He'd like to stop and shake each man's hand, swap quick kisses on the cheeks of the women; ask them how they were, what they dreamed of, how they dealt with their confinement. He saw himself as a role model, impatiently wished that he could tell them of his and Sheena's plans.

As he approached his desk Ezra felt a sudden urge to break into a run, to place his hands upon its veneered surface and vault over to the other side. When he'd walked around to his chair he wondered why on earth he'd not obeyed the insubordinate impulse, chuckling as he logged on to his computer.

'What's the joke?' Chrissie demanded.

'Whatever it is,' he replied, 'it's on us.'

'You're right, Ezra. Jim just told me they want us to prepare costings not just for production of the bottles, but for a new bottling plant as well.'

'They?'

'I didn't ask,' Chrissie frowned. 'Yeh, who are they?'

Ezra shrugged. 'The Germans, I guess. Where?'

'Turkey.'

Blaise heeled the four-pronged fork into soft black soil.

'Easy,' Zack murmured. 'We don't want to spike one. That's it. As far as you can, then lever up as big a clod as possible.'

Blaise leaned her weight on the fork: a clump of soil all around the stalk rose, then began to break and crumble back into the earth, unmasking a score of new potatoes like white eggs. Blaise knelt beside Zack and felt in the soil for more – she was reminded of rustling in bran tubs for hidden gifts – off which she rubbed what little black soil still clung to the potatoes' diaphanous skins. It was incredible to her if, as he claimed, Zack had planted what were

163

now rotten seed potatoes, at the root of each plant, less than three months earlier. It seemed more likely that some tortoiselike animal had lumbered across Port Meadow and lain them here. Either way, she conceded, they were miraculous.

'You change the world by doing this, do you?' she asked. 'By growing these, and then eating them?'

'Wait till you taste my Maris Bard,' Zack smiled. 'We'll boil them back at the squat, and we'll eat them on their own, with nothing but a little butter and mint.'

The lines in Zack's big hands were etched with black soil, as if the earth had fingerprinted him.

'So I'll change as well,' Blaise said. 'And that'll change the world.'

Zack stood up. 'There's a Palestinian family round the corner from us. I was going to take them some. You can come too, if you like.' He handed Blaise the fork. 'Here. We've still got broad beans to pick after this lot.'

Ezra checked his emails, engaged with those concerned with the prototypes, dealt with others. Then he noticed that the screen held the information that he had a store of 317 emails. For the first time that morning he felt weighed down. The backlog was clogging the bowels of his system. He went through them, putting a tick beside those he recognised as once imperative to retain. After every twenty-five he clicked on *Next*: in each batch there were more that were clearly redundant, and by the end he was confronting vital emails a year old that he couldn't remember ever reading.

Ezra clicked *Delete*, the screen swooned out of sight, a brief abracadabra shimmy, and returned with only 163 emails left. He was decisive and it was easy. He felt less burdened but there was still ballast in the basket, so he ploughed through the rest, ticking aggressively, and deleted a further 142. Only twenty-one left. These were recent, significant emails – all of which he'd replied to. His eyes were sharp, his brain focused, the mouse was a knife, and Ezra Pepin sliced a tick beside all but one of them and cut loose from the moorings. You have one email. You have no obligations. You are a free man.

Almost. The last surviving email was one forwarded to him from Jim Gould: the Chief Executive's request for a bit of forward thinking. Ezra opened a new document, titled it *Do We Have the Bottle for the Future?*, fetched himself a coffee from the mezzanine, and started typing.

Water is the most precious commodity on our planet.

Owing to a deepening sense of the interconnectedness of life on earth, people are beginning to appreciate this, even in those parts of the world where there is no shortage of water.

Yes, Ezra thought, that's a good beginning. I'm not sure where it came from. Or where it's going. But let's find out.

The bottled-water industry in the UK has grown in fifteen years from one selling exclusive, largely imported mineral water to one selling over a thousand million litres of mostly UK-sourced spring and table water per annum. Sales have risen in both volume and value by an average of between 10 and 15 per cent year on year.

It would be easy to explain this extraordinary growth by saying that we have created a demand and met it. A triumph of marketing. But something more is happening, surely, when test after test has shown that tap water is a thousand times cheaper, just as bacterially clean and generally indistinguishable in taste from all bottled waters. Except for those noted and sold for their mineral content – which most consumers in tests actually declare to be unappealing.

No, our industry is surely one that has responded to a profound thirst of the public.

Ezra Pepin enjoyed writing reports, but it was a painstaking process: harking back to his essay-writing days, he'd marshal the research material before designing the structure of the piece. Then he'd write something that so dissatisfied him he could barely reread it himself, never mind show it to anyone else, and would rewrite endlessly, shuffling between computer edits and printouts he took to quiet corners of the building to pore over with a red pen and scissors.

'Like some prevaricating bloody novelist,' Jim Gould would

complain, hovering over him as one failed deadline followed another.

'You're such a perfectionist,' Chrissie said. If only, Ezra thought, grateful for the illusion. It was more that his mind was naturally turbid: he was obliged to sift, and filter, and distil, to achieve any kind of clarity.

Today, however, was different: he wrote, and as he wrote he thought, I may hardly have to change a word. And why should I?

What is that thirst, exactly? Of course it's easy to come up with glib answers: convenience; lifestyle choice; the prestige of conspicuous consumption; health.

But what lies behind these words? If we and consumers talk often of the purity of water, what are we really saying?

What we're saying is that in a post-religious age the sanctity of life, of each sovereign individual, is heightened. The loss of life in war, famine, catastrophe appears to us ever more horrific; while each person's own life, the only one we're ever going to have, becomes ever more precious. We want to enjoy it, with all our faculties intact, for as long as possible.

Drinking pure water is an expression, and also a perfect symbol, of this evolutionary process of self-awareness.

While Ezra watched his two dextrous forefingers scuttle to and fro across the keyboard, Sheena Pepin willed her footsteps across Aristotle Lane allotments. The bright sky made her photophobic eyes ache, which was why she kept her gaze on the ground as she walked. How had she forgotten her sunglasses *again*? When, nearing the corner where Mole's bender was hidden, she did look around, there seemed to be no one there. But then she realised that the silhouette over here, and the motionless sentinel over there, were not scarecrows but people. Looking in her direction, perhaps, watching her; it was impossible to tell. She peered back, her eyes screwed up, and in time the outlined figures bent again to their labours.

Stamping down brambles, Sheena trod through the thicket and into the clearing, her heart beating faster now, coming to tell him it was over, than on any previous visit. What she was about to have to do might be difficult, but it was necessary. The trip to Brazil, the idea for which had come to her with such originality and force, demanded this act. On top of which, making love with Ezra the night before had been their best in years – who knew what that augured for the future?

The clearing, when she reached it, was empty. The only sign of Mole's presence was an unreal flatness to the grass. The clearing seemed too small for the bender and a space in front in which to squat and cook and take one's ease; a mean allotment for a man. Had he been evicted? Or had he moved on of his own accord, eternal drifter? The men she'd chosen intermittently were all the kind to up and leave, weren't they?

If there was some disappointment in not seeing Mole, the relief was greater. There might be a certain thrill of power, that was true, but still it's never easy telling someone you don't want to see them any more, however casual or brief a liaison. Thank goodness, really, the calculation appeared likely, in balance, to have been mutual. Sheena was not obliged to come. Mole was so impenetrable – so unexplored – that she had been forced to make every advance: it would have been easy enough for her to let it fade through neglect. The fact that Mole had already left was reward for her courage.

Sheena wanted the past tidied up, so that the future could proceed without impediment. She strolled back out of the clearing smiling to herself, unbothered by the sun, and through the allotments, back towards her bicycle on the other side of the railway line.

Blaise watched her go. 'That woman,' she pointed out to Zack. 'Do you know what she's doing here?'

'There used to be a guy there,' he said. 'Mole.'

'Of course,' said Blaise. Someone had told her he was camping in scrubland somewhere.

'We chatted once or twice,' Zack said. 'Never mentioned he had an older woman.'

*　　*　　*

The British Medical Association recommends that for optimum health a person should drink at least 1.5 to 2 litres – six to eight glasses – of water a day.

According to the Natural Mineral Water Information Service, more than eight out of ten people in the UK don't drink enough water. Ezra typed, nearing what he sensed was the conclusion of his discussion paper.

The bottled-water industry's potential market is thus still, despite its rapid growth, relatively untapped.

How can we claim that market? Well, in the same way that when motorways are built, cars swiftly appear on them, so it is safe to say that with our consumer profile we could flood the market with increased quantities of our product and see it absorbed. But we want to do much more than that.

It might be expected that if, in Britain, rich people drink more mineral water, so poor people drink more tap water. This is hardly the case. In fact, the poorer people are, the less water of any kind they drink – cash rich (that splendid euphemism) they drink alcohol, tea, instant coffee; colas, flavoured carbonates and lemonades. But not water.

They also smoke more than wealthier people, eat more junk food, take less exercise, are in every way less healthy, and die earlier. Why? Because among them there remains an authentic residue of religious faith: hope of a better life to come – through the Lottery rather than reincarnation, maybe – and a fatalism, an acceptance of today's meagre existence. Not only do circumstances limit a person's view of themselves in the world, but lack of education means a limited imagination. Poor people value themselves less than the rich.

If with the right aggressive marketing we can play a part in convincing the poor of this country of their inherent and equal worth, we shall not only conquer the market, but we shall do so as a powerful force for good in our world.

Ezra spellchecked his document and read it through once. He then sent a copy to the Chief Executive, and forgot all about it, and such was his mood in the following days: Ezra Pepin bounded into the office, jovially greeting one and all along the way, worked incisively, moved from one task to the next, and bustled home.

Because home was where real life occurred, in the light evenings after the children had retired reluctantly to their bedrooms to study, read, sleep. Sheena and Ezra stepped out on the decking. Arrayed upon the marble table top were crisps and olives and nuts; tubs of hummus, salsa dip, tapenade; anchovy on toast, new-potato salad. Light tapas-style meals were all they desired, neither of them hungry, as if the words they shared to describe their move nourished them. Or as if it was important not to weigh themselves down, for their bodies to sag their spirits with full and heavy stomachs, as they scanned the brochures, the website pages and the emails – for schools, houses, flights – that Sheena flourished daily.

Ezra would open a bottle of wine, and they would weave the fantastic details of their dream with threads of excited speech.

'You've got everyone growling their way to work every damnable morning,' Ezra heard himself saying. 'There's going to be so much gridlock in ten years' time that the government are already ordering health trusts to plan policies for reaching medical emergencies stuck in traffic jams.'

'You mean births?'

'Right. And heart attacks. Strokes.'

'Helicopters?'

'I guess. Yeh.' Ezra found it hard to stay seated. He got up and paced the deck, glass in hand, his lanky frame a little awkward with excess energy, muscles ill-contained in skin, as if at any moment if he obeyed his body's impulse he'd vault the balustrade, to land lightly on the lawn and take off into the gathering dusk.

'And I was thinking, this is England, isn't it, what a perfect metaphor, all snarled up. And how do people escape? When they finally get to work? Or if they've had the good luck and sense to work from home? Through the portals of the net, for Christ's sake. Into virtual reality. And no wonder. It's the only space left to us – okay, it's getting clogged up already, true. But the point is, and why our plan, I mean your plan, darling, is so great is because, is this living? No. It's not. And that's what Brazil means to me. A stab at reality.'

They told the children over supper the first weekend. Sheena laid out the plan in the shape of an adventure, made it sound to Ezra, nodding in parental agreement, like they were off on a voyage in search of Spanish galleons.

Blaise nodded intelligently, and said, 'Brazil? Very good. Yes. Brazil,' as if this hare-brained escapade were no great surprise to her, she'd been expecting it, in fact, and it was moderately interesting to hear which specific dot on the globe the grown-ups had decided on.

Louie responded to the football lure with an excited, 'Mummy. Daddy. I'm is David Beckham.'

'Yes, Peanut,' Sheena agreed. 'Ronaldo is from Brazil. Do you know Ronaldo?'

'Daddy is Ronaldo.'

'Excuse me?'

'I'm is David Beckham.'

'Yes. But Daddy's not –'

'Actually I am, darling,' Ezra confessed. 'Quite often, when we play in the park.'

'Yes,' Louie frowned, still worried they were missing the point. 'But *I'm* is David Beckham.'

Hector listened in silence.

'Well?' Sheena asked him. 'What do you think, Hec?'

'It's to do with Daddy's work, isn't it?'

'Yes,' she agreed. 'Absolutely.'

'I knew it. I told you, Daddy. You denied it.'

'What did you deny, Ezra?' Sheena wondered.

'They're sending you to Brazil, Daddy.'

'No one's sending him, Hector,' Sheena said. 'And we're all going, that's the beauty of it.'

'I don't get it,' Hector scowled. 'Wait. They're sending the whole family? Oh. I see.'

'No one's sending us. Are you being deliberately obtuse, Hec? We're going of our own accord.'

'Hang on, darling,' Ezra interrupted, laying a hand on Sheena's arm, as he recognised in Hector his own barely conscious habit of playing for time, sowing confusion in which he might absorb at his own pace surprising information.

'It's not my work now that Mummy's talking about,' he explained. 'I'm leaving my job, you see, and I'll resume the work I had to lay aside back when Blaise was little.'

'What work?' Hector asked, eyes widening melodramatically, as if in some movie in which his father was about to reveal a secret career in espionage. On the face of their introvert boy the effect was extremely comical, and it was all Ezra could do to keep from laughing.

'He doesn't understand,' Blaise told her parents, and turned to Hector. 'It's those Indians. The jungle stuff. The lost-tribe stories Dad's been telling us all our lives.'

'I didn't know that was *work*,' Hector said in a defensive tone. 'No one told me it was work. I thought they were stories.'

Sheena and Ezra made clear that they weren't leaving until the end of the summer – not for months – which calmed the children's anxiety, and made it easier for them to ask questions.

'Can I take my slide?' Louie wondered. '*And* the trampoline.'

'Do you want me to fight or dance?' Hector demanded. 'Is capoeira self-defence or disco or what?'

'Both,' Sheena replied patiently.

Blaise seemed unworried, calm, distracted. Although this may have had something to do with the Asian boy Sheena also happened to glimpse her with on Churchill Way, walking her home from school. In between Blaise's sporadic end-of-year exams, Sheena looked for an opportunity to talk.

That hot Saturday lunchtime Blaise said, 'My head's crammed full. I can't get any more in it.'

'Do you want to come and pick strawberries?' Sheena asked. 'The first ones must be ready. I pumped your bike tyres up for you, by the way.'

They cycled across Port Meadow, over the loose drum-rolling

171

planks of one bridge and the steep iron of the next, and on round to Binsey Lane. Sheena wore sunglasses and a floppy cotton hat Ezra referred to as her cricketing one. She knew how unfetching it was, and would discard it as soon as her white skin was a little tanned. Every summer the sun unsettled her. Sheena regarded her body as an efficient machine, she even admired it, but especially so when clothed, equipped for action in tops, leggings, boots. Summer forced her to peel layers of clothing, bare her white flesh. Perhaps, Sheena thought, two years on the beaches of Brazil might be good for her too, might coax more vanity than she allowed herself, as she watched Blaise cycling abreast, a yard or two ahead, her daughter's almond hair flowing around her nut-brown face, tanned since the first sunny day of the year. As was her body: who knows what genetic shakedown had given Blaise skin that appeared to colour without the need of direct sunlight; the sun shone on exposed areas – her face and hands – and the rest of her body seemed to blush brown beneath her clothes. It was uncanny.

Having shed her grungy and hippieish attire, forgoing her sartorial emblems of allegiance for a summer truce, today Blaise was wearing a white T-shirt and a pair of last year's tennis shorts. She looked to Sheena to have grown half a foot in a few weeks; her legs were clearly too long for the bicycle pedals – Sheena should have raised the seat as well.

'You don't have the studious pallor of a girl confined to a dungeon of revision, do you?' Sheena observed loudly above the rattle of her old bicycle.

Blaise glanced across her shoulder, perhaps to check her mother's intent from her expression. 'Just lucky, I guess,' she said.

'You take it so lightly, you lot,' Sheena said. 'When I think how I worried at your age.' Sheena could see her daughter smile. What this smile might mean she declined to decipher or interrogate, as they cycled along Binsey Lane.

At the Pick Your Own stall they collected a couple of punnets each from a tall man far gone into middle age who, to Sheena's annoyance, seemed unable to keep his eyes from straying to Blaise's youthful legs. His gaze kept being drawn back, as if he'd seen something he couldn't quite believe and had repeatedly to ascertain was true. Sheena wasn't sure, as she removed her hat, whether she should feel more irked on Blaise's behalf or her own. She hoped that her daughter was not aware of the lecher's attention. But then Blaise did something that seemed to mock such naivety: standing in front of the man, she put the punnets back down on the table, crossed her hands at her waist, grasped the hem of her T-shirt and slowly pulled it up over the top of her head. A pale blue bikini top – like the tennis shorts last year's – barely secured her developing breasts. With her head bent slightly forward, Blaise wrapped the T-shirt around her hair, with a practised and impressive dexterity, so as to improvise a turban.

Seeing her standing there, her burgeoning youth ill-contained in minimal bikini top and tight shorts, Sheena thought her daughter's action might provoke the open-mouthed paedophile to blood-draining collapse. But then after a final efficient little twist of fabric Blaise secured her headgear, picked up the punnets, and turned and walked away, in the direction of strawberries which their hapless custodian had indicated.

Sheena trotted after her. 'What was that?' she asked as she caught Blaise up.

'What was what, Mum?'

'What you just did.'

'What did I just do?' Blaise wondered.

'With the T-shirt.'

Blaise shrugged as she walked. 'I took it off. It's hot.'

They squatted along the rows of berries on beds of straw, ripening in the heat. Sheena lifted green leaves to find the crimson fruit, and broke off their stalks.

'They last longer if you pick them like this,' she said.

'What's the point?' Blaise asked, sliding succulent berries loose from their fleshy pegs. 'You'll only be destalking them in a couple of hours back home.'

Sometimes it seemed to Sheena that Blaise was programmed to say things to make her rise, with little idea she was doing it. 'No, I won't,' Sheena replied. 'We'll make the boys do it.'

As they picked they chatted, an intermittent, grazing conversation that touched on grandparents, Brazil, exams, until they were well into their second punnets, and Sheena realised she was running out of time.

'So, who's the good-looking young man you've been seen with lately?' she asked, in as nonchalant a voice as she could muster.

Blaise neither blushed nor flinched. 'No one.'

Sheena tried to inject into her voice a tone equivalent to a raised eyebrow. 'Really?'

Blaise put a strawberry into her mouth, pulling it off its stalk with her lips. 'I don't know what you're talking about, Mum.'

'I just heard about a boy, called Ahmed or something. That's all.'

'Oh,' Blaise intoned, a long, sighing vowel that suggested how obtuse her mother was being. 'You mean Akhmed.'

'Akhmed? Is it important to make that throat-clearing sound when you say it?'

'It's his name, Mum,' Blaise explained good-naturedly. 'It's like some foreigner calling you Shinna. It's not your name. You wouldn't like it. Your name's Sheena. His name's Akhmed.'

'Is he a foreigner?'

'Of course not.'

'Well, anyway, I heard he was good-looking. Is he Moroccan?'

'No.'

'Indian?'

'I just told you. He's English.'

'No, but you know what I mean.'

Blaise glared at her mother, then seemed to change her mind in mid-thought, and shrugged. 'His parents are from Bangladesh. But Akhmed and all his older brothers and sisters were born here. His dad owns The Raj Cuisine.'

'On Walton Street?'

'Right.'

'We used to go there all the time. Daddy and I. I wonder if it's the same guy.'

'Probably. I think he's been there for ever.'

'But I can't picture now who was the owner and who were the

waiters,' Sheena said. 'The waiters were always changing. Daddy might remember. We lived practically next door. Delicious peshwari nan. And their channa marsala side dish. I've no idea why we've not got a takeaway, even, in years, when Dad could pick one up on his way home from work. Probably all changed now, though. Nouvelle Indian and all that? Fusion?'

'I don't know, Mum.'

'Well. Listen, Bee, anyway, I mean if you want to bring Akhmed round –'

'Not so much, Mum,' Blaise interrupted. 'You're not hawking up a gob of phlegm. They're not Arabs.'

'Sorry, thanks, okay. But if you want to bring Akhmed round, please feel free. I know we're embarrassing, but –'

'No, you're not.'

'All parents are embarrassing at your age,' Sheena insisted, trusting, however, the truism was less true of herself than of Ezra.

'How can you say –' Blaise began indignantly, but then stopped herself. 'Well,' she allowed. 'Okay. Lose the hat, maybe, Mum. And it is time you bought a new pair of sunglasses. Those *are* kind of scary. The owl has landed.'

The weather was unsettled: with weak Atlantic fronts and low-pressure centres that roamed above the region; thundery showers broke and fell. There were breezy mornings, and afternoons of rain, after which the urban air filled with the smell of buddleia and lilac, and excrement, a sweet decay underlying the fruitfulness of summer. One evening Sheena and Ezra sat outside despite a drizzle pattering on the lean-to roof and murmuring into the lawn.

'Did Louie show you his Brazil football shirt?' Sheena asked. 'I saw it in Next, I couldn't resist it. I mean, all part of the preparation, don't you think?'

Ezra rolled himself a cigarette. He'd given up smoking many years earlier, soon after Sheena confided she had begun to imagine the prospect of having children with him. 'Of course, you'd have to quit smoking,' she'd added.

'Maybe,' he'd said.

'Let me put it this way, sweetheart: if you don't, I'm leaving you.'

'But that is the most unreasonable thing I've ever heard,' Ezra had complained. 'You can't just spring something like this on a person.'

'I don't mean immediately, Ez. Of course not. What do you think I am? I mean *some* time. If we're committed to each other. To having children.'

'Oh, sure.'

'And if you don't want children I'm leaving you anyway.'

'Okay.'

'I'm not having children lose their father to lung cancer.'

'That is reasonable,' he'd said, lighting up.

'Like your mother.'

'I know,' Ezra nodded. 'Although you know she didn't actually smoke, darling?'

'Let's say in about six months' time?'

'No problem.'

'How about the 1st of September, then?'

'That's fine,' he'd said, removing a strand of tobacco from his tongue. 'Let's do it.'

And they did. As the date ground nearer Ezra rolled his cigarettes ever thinner, he joined the college gym, he steered away from pubs. At the beginning of September 1988, Sheena put up with a bad-tempered grizzler of a boyfriend for a weekend, during which, she would claim, she tried so hard to palliate – and reward – his withdrawal symptoms with sex that Blaise was conceived.

'A nicotine-free baby but a crotchety one,' Sheena would joke.

Over the ensuing years, once he'd established, for both Sheena's benefit and his own, that he was free of the habit, Ezra would scrounge the occasional party cigarette – an old flame whose acrid kiss he relished, then once more abandoned.

Now, however, he broke a fundamental rule and bought himself a small pouch of Golden Virginia, green Rizlas, a disposable lighter.

'I'm sorry, darling,' he said, 'but I guess I'm just so excited.'

'No, it's fine, Ez,' Sheena laughed, indulgent and confident that this was a temporary prop in the drama of their evening performances. 'I only wish you'd bought matches. Really. Throwaway lighters. What an obscene technological breakthrough that one was.'

'You're right, darling. It really was.'

'Imagine a pyramid of all the lighters that have been thrown away. Being incinerated. Metal and plastic burning. The black smoke. I mean, how did they ever come into fashion? I'll tell you how. Because we're a gutless people, that's how, we're always hedging our bets. Always saying, "Yes, actually I'm about to give up, maybe." Have the courage to smoke, for God's sake, or the balls to quit. One or the other. Am I right?'

'Yes, Sheena,' Ezra agreed, lighting up a perfectly shaped cigarette, rolled with a facility that pleased him. 'You're bloody well right.'

He popped a green olive into his mouth, stoned it with his tongue and teeth and spat the pip towards the flowerbed. He took a gulp of cold white Riesling, cleaned his mouth and then imbibed it with a swift swallow which as he closed his eyes he could feel followed by a giddying wave of inebriation through his brain.

'You know what this is like, darling?' Ezra asked. 'It's like waking up. I feel like Rip van Winkle.'

'Me too,' Sheena smiled. 'Sleeping Beauty.'

'Woken with a kiss.' Ezra inhaled from his cigarette; exhaled. 'When you're stuck in a rut,' he said, 'you might as well be asleep. There's no change from one day to another, one year to the next.'

'Apart from the children growing, Ez.'

'You know what I'm reminded of? The times I found myself in the jungle all alone. Very, very rarely. Because you know I was clumsy, they never took me hunting, so I'd hang out in the village. Just as well, of course, because I saw aspects of life few other anthropologists had seen. But every now and again I forced myself to walk off into the dense forest. Right out of sight of the village, far enough to risk becoming disorientated, and losing my bearings. And I was terrified. The jungle seethed with lurking threat: there was a jaguar behind every tree, a snake crawling just ahead of me.

177

My heart was juddering against my ribs.' Ezra stubbed out his cigarette. 'I never felt so bloody alive in all my life.'

Sheena leaned forward from her chair towards him. 'Give me that kiss, Prince Charming.'

'The wake-up one?'

'No, the one to help me sleep at night.'

Some evenings they pursued each other upstairs without clearing away, and made love, urgent co-conspirators of change, in flight from the forces of mediocrity that would stifle and deny them. And Sheena, as she chuckled to carnality's liberating rhythm, congratulated herself on having orchestrated that flight.

While outside on the marble slab, amid dying candles, sat bowls of sauce and tubs of dip, and unfinished glasses of wine, paraphernalia of some hallucinatory rite, which night insects devoured, and by morning were drowned in.

Blaise joined her parents once or twice, and seemed happy to turn their duet of anticipation into a trio, if as a minor instrument, content to listen while she waited for a cue. She was preoccupied, and her parents assumed it to be with Akhmed, who was there in the house one afternoon soon after the strawberry-picking expedition. As the members of the family came home, each was introduced to him. He was a slight, fresh-faced boy who didn't look to Ezra as if he'd fully entered puberty. He didn't say a word but nodded, and shook hands. And from then on he was there often, hovering. Eating food Blaise took him from the fridge. Helping with her revision – 'He took the same subjects last year,' she explained. Ezra would glimpse Akhmed drifting upstairs, gliding along a corridor, a silent presence in his house who acknowledged him with a polite and possibly condescending nod; a bow, almost. Akhmed looked to Ezra juvenile, unready, unprepared, for sex, which innocence only worried him all the more.

'What's wrong with Akhmed?' he asked Sheena in bed one night. 'He doesn't say anything.'

'Ezra, he's very shy, obviously. And use the back of your mouth, not your throat.'

'I haven't heard a word issue from his lips. And he won't look at me.'

'What were you like at that age? A witty conversationalist? A gifted raconteur? It's difficult for boys. His voice is still a little unbroken.'

'However would one know?'

'That's why he's so quiet. I think he's rather sweet.'

'I damn well hope so,' Ezra worried, 'considering the amount of time he spends in our daughter's bedroom.'

'Don't worry, Ez.'

'I can't help worrying. I'm her father. I'm supposed to worry.'

'They're not doing anything, believe me.'

'How would you know?'

'She'd tell me.'

'She would?' Ezra frowned. Could this be true? Blaise hardly told *him* anything any more. Was their father–daughter bond almost broken, or would it be regained after this adolescent phase? He was prepared one day to give her away, with due ceremony. 'Don't you think we need some house rules?' he demanded.

'Of course. That's why we've got them already.'

'We have?'

'I've told Blaise, One: no one stays the night. Two: if she wants to have sex, she's got to speak to me about birth control first.'

'Sex. Birth control. For God's sake, Sheena.'

'Three: if she gets pregnant, tell me immediately. Those are the rules.'

Ezra stared at Sheena. 'I'm glad we discussed them fully,' he said. 'They sound draconian yet woefully inadequate.'

'I beg your pardon?'

'I'm supposed to be reassured.' Ezra shook his head. 'She's fourteen,' he said. 'Barely.'

'Fourteen is not so young for sex. Not these days.'

'Not so young? Are you serious? It's two years under the legal age of consent, for one thing.'

'And about ten years under the age you want your daughter to enjoy her body, I suppose. What is it with men?' Sheena wondered,

179

turning on to her back, as if addressing a third person up above them who'd slipped into the room without Ezra noticing. 'This hang-up about their daughters' sexuality?'

'It's not a hang-up,' Ezra said. 'It's a taboo. There are good reasons for its existence.'

'Look at Blaise, Ezra. Have you actually seen her recently? She's sexually mature. Girls are at that age, more than ever nowadays. In many cultures she'd have been sexually active for years by now.'

Ezra hiccuped an indignant laugh. 'I'm probably aware of that more than most, wouldn't you say?'

'She's not a child. She's a woman. It's your problem. Deal with it.'

Ezra found the conversation creepily uncomfortable. He wanted neither to discuss nor to ponder the subject. And why did Sheena use the word sex or sexual or sexuality in her every sentence, rubbing Ezra's nose in it, relishing their daughter's ripeness?

'She's going to lose her virginity sooner or later. I mean, ask yourself: what's the best way for that to happen?'

'I don't wish to ask that.'

'With some much older pervert, maybe?'

'Sheena –'

'The fact is, maybe she could do worse than a nice, quiet, steady boy, as ignorant as her, who she can teach as she learns as they go along.'

Ezra was silent.

Sheena addressed her invisible companion again. 'I just don't know where this distaste for female sexuality that men seem to have comes from.'

'Don't give me your crass generalisations, Sheena.'

'She's a healthy girl, our Blaise. She'll have appetites, Ezra, desires.'

'Of course!'

Sheena yawned. Then she leaned towards Ezra and planted a perfunctory kiss upon his lips. 'I am *egg*shausted,' she said. 'Now, if this conversation has run its course, I'd like to try and get some sleep.' She rolled over, patted her pillows, dropped towards them and exhaled with a loud sigh. Ezra switched off his bedside light. Sheena rolled back halfway towards him, so that her mouth once more addressed the ceiling in the dark.

'Did you even know when she started her periods?' Sheena demanded. He heard what was almost a giggle, a light-hearted derision, in her voice.

'Yes,' Ezra murmured.

'It must be almost two years now.' Sheena rolled back.

Ezra listened to her breathing, sensed a pacification of her movement that suggested she was intent on her path to sleep now, and would disturb him no more. Yes, he thought: he did know when Blaise had begun to menstruate. It was him she came to. 'Look, Daddy,' she said, tears in her eyes. She led him to the bathroom, and to spots of blood on the floor. 'It's coming from inside me,' she said.

'But Blaise,' he said, 'you know what that is, don't you?'

'I suppose so,' Blaise murmured, her expression despairing, mournful.

'But it's wonderful, darling,' Ezra told her, and Blaise's gaze had flickered towards him and then away, and she summoned a brave smile to her face. That very evening Blaise came and sat on his lap before going up to bed, as she had a thousand times before, and she told him that Sheena had taken her to Boots in Summertown. She was equipped, she said, with a smile that suggested she'd done more than simply come to terms with her new condition; it was more coy and self-satisfied than that, the smile of one admitted by her mother to an ancient sisterhood.

As he hugged the child nestled in his embrace, Ezra attempted to refute the information his body was feeding him. Beyond intellectual understanding, beneath consciousness, knowledge entered him that he would have liked to turn back. It came to him from the warm body in his lap. It reached him in a direct connection from his daughter's womb, through her genitalia and on through his, into his body, his nervous system, his brain. The knowledge that there should be no more of such physical intimacy. That blood drew a

181

line between the relationship they'd had and a reserve, a discretion that they would henceforth obey.

Ezra squeezed his daughter then – two years ago – kissed her cheek and said, 'Go on up to bed, darling.' He'd watched her go that evening, and now he could feel again the pain of that swift and necessary bereavement. And now this, the prospect of his girl's virginity given to a gormless boy. Except, Ezra recalled with an impatient eruption of hope, they might get to Brazil before it happened.

The unsettled weather lifted. Patchy mist and fog in the mornings gave way to sunshine and warmth again. And a Sunday evening soon came along when they were due to leave Blaise in charge and go over to the Carlyles'.

The day before, Sheena had come home from work with a Blackwell's bag from which she slid on to the sitting-room coffee table a Portuguese–English dictionary and a *Teach Yourself Portuguese* CD.

'Of course *you* won't need it, Ez,' she said approvingly. 'But we will.'

'Me?' he laughed.

'Maybe you might want to brush up a little, though.'

'Brush up?'

'I guess we'll be relying on you to get us settled in the first week or two, but I'm sure we'll pick it up soon.'

'Week or two?'

'Dad!' Blaise yelled across from the kitchen. 'Help! There's an echo in the house.'

'Anyone want a cup of tea?' Sheena offered, leaving Ezra to try and recollect whether all those years ago he could possibly have led Sheena to believe he could speak Portuguese. Surely not. He was always reasonably modest, wasn't he? He'd learned a little Spanish before going to Paraguay; and he'd acquired some rudiments of the Achia's language while with them, that was true; but they wouldn't be much help to the Pepin family starting out in São Paulo. Did Sheena think that his tribe were in Brazil? Wait a minute. Did she

182

imagine that they would put the children in the International School and all be speaking fluent Portuguese in a month? The truth was they'd mix with other visitors, of course. They'd live there as ex-pats. Drawn into the colony of English-speaking peoples.

Perhaps it was that jab of idiocy that disconcerted Ezra and made him say to Sheena, as they got ready to go round to Simon and Minty's on Sunday evening, 'Let's tell them.'

'Who? What? Already?'

'Yes. Why not? We're going, aren't we?'

'Of course we are, Ez.'

'No turning back, darling?'

'No.'

'So let's tell our friends already.'

'Okay. Yes. Let's.'

The phone rang. Ezra strolled out to the landing, and saw downstairs Blaise lunge for the cordless handset and reach it before Hector. She said hello, then responded to the other person's voice by trotting upstairs to her room, at the same time twisting her head, raising her shoulders and bending her back, so as to bury the phone in her protective embrace like a baby. She passed by her father, ignoring him. He returned to the bedroom.

'Who was that?' Sheena asked.

'One of Blaise's friends.'

'What friends? They never come round. Does she have any more?'

A recent image recalled itself to Ezra's mind: he was cycling through Wellington Square and, glancing to his right to the lawn in its centre, he'd spotted Blaise in amongst a group of half a dozen friends. They were chatting away, not to each other but on mobile phones. To the friends who hadn't made it to this little gathering; ghosts who augmented it with their busy absence.

But that was months ago, he conceded. A year, maybe.

'Must have been Akhmed,' he said.

'Oh, my God. How could I forget? His father rang today, while you and Louie were at the park.'

'Mr Raj Cuisine?'

'Abdul Azam. He wants to see you. I said he could come round tomorrow before supper; he said six would suit him.'

'Why does he want to see me?'

'Good question!' Sheena spat. 'I mean obviously about Akhmed and Blaise, but why *you*? I'm the girl's mother!'

'Hey, don't shout at me, darling, I didn't say a thing.'

'He spoke to me, introduced himself as Akhmed's father, and said, "Could I speak to Mr Pepin?" I mean, excuse me, Ezra, but what century is this?'

'If the last one was the American,' Ezra said, doing up the buttons of a blue cotton shirt. 'I guess this'll be the Chinese.'

'You know what I mean, Ez.'

'Or the Indian.'

'You men are just so . . .'

'Just so what? Hey, I'd be quite happy for you to deal with it, if that's what you want. I can work late at the office – you talk to him.'

'You're missing the point, Ezra Pepin. It's one of principle.'

'That means I have to see him, does it?'

'Of course. Are you ready?'

'Almost.'

'We're late, Ez.'

'I'm coming.' He buckled his sandals, and stood up, frowning. 'I wonder what he wants?' he said.

9

An Announcement

Sunday 6 July

Minty Carlyle headed home with the car boot full of plastic-bagged provisions from the Sainsbury's in Kidlington. How refreshing it was, she thought to herself as she drove down Woodstock Road, braking for the speed camera then cruising on past Squitchey Lane, to have clichés skewered, and shown up for the rubbish they are. This morning she'd come with gratitude upon lines by Ivy Compton-Burnett, to the effect that time has too much credit: it's not a great healer, it's an indifferent and perfunctory one, and often it doesn't heal at all.

Yes, and sometimes it only muffles the cries of the wounded, or it covers the wound with its thin tissue, to fester and rupture and break through in the future. Because you simply couldn't tell the consequences of a particular cause; you could only wait for the rupture and hunt the cause down with hindsight. Then it was easy, Minty thought. You didn't have to be a student of Freud or Klein to work it out. Like the way her widowed mother had withheld affection. For example. Unimpressed by her daughter's achievements, unamused by her conversation, undesiring of her bodily presence. The girl's response a childhood-long, a lifelong, vain courtship of her mother; the pained withdrawals of a rejected suitor. One of whose legacies, it was pretty obvious, was a refusal to give up on anything or anyone.

185

'Your determination is tectonic,' Simon told her when, years into their marriage, he perceived the extent of his partner's will. 'It's glacial,' he said, impressed and unsettled, and grateful that her ambitions were modest ones.

Another truism ripe for the compost heap: you can choose your friends but not your family. Oh, sure, fundamentally it was so but ever less so, it seemed to Minty, as families cracked and scattered; while friends you found yourself attached to for ever, by all sorts of sinews and threads.

Take the Pepins. Their best friends, after all. Simon and Ezra had met – along with Ian Flegg – one winter at a Saturday dads' club, in a church hall on New Inn Hall Street. They got talking as their first-borns toddled between tricycle and slide, watching in that self-denigratory, deflective way which seemed to come naturally to men: of course, this is not me, mate, or us, is it, we know that, we're just temporary guardians of these little beauties; let us share with each other such acknowledgement.

Over one dinner back then, with their infants asleep, she and Sheena had joked what a wonder it was how rarely Blaise and Ed were brought home from that danger zone with neither cut nor bruise nor broken bone.

'It's because, Minty, they're so bloody unobservant,' Sheena explained, the men cowering but amused, 'I swear they forget they're there to babysit at all. The kids move into self-protective mode. When they're on their own – studies prove this – children have fewer accidents than when supervised by adults.'

'I say, that makes sense, Sheena,' Simon agreed. 'Next week we'll leave them there while we pop down to the Nag's Head for a quick one.'

'A quick one?' Sheena smirked. 'I suppose there's a pretty barmaid there, am I right? I won't have you leading my poor husband astray, Simon Carlyle.' Laughing that ugly guttural laugh Simon would continue to provoke in her over the years to come.

Anyhow, there you had it already: legends of family and of friendship entwined from the start. By the following spring, instead of Saturday child duty the three men were slipping out of bawling houses early on a Friday morning to play tennis together, a regime they'd practised – along with a fourth partner whose identity had changed periodically – ever since.

Ed and Blaise were best friends for years, really only cooling off this last winter. Which, Minty admitted to no one, she wouldn't say she was sorry about. Although Ed adored Blaise, it had irked Minty to see the girl lead her son by the nose; not out of some precocious feminine allure but, even worse, greater strength of personality – or vehemence, as she would rather put it, real strength being more profound for being hidden. It relieved Minty to see Ed pull back; realising he didn't need to be pulled across the terrain of his own life by someone else.

Of course – you might as well say it, Minty thought to herself, driving down Woodstock Road – it was hardly Blaise's fault if she reminded Minty too much of her mother. The odd thing about their interfamilial relationship – recently tangled further by Jack and Hector's intense boyish camaraderie – the really absurd thing was that amongst the various shifting ties between them it had come to be universally assumed that the strongest bond was that between herself and Sheena. How this had been reached, Minty understood, was cumulative. Being each the chief organiser of their households, so arrangements, messages, reminders came through them, imposing daily the foundations of a friendship that actually, if you looked for it up above the surface, out in the open, barely existed at all.

Except that that wasn't true, was it, because like ties of blood those of friendship were bound in experience – shared births and child-raising, shared holidays, shared meals and argument and drunkenness – knotty moments that held awkward truths about each other, and brought with them tolerance. And loyalty. And . . . she thought, turning right into Bainton Road, and . . . nothing.

Simon Carlyle first saw Minty Flippence the night he met some friends at Catweazle club, and a thin, dark waif stumbled to the open mike and with a cracked and trembling voice broke his heart.

He pursued and seduced her, and for ever after one of the many things Simon Carlyle admired about his tough, generous, laconic, stylish, spiky wit of a wife was that she didn't give a damn what people thought of her, as long as they liked her poetry. Minty was cool, steely and sardonic, but poetry made her anxious. She got agitated writing it, which stopped her writing it, which made her nervous and depressed. Submitting poems for publication rendered her wretched and she spent weeks in a state of misery waiting for the rejection slips.

As for reading her poetry in public, it transformed the carefree young graduate student into a highly-strung, haunted creature for days leading up to performance. The trouble was that Minty hated the spotlight but she needed the attention. Or vice versa, Simon never could work it out: Minty shrank from the attention but she needed the spotlight, so she joined one poetry session at the Prince of Wales on Walton Street and organised another, St Clements Poetry Group, which met once a week at the Elm Tree on Cowley Road.

The night before a reading Minty couldn't sleep, on the day itself she couldn't eat, and as the hour approached she lost control of one after another of her bodily functions. By the time she got on stage she had a tension migraine and stress toothache, and the poems on the sheets of paper in her hand trembled from all the caffeine she'd drunk. So she downed three vodkas to steady her nerves, which caused her to slur the words. While the thick reek of cigarettes she'd been churning through for days tarred her throat and made the words crackle and break as they issued from her mouth, lending every confessional, declarative, rhetorical line a compelling authenticity.

During the year of her engagement to Simon Carlyle, Minty Flippence worked alternately on her academic thesis on English Medieval Latin Lyrics and on her own self-absorbing epic poem, switching from one to the other in a disciplined fashion: when she felt inspired she wrote more cantos about the aridity of contemporary life; when not, she went to the Bodleian Library. Her own poetry demanded intuitive concentration. The thesis required a mole's blind obedience to hope for what could have survived the centuries. It wasn't long before one activity began to inhibit and thwart the other: before she'd even put pen to blank white paper she knew her personal outpourings could not measure up to what others had written before, while the search for fragments of charred remains from long-ruined monasteries took place in a world of ghosts: Minty would emerge from the Bodleian like a pallid, ashen version of her fulsome self.

Before Minty knew it, she was not working alternately on her doctorate and her epic, switching from one to the other, not working just as hard on each of them. Then, out of the blue, six months after the Carlyles were married and living in Simon's family home on Bainton Road, a small press in North Wales thanked Minty for the collection of extracts she'd sent out a couple of years previously, and offered to print them. It was the break-through she'd dreamed of, a life-changing moment. Seeing the book from final revisions through proof stage to publication took up the following year, during which she didn't even attempt to produce new work, and then came the suspense of waiting for the reviews. She also became pregnant with their first child. If she'd been nervous before, that was nothing compared to this nauseating period of daily purchase of newspapers and magazines, of tuning in to distant radio programmes, of phone calls and conversations with people who might have heard a rumour of a round-up of debut collections that may be about to appear in . . .

As the weeks and then the months went by and it became clear that her pamphlet, *The Desert Wanderers*, wasn't going to get a review, and wouldn't sell many more than the thirty copies she'd sold herself to friends, relatives and fellow poets, Minty retreated behind a bitter resentment of the injustice of the literary life. As if she'd ever *asked* for this gift and burden.

Eventually, when she'd stopped looking, six months after publication a small magazine in Northumberland ran a short review by some nobody no one had ever heard of describing Minty's book as *an impressive and promising debut from an intriguing new voice,* identifying the influence of Elizabeth Bishop no less than Sylvia Plath, and expressing reservations only about one single canto, which seemed *out of kilter* with the rest.

'*Out of kilter*?' Minty demanded of Simon and anyone else she showed the review to. 'Does she think I didn't *mean* to use a different metre? That that might be the *point*? I mean, why give poems to an idiot if she knows *nothing* about *poetry*?'

The first reading of Minty's that Ezra and Sheena went to was also her last. She never felt more vulnerable than when she read, and hated friends hearing her, but couldn't stop herself inviting every acquaintance she knew. Ezra and Sheena joined Simon Carlyle to huddle into the packed room at the back of the Elm Tree one winter Wednesday evening. They remained fixed to their rickety stools as one poet after another rose from the crush around them, barrelled his or her way to the front and read for ten minutes or more.

Ezra and Sheena listened to their friend as she blushed, perspired, mumbled and stuttered through half a dozen terse, unhappy cantos of what she called her ongoing work-in-progress: the forensic dissection of the feelings of a woman subtly unlike the poet herself. The confession of slights and hurts addressed to a 'you' who seemed to Ezra to be different people: here a father, there a mother; a husband, an unknown man. A resentful yearning to close the gap between the actual and the possible.

Lingering to sympathise with her afterwards they found Minty not suicidal, as they'd feared, but gleefully herself again. The sociophobe on stage became the wit in the saloon. From that night she stopped taking part in readings altogether, because there were only so many times you could read the same cantos to the same people. Soon she was more relaxed than she had been in years.

Poor Minty, they sometimes referred to her, the Carlyles' friends. She'd become aware of that. And who could blame them? Her ambition and frustration, her need, had been so unconcealed all these years how could they not impute to Minty disappointment at her failure? Not feel in their pity at least a little of the pain of peeling herself open to the world in confessional poetry, frank, naked, honest – of relinquishing every sovereign individual's last bastion, his or her interior life – only for the world to say, 'Actually, no thanks. Not interested.'

But it was just where they were wrong. Because what she'd learned over the years was not that success and failure are the same imposters, exactly, but that they're beside the point. Wasn't it Joseph Brodsky who wrote that if art teaches us anything it's that the human condition is private? It was about as difficult a notion as Minty thought she'd ever read, because didn't we also dream, above all, of finding another – a Platonic partner or a multitude – with whom we might share the very essence of our being?

Minty finished unpacking. She lit a Camel and watched Simon who was at this moment this Sunday evening jerking and gasping, bent over a wine bottle held between his knees, struggling to extract the cork like some deranged dentist. Minty left the room; Simon may not even have been aware of her presence, even with the cigarette smoke. As unobservant as he was obstinate. Over the years he'd been given modern corkscrews at Christmas of increasingly sophisticated engineering. Leverage; hydraulics; suction. Simon was offended by their effortlessness. They collected in a drawer, items in a neglected archive, except that Minty used them, of course. He preferred the simple handle you wrapped your fingers round, took a breath and set yourself, and then gave the bloody thing a good heave; the exertion a price to pay for the pleasure to come; or part of the pleasure, perhaps. It was beyond her.

The sudden sound of the piano halted Minty on the stairs. Ed had plunged without ceremony into the middle of the allegro of, she guessed, a Chopin concerto; notes tumbled from the sitting-room, spun into the hallway. They danced like scintillae around the edges of her vision.

Ed stopped abruptly as he'd begun. Then started again in the same place, repeating the passage – as he'd probably do for an hour now: he'd be seized by the compulsion to attack a section, with an emotion that looked like anger, as if the thought of the music had jumped into his head, challenging him to solve some riddle hidden deep within it. And there would follow a duel upon the keyboard, Ed fighting the music over and over, until he forced it to reveal its secret to him. And then, victory won, Ed would set off into a startling improvised departure from the concerto, in which you could hear faint derisive echoes of Chopin.

Minty stood now on the stairs, smoking down her cigarette and listening to her son's pursuit, between the tones and semitones, of an invisible, elusive quarry. She knew – perhaps she'd always known – that she herself was like that novice who sent a sheaf of poems to W.H. Auden. Auden told him he appeared to have the most important qualities for a poet: persistence, a good ear, a good eye, curiosity and a greed for language; all he lacked was talent. Not that this would stop her writing, Minty assured herself. No, she was in for the long haul; she'd always write. It was just ironic she had a son whose talent was undeniable. Minty headed up the stairs, Ed at fourteen hunting along the keyboard with his mind more concentrated in the moment than she had ever written a single line.

'Minty!'

She heard Simon's voice calling upstairs as, after a long shower, she gathered one leg of a pair of black tights in her fingers.

'Minty!'

She drew them on, before walking to the top of the stairs. Simon was in the hallway looking up at her, wrapped in an apron, cradling a mixing bowl against his soft tummy with his left arm. His right arm supported the extravagant gesture of his hand as he exclaimed, 'Minty. I've looked everywhere for the mace.'

'Mace?' Minty asked. 'Couldn't you use a rolling pin?'

'Ground mace,' Simon said impatiently. 'I need a pinch. Where the hell have you put it?'

'It's in the usual place, sport,' she told him in her tarry voice. 'Cupboard to the left of the sink.'

'I've *looked* there.'

'Look again.'

Minty returned to their bedroom. She clipped her black bra behind her. Seventeen years married and he still yelled. Through the house. Marching towards the stairwell, shouting up or down. The boys yelled back like soldiers.

'Breakfast!' 'Coming!'

'We're leaving!' 'Just a sec!'

She must have asked him a hundred times not to yell. He still did.

At her mother-in-law's old dressing-table Minty applied bright-red lipstick. Black mascara. She studied the creases that even in repose now were there at the sides of her eyes; little threads of time. They didn't bother her, though the white hairs did: she'd been dying her hair for five years, and she now ran her fingers through it with gel. Short, thick, lustrous hair: scraping it away from her face gave Minty a masculine elegance that appealed to her.

Weird, perverse it was, that Sheena could only be sporadically bothered to unpluck those white hairs of hers. In her long, jet-black mane they stood out. It wasn't just a question of vanity, Minty considered: they looked like typographical errors.

How strangely we aged. Now, which dress should she wear?

'Minty!'

Good lord, not again. She waited. Heard the racket of drums and cymbals from the kitchen. No more yells, he must have found his pan or colander. He was a complete clown in the kitchen, Simon, recently lured there by a glamorous television chef. 'The ideal woman,' he called her. 'Apart from you, Minty.' His panic-stricken performances around the kitchen he offered as homages to his mentor from a humble admirer. Offered to the family and to guests, too, and increasingly successful, if owing more to the richness of the recipes than to Simon's culinary instincts.

Not, Minty conceded, that she'd complain about this middle-aged development. She suspected that Simon would do ever more cooking as time went by. If she'd kept a record in her diary there'd be a direct correlation, she was sure, between Simon's rise in the kitchen and the decline of their sex life. Their lacklustre fucks, petering out. It seemed entirely conceivable that they'd never have sex again. In his late forties, Simon had the pink and swollen complexion of the bibulous Englishman. It amused Minty to picture him playing tennis with Ezra and the others: Simon's flesh was a loose mass about him. His ponderous bollocks hung below his stubby penis like something gamey, some butcher's sac, left to keep there a while.

Minty had reached a point a year or two ago when she could no longer pretend desire for him, and Simon had persisted only briefly, forlorn alcoholic assaults that were like some throwback of time and class, before letting go entirely. He seemed relieved.

It was hard to believe she'd ever found his foul tongue, his stream of scabrous comment on the world, charming, but it had been, once, when it issued from the mouth of a dashing young architect. People indulged him now, didn't they? They made allowances. Though not Sheena Pepin; no, some women still enjoyed it. He made Minty think, as she lit another cigarette, of an aged putto.

How could she want him, though, a defeated man – her rejection another defeat? Simon barely scraped a living, was given one or two small commissions a year by friends, and friends of people they knew. He relied on family money, in trust funds, stock and share portfolios, ISAs, TESSAs, PEPs, that Simon watched anxiously, their various savings inadequately caged birds. Rage fermented inside him. He didn't explode. Or throw things. Or hit anyone. He only yelled, his rage expressed in impatience with objects lost, sons late. And he sulked. Could spend hours in one of the loungers in the garden nursing a bourbon, brooding into the gathering dark, furious, thrown.

Minty wouldn't give up on him, though; she was going to stick with him. Persist, wouldn't she? Ezra Pepin, on the other hand, who'll be here soon. For example. Less than ten years younger than Simon – a few months younger than Minty herself – but a different generation. No, not that exactly, rather in a different relation to his physical self. Like a subtly altered breed. Approaching at forty not his ruin but his prime. Because Ezra was one of those men, Minty thought, he was a man improving with age, the bland handsomeness of youth having given way to character that was increasingly apparent in the lines of his face, his rumpled hair, the well-cut suits he had made by that Italian guy on Walton Street, his broad shoulders.

They'd be here soon. Minty stubbed out her cigarette, returned her gaze to the mirror, fingered her hair back once more from the sides of her face. Yes, she was pretty fortunate, she allowed. She still had, what? A kind of gothic undergraduate glamour, she thought, and laughed at the absurd self-delusion. And the laughter, even as it betrayed so many more lines around her eyes, made her look humorous and chic and fun. And then, quite suddenly, there happened that shift, that awful lurch in perspective she sometimes got, a revulsion with herself. The sick feeling that it was a stranger looking back at her. No, not that, exactly. The opposite, in fact: that she was staring at someone she knew too well, knew deep into her rotten bones. A nauseating familiarity. Wincing, she turned away.

'Minty!'

She checked her watch. Seven-thirty-five. The short black agnès b dress, her best one.

'Coming!' she yelled back. How, though, did Sheena not appreciate him? That Minty couldn't understand. In all these years of friendship she'd not been able to work it out. How could that woman so obviously, so carelessly, take Ezra for granted? How could she be comfortable emotionally, morally, pushing him out of the door each morning to go to work in some bottled-water company, finding ways to increase the efficiency and the sales and the profit of bottles of drinking water in a country where good God-given water fell from the sky for months on end? When what he needed was the opposite, poor brave and halting man, to be pushed the other way, back into his study to pursue his research. How could she hear those stories Ezra told, the delicacy and precision, and not do everything in her power to have that thesis – and many other books – written and published?

No, Minty didn't understand! And she couldn't interfere. When she'd tried oh so tentatively Ezra retreated into his diffident modesty. Sheena laughed it off like it was *her* problem but she was dealing with it as best she could. Yes, indeed: setting up that stupid business of hers (wasn't there something distasteful, Minty reckoned, about all these female entrepreneurs nowadays?) Not to mention throwing herself into one environmental campaign after another – Simon happily roped into this last one. 'An architect protesting against house-building!' he'd chirp. 'Isn't that marvellous? Aren't I just woefully paradoxical?' The perversity of it positively erotic for Simon; another sublimation, poor man.

Minty stepped into her black Pradas, with their heels that would elevate her eyeline from an inch below to an inch above Sheena's. Took a last look at her reflection, gave a deep sigh: the unfair mystery of other people. If there was one thing her mother had taught her, Minty thought, it was to expect nothing.

Yet hope for everything, her ambition thin and boundless.

Sheena and Ezra Pepin strolled along the fresh pavements of Blenheim Orchard hand in hand, and through to Bainton Road. Ezra turned right. The Carlyles' house was the third one along. He anticipated Sheena's voice, 'Does she think we don't all want *peace*?' Ezra prepared to mollify his wife, so that the evening did not begin with antipathy amongst them. But then he saw that the rainbow flag – horizontal stripes overlaid with the word *PACE* in white – had been taken down from the upstairs window.

There was a builders' skip outside the house next door. One of a multitude these last two or three years along Bainton Road, whose Edwardian houses had looked appealingly faded and comfortable until, four years earlier, there rose behind them the bright, hard fake-Victorian dwellings of Blenheim Orchard, coltish, mocking, and the houses on Bainton Road were suddenly exposed for what they were: scruffy, tired, down-at-heel.

One house after another had been besieged by scaffolding. Small men clambered over roofs, repointed brickwork, painted windows. Then they disappeared inside, came out like robbers stealing carpets, sofas, radiators, which they threw into their getaway skips. The Carlyles must have filled half a dozen with their make-over. The house had been Simon's parents' home, he'd lived there all his life, and it enveloped first Minty and then the boys with little need to change. When Simon's mother moved to a nursing home on Moreton Road, contemporaneous with the Pepins moving into Blenheim Orchard round the corner from their old friends, Simon applied his skills to his own dwelling, designing a kitchen extension and a basement conversion. They had wooden floors sanded, walls stripped of dark wallpaper and painted white. Minty decluttered the house of gloomy furniture, faded paintings, thick curtains; bought white lampshades and bright Iranian carpets.

'Minty!'

'I'm here,' she growled.

'There you are, thank God! Where the hell have you been?' Simon was beating potatoes that he'd already mashed in a large saucepan on the sideboard. Around it a fork, a manual whisk and an electric one lay rejected; globules of the off-white mixture were scattered across surfaces, objects, Simon's apron with a food-stained picture of the Colosseum. 'I was calling you!'

'And how often have I asked –'

'How the hell do I know when this is supple and light? She doesn't say, damn the woman.'

'Let me see.'

'And where's the nutmeg? I asked you to get me one when you went shopping.'

They heard their guests' voices, with Ed's, in the hallway: by the time the Pepins reached the kitchen Simon had accomplished a swift change of persona, covering his frustration with the mask of a buffoon. And within a further minute he had them all, not just Sheena but Ezra, too, and yes, Minty as well, laughing at his hopeless tomfoolery, as he dragged them into a whirlwind of panic to lay the table, you won't believe this salad, get the plates, quick, quick, not those ones, they're hot, Ezra pour that wine, girls you grate, you squeeze, thirty seconds, help, Minty, where the hell's our pie dish, the ceramic one, no, enamel then, yes whatever, for the fish pie?

Until the implements and the crockery, the friends and the first course all arrived more or less together at the dining-room table,

197

breathless and middle-aged and giggling, Simon still playing the fool as he mixed up lemon juice with salad dressing and pretended to pour a glass of Ostertag Pinot Blanc over Sheena's lap. What a ridiculous dexterity he had! And Sheena was hooting with laughter, Ezra chuckling, the salad had iron and wit, the wine was as chilled as it needed to be. There was something worthwhile in this room, Minty conceded: a true conviviality. If she had to make do with this, if this was the sum of it, then she would. Be here with these friends, be this close to Ezra, put up with Sheena with good grace, discover she could still feel some kind of fondness for this overgrown boy of a husband.

It wasn't until they'd finished a bottle of Brouilly and another of Pinot Blanc with three delicious and companionable courses, and Minty had stubbed one cigarette out in the remains of chocolate mousse on her plate, and leaned over to light Ezra's rollie, and Simon had carried in a tray of coffee and After Eight mints the Pepins had brought, that Sheena said, 'Listen. We've got something to tell you.'

'Yes,' Ezra said, twisting his head to blow smoke away from his companions, then turning back to face them. 'We've got something to share with you chaps. We haven't told anyone else yet.'

'You're the first,' Sheena emphasised. 'You tell them, Ez.'

'Me? You sure, darling?'

'Yes, you go ahead.'

It struck Minty all of a sudden, from the way their upper bodies were leaning slightly towards each other, that Ezra and Sheena were holding coy hands under the table, like a couple of teenagers.

'Don't you want to?'

'No, you go ahead.'

Good lord, Minty realised: Oh no. Surely not. Not another Pepin baby. Incredible! Can you believe the selfishness of that –

'We're going to Brazil,' said Ezra, smiling, looking pleased with himself for having said so.

There was a pause. The announcement was too facile to make any sense. Except that Sheena turned to Ezra, and her face appeared to reflect a painful stab of indigestion.

'Well,' she squawked. 'I'm certainly glad I asked *you* to tell them. Context, a little? Background, maybe?'

'No, no,' Simon rallied. 'Why, what a marvellous idea. We've not been on an adventurous vacation in years, have we, Minty? Always go to the same island. As you both know. That same bloody villa!'

'Especially brave of you,' Minty joined in, relieved by Simon's deciphering of Ezra's statement, 'for people who rarely holiday anywhere further than the Lake District.'

'I haven't been to South America in years,' Simon admitted.

'Amazing resorts, aren't they?' Minty said. 'I was reading in the travel section. Bermuda at half the price. That is Brazil, isn't it? In the north, right?'

'Bloody long flight,' said Simon. 'Wouldn't just go for a week or two. Make it a month, I should.'

'We're going to live there,' Sheena grinned.

Again it took the Carlyles some moments to respond. Minty frowned. 'You're going to *live* there? Are you, in . . . ? In *Brazil*?'

'But your business, Sheena?' Simon queried. 'The children? Blaise,' he said. 'Hector!' Suggesting with each name in turn a mounting incredulity. 'Little Louie!'

So then the Pepins took the Carlyles through their scheme, and the Carlyles raised objections like lawyers, which the Pepins answered patiently, the Carlyles occasionally shaking their heads.

'And you see the best thing,' Sheena said, 'is that Ez can go back to that tribe and complete his work with them?'

'In Paraguay?' Minty said.

'What?' said Sheena.

'It's very close to the border,' Ezra clarified. 'Which, after all, as you can imagine, is a bit of an abstract concept out there in the middle of rainforest.'

'But seriously, Sheena, what about Blaise?' Simon asked. 'I mean, she can't be too happy about it, can she?'

'Why on earth not?'

'Well, with this young man of hers.'

'Oh, it's nothing serious,' Sheena assured him.

'Really? Oh.' Simon blinked. 'Wasn't Ed telling you, Minty?'

'Don't take school gossip too seriously,' Sheena advised. 'Puppy love: of course they think it's for ever.'

Notwithstanding their caveats and questions, the Carlyles expressed admiration and approval for the enterprise, much as Sheena had once done for the refurbishment of their house. Simon opened a fourth bottle of wine, a Château de Sours rosé with a tight cork which he grappled and cursed at in an Arthurian trial of strength. The others broke into a round of applause when he passed it.

After they'd made another toast to freedom and adventure, Simon said, 'But really it's not a bad intoxicant, is it, the fruit of Bacchus?'

'I've forgotten, Ezra,' said Minty. 'Did you take stuff with those people? Those Indians of yours? Ayahuasca and whatnot?'

'A similar substance,' said Ezra, groggy with wine. 'Yes, I did.'

'Often?'

'They performed a ritual half a dozen times a year. Though no one took part every time. It would have been overwhelming.'

'It's been years since I took anything,' Minty said.

'I say, that's not entirely true, is it?' Simon corrected her. 'You were puffing away on that thing at the Fleggs the other week.'

'Pot, sure. I mean something trippy. And if I don't take it again soon I never will.'

'I know what you mean,' said Ezra.

'Ha!' said Sheena. 'You have something every time you go to London with your workmates.'

'No, I mean literally,' said Minty. 'I'm giving up when I'm forty.'

'You're giving up what you no longer indulge in?' Sheena asked. 'That's admirable, Minty. It really is.'

'She's going to quit drinking,' Simon said, shrugging extravagantly to make clear it was all Minty's own idea. 'Cigarettes, too. Dope. You name it, she's going to abstain. Totally. Not a drag, not a drop.'

200

'A bit extreme, isn't it?' Sheena asked. 'I mean, surely you'll indulge a little. Like at weddings and new years and . . .'

'Oh, don't underestimate this woman, Sheena,' Simon laughed. 'What she resolves to do, Minty does, I can assure you.'

'In that case,' said Ezra, 'you deserve a final splurge. Don't you think?'

'Why, yes, sport,' Minty agreed. 'Would I not?'

'When's your birthday again?'

'You don't know it?' Sheena demanded. 'That is just so typical,' she told Minty. 'August, Ez. The 17th.'

'It's a Sunday this year,' Minty said.

'Perfect,' said Ezra. 'We'll make it a farewell blowout. There's a gang at work I sometimes tag along with, they know the best stuff –'

'Stuff?' Simon asked.

'I'll find out from them something happening somewhere that Saturday. We'll go. All of us. Leave it with me.'

Instead of the perfunctory 'have a good week' farewells of their social Sunday evenings, it took the Pepins and the Carlyles till after midnight to let each other part on the porch.

'We'll miss you so much, you know that,' said Minty.

'Are you kidding?' said Ezra. 'You chaps are going to be the one most difficult thing to leave behind.'

'Jack'll be devastated,' said Simon.

'Hector insists he come out to visit,' said Sheena. 'And that goes for all of you.'

Eventually the Pepins stumbled away, and the Carlyles retreated inside, and Simon turned off the porch light and locked the door.

Since Simon had cooked the meal, it was Minty's job to load the dishwasher, scour pans, rinse wine glasses. But Simon hovered near by, not helping but talking.

'I don't care what you say, Minty,' he said, scowling. 'Ridiculous thing to do. Taking the children out of a perfectly good school that people pay thousands to buy into the catchment area for, away

201

from their friends, not to mention the boyfriend about whom they seem to have not a clue.'

The last thing Minty needed was the boozy drone of Simon's voice. She needed to be alone, so she banged pans and rattled cutlery to shut him up. But he just maundered on a little louder.

'No, you have to admit, Minty, it's very odd. All right: if there was a reason. But does it make sense, him going back into the jungle after all these years? I mean, he didn't have the spunk to write the bloody thing in his twenties, with what? A grant, a supervisor, a college behind him. How's he going to do it alone, in his forties?'

As, finally, Minty laid the table for Monday morning, Simon disappeared abruptly from the kitchen. Turning off lights, Minty made her way upstairs and to the blessedly vacant bathroom. She'd just sat on the loo when Simon burst in, and made for his tooth-brush.

'But really,' he said, squeezing Colgate on to the brush, 'when you think about it . . .' Then he began to scrub his teeth, which crunched and mangled his words into gobbledegook. So he ceased. Simon finished brushing his teeth, fed himself water from a cupped hand, gargled noisily, and spat a froth into the sink. He then hawked, slurped and tasted on his tongue whatever had come up, before repeating the gargling process.

Minty removed her tights and knickers, tore off some loo paper. She didn't want to despise him, for goodness sake. But how could she avoid it? How could disgust not turn into repulsion and on into contempt? Unless their bodies led entirely separate lives.

But he'd still talk, wouldn't he?

Simon splashed water on his face, buried it in a towel, rubbed vigorously, and re-emerged saying, 'No, it's an amazing project, actually, you really have to hand it to her, you know. Bloody brave. And they don't have to do it, you see, Minty, that's the thing. Sheena's taking a chance. If you ask me, it's rather heroic.'

They swapped positions, Minty with her electric toothbrush that she hoped might shut him up. Not to mention the sound of him peeing, which only made him puff out his chest and take a deep breath and speak louder.

'It's making me rethink, sweetheart, we've been too bloody conservative. I know it's too late now for this July, but let's not go to Greece *next* year. Let's go somewhere different. Like Turkey. What? Or Crete.'

She knew she'd not have solitude until Simon had gone to sleep. Sure enough, within minutes of turning out the light he dropped off, and before long commenced a cautious, grumbling snore.

Minty slipped back out of bed, pulled on her silk dressing-gown and crept barefoot downstairs. Down, away from her three boys left hanging up there on the first floor, safe from the tamed animals of Albion. Up in the branches while she climbed silently down to the ground and out of the back door to the garden.

1 a.m. Monday morning. Cars from the ring-road were isolated insects in the silent summer night. The click of her lighter much louder. Minty looked up to the sky, but there was nothing to see above the urban glare. She lowered her gaze, and an idea came to her: she imagined walking in a straight line west towards Port Meadow. Over the side fence and through their neighbours' garden. Jumping over their hedge and on over Gladstone Lane and through the rest of the gardens, vaulting the fences, until she got to the canal. And leapt in one easy bound across it.

On in the same way through the Waterways estate and then up spring-heeled over the chainlink fence, levitating across the railway line, floating over the fence on the other side. Then she would run like a girl across Burgess Field, jump the stile by the gate, and walk on, barefoot, her nightdress cool in the warm night. Treading over the mint and the fading buttercups, past the cows sleeping like statues and the tired horses, out to the empty centre of the great Meadow.

Maybe there, Minty thought, she'd be able to see the stars, and get just a little perspective. Beyond the limits of her life closing in around her. Ezra Pepin was leaving the neighbourhood. He was leaving the country. There was to be no more consolation in proximity; no longer the tantalising possibility of one day

203

something too good and wrong and dangerous to ever hope for happening. He was going to another continent. Might as well be another planet. A little perspective was what she needed.

But a trek to the Meadow was only going to happen in her mind. Instead Minty walked past Simon's deckchair and over to the middle of the lawn. She sank down, stubbed her cigarette out on the dry grass, put her forehead to the hard earth, and wept.

10

The Pitt Rivers Museum

Monday 7 July

'It won't be open,' Akhmed said, a little out of breath. Every half-dozen strides or so Blaise began to edge ahead of him, and he had to trot three or four quick steps to catch up with her. Whenever he did so the books in his black plastic rucksack jiggled against his back.

'Museums are always closed on Mondays,' Akhmed gasped. 'Everyone knows that.'

Blaise walked at a medium pace. The warmth and movement made her skin bristle and tingle, the outer reaches of her body fully inhabited and grateful to be so. Each footstep on this hot afternoon took her further away from school. She'd begun skipping dull lessons when her senses disengaged like cogs inside her head, and she'd lose herself for stretches of time in the sight of the sun decoding a prism of colour on the white wall. She never used to dream so much at school. A sign of age, perhaps; she was growing old.

It had also made a difference that she'd stopped using her bike: she felt less visible on foot. For walking had become both the means of escape and the reason for it. Blaise slipped out of school so that she could go for a stroll. For the articulation of her joints, the stretching of her muscles; breath in her lungs, thought in her head.

'Why are you walking so fast?' Akhmed demanded. 'It's either open or closed. Going quicker's not going to make any difference.'

She used to go to the Wasteland. Now she and Akhmed ambled along Charlbury Road, through the north Oxford conservation area of large, detached houses and their spacious, tousled gardens. It was eerily quiet. There was no traffic here.

'Who lives in these houses?' Blaise wondered.

'Rich people,' Akhmed said. He looked around. 'Where've they all gone?'

'Nowhere,' Blaise murmured. The whole area seemed abandoned. She felt like she was passing through some emergency they'd read about in the news tomorrow. Some upper-class catastrophe.

'You're right,' Akhmed nodded, judiciously, as if it were his confirmation that made it so. 'See, they've all got cars parked in the driveways.' He frowned. 'Maybe they're asleep.' Perhaps the wealthy too said prayers at odd hours of the night like his pious brother, and needed to catch up in the afternoon.

Blaise walked the deserted streets, past the still houses. This silence could feed you, she thought. If you had money this is what you'd do, you'd buy a big house with a big garden where you could be quiet, surrounded by other people who chose the same thing.

Akhmed skipped quickly to catch up with her. 'You know what's crazy,' he said, 'is that it's English *I'm* missing. English. I mean, I wouldn't mind dodging geography, either.'

His momentum had taken Akhmed a few feet beyond Blaise by the time he registered that she'd stopped still. He turned to find her glaring at him.

'I told you you didn't need to come,' Blaise said, and set off again. 'Didn't I?' she asked as she passed him.

Akhmed stood for a moment, staring at the spot on the pavement that her trainer-shod feet had just occupied. He turned, and glanced towards the withdrawing figure, until the gap opening up between them provoked an energy that overcame his paralysis. He jogged after her, the textbooks in his rucksack thumping against his spine. 'Someone has to look after you,' he said, as they crossed Bardwell Road, into Dragon Lane. 'I mean, what if you get caught?'

'It's creepy here,' Akhmed whispered, edging closer to Blaise. 'All these bones. I never liked it here.'

The lower jaw of a sperm whale pointed straight up, a Gothic arch. In a side bay a procession of skeletons made ready to set off, two by two. Tiger and rhino, red deer and pig, reindeer and horse. They advanced placidly across the tiled floor of the museum, stunned in the act of embarkation upon a prehistoric ark. One-humped camel, Irish elk, giraffe. Bringing up the rear, calmly meeting their doom, an Asian elephant with its calf.

There didn't seem to be any ventilation. Blaise stripped off another layer of clothing. The only other people here were young women with foreign accents chasing after red-faced toddlers. Blaise wished she could take off her sweaty T-shirt. From the top of marble columns, cast-iron ribs rose in arches to the apex of the glazed roof. The great hall was a giant greenhouse. It was wrong, Blaise thought. An error. A room so full of bones should be cold.

The skeleton of a Nile crocodile feigned lifelessness, ready to pounce. Akhmed skirted the undisguised malice of its sharp-toothed jaws, his hand on Blaise's arm, half grasping her for reassurance, half pushing her to safety.

'Come on,' Blaise said, setting off towards the back of the Natural History Museum. 'Let's go in the Pitt Rivers.'

'Where do you start?' Akhmed wondered. 'In a place like this?' He shook his head. 'There's no order.'

They wandered through the maze of cluttered display cases, each one packed with ethnographic objects that had been collected together according not to where they came from or their age but to a general theme. Musical instruments. Weapons. Tools. Magic objects: amulets and charms from Africa, Melanesia, the Americas.

'Each case is like an Ark of the Covenant,' Blaise said.

'An ark?' Akhmed demanded.

207

'You know,' she said. 'It contained the tablets of the laws of the ancient Israelites. My dad says these cases are like that. *Densely packed with meaning.*'

Akhmed analysed her tone of voice, to see whether there was sarcasm or irony there that would invite him to participate. He was unable to detect any. 'Why am I whispering?' he asked.

Blaise offered no explanation, so Akhmed tried to answer himself. 'It's either cos it's so dim in here, or cos of those shrunken heads.'

Blaise ambled on. 'My dad used to bring me here when I was younger,' she said. 'Whenever we were in town, him and me, we'd drop in here on the way home. We had five minutes to each choose one thing.'

'What thing?'

'Something different. Then I had to show it to him, and explain why I liked it, and wanted to share it with him. And he'd do the same with me.'

Akhmed nodded, unsurprised, as if he and his father had played similar games.

They strayed among the display cases. Blaise liked the tiny handwritten labels, attached to artefacts with cotton thread; sometimes the items themselves were written on. She appreciated the clutter; the atmosphere of Victorian curiosity and quest. She recalled Ezra telling her about a professor of anthropology in the university, who studied the work of Victorian ethnographers in order to reveal more about nineteenth-century Englishmen. Her father had given a disbelieving chuckle.

'Look,' Blaise exclaimed. 'I chose this once. I remember.' It was an ivory globe, a little larger than a tennis ball. There were a number of circular holes in its surface. Inside was another ball, inside that one another, and so on and on. Eleven graduated hollow spheres. Each one was elaborately carved and fretted.

'Chinese,' Blaise said. 'Imagine how long it must have taken to carve that.'

Akhmed frowned. 'You'd make it with a computerised machine tool today,' he assured her. 'You wouldn't touch it.'

208

'My dad reckoned it would have taken more than one crafts-man's lifetime.'

'What?' Akhmed said. He wrinkled his nose with mistrust. He peered a little closer at the ivory sphere, as if to interrogate it. Its smallness. Its absurd, superfluous complexity.

'That's what Dad figured,' Blaise said. 'That's what he told me.'

The battered, pale-grey Ford Escort that limped into Blenheim Orchard early Monday evening, with its dents and scrapes worn proud as war wounds, and rust spots spread like some automobile skin condition, was the oldest car Hector Pepin had ever seen trundle on to their estate.

It had been another hot, bright afternoon that was beginning to give way, with the sun drained of its ferocity as it fell in a slow arc towards the edge of the earth, to a pleasant evening.

The old Escort drew to a halt behind the two cars parked outside the Pepins' house, hemming them both in. A slight, balding man dressed in a black suit, white shirt and thin black tie climbed out. He turned and fed the loose seat belt all the way back into its sprung holster, and when he closed the door Hector watched him less slam it shut than feel it home; inviting bolt to click solicitously into mechanism. The man walked along the short avenue between the Pepins' cars towards the front door, and as Hector tentatively descended the stairs he heard the doorbell ring.

After waiting a moment to allow anyone more eager than himself to answer the door, Hector did so, and with the awkward deference of a shy eleven-year-old he invited the man inside. If he'd not been too timid to look at him when he spoke, their eyes would have met at almost the same level.

'Kindly tell your father, my boy,' the visitor said, in a tone that sounded like a friendly proclamation, 'that Abdul Azam is here.'

'I don't think he's back from –' Hector began, but then stopped himself as he heard the distinct familiar sound of their side gate banging against the wall of the house. 'I think he just came home,' Hector said, and stood there, waiting. Not sure whether it was more polite to go and tell his father they had a visitor or to stay with their visitor until his father reached the hallway of his own accord. He gazed at the corn-coloured carpet, taking in the man's black shoes: the leather was cracked in thin lines across the bridges. Hector glanced up briefly: the man stood with a serene, incurious smile on his face. At ease, Hector observed with admiration.

The back door opened and closed. Ezra came rushing through from the kitchen, sweating and breathless.

'Daddy, this is Mr Azam,' Hector said.

'Hello,' said Ezra, offering his hand. 'Ezra Pepin. How nice to meet you. I hope you haven't been waiting long, Mr Azam.'

'Please, call me Abdul.'

'I will, I will. Now, let's see, Sheena's in there, and there'll be kids everywhere down here. Oh, first of all, can I get you a drink of something?'

'No, thank you.'

'Tea? Water?'

'No, no. Abdul doesn't need a drink. You want to send them to their rooms?'

'The children? Oh, no, much easier for us to go up to the spare room. My study, I should say. Do come with me.'

The sofabed had been flipped up. Ezra ushered Abdul Azam in, relieved that the room was tidy: he hadn't yet found time to start working through his papers, in preparation for the trip. When he did, this study would become chaotic. For himself he swivelled the chair out from his desk. Ezra sat side-on to his desk, facing his guest like a doctor. He was relieved to sit down. Abdul must be about a foot shorter than me, Ezra thought. The height of the average Achia, he realised, recalling how it had taken him weeks to over-come his awkwardness with people he towered over.

'The Raj Cuisine, isn't it?' Ezra began.

'That's right.'

'We used to go there all the time, Abdul. When we were first, you know, together. And married. And had Blaise.'

'Ah, yes. Blaise.'

'We lived on Walton Street. Then we moved along to Kingston Road. Then a bit further, here to Blenheim Orchard.'

'Always moving away from restaurant. That what it is.'

'Oh, but I miss those days. Remember when Raymond Blanc's used to be a piano shop?'

Abdul raised his eyebrows. 'Long time ago, Ezra.'

'You remember the locksmith's where Branca's is? And when the Jericho Café was Lancelyn Lighting?'

'Of course Abdul remember.'

'Loch Fyne was that cheap bicycle shop? And now Sip. See their posters? *Opening soon: a new concept in eating.* I thought, What, through the ears?'

Ezra laughed at his own wry observation. 'Am I right, Abdul? I mean, really.' Abdul Azam smiled back, though possibly not at Ezra's humour.

'It used to be that expensive junk shop?' Ezra continued. 'Before that there was a guy who welded together his own iron bedsteads. We bought our marital bed from him. A beautiful thing. Fell apart eventually. Too much . . . well, children bouncing on it, I guess.'

'Over thirty years Abdul is there,' Azam smiled. 'A lot of changes.'

'Have they been good for you? More restaurants. Are they unwanted competition, or do they drag customers to Walton Street for all of you?'

'Ah, business, Ezra,' Abdul drawled, as if to indicate that Ezra need not bother himself with such weighty matters. 'Sometime good, sometime bad. Sometime you know why, sometime you don't. It's like that. But people they come to my restaurant. Always they come.'

'We certainly did.' Abdul had not changed since the last time Ezra had been in the Raj Cuisine. He was instantly recognisable, with his narrow moustache, his thinning hair. Ezra must have spoken with him – of items on the menu, the weather outside, the popularity or otherwise of whatever films were playing at the cinema across the road – fifty times. There was a familiarity between them. Except that he wasn't sure whether or not Abdul remembered him. Another English customer from years ago.

'Everybody come to Abdul.'

Abdul Azam wore a smile of disconcerting constancy on his face. It seemed to suggest wry amusement at something shared with his companion, the acknowledgement of a mutual understanding.

'Thing is, Ezra,' Abdul was saying. 'Thing is, everything change, but Raj Cuisine don't change, no, Abdul still there.'

'That's true.'

'Other people, they can run around. Abdul try to take what is called the long view.'

'That's very sensible, I think.'

'Thing iz, everybody struggle with time,' Abdul spoke with a nasal twang, stretching every vowel. The voice of a patient man. 'Everybody have trouble with time. Even Abdul.' The same fixed smile remained on Abdul's face as he spoke, in his slow insistent drawl. 'Always I am asking, time does it go in straight line? Everywhere I look I don't see lines. I see circles: of sun and moon, of planets around sun. Any place we look how man has measured time, we see circles and wheels.' Abdul's hands described small globes. 'Cogs revolve in mechanical clock, Ezra. Hands of clock ticktock round and around. Why? If time is linear. Why?'

Abdul raised his head and gazed at the ceiling. After some seconds he was still looking up, so Ezra found himself following Abdul's gaze, as if there might be crib notes there; or Sheena had just had a Velux window installed in the spare room without telling him, opening a view through the attic right up to the horological stars. Even though of course it was still light outside.

Abdul lowered his gaze towards his host, smiling.

Ezra said, 'You're right. We clearly want to believe that time is circular. Why? I don't know. For comfort?'

Abdul grinned. 'Fear of eternity,' he said.

Ezra nodded, in cautious agreement. 'Is it an interest of yours?' he asked. 'You study time?'

'Abdul no time to read books,' he said with a regretful chuckle. 'I have very clever customers, Ezra. They talk to me. I listen.'

'I see.'

'They all come to Abdul.'

'Right.' Ezra pictured a stream of lonely dons dropping in to eat at the Raj Cuisine.

'You have heard of computer engineer, Ezra?' Abdul asked in his slow-motion nasal sing-song. 'In Arizona? Building big clock. Because he know that everybody only think about today. Tomorrow. People forget how to take long view, you see. That what I'm saying. He want to make clock that stay accurate for ten thousand years.'

'You're winding me up,' popped out of Ezra's mouth.

'It tick once a year,' Abdul continued, holding up a delicate index finger. 'No hour hand, only century hand. You see?'

'Yes. No. See what?'

'Thing is, Ezra, clock like this help people take long view.'

'Yes, yes, I see that, Abdul. Think in the long term.'

'That what it is,' Abdul smiled, glad the point had been made. 'Take long view. But now I take too much of *your* time, Ezra.'

'Not at all. Do you need to get back to the restaurant?'

'Oh, they can wait for Abdul. But one thing, Ezra, before I go.' Abdul placed a hand on his chest. 'I can tell you. You are father. I am father. In an actual fact, I am worried.

'So am I,' Ezra nodded. 'I'm worried, too.'

'What my son he is doing with your daughter?'

'Well, Abdul, that's a damn good question. I've asked it myself. What is your son doing with my daughter?'

'And other question. What your daughter she is doing with my son?'

'Yes, indeed.'

'Abdul not old-fashioned, Ezra. But Akhmed, we don't see him. Mother worried. Abdul worried. Because Abdul, he take the long view.'

'Yes, I see,' said Ezra. 'I understand,' he nodded, wondering what Abdul meant. Abdul smiled at him, and he nodded back. Ezra tried smiling too; he shook his head ruefully. Still Abdul smiled. Ezra returned to nodding sagely, with a meditative frown, to give the impression that he was working through the deep layers of this conundrum before saying anything, an approach he suspected Abdul Azam would appreciate.

And then suddenly Ezra Pepin remembered something significant. 'But look,' he said, 'it doesn't matter, Abdul, not at all, because didn't Akhmed tell you?'

'Tell me?'

'Why, we're off to Brazil. In a matter of months. Weeks, really! The whole family. We're going to Brazil for two years.'

'All of you?' Abdul's smile might just have widened a little then, Ezra wasn't quite sure.

'All of us. To live and work there. Blaise and our son, Hector, will go to school there.'

'That very good news,' Abdul said. He stood up. 'Thank you. Because they so young, that why.'

'Exactly,' Ezra agreed, as he followed Abdul out of the spare room. 'So young.'

'Very good news,' Abdul repeated. 'Abdul don't think it good for a man to get married until he's older.'

They went downstairs. The house was strangely silent.

'I agree,' said Ezra.

'Akhmed get married like brother, after he finish university. Twenty-two, twenty-three.'

'At least,' Ezra said, opening the front door and stepping outside with his visitor. He walked him to his car.

'You and your wife,' Abdul said, 'please, you come to Raj Cuisine again.'

'We should.'

'Have favourite dishes. Guest of Abdul.'

'That's very kind, thank you. We will.'

They shook hands, and Abdul Azam got into his decrepit old car. It gargled into life, and crawled ponderously away.

As Ezra re-entered the house he heard raised voices, the velocity of whose utterances accelerated, their volume increased, as he approached the living-room; and then stopped a split second before he came through the door.

Sheena and Blaise looked to be involved in a game, which for the moment was played in silence: Blaise jigged backwards in loops and spirals and figures-of-eight around and between sofas and coffee table. Sheena pursued her, making periodic lunges for an object Blaise held in her fist and kept managing to flick away from her mother's grasp. It looked like a relay race, with strange new rules: each time, retreating further, Blaise taunted Sheena with the object. So that Sheena was lured into coming forward and making another angry lunge, and Blaise again flicked the baton away.

Hector watched from a windowsill. Louie stood on a kitchen chair in his pyjamas, clutching a banana.

Then the sound, the voices, erupted again. Though it was possible that Ezra had cut them out in order to make sense of the scene in silence.

'Give me that thing.'

'No.'

'I'm ordering you.'

'But why should I?' Blaise hissed. 'Why?'

'Because I'm your mother,' Sheena yelled. 'That's why.'

Then Blaise noticed her father standing in the doorway. 'Daddy! You tell her!'

'What is going on?' Ezra asked. He could hear his own voice sag with disappointment at what he was seeing, after weeks of harmony between them that he'd allowed himself to hope was the eternal future. 'What are you doing?'

'I want,' Sheena said, enunciating each livid syllable, 'to . . . see . . . the . . . news.' She ceased the pursuit of her daughter.

'Daddy!' Blaise said, coming to a stop. 'Tell her!'

'It's seven o'clock,' Sheena said. 'It's time for the news.'

'Tell her, Daddy,' Blaise pleaded.

'What, Blaise?' Ezra asked. 'Tell her what?'

'Tell her *The Simpsons* is better than the news.'

Ezra swallowed a laugh. He shook his head. 'Of course *The Simpsons* is better than the news,' he said. 'Everyone knows that. But it's not the point. The point is Mum wants to see the news. Why don't you record *The Simpsons*, Blaise?'

'She can video the news!'

'Don't be ridiculous!' Sheena spat.

215

'Then it won't be news,' Ezra explained. 'But *The Simpsons* will still be itself in an hour's time.'

'But it's not fair,' Blaise complained. '"The human rights of children are respected in this house,"' she announced, in parody of one or other, or maybe both, of her parents. 'But it's not even about this. She doesn't even like watching the news. Mum's annoyed because Akhmed's dad only wanted to talk to you.'

'Don't be so bloody rude,' Sheena said. 'You're not too old to be grounded. I had a phone call from school today. "Is Blaise all right? Why didn't she come in for her geography exam?"'

'Exam?' Ezra asked. 'You didn't sit one of your exams?'

Blaise shook her head as if to deter an irritating fly from her cheek. 'It's geography, Dad. I was going to fail. It'll have nothing to do with my GCSE options.'

'But Blaise,' he responded, 'this is not the sort of decision you make alone. You have to discuss it with us. Your parents. You have to consult us.'

With her daughter's attention diverted towards her father, Sheena made a sudden lunge for the remote and plucked it from Blaise's surprised grasp.

'Hey! That's not fair,' Blaise cried. 'We were talking.'

Ezra had to admit that he agreed with Blaise: that really wasn't fair. Sheena had broken an informal truce. So what should he say or do now? He was flummoxed; he couldn't cope. Blaise stood frozen with indignation, surely primed to burst into tears. Sheena stepped towards the television, deftly summoning Channel Four. A solemnly excited voice spoke, followed seconds later by images of carnage under a hot sun.

'You see?' Blaise yelled, pointing at the screen. 'You see?'

Sheena ignored Blaise and everyone else, focusing her attention on the television. She perched herself on the arm of one of the sofas.

How could she have done that? Ezra was still asking himself. Surely she wasn't allowed to. He glanced at Hector, then at Louie, staring at their mother and sister, waiting for the next move.

Blaise made it. She looked like she was going for the remote, which Sheena had buried beneath her crossed arms. Instead she

216

gave her mother a good push. Sheena tumbled backwards, head over heels, on to the sofa.

'Oh, for Christ's sake!' Ezra shouted. 'You two sort it out,' he managed, before slamming the door behind him and running to the stairs. He was confounded, annoyed and deeply saddened. Dismayed by his wife and his daughter's behaviour. But he also knew that he had to get out of there, immediately, because what Blaise had just done was very funny – and if they heard him laugh, Ezra suspected that he would suddenly become the one in trouble.

He bounded up the stairs with giggles bouncing in his throat. He leapt into the spare room, closed the door and let it go: a painful paroxysm, snorts of helpless mirth. Pockets of guff found urgent release from his lungs. Bubbling laughter.

The hilarity evaporated. And what he'd witnessed was no longer funny. It just meant that Blaise and Sheena were at loggerheads again, unable to cope with each other's such similar behaviour. To bend a little. As if they were under some fateful obligation to express, to punish, their DNA, their common make-up, in a double helix of inevitable argument.

He'd have to return to Blaise skipping this exam. What did she mean it had no bearing on her GCSEs? She wasn't doing GCSEs; maybe it would have a bearing on her baccalaureate. What else was she not telling them?

And it sounded like he'd have to pay with Sheena for that man-to-man session – as if it was anything he'd asked for or wanted! Although, come to think of it, if he were honest, there was a moment in the pantomime when it had struck Ezra that he could have been talking with a fellow patriarch about matters that men dealt with.

But wait a second: why did Blaise make a point of Sheena, her mother, being pissed off about Abdul Azam's visit? Surely Blaise was the one to be most troubled by its implications? Why call attention to it? And wasn't she interested in what was said?

Still, Ezra thought, it was good to get out of there. Let those two work it out between them; let them grant each other some respect or be condemned to endlessly renegotiate their positions. He was not obliged to intervene. Except that an awful sound reached Ezra's ears, and he thrust open the spare-room door. A banshee shriek. He pell-melled down the stairs and reentered the sitting-room, to be greeted by the sight of his wife and his daughter wrestling on the sofa and off it to the coffee table, scattering books and magazines. They were well matched. Sheena was heavier, but Blaise was supple and springy. Ezra watched for a moment. Summoning resolve. Hoping one of them would submit and walk away. Or that their combat would melt into an embrace. For how could he, wretched man, help but see a single ugly eight-limbed organism fighting with itself?

Ezra Pepin walked over and, squeezing his eyes and flinching in a vain attempt to protect himself, pushed himself between them. He was temperamentally as well as physically unsuited to violence; a coward and over six feet tall and thin, ungainly: handicapped by a high centre of gravity and a low resistance to pain. Women's bodies were unpredictable. Flailing knuckles, kneebones; razorlike finger-nails came out of nowhere. Random collateral damage. Flinching, Ezra clutched a wrist, put his arm around a torso, and began pulling them apart.

Sheena pulled on her Speedo swimsuit. Once the bottom was up over her groin and around her waist, she paused to remove her bra, before lifting the straps up over her shoulders. The swimsuit stretched and moulded itself to her torso, a polyester elastane corset, which modified the female swellings of her body to an aquadynamic androgyny. She restrained her hair in a blue cap, tied the locker key around her left wrist by its rubber strap, showered, splashed through the footbath, soon pushed off into the cold, chlorinated water.

Monday evenings after seven were for lengths. There were signs that indicated that swimmers were expected to turn at each end in a clockwise direction; to their right. A woman just ahead of Sheena reached the end and turned to her left. Sheena turned the correct way, and kicked off from the wall underwater. She soon overtook the woman. There were maybe a dozen people in the pool. Sheena paid them little attention, but as she accumulated her lengths so she passed them, and made her customary assessment. There were wanderers, incapable of swimming in a straight line, inept front crawlers mostly, frantically gulping air and veering when they should have been checking a marker towards which to aim, or following one of the lines below them, painted on the bottom of the pool. You had to watch out for them: they might as well have been blind, swimming without a guide dog, they'd crash into you with a flurry of splashing limbs.

Then there were idlers, like those two over there, fat women who always seemed to come in pairs, swam two or three sluggish lengths, then floated by the side, wobbly arms spread along the tiles, gasbags self-satisfied with their exercise.

The blurry clock on the wall at the shallow end told Sheena it had taken her fifteen minutes to complete the first twenty lengths. She was on target, as long as she didn't slacken her pace. She derived pleasure from making every stroke exemplary: arms conducting graceful displacement of water; streamlined body in smooth motion; muscled legs amphibian. Swimming was Sheena's refuge. An anonymity where she answered to no one. Where she tried not to think of work or family although, strangely enough, it was precisely here that doubt, when it wanted, came for her. Maybe it was her fault. Maybe she was the unreasonable one, after all, and not her adolescent daughter. Maybe strength, consistency, purpose, did, as she believed, give some children – like Hector – security, but others, who were already strong themselves, needed something else. Something she was incapable of giving.

It was necessary, sometimes, to concentrate on your stroke, in order to lose yourself once again within it. A man came slowly up from behind her, into the compass of her vision. He pulled gradually ahead of her. He'd only just arrived: it was unlikely he'd keep up that pace. She hoped that she'd have time to prove this before she completed her schedule, and begin slowly to overtake him.

Another man was sitting on the side and lowering himself in at the shallow end, up ahead: right in front of her. Was he oblivious?

He had on long, baggy, apologetic shorts, like the ones Ezra wore. He couldn't be serious, that much was certain. If a man wore anything other than a pair of tight trunks, with its jumble of genitalia, you could be sure he only came to flounder around. Sheena couldn't see the point of that. She would swim forty lengths, she always did, and then she'd get out, and for the next two or three days her body would belong to her. She would inhabit it; it would fit her.

The next day, the house seemed empty when Hector came home from school. He went to the bathroom. The smell of pear drops hung in the steamy atmosphere. Torso wrapped in a blue towel, Blaise sat on the edge of the bath, painting her toenails a bright red.

'Hey!' she objected. 'Anyone ever teach you respect for people's privacy?' She stood up.

'The door was unlocked,' Hector pointed out. 'It wasn't even closed.'

'I left and came back. And now, see? I'm leaving again.'

'Stop looking in the mirror then.'

Blaise gathered together items of her toilette. A make-up bag. Nail clippers. 'I'm not.'

'I've seen you,' Hector said. 'Looking at those lumps.'

'Rubbish.' She lifted the floormat and draped it over the side of the bath.

Hector began stepping agitatedly from one foot to the other.

'There is a loo downstairs, you know,' Blaise told him. 'Anyway, you can go ahead and use this one. I don't care.'

Hector narrowed his eyes. 'You're always looking in the mirror.'

'I hate looking in the mirror.'

'Don't blame you. It's not a pretty sight.'

Blaise passed Hector in the doorway. She stopped and stared at him. 'Look. Who's. Talking.'

'Well, I don't, see, Blaise, and that's the difference.'

Blaise groaned. 'Oh, shut it, Hec, you little spod. Out of the way.'

'Where are you going, anyway?'

'None of your business.'

'I was only asking.' Hector trailed along the corridor after his sister. 'I'm just a bit bored, that's all.'

Blaise stopped outside her room, and turned. 'Actually, I'll let you come with me if you like.'

Hector frowned.

'If you promise not to tell Mum or Dad.'

'Promise what?'

Blaise sighed impatiently. 'Do you or not?'

Hector thought about it a moment. 'Promise.'

'If you break your promise what happens?'

'I'll rot in hell.'

They walked up Churchill Drive towards Woodstock Road.

'What are we doing?' Hector asked.

'We're meeting someone,' Blaise told him.

'Who?'

'Shush and you might find out.'

They crossed Woodstock Road at the lights, and walked up to Oakthorpe Road.

'Blaise?'

'Hec, I said you'll find out.'

'No, this is about something else,' Hector claimed.

Blaise looked at Hector as they strolled. 'Well, what?' she said.

'What did it feel like?'

'Did what?'

'When you hit him. That man. Were you scared? I was just wondering, that's all.'

Blaise looked away. 'I don't want to talk about it.'

'Did you want to hurt him? Was that part of it?'

Blaise stopped walking. She stared at the ground. Then she turned to her brother. 'You're just like Dad sometimes, you know that? I said I don't want to talk about it. Now stop talking. You're no use to me if you can't keep quiet.'

They crossed Banbury Road at the pedestrian lights. Blaise

approached a tall, thin man who was leaning against the brick flowerbeds outside the Co-op. He smiled when he saw her.

'Who's this?' Zack asked. 'Is this your brother? Yes, I can see the resemblance.'

Blaise grimaced. 'Don't flatter yourself,' she told Hector. She turned to Zack and said, 'I thought he could watch.'

Zack took a sheet of paper from a shopping bag, and handed it to Blaise, who looked at it and frowned.

'Only twenty?' she asked.

'We've got someone else coming after you, and then there's me,' he explained. 'We want to get them all on without being stopped.'

'No scenes,' Blaise said.

'Not today. That's the plan.'

Hector noticed a badge on the man's lapel, with the letters *PSC*, and he leaned nearer to see the small words underneath. Zack noticed Hector's movement, looked down, and removed the badge.

'Well spotted,' he said. 'Don't want to give the game away, do we?'

Hector accompanied Blaise along the grey precinct set back from the road, and into Marks & Spencer. 'We're buying fruit,' she told him. 'Get a trolley.'

'Who's that man?' Hector asked.

'Get the trolley.'

Hector caught up with his sister. 'What are we after?'

'Here,' she said. 'I got a list off Mum. Fruit and veg first. Have a look. You can choose what sorts.'

Hector pushed the empty trolley slowly along the stall, studying the apples and pears, peaches and grapes, bananas and kiwi fruit. He tried to work out why every loose apple in one box had a sticker on it that read, *Braeburn*. It didn't make any sense. Did some adults follow strict diets that ordered them not only to eat an apple, but a particular variety? There was a box of *Pink Lady* apples with the same identification. Hector couldn't fathom it. It would be like every chocolate button in a bag having a sticker on it, saying, *Milk Chocolate:* you'd have to remove the sticker from each button before you could eat it.

Hector couldn't decide what he wanted. He was ambling back towards Blaise when he saw that she was peeling stickers off the sheet of paper the man had given her and attaching them to transparent plastic boxes. Inside each box nestled four large, identical nectarines. On each sticker were the words, *BOYCOTT ISRAELI GOODS.*

11

Tennis in Summertown

Friday 11 July

From below the horizon the sun had breathed pink and turquoise into a vaulting sky, and now was rising. It poked its light between the spires and towers of town, sending fingery shadows across the grass of the fourteen Alexandra Tennis Courts. There was a tang of moisture in the air, left over from the night's thirsty dreams, an aftertaste of dew on the surface of the earth: the weather remained dry and hot during this, the first summer of the twenty-first century that dazzling days duplicated themselves for week after week, until England appeared to be creaking.

Four middle-aged men in scruffy shorts and loose tops strode past the chestnut trees. Simon Carlyle let his bike fall against the fence, then he and Dan and Ian tossed their padded racket holders and tubes of fluoro balls over the wire fence around the council courts.

Another night without rain, another bright lifeless morning, and it was fine, Ezra Pepin reckoned, it was splendid, to be up before the day showed its hand. He was the youngest of the four, his companions already into their mid and late forties: he rolled plastic bottles of Isis Water under the fence while the others launched themselves at it. They grabbed the stanchions around the pad-locked gate and hooked their fingers in the grey diamond mesh, glancing down for footholds. As if they could scale the fence like nimble scrumping lads. Could overcome gravity. Not this time, though, and no more. They were men of authority, in their prime, risen as far as they were likely to. Inelastic limbs, obdurate joints betrayed them; their girth weighed them down; so that as they scrambled up they found they had to use all the brute, inelegant male force with which they'd been endowed to heave their loosening bulk up and over the top of the fence.

They scrabbled and dropped to the ground. Planting their feet on the surface of the green spinning earth the men stood up straight, and breathless, and recomposed themselves, looking not at each other but out across the white, inviting grids arrayed before them on the vast lawn.

Ezra climbed over, and landed beside the others. 'They've marked the courts out for us,' he observed. 'Maybe we'll have less of your dodgy line calls this week, Ian.'

'The chalk never lies,' said Simon, in a bumptious tone that suggested it often did.

'I love the smell of lime chalk in the morning,' said Dan, breathing deeply, as they broke into their usual pairs, Ezra with Simon, and knocked up from the back, belting balls at each other that were soon trawled by the net.

'Give me a volley,' Ian called across to Simon as he jogged forward.

'Try a serve?' Ezra shouted a moment later, batting some balls to Dan. Their voices were fresh, hopeful, sonorous in the empty morning.

'Rough or smooth?' Simon offered.

The men grunted and lunged, scampered to and fro. Games went against serve. Simon's service action was that of a madcap English inventor who'd spent years perfecting it in his garden shed, only to watch it fall to pieces in the open air. He tossed the ball towards his shoulder, then crouched down to swipe it. It looked like he was swatting a fly, straight into the net. One time in ten the ball shot over, back-spin grabbed it by its scruff and drove it into the ground, and an unplayable ace sped past the receiver. For his ground shots, instead of stepping aside in preparation for hitting a tennis ball, opening his body for a wide sweet swing, Simon stepped *into* the flight-path, and had to dig the ball out of his body with the racket, producing soft lobs his opponents generally failed to put away.

'It's tennis, Jim,' Ezra cursed, when for once Ian smashed one past him. 'It's tennis, Jim, but not as we know it.'

Simon was well partnered: Ezra scurried after every lost cause, his shirt awash with sweat. 'Out!' he called, early and loud, just before a shot of Dan's landed on the line. Overruled, Ezra was left to rail at the injustice of the straight white lines; at puffs of chalk conspiracies.

The men assured themselves they could play metronomic, transatlantic tennis if they wanted to, echoing shots back and forth for hour after tedious hour. Any club member all in white could do that. No, the four of them were mavericks, cursing loudly when a shot failed to match the magnificence of which they were capable.

Early commuters cutting through from Middle Way to Woodstock Road, dog walkers letting their pets off the leash for a loop around the tennis courts, would stand stock-still and peer at the players from a distance, as if given just a little more information they'd be able to make sense of what they were seeing. The inexplicable trajectory of the ball; the ambition of these untutored eccentrics. As if the Corinthian ideal were insufficient. It wasn't enough to be a sporting loser, Ezra conceded, a happy amateur, you had to be useless, too, you had to carry the handicap of being stubbornly self-taught, of never acquiring the most basic technique, so that every single ball towards you was a fresh challenge, each shot the first you've ever played, you're forever improvising, and the only thing that saves you is your English schoolboy's eye for a ball, aided by the occasional shameless fluke of physics. All of which explained why tennis was an ideal sport, inspired and clumsy as life itself.

In the second set play improved: Dan found his range, Simon made fewer errors, Ian got his eye in, and Ezra entered the zone: he anticipated his opponents' perfect passing shots and, stepping forward, interrupted them, to thump solid volleys from the sweet spot in the middle of his racket. He hit groundstrokes with the ball still on the rise, sending it back unexpected as a rabbit punch. The match was tied at one set all.

The men gathered to swig from their water bottles and to confer. 'It's ten-past eight,' Simon puffed.

'How's your back?' Ezra asked.

'Holding up.'

'Plenty of time for a decider,' Dan gasped, lighting a cigarette.

'Let me call Carol,' Ian decided, groping in his rucksack.

'I can manage another set,' Ezra agreed. 'Work can wait for us, can't it?'

'There's no way,' said Simon, 'I'm stopping with those two fellows on the up.'

In the third set the standard reverted to that of the first, then plummeted further. Ian found himself unable to achieve any power: however fiercely he wielded his racket the ball floated over the net. It was a tactical masterstroke: Ezra and Simon pounced on these gifts, and blasted them wide and long. Simon grew more agitated, so that he was soon trying to hit balls directly in front of him, while Ezra's game simply unravelled.

'Eat that!' he yelled, making winners that turned in front of his eyes into wild losers. At 2–5, 0–30 he hit a firm, swinging deep serve and followed it in. Ian managed a feeble return, a gentle chip at which Ezra took a lungeing, hopeless swipe. In slow motion, the ball drifted gently beyond his reach.

'Fuck!' Ezra yelled in the bright morning. He hurled his racket at the back fence, where with a loud crack the guaranteed-for-life titanium frame fractured like bone.

'Game over, chaps,' said Simon.

Ezra joined the others gathering their stuff, bearing his broken racket sheepishly. 'You big girl,' Dan cursed him.

'You just robbed yourselves of the possibility,' Ian said, 'of one of the great comebacks in the modern era.'

They strolled across the grass, knowing they were late for work, asserting their seniority, their independence, their sense of perspective in these hectic times, and they clambered tiredly back over the fence, and set off in various directions for bikes and cars and the working day awaiting.

Ezra Pepin had a shower at home and got to work at nine thirty. Walking from the bike rack he realised how much he was still sweating in the heat and thought he might need another shower in the basement gym. But then he entered the air-conditioned building and soon felt more at ease.

'Where have you been?' Chrissie demanded, when he reached the Operations area. 'I emailed you. I tried your home. I tried your mobile.'

'Switched off. Sorry.'

'The CEO's looking for you.'

'I thought he was in Berlin this week.'

'He's back, apparently.'

Gideon Juffkin came over. 'He says you're the first person he wants to see,' he frowned.

'Be gone,' Ezra replied.

'Ezra!' said Jim Gould. 'Where have you been? How do you think this looks for us? Gideon: buzz through to the Chief Executive's PA. Tell him Ezra's here and available.'

'Jim,' Ezra said. 'What does he want?'

'He didn't tell me.' Gould said. He glanced over his shoulder.

The three of them stood in an anxious crescent around Ezra's desk, watching him in jittery silence. Well, to hell with them, Ezra decided, as he climbed the wide stairs at a leisurely pace. He'd been summoned by the new boss: he was damned if he was going to panic about it. Their obsequiousness was demeaning; it was pathetic – although, he reminded himself, *they* weren't leaving Isis Water and going off to Brazil in a couple of months' time. He was a fortunate man.

The Chief Executive of Isis Water was standing by the window when his male secretary ushered Ezra Pepin into his office. He turned abruptly and strode over, arm extended.

'Mr Pepin,' he said.

'Good morning, Mr Kuuzik.'

'It's time you called me Klaus,' he smiled. 'And I will call you Ezra, if I may?'

'Of course.'

Kuuzik was a couple of inches shorter than Ezra, with cropped brown hair, a tanned complexion and pale blue eyes. He wore a thin grey cotton suit which fitted him so well that Ezra's own bespoke threads might as well have been off the peg from some Cornmarket store.

'Come, let us sit down, Ezra. Tell me, your people couldn't find you.' He held his arms out to the sides. 'They didn't know where you were.'

Had his new boss just begun to tell him off? Ezra wondered. That was one thing he didn't need, especially since it was highly unlikely he'd see him again in the next couple of months, and certainly not ever afterwards.

'They knew where I was,' Ezra said. 'Friday morning. They were covering for me, Klaus. I was playing tennis.'

'Tennis?' Kuuzik's face broke into a smile. 'I think it's a good idea to exercise before work. I think it's essential.'

'You do?'

'Every day.'

'You play tennis?'

Kuuzik lowered his head into his rising shoulders, in a gesture of modesty. 'I play many sports,' he said. 'My trainer keeps me from getting bored. But please. Would you like a tea, coffee?'

'Coffee, yes.'

'Espresso? Cappuccino?'

'Cappuccino would be good.'

Kuuzik went to the door and asked his secretary to bring the drinks. 'Of course, this will be Italian cappuccino, Ezra. I cannot understand how you can serve in England this huge mug of filter coffee and brown foam and call it cappuccino. Cappuccino is an espresso with *ein bischen* of frothy milk added.'

'It is?'

'Yes. You will see.' Kuuzik ushered Ezra towards one of a pair of awkward, angular chairs designed, perhaps, to keep tired executives awake. When he sat down, however, the chair received him with such a comfortable embrace that he suffered a kind of corporeal astonishment. 'But first, Ezra,' Kuuzik said, 'I want you to tell me. How did you know?'

'Know what, Klaus?'

'Don't be reticent. You must have done a good deal of research. Did you find someone who used to work with me?'

'You're referring to the paper I wrote?'

'Of course.'

Ezra took a deep breath. 'I did no research at all, Klaus. That's the truth. I thought I would risk the opportunity to look beyond the constraints within which we customarily labour and speculate. It was self-indulgent, I know.'

'But what you said about making the world a better place?'

'I don't know why I said that.' Ezra shrugged apologetically. 'It came out.'

Kuuzik frowned, then let his face relax into a smile. He gazed at Ezra, wondering, perhaps, whether or not to believe him.

'You didn't speak to someone from Leipzig?'

'Leipzig?' Ezra asked.

Kuuzik smiled, as if he still wasn't sure, Ezra's apparent ignorance being too unlikely. 'The Graduate School of Management,' he said.

Klaus Kuuzik spoke with the accent of one who'd rehearsed his second language in different countries, in a quiet, constrained voice. Ezra leaned towards him. He discerned the aroma of Kuuzik's aftershave: it was a subtle musky scent he'd not been aware of before.

Kuuzik raised his arms and his shoulders a little; enough to suggest he'd come to a decision; to reveal something, perhaps. But before he could say anything his secretary entered.

'Ah, coffee, Bernhard.'

When Ezra sipped his he said, 'You're right, Klaus, what our machines call cappuccino is an abomination.'

'Mine is a macchiato. Literally it means the hot milk is *stained* with coffee.' Kuuzik leaned back in his seat and smiled. He kept steady eye contact, when he was both speaking and listening. It demanded the same from Ezra. Usually, he found such intensity draining: someone looking in your eyes, gazing into you. With Kuuzik, however, he felt energy coming the other way. He also thought that the other man's eyes were not strictly blue, as he'd first imagined, but, when you really studied them, almost green.

'How old are you, Ezra? You are thirty-seven, thirty-eight?'

'Thirty-nine,' Ezra smiled.

'I am a year younger. I suspect a man doesn't really know what it is to be a man until he's forty.'

'I don't mind the sound of that,' Ezra admitted. He found his focus of attention narrowing, gradually, towards Kuuzik's eyes. They were neither blue nor green, he saw now, but both. Aquamarine. He was reminded briefly of the sea off a Dalmatian island he and Sheena had swum in, on their backpacking honeymoon: Kuuzik's eyes were the colour of ocean you could see the bottom of, as if light were reflecting back up through them, from some inner source.

'Yes, but then we don't have long, I believe. Forty to what? Sixty? And soon we are not so much of a man any more. That is why we have to achieve a great deal in those years.'

'You think so?'

'I know it. Ezra, your paper is intriguing. I have been told also about your other work. I am impressed with what I hear of your input into children's sales.'

'Thank you,' said Ezra. There was a sudden warmth in the room. In the air around Ezra's face. He suspected he was blushing. For the first time in years. 'I assisted the marketing guys a little.'

'Yes, I like this flexibility. Sales, marketing. Operations, policy. Overlapping areas. But the children, it was an impressive project. You have children?'

'Three,' Ezra nodded.

'Me, too,' Klaus said. 'Three girls. You have daughters?'

'One.'

'We'll have to institute Bring Your Daughter to Work Day. We did it once a year in Vancouver.'

'I'd have to work hard to persuade our Blaise to come in.'

'Oh, don't worry, Ezra, we make it fun for her. So tell me, what was your involvement in the campaign?'

'Well, let me see.' Ezra cast his mind back. 'Children under ten, we discovered, drink more than three billion litres a year of soft drinks. Which they buy. They drink less than two per cent of that amount of water. Most of it from the tap, for free. It's an insanity, which we began to redress. The marketing guys targeted the parents: *What do you want to put in the kids' lunch box – fizzy pop or natural spring water? Make the healthy choice.*'

'Sensible enough.'

'What *we* did was to work directly with children, to generate authentic word of mouth. We worked our way into primary schools in target areas. Found out who were regarded as the coolest individuals amongst the senior year, the ten- and eleven-year-olds, and gave them bottles for free.'

'That was it?'

'That was it.'

'What was the effect?'

'Unquantifiable. But as you will know, our sales of Dinosaur Water far outstripped our competitors' similar items.'

'Good news, Ezra, for children's health. They're driven to school, watch TV, eat junk food, so they get fat. Skinny celebrities say, *Look like us.* So they starve themselves. They can't find a middle path. How can they?'

'All we're constrained by, after all,' Ezra said, 'is a small matter of the need to make a profit.'

Kuuzik gazed at the far wall of his office. There was a very large abstract painting, the shape of CinemaScope. It could almost, it struck Ezra, be a portrait of the colour of Kuuzik's eyes.

He turned back to Ezra. 'The money will follow,' he said. 'It's not difficult to make money. People who can't make money shouldn't be in business. They are not needed.'

Kuuzik's eyes, Ezra considered, had something remote about

them. It was as if although he was fully engaged with what the two of them were discussing, he really was, maybe he was also thinking of other things. The eyes of a man who wants something more.

'Consider this, please, Ezra,' Kuuzik was saying. 'Coca-Cola sold worldwide because it was American. Because the whole world aspired to be American. Not because Coke is in some way universal. Now the backlash has begun, of course. They won't recover. We all want to find a universal selling point. Global appeal. Let us say, for a bottled water, sold all over the world. Do you think that's possible?'

'I don't see how it can be,' Ezra said. 'But I should admit that my background, in anthropology, means that I'm naturally attracted to what is specific in a culture. Cultural diversity is what interests me.'

Kuuzik's attention upon Ezra was strangely unwavering. He listened to every word Ezra spoke, and every word he spoke drew Ezra's attention towards him. He made Ezra feel as if Kuuzik was discovering more than a colleague; he'd recognised a friend. They leaned close as they talked, in what had become an intimate but excited whisper. The smell of Kuuzik's breath had a resinous edge to it, sappy, alpine.

'It might be possible,' Ezra said, 'to have a universal product, but one whose identity changes from one region to another.'

Klaus nodded gratefully, suggesting that this was exactly what he'd been hoping to hear. He drew closer, as if the room might be bugged. 'I'm putting together a team,' he said quietly. 'I want to move fast. This is why I'm looking for men and women in their prime and ready to do something, how shall we say, extraordinary. I want you in my team, Ezra Pepin.'

Ezra tried to recall whether anyone had spoken to him in this way in years. Ever. His mother, but she didn't count. His history teacher at Devizes Comprehensive, Mr Ash: his face ballooned in Ezra's mind's eye, circular behind black-rimmed glasses, Ash took groups of five or six boys in his Volkswagen camper van on eye-opening weekend field trips to Avebury, Stonehenge, the Cerne Abbas Giant, that were for Ezra Pepin full of wonder at the lost

233

people who'd built these monuments. The teacher restraining himself – so far as Ezra knew – from anything more than hands lingering on a boy's shoulders. Kneading them gently. At Oxford? No, apart from Ash's lonely encouragement no one had spoken to him as Kuuzik did now, and made energy emanate from the pit of Ezra's stomach, the embers of something kindling, some hope that had almost gone out.

'The truth is,' said Kuuzik, 'that I got the short straw. Not officially, of course. To come here was for me a promotion. But England? I understand how Julius Caesar felt. Sent to the outpost of the empire, no? So what I want is for us to show the cynics in Berlin something a little special. More than special. If I have the right people we can do anything. We can change the world, Ezra, yes?'

Ezra saw and felt Kuuzik's eyes looking into his own. He felt undefended; that he'd been identified by a rare individual as an equal. Klaus saw through Ezra's eyes, past the hiding places where we conceal our fear and desire and discontent, to where he could see another dynamic and greedy man asleep inside Ezra Pepin, capable of incredible things.

'Yes,' Ezra said. 'Oh, yes. We really can.'

It was lunchtime, in the squat on Islip Road. Blaise unwrapped butter and cheese and bread, unbagged the fruit, and placed them on the newspaper beside her. There was no furniture. She sat cross-legged on the wooden floor. An indoor picnic. Zack filled two enamel mugs with water in the kitchen, and brought them back. Blaise was glad that neither Jed nor Bobby was here; she didn't know where they were, and Zack didn't say. Maybe they'd moved on somewhere else and left him here, alone. The sun poured through the dusty French windows on to the floorboards.

Blaise had had to get out. She'd lain in bed all morning with the curtains closed. Her brain wouldn't work any more. It was like a swamp bubbling inside her skull, stupefied. Was she going to change into her future adult self, or did that adult self already exist inside her? The question oozed around her head, into consciousness and out of it and in again.

When, finally, she'd stirred, Blaise had found herself in front of the bathroom mirror: it was a place where her face altered from one day to the next. Her cranium was changing shape. Her jaw was flatter than it used to be; her eyes had lost their symmetry. Pressing through hair, Blaise ran her fingers over bone on the top of her head, expecting to find some horrific knob or ridge that would give away the havoc being wrought inside. Tumour, probably. Haemorrhage, perhaps. She'd looked the words up in the family medical encyclopaedia. Bovine spongiform encephalopathy, quite possibly. She gazed at dark crescents beneath eyes that looked reproachfully back at her. It was odd. She studied her reflection yet what Blaise felt, above all, was unknown; unseen. She was fourteen. She wondered whether she was a shell, coming close to cracking.

Zack put the mugs of water down next to Blaise, on the other side from the food, and sat cross-legged himself, facing her. As if he'd underestimated how long his legs were, their bent knees touched, and each shrank a fraction back from the other. He was wearing cut-off jeans, Blaise blue shorts. Zack cut the white bread with an unserrated carving knife: the blade hacked bluntly through the crust, splitting it. He tried again, with a thicker slice, and was more successful. His big, soil-lined hands, with their long fingers, had a certain autonomous competence about them, as if, even without orders from Zack's brain, there were many things they could do on their own.

It was too hot. Was every single window in the house closed? That was what it felt like. The air was stifling. Zack ought to open the French windows. Blaise realised she had too many clothes on, having thrown a cardigan over her blouse before she'd gauged the day. Her skin prickled. Her face felt red, and ugly. There was a sudden throb in her thigh: the mobile in her cardigan pocket. She ignored it, hoping its alert was not evident to Zack. She didn't want to have to justify not answering it. It was probably Akhmed.

With the big carving knife, Zack spread butter on the slices of bread. Smoothly, patiently. There was nothing to betray any expectation he might have that she should do anything to help. Well, perhaps there was only the one knife: he used it to cut cheese, too. He laid strips of cheese on each slice of buttered bread, then he put the knife down, and rested his hands in his lap.

Blaise stared at her knees; at the millimetres between her knees and his. When she looked up at Zack, he was smiling at her. He seemed to have been waiting for her eyes, just as she'd been convinced he had. She liked the way Zack, his blond moustache crinkling, smiled: it was as if he knew what Blaise was thinking, and thought the same thing. Unless, she admitted, his smile didn't mean that at all. Maybe it meant he was too shy to say or do anything more. Even though he was almost ten years older than her.

Blaise didn't know what Zack's smile meant. She wanted him to do something that might reveal what its meaning had been, so that in retrospect she could understand. In psychic response, he reached out his right hand, and placed it on her left knee. Blaise felt a quiver of warmth surge up her thigh.

Zack's smile appeared sad. He shook his head, slowly. 'You're thirteen,' he said.

'No,' Blaise told him quickly. 'Fourteen.'

She knew he was going to pull his hand away. She put her left hand on top of his hand.

Zack's smile began to mean something else now. It was wry; rueful. 'It's dangerous,' he said.

'Why?' she asked. 'What do you mean?' She knew what he meant. But until he explained, she could pretend that she didn't.

Zack took her hand, and held it. In doing so, he'd lifted his hand from her knee, but Blaise didn't mind. His fingers were interlaced with hers, the pads of each of their fingers on the back of the other's hand, Zack's thumb massaging her palm. The whole surface of her hand was alive with feeling; it was covered by tiny spots that tingled with pleasure. Maybe this was why Zack had been smiling: he'd known he had the power to activate these pleasure spots with his touch.

With his free hand Zack took a piece of bread and cheese. 'Come on,' he said. 'Let's eat.'

Copying Zack, Blaise folded over a slice of bread to make a sandwich. They chewed mouthfuls of food slowly, holding hands. Blaise stroked Zack's skin. He kneaded her flesh. Blaise drank water from one of the enamel mugs. She watched her fingers roam over the soily knuckles and squeeze the veined back of Zack's large hand. She was starving, but she didn't want to eat any more, but she was so hungry, but . . . She lifted Zack's hand to her mouth, took his middle finger and bit into it. Zack let out a gasp, but he didn't pull his finger away. She grasped the finger in her fist and fed it into her mouth. She took it all. Sucking it, she knew that this was what she was hungry for.

Blaise braved a glance at Zack. He wasn't smiling any more. He looked hot, and scared, and his eyes seemed bigger than they had moments before. The pupils were dilated. As she licked his finger, it seemed to Blaise as if the taste and the sensation could feed her as well as any food. Zack slid his finger out of her mouth, and pulled his hand from her grip. Blaise blanched with disappointment. Zack reached around the back of her head and pulled her towards him.

Zack's lips and mouth were slippery, his tongue fell upon hers and somehow she knew what to do with it now. Her eyes were closed. Their tongues connived in urgent slithering conversation. There were colours on the inside of her eyelids. Purple, red, liquid colours melding, not just in her eyes but all over her body, indigo and crimson warm and melting from her mouth down through her torso.

It took Blaise some moments to realise that Zack had withdrawn. She opened her eyes. He was sitting back, breathing hard. He looked confused, like a soldier given an inexplicable order. He began to shake his head. 'No,' he muttered, and looked at her. 'No, Blaise,' he said. 'You're too much, girl. We can't do this.' He shuffled back some inches across the wooden floorboards. 'You're too much.'

When Ezra cycled home that evening, he resolved not to mention to Sheena his meeting with the new Chief Executive. Twelve years he'd been working for Isis Water, cruising with his colleagues as before their eyes their product became a profitable necessity in the lives of consumers. All over the country people were paying hard-earned money to drink water from a bottle instead of out of the tap. Oh, sure, Isis Water had to battle for its market share but Ezra Pepin and his colleagues had found their prestige growing and their incomes rising with little effort.

And now, just as, finally, he was returning from this illusory world to his real life, a bright unexpected prospect seemed to have opened up before him. The timing of it bamboozled him. His destiny was being toyed with.

Fridays were Ezra's evenings to cook, and the family ate together, to be joined, today, by Jack Carlyle, who when Ezra came home was teaching Louie to play chess.

'No, the *knight* eats them on this level,' he was patiently explaining. 'The bishop *stabs* them.' The boys lay on their sto-machs, knees bent behind them, bare feet swaying in the air.

'Where's Hector?' Ezra demanded, surprised that it was Jack and not Louie's brother who was initiating him into the virtual violence.

'Upstairs,' said Jack, his voice crackling, the tremors of a boy's voice in the process of breaking. 'I suppose.'

Ezra welcomed Friday evenings. It was where the weekend began, and he'd almost always managed to protect it from the encroach-ment of work. It struck him now how much more demanding life would be in a team with Klaus Kuuzik, and for the first time that day he didn't feel regretful that he'd not be able to join it.

'Help!'

Panic zipped through Ezra's body, a surge of electric adrenaline.

'Help, Daddy!'

He was at the stairs in two strides. It was Blaise's voice. Using the banister for extra leverage and momentum, Ezra took the stairs three at a time, and reached the top. Blaise was sitting on the landing. With her right arm she held Hector in a head-lock. Any sign of sweat or struggle was long gone: they appeared both to be waiting for something.

Blaise looked up at her father. 'Help me, Daddy,' she pleaded.

It was definitely Hector in that arm-lock, Ezra confirmed, although all he could see was the brown hair on the top of Hector's head.

'Come on, Daddy. Please!' Blaise appeared genuinely afraid, Ezra could see it in her eyes. He tried hard to figure it out. Was there some kind of ventriloquism going on? Was Hector using Blaise's mouth, her voice, to communicate?

'What are you doing?' Ezra asked his daughter.

She looked distressed. 'If I let him go,' she said, 'he'll punch me.'

Hector tried suddenly to wriggle and heave his way loose. A long grunt broke free from his lips. Blaise held her grip tight. It looked like a game, a variation of a bucking bronco. It wound down, and they were still again.

'Hector wouldn't admit there's no such thing as life after death,' Blaise said.

Ezra tried to understand how such a dispute might have led to the crisis displayed before him. I'm only about four hundred years too late, he thought. 'I beg your pardon?'

'I told him that when he admits it,' Blaise said, 'I'd let him go.'

'Do you have any idea how ridiculous that sounds?'

'But he only said there was,' Blaise explained, indignant, 'to annoy me.'

Hector was kneeling, his forehead almost touching the landing carpet; being forced to pray for the heresy of insisting there was an afterlife.

'I was only joking,' Blaise told her father. 'But then he got all furious. If I let him go he'll kick me, I know he will. Help, Daddy.'

'No, he won't,' Ezra said. 'Will you, Hec? Let him go.'

Frowning, Blaise relaxed her grip. Hector shuffled backwards, and pulled himself slowly loose. He climbed to his feet.

'Why do this?' Ezra asked. 'Does it have any part in normal human discourse, do you think?'

Blaise shrugged. Hector stared at the carpet. He'd grown accustomed to its sight, did not wish to relinquish it.

'Do you have any idea how long you two will be brother and sister? Always.'

'He knows I love him, really,' Blaise said. 'Don't you, Hec?'

Hector made no reply. He walked slowly past them, and stepped downstairs.

Ezra slipped free from his working clothes. He worried whether it might be possible for his daughter to have some renegade trace of psychosis in her personality. But as he showered he let such idle anxiety be rinsed away. He pulled on shorts and Hawaiian shirt and, feeling oddly energised by the confusions of his day, trotted down the stairs. Louie was now a spectator, watching Hector and Jack do digital battle. Blaise lay on the sofa, browsing through a large photographic book.

'Hey,' Ezra said. 'Life is good, kids.'

'No,' said Louie. 'Life not good, Daddy. Cos there is dying.'

'Well, yeh, okay,' Ezra conceded. 'There is that, Peanut. But I mean, apart from death, life is great, isn't it? Now, who wants to help Dad rustle up some supper?'

It was a question that brought no response, but Ezra was in no mood to care. His custom on Fridays was to conjure a meal from whatever he found in the fridge and the cupboards, before the weekly internet order from Tesco was delivered on Saturday morning. It was a challenge that was half a culinary and half a survivalist test – either of which, Sheena reckoned, would have strained a more competent cook than her husband.

Ezra found enough vegetables to fill a roasting pan so he whacked the oven up high, and set to peeling parsnips, potatoes, carrots, peppers and garlic. There was no cheese in the fridge but there were eight eggs and a little bacon, so he whisked an omelette, and there were plenty of salad ingredients. And in the freezer he found a couple of packets of half-baked baguettes, so he crushed some cloves of garlic: he was mashing them with butter, garlic bread being always popular in their house, when Sheena came in.

240

'Hi, Ez,' she said, and leaned forward to kiss him. Her hands were full with bags and his were messy with food, so that their only contact was with their lips. Yet there they met each other, briefly, with a true and fond acknowledgement. She smelled of perspiring skin and damp hair. How natural, Ezra thought, this marital affection; how absurd that for years they'd trudged along without it.

'Are there any beers in the fridge?' Sheena asked. 'I'm thirsty.'

'I think so. Stick some more in anyway.'

'This heat. We had to send Stella to Gills for another fan. What are you making?'

'Spaghetti Bolognese.'

'Surely we don't have any beef?'

'I'm making a vegetarian version.'

'But then it's not . . . wait a minute, there aren't any tomatoes left, are there?'

'That's nothing. There's no spaghetti either.'

'Oh, Ez,' Sheena sighed, with a certain rediscovered tolerance for his humour where for so long there'd been only irritation. 'How was your day, anyway?'

'My day? You don't want to . . .' Ezra hesitated. 'Well, actually,' he said, 'it was remarkable. The new CEO of the company, Herr Kuuzik, asked me in for a meeting.'

Sheena was clinking bottles of Pilsner in and out of the fridge. 'You want one?'

'I'll stick with wine, thanks. And he wants me to join a hand-picked team.'

'Oh. Team of what? Can you pass that opener?'

'Well, I'm not sure exactly,' Ezra admitted. 'He's an extraordinary man, darling, and he seems to want me with him.'

'Right. Big man in a small world.' She flipped the top off the bottle, which bounced on the tiled floor. 'Who can't have you. Was he disappointed?'

'What about?'

'Brazil, of course.'

'I didn't tell him.'

241

'You didn't. Why not? You want a sip?'

'Because I'll give a month's notice, a month before we go right?'

'I said a sip! Not a glug! Yes, of course, you're right. I suppose they'd fire you if you told them too early. "You have fifteen minutes to vacate your office and leave the building. Security!"'

Ezra wanted to disagree. 'It's possible,' he said. Such things happened, but he was sure they wouldn't do that to him.

'I'm going to drink what little's left of this through there.'

'But don't you think . . . ?' Ezra began.

'What?'

'I mean, it's a compliment, isn't it?'

'Who needs it? I mean, sure.' Sheena kissed him again. 'But I'd expect nothing less for you, sweetheart. How long's it going to be?'

'Oh, about ten minutes,' Ezra said.

'I'll be back to lay the table.'

'No, no, I'll do it,' Ezra said. 'Go on. I'll give you all a shout when everything's ready.'

12

The Path of Resistance

Saturday 12 July

Ezra lay on the sofa. It was seven-fifteen, and three mugs of strong coffee had gone the way of two bowls of cereal. His eyes ached. Caffeine was making his blood course gleefully around his veins; it seemed to be trying to whip up enthusiasm for some vascular sport. His head throbbed. He wondered what he'd done to deserve insomnia, this most self-punishing of afflictions. He tracked a pocket of wind along his colon until, with an agreeable report, it left his body.

It had been too long, he thought, since he'd seen his father. A neglectful son. If their grandfather were to die while they were in Brazil, he wondered, would the children remember him? For the Achia, Ezra recalled, the break between life and death was total: those who died were buried with proper ceremony and would depart freely on a journey to the Invisible Forest. They could then be forgotten with good grace. To forget the dead was the way it should be.

There were those, however, who went hunting and never returned; who, out in the forest, had died alone. Unable to leave this realm with due ceremony, the spirit of a dead person remained in limbo and, in his or her loneliness, would try to lure relatives, especially children, to join them. How to forget such a dangerous spirit? That was the challenge.

Funeral rites were enacted which included special chants, and the consumption of certain plants, designed not to commemorate the deceased but to wipe out all memory of him. Memories in the minds of the living were the very substance that kept a dead person in limbo: by fading from their thoughts, the ghost would be able to complete the process of departure. When trapped in limbo, however, a dead spirit would try to trigger unhealthy excitations – memories – in the minds of the living, in a vicious circle of unwanted attachment.

The aim of the Achia's funeral rites was a collective amnesia that wiped out earlier generations. Just as the dead were given no tombs in their own names, so they were allowed no memorials in the minds of those who survived them.

To live in the present was uncivilised, perhaps. Perhaps memory was civilisation. In its decline, Ezra mused, did every civilisation again reach this point? A collective, willed amnesia. A drift from history, out on to open seas. How wonderful it would be, he thought, if he, Ezra Pepin, could forget. Perhaps the new project would let him. Perhaps this was what was being offered by Klaus Kuuzik.

Eventually the members of the Pepin clan emerged, groggy in the sunlight besieging the house, as if from a fairy-tale sleep.

'How come the rest of my family can doze at the weekend,' Ezra moaned, 'when I wake up even earlier than during the week?'

'It's a leftover, Daddy, from your Catholic upbringing,' Hector suggested.

'I wasn't brought up a Catholic, Hector.'

'Catholic, Protestant,' said Blaise. 'Whatever.'

'Okay, Peanut,' Ezra explained, once Louie was fed and now, in the bathroom, washed and dressed and teeth brushed. 'Let's Daddy and you go to town.'

'Don't want to.'

'I need to pick up a couple of maps Blackwell's have got in for me. See, Sheena?' he called out. 'I'm on to it. Tell you what,

Louie, we can take a football and play in the Parks on our way home.'

'Want to play with my trains.'

'Come on, darling. Let's get in there before the crowd. It's after ten already.'

'Want to play with my trains,' Louie said, and walked out of the bathroom and into his bedroom.

Ezra followed his son, who was already crouched on the tiger rug taking sections of Brio out of the red plastic box in which Sheena or Ezra put them back practically every night. He coupled and extended the wooden track with whatever piece came to hand.

'Peanut,' Ezra said. 'Mummy and Blaise are going shopping now. I can't leave you here. You have to come with me.'

'Lou stay here,' Louie told the rug.

Ezra looked down, at his three-year-old boy improvising a railway line with a viaduct, a tunnel, bridges over easily imaginable rivers. It was obvious Louie was fitting one to the next automatically, in a sort of stubborn trance. His disobedient autonomy.

'I tell you what,' Ezra said, his joints cracking as he knelt beside Louie on the floor. 'I'll see if Mummy can pick up the maps. Shall I play trains with you? And you play football with me in a bit, out in the garden?'

It was immediately clear that Ezra had done the right, the good parent, thing: Louie's bent, frowning face rose, transformed by a smile it was barely large enough to contain. 'Yes!' he said.

Ezra had mixed a green salad in the white pasta bowl and placed it in the centre of the kitchen table, surrounded by cheeses and savoury pastries, dips and bread, when Blaise came home, giggling through the back door, accompanied by a woman with dark hair cut close around her head in a style that reminded Ezra of some glamorous TV character whom he couldn't quite identify. He didn't think he'd met this friend of Blaise's before, until he realised that it was her mother. His wife. Sheena.

'That is incredible,' he said.

'There's no need to gape, Daddy,' Blaise admonished him.

'I'm stunned,' he said.

'Yes, but do you like it?' Sheena asked.

'It makes you look ten years younger, darling,' Ezra said. Sheena had not changed her hairstyle, so far as he was aware, in all the years of their marriage. When she went to the hairdresser, he assumed she always said, *Same again, please*. 'I love it,' Ezra managed.

'Fashion show before lunch!' Blaise demanded. 'Wait till you see her clothes.'

Hector arrived home in time to join Ezra and Louie on the white sofa. Blaise and Sheena kneed and shoved the pink sofa back, and spread out clothes from bags that said *White Stuff, Cult Clothing, Fat Face*. Sheena removed her white T-shirt and blue jeans and stood there, a bewildered mannequin in bra and knickers, awaiting her daughter's instruction.

'Put those trousers on, with the slinky top,' Blaise ordered. Sheena obeyed. Thin cotton slacks hung loose to the floor; they made her look a little heavy, thought Ezra, but more comfortable in the heat than thick denim.

'Give us a twirl,' Ezra requested, and he and the boys applauded.

'Now show them with the other top,' Blaise decided. It was tight, short-sleeved, in ribbed layers, alternating ones of which were see-through. It made the most of Sheena's athletic arms and shoulders, her straight back. This sudden departure from her floppy T-shirts and faded jeans, along with the shock of the radical haircut, made Sheena look like a long-lost close relative of herself.

'You look fantastic, darling,' Ezra said.

Sheena smiled. 'I wasn't sure.'

'No, it's perfect, Mum,' Blaise assured her.

'My new fashion consultant!' Sheena said, in a ditzy tone of voice.

'They look like your kind of clothes, Blaise,' Ezra said.

'Excuse me?' she howled.

Hector laughed knowingly; whether at his father or sister, or even his mother, wasn't clear.

'Well, don't they?' Ezra frowned. 'That cool, sort of casual, put-together messy look?'

'Dad!' Blaise exclaimed.

'Thanks a lot,' said Sheena. 'Messy. Thank you.'

'I meant sexy, darling. You know.'

'It was months ago,' Blaise said. 'I never wear grunge chic now. Anyway, wait. There's more.'

When the fashion parade was over, when Ezra had witnessed Sheena transformed, in a morning's shopping with her fourteen-year-old adviser, into a younger and more modern woman than the wife he'd woken up next to at the beginning of the day, he asked whether or not Blaise hadn't been allowed to get something for herself.

'No.'

'Oh, go on, sweetie,' Sheena said.

'I don't want to.'

'Why not?'

'Oh, all right,' Blaise said, picking up a tiny plastic bag and taking it from the room. The others went through to start lunch. Sheena put on a CD she'd bought, thick with samba rhythm. Blaise re-entered the kitchen weaving to the beat, wearing a synthetic gold bikini.

'Mum chose it,' Blaise said.

'All set for the carnival,' Sheena approved, pulling Louie from his seat to join her on the kitchen dance floor, as Blaise gyrated round in a top that less covered than drew attention to her firm, emerging breasts, and a thong bottom. Her puppy fat had become a plumpness defined by adult curves, Ezra saw, joining the dance himself with a clumsy reluctance. Blaise possessed at one and the same time the sweet blunt body of a child and the enticing, declarative flesh of a woman. As if the whole of her body had undergone a sexual transubstantiation separate from its specific, zonal development. Ezra felt a despairing rent inside, torn between pride in his daughter's body and dismay at its inevitable plunder. The women had chosen for each other. Sheena had been altered superficially by their shopping trip, but it was negligible compared to Blaise's transformation from within.

*   *   *

247

They were eating fruit and yoghurt and no one had spoken for some minutes when Hector said, 'Mum?'

'Yes?'

'Dad?'

'What, Hector?'

Hector looked at Sheena, and then at Ezra. Then, gazing in the direction of the open doorway, he said, 'I don't want to go, really.'

Ezra hesitated, turned to Sheena.

'That's okay, Hector,' she said. 'It's fine to be a little anxious. I think we all are.'

'But I want to stay here.'

'But you can't stay, Hector, you know that. So you might as well not worry about it. We're all in this together, you see? We can lean on each other.'

'What is it, darling?' Ezra asked him. 'Why don't you want to go?'

'I just explained, Ezra,' Sheena said. 'It doesn't matter. Let's not rehash our worries.'

'Oh, I get it,' said Blaise, as if solving a riddle before anyone else did. 'You really don't know,' she asked Ezra and Sheena, 'do you?'

'Know what?' Ezra asked.

'It's so obvious,' Blaise said, shaking her head. 'I can't believe you don't know.'

'Well, let us in on the secret, honey,' said Sheena.

Blaise shrugged. 'He's gay.'

'What?' Sheena winced.

'He doesn't want to leave Jack.'

Hector let out a hyena kind of snorting laugh: angry, dismissive, outraged, embarrassed, all at once. It felt like he needed to say something, but couldn't take the risk of stopping this hiccuping snarl to do so, for fear of what else might happen. In the meantime his face reddened in front of their eyes, blood suffusing the capillaries beneath his skin and colouring it like crimson light.

Ezra leaned over to Hector and touched his arm. 'Don't take any notice,' he said, shaking his head.

Hector stood up and walked from the room, with as much slow dignity as he could muster.

'Number one,' Sheena told Blaise, 'it doesn't matter if Hector's gay. And number two, he isn't.'

'Did I say there's anything wrong with it?' Blaise asked innocently.

'None of us wants to leave our friends,' Ezra said.

'Oh, for God's sake,' said Sheena, getting up from the table and carrying her plate and glass to the sink. She opened the cupboard underneath and scraped remnants of pear and pineapple into the compost bin.

'Just cos he doesn't know he's gay yet,' Blaise said. 'I mean, of course he knows at some level. Boys can realise it when they're six or seven but still not have admitted it when they're fifteen.'

Sheena laughed. 'Blaise, honey,' she said. 'As far as fashion goes, you're my new guru. But just wait a while longer before you become a sex expert, okay? I've got to run, everyone. I'll see you later.'

They watched Sheena walk straight out of the kitchen door, grabbing her handbag off the side, and wheel her bike away along the side of the house.

'Mummy did say run,' Louie frowned. 'Mummy not run. Mummy do ride her bike.' He pottered off towards the sitting-room.

While Ezra rewrapped bits of cheese in their Tesco plastic, Blaise loaded the dishwasher. She did so slowly, as if she was a domestic robot, gradually losing battery power. Eventually, holding a dessert spoon in each hand, from which banana yoghurt splodged on to the terracotta floor tiles, Blaise said, 'I may not want to go either.'

'Darling.'

'I mean, you do know that, don't you, Daddy?'

Ezra took care to wrap each morsel in the same plastic it came in. 'Why wouldn't you want to, Blaise? Because of Akhmed?'

'Of course not,' she said, smiling to herself. 'Lots of reasons.'

Ezra opened the fridge door to return the wrapped portions to cool hygiene and the light's hideous clarity. 'We'll be back in two years, don't forget.'

'Two years?' Blaise said, in a tone of voice that suggested there was no point in Ezra trying to pull the wool over her eyes, that she was fourteen; she understood time now. 'I'll be old by then.'

Ezra smiled. 'Is time so precious, already?' he asked.

'Of course it is.'

'What is time?' Ezra shut the fridge. 'It's the unfolding of the essence of the universe.'

'Oh, Daddy,' Blaise said, impatiently. 'All I'm saying is: just supposing.'

That early evening, Sheena lay in a hot oily bath with her eyes closed. Ezra lowered the toilet lid and sat down on it. Nursing a cognac, he told Sheena of the rumblings of doubt and dissent inside the family. He made a little more of Louie's rebellion that morning than there was; identified a connection to Brazil where perhaps, he knew, there was none; tried to explain his acquiescence as the only thing possible to avert fury and tears – though on that point Sheena wasn't fooled.

'Ezra,' she said, 'I wish you would just put your foot down. It's not fair to children not to give them boundaries. You know that.'

He analysed Hector's reluctance to leave, using Blaise's accusation, or revelation, of their son's possible sexual orientation to identify this point in Hector's life as the most emotionally complicated and confusing, when he more than any of the rest of them needed stability, a secure berth.

Sheena lay still, eyes closed, breathing in the scent of lavender. Every now and again she shoved her backside along the bottom of the bath to agitate the hot water, and feel it wash across her. 'As we've explained, to each other and to him,' she said, 'for precisely all these reasons, this is the best possible time for Hec to live in a sexually liberated society.'

Sheena liked to soak in water so hot Ezra could use the same bath half an hour after she'd left it. Her face had coloured; perspiration glazed her countenance. She looked feverish.

Ezra rehashed his conversation with Blaise, which had carried on in a strange, niggly fashion. He didn't tell Sheena that Blaise had said, 'Akhmed's brother believes that gay people should be stoned.' She'd waited for her father's reaction to this provocation.

'I'm sure he doesn't,' Ezra had replied, calmly. 'That would be barbaric, don't you think?'

'Not to death, Daddy,' Blaise had said. 'Unless they'd, you know, done it.'

'Anyway,' she'd also said, and Ezra did repeat this to Sheena, 'Akhmed says if I don't want to go, I could move into their house.'

The first thing that came to Ezra's mind had been the image of Blaise in her gold bikini. 'I'm really not sure his father would be happy with that, darling,' he'd said.

'Ezra,' Sheena interrupted his recollection. 'I thought we'd gone over this. The family's like a car, and we're driving it. You and me. That's our job. The kids are in the back seat. One day they'll grow up and leave home, and get their own car if they want.'

'Yes, darling, but –'

'Or they can get a motorbike if they prefer,' Sheena said brightly. She had nothing against introspection: it was indulgence that annoyed her. It seemed like Ezra ignored how hard it was to bring up children. Any halfway happy family, Sheena considered, was a rare enough achievement. It didn't help to confuse things. 'And they can ride it on their own,' she said. 'Or have a passenger riding pillion. Hey!' Her hand shot out of the water, spraying Ezra across the floor. 'They could have someone in a sidecar. You don't see those around any more, do you, Ez? I remember whole families in them, when I was a child. Dad on the motorbike, Mum and one or two kids in the sidecar. So reckless, and romantic.'

'Sheena,' Ezra said sternly. 'Our children have anxieties. They have a right to them. Surely we owe it to them to address those anxieties.'

'Ezra Pepin,' Sheena laughed, causing the bathwater to sway, and her breasts to rise and slackly fall. 'Who do you think for the last fourteen years has been doing the anxiety addressing around here? What a cheek. Oh, and how about a mobile home? Or a caravan. They could have a caravan if they want. God, I hope not. What would that say?' Sheena raised her wet hands to her head and stroked her thick hair back from her face. 'Families as vehicles, though: nice poetic metaphor, isn't it? I think I'll tell Minty. She might like to use it. What do you think?'

Before Ezra could answer, Sheena pulled herself to her feet. The water fell from her body into the steaming bath. 'Pass the towel, Ezra,' she asked. She stood undissembling, beads of water collecting across her skin, a middle-aged Venus.

Ezra grasped the white towel from the floor, and held it open for her. The door swung open. Their youngest child burst in, scanned the scene, and said, 'Lou want bubbles!'

Cold water cascaded, and bubbles bloomed. Ezra knelt down, checked depth and temperature, and turned off the taps. Louie climbed in and wiped white foam on his father's face for a moustache, and a beard. Enjoying himself, he spread out, dabbing bubbles on Ezra's nose, and hair, and ears. Ezra could hear them hiss and whisper as they dissolved upon him.

Hector came in and changed into his pyjamas. Then he dropped the trousers, sat on the lavatory and read out loud from the paper.

'*A teenager has been sent to prison for three and a half years for smashing a glass into the face of a pilot in a jealous rage,*' he intoned softly.

Louie splashed his plastic ducks and other aquatic animals in the water. 'Where is that dolphin?' he asked, face scrunched in bemusement, hands outspread.

'I have no idea,' Ezra admitted. 'Where is that pesky fish?'

Louie looked aghast at his father's stupidity. 'That not a fish,' he said. 'That is a dolphin.' His hand shot up out of the bubbles, clutching the animal. 'Here it is!' he exclaimed. 'It was hiding!'

'*Dean Harper, 19, had met Miss Carter earlier in the evening of October the 4th, last year,*' Hector read, his voice soft yet insistent, '*and they had gone on to the George Street night spot. Harper walked across the dance floor and smashed a beer glass into Mr Nassim's face, causing serious cuts to his nose and jawline which may leave him scarred for life, Oxford Crown Court was told on Friday.'*

Perhaps Sheena was right, Ezra considered: she reckoned that Hector suffered some learning disorder that meant he needed to vocalise the written word in order to comprehend it. Louie had hold of his penis like a rubbery toy, to be stretched and sprung and elongated. An unbearable sight. Ezra pulled out the bath plug.

After Ezra had towelled Louie dry and put cream on his sore places, behind his left ear and right knee, and the boys had brushed their teeth, Hector went back downstairs while Ezra read Louie two books in bed. The boy then had a last drink of water, turned off his light, kissed his father and snuggled under his duvet.

On the way out of Louie's room Ezra noticed Blaise's light on, and pushed the door open. She was sitting up in bed. 'Tired?' he asked.

Blaise nodded. 'A bit.'

'What are you reading?'

Blaise lifted towards her the large book that had been resting against her knees, and let her legs stretch flat. *Aftermath*. A book of photographs, which Blaise had studied for a school project.

'Is it good?' he asked.

She thought about it. 'I don't know,' she said. 'It's sad. Daddy,' Blaise said, changing the subject, 'does Mum know I may not go to Brazil?'

'If you don't go, none of us go, darling,' Ezra told her. 'Mum believes you'll *want* to go.'

Blaise shook her head. 'You know what she says: *The path of resistance –*'

'*Is the point of resistance.* Yes, that's right.'

'So she should understand if I resist her, Dad.'

'I don't think that's what she had in mind,' Ezra said. He gestured towards the book. 'You think you might want to be a photographer one day?'

'Maybe, Daddy,' Blaise said.

'Or filmmaker, maybe. You should see the film Werner Herzog

253

made. I don't remember what it's called. Images of the oil fields of Kuwait burning.'

Blaise smiled up at her father.

'What's funny?' he asked.

'I don't know. Nothing, Daddy. Just that you don't want to listen.'

'Of course I do, darling. I'm interested in what you do and what you think. I mean, can I have a look at this book some time?'

'You can look at it now if you like. I was about to turn off the light.'

'Okay, honey, I will, thanks.'

Ezra leaned towards his daughter. There was a flavour of tangerines on her breath. He kissed her goodnight, and left the room.

Blaise had come across a copy of the book in the Westgate Library, browsing for an essay about visual representation of conflict, and she knew within a few pages that a borrowed copy would not be sufficient: despite the price of photography books, Blaise saved up pocket money and ordered a new copy from Blackwell's. A week after she finished the essay, she was notified that the book was waiting for her at the customer collection point on the second floor: there it was sealed in Cellophane, which, back home, she had sliced open very slowly with Sheena's Quick-Unpick.

This evening Ezra sat in his spare-room study and leafed through his daughter's book, in the light of the Anglepoise, while outside the summer dusk gathered, closing in around his house. *Aftermath* was a collection of images of bombed cities, by assorted photographers. Mounds of rubble in London during the Blitz, St Paul's untouched in the background, a beacon emitting its fragile bravado. The awesome obliteration of Nagasaki and Hiroshima, cities turned into the blueprints of cities. Leningrad, a destroyed mausoleum, impossible to believe ten or a hundred people, never mind millions, survived in its cellars through the terrible siege.

There was not a single person in the book; no human body, alive or dead.

Apocalyptic cityscapes. Grozny and Vukovar. The bare bones of

254

cities, blasted clean by the breath of dragons. In the book was an essay about the development of explosive material. Gunpowder and dynamite. Nitroglycerine, gelignite, TNT. Chemists in their laboratories, studiously separating elements. The A-bomb, the H-bomb. Plutonium, uranium. Napalm, Agent Orange. The urge towards eradication of one's enemies.

Black-and-white photographs: long avenues lined by shells of buildings. They looked pretty; decorative. Buildings gutted by fire: wooden joists, floorboards, roof beams burnt out, leaving hulks behind. Firebombed Dresden. Stalingrad bearing multiple scars, from long-range artillery to the Molotov cocktails and ricochet nicks of hand-to-hand fighting.

V-2s and doodlebugs. Bazookas and Exocets. Cluster bombs. Intercontinental ballistic missiles.

Although the book was a compilation of the work of many different photographers, there was some quality the images shared. The lens made sense of what it captured, with a particular lucidity. What was it? Ezra wondered. It felt almost like an avidity. As if a camera – whoever happened to be behind it – adored this spectacle: the destruction of what other human beings had built. As if the photographic frame understood the meaning of this sight; as photographic emulsion, perhaps, understood light, and shadow. Unless, Ezra reconsidered, the avidity was not in the medium, or the apparatus, but in the viewer's eye, and brought hungrily to each picture. He gazed, in a rapture of devastation. In colour: massive bridges taking off from the banks of wide city rivers, then not there any more, torn limbs. What had once been a bus, mangled in a suicide bombing, an impossible riddle in three dimensions.

Belgrade: the police headquarters, at first glance intact, until you realised that every single window was missing. Kabul: sandstone dwellings that looked more like the ruins of an ancient civilisation than a residential district levelled by smart missiles. Ramallah: a row of concrete houses whose fronts had been torn off, the rooms baring their contents like dolls' houses.

*   *   *

Ezra bent forward and lowered the book to the floor. Barely consciously, he slid it under his desk. He switched off the Anglepoise lamp and closed his eyes. For a while Ezra sat in the darkness. In his mind's eye he saw himself, his body – or could it be Blaise, and her body? – in the midst of scenes in the book. At the moments before the scenes became what the photographs showed, and the people vanished.

13

The Phoenix Cinema

Tuesday 22 July

One unclouded Tuesday noon, Ezra Pepin and Klaus Kuuzik strode side by loose-shouldered side along Hythe Bridge Street, and on past Gloucester Green bus station, then Worcester College. Although he was wearing a jacket, Kuuzik looked to Ezra a little cooler than Ezra felt, sweating in his rolled-up shirtsleeves. As if the fabric of the ice-blue lightweight suit possessed a chill intelligence.

'So, okay,' Kuuzik was saying, 'organisations as we knew them have virtually disappeared. They're no longer employers, they are yes, indeed, organisers. Of a free agent nation; of mavericks with portfolio careers. Each of us entrepreneur-in-chief of our own service company. This is good. Because we all crave control. Every man hungers for power over his own life. Isn't that true, Ezra?'

Kuuzik's eyes were hidden behind a pair of letterbox ebony shades. The glassy midday light forced Ezra to narrow his eyes, which he suspected gave him the look of steely resolve appropriate to a free and powerful agent. 'Certainly,' he agreed. 'But power is both quantifiable and a state of mind. If you think you're powerless then you surely will be. Power is not something that can be given to you. You have to take it.'

'Or believe you've taken it.'

'Indeed.'

'What an organisation has to provide – apart from network coherence, of course – is vision. We can't give power to people, as you say, but we can offer them inspiration.'

The men walked along Beaumont Street, between the Ashmolean Museum and the Randolph Hotel and round into St Giles. Ezra imagined that pedestrians coming the other way had all seen the photograph and read the profile of Klaus Kuuzik in the business section of last week's *Oxford Times*, recognised him now and noted the dapper colleague beside him. Authority, and stature.

'A friend of mine,' Kuuzik continued, 'says to his people, "We run like mad and then we change direction." And he's right. A sense of restlessness with the status quo is necessary to create the conditions for change and opportunity.'

'Always,' Ezra agreed.

'Do you ever wonder,' Klaus said, 'whether teenage alienation is a product of technological society, or whether it's always existed, and is the true engine of this restlessness?'

'That is an interesting question,' Ezra agreed. 'What makes young people break with tradition? It's something I was studying in tribal culture. Is that drive to be ourselves satisfied by appropriate coming of age rituals?'

They strolled along the wide boulevard of St Giles, and forked right up Banbury Road. One of the things about talking as you walked was that your every utterance was a projection into the future which you stepped into. As if it was your conversation together that led you forward; that was your direction.

'In classical Hindu tradition,' Klaus said, 'there was a trinity of gods: Brahma the Creator; Vishnu the Preserver; Shiva the Destroyer. It strikes me that we need all these qualities at the head of an organisation. We might call them different temperaments, and of course no one man can hold all three within him. Which is why a team is needed.'

They passed the first of the ugly scientific institutes in silence.

Might I embody one of these qualities? Ezra wondered. Is that what he's saying?

'Last time I was in India, you know,' Klaus resumed, 'I was on the train from Delhi to Rajasthan. We were served bottled water. Aqualina – Pepsi's Indian line. When we got to Jaipur it was incredibly hot, and people had put up small thatched huts, water temples, to give water from earthen pots as a free gift to the thirsty.'

Ezra nodded. It crossed his mind that on a day like today England could do with a few such temples. Whatever happened to drinking fountains, anyway?

'An ancient tradition across India,' Klaus said. 'And right there you have a fundamental clash: water as profitable commodity, water as sacred gift. The question is: where do we at Isis Water stand?'

Before Ezra was obliged to answer this odd question, Klaus said, 'Well, here we are. There's someone I want you to meet.'

Gees restaurant was in an elegant Victorian conservatory. Air conditioning and ceiling blinds held back the dazzle and heat of the summer day. They were led to a table on which upside-down glasses, reflecting light from the many windows, vied for supremacy of cleanliness with chemical-white tablecloth and napkins. A slight, saturnine man stood to greet them.

'This is Carl Buchannan,' Klaus introduced him. 'A hydrologist of rare curiosity. I've dragged him here from Vancouver to work with us. Carl, meet Ezra Pepin. I thought they must have been hiding Ezra from me, Carl, but in fact he was hiding from everyone, including himself. Am I right?'

'I don't know about that,' Ezra shrugged.

'Ah, they're too modest, these English,' Klaus told Carl. 'The world is full of ambitious men who lack talent. Intelligence. You can't create these qualities. But ambition you can inspire, even in a modest Englishman.'

The Canadian fidgeted with his napkin. He had an energy, a restlessness, about him.

'You worked together in Vancouver?' Ezra asked him.

'Listen,' Buchannan said, 'until Klaus appeared, I still kind of agreed with Joe Stalin that water allowed to enter the sea is wasted, you know?'

'You mean that anything is possible? Or was, at least.'

Buchannan frowned. He gave the impression he'd already had enough of Ezra's company. 'Sure,' he said, abruptly, in a tone which suggested that no, actually that wasn't what he meant. 'I mean I came to realise that if the way we use our knowledge damages the world, would it not be better if we hadn't been born?'

'A Hippocratic oath for engineers.'

'Why not?' Klaus interjected. 'Yes, I like that idea. Let us not forget that with every generation we are removed further in time from the Garden of Eden.'

'The Garden of Eden?' Ezra asked.

'From simplicity, if you prefer, Ezra. From the Golden Age, let us say. "He that increaseth knowledge, increaseth sorrow." This is the great challenge of progress. But gentlemen, please, an aperitif? Let us relax. I know it's a little old-fashioned, but I propose that we do not expect too much from our labours this afternoon.'

They ordered gin martinis and vermouths, which came with olives on sticks, in glasses the shape of windblown umbrellas. The first bitter sip gave Ezra Pepin a taste of illicit decadence all the more potent for being from another, more complicated era. They assessed the menu.

'I can recommend the king scallops to start with,' said Klaus. 'Although myself, today I think I'll try the roast partridge. Here's a question for you, gentlemen,' he said. 'Is it better to give people what they want but don't need? Or what they need but don't want?'

'What they need, of course,' said Buchannan without hesitation.

'If they need it badly, yes,' said Ezra, in more measured tone. 'For survival. Otherwise, what they want. Because this may bring happiness.'

'A consumer's happiness,' said Buchannan. 'The addict's happiness, which needs to be fed again tomorrow.'

'It depends what we're talking about,' Ezra stood his ground. 'Shoddy products, then you're right. But –'

'Gentlemen,' Kuuzik interrupted, 'please, forgive me. It was a trick question. A false dichotomy. Because the answer is both: we have to give people what they want *and* what they need. Ah, here comes something for us, I suspect.'

Ezra ate his king scallops, pan-fried to a juicy tenderness, served on a pile of *al dente* green beans, with a leek-and-shallot vinaigrette dressing. Buchannan had gnocchi, with juicy mushrooms, pine nuts and salsa verde. Klaus refilled their wine glasses with Pinotage. He put his knife and fork on his plate and slid them gently together, like palms to prayer.

'Water,' he said, 'is meant to flow. When it's unable to flow, it stagnates. The same is true of trade. You know our approach to trade, Ezra: we want to offer water to the thirsty. I wonder, does this make us radical or traditional?'

'Both.'

'Exactly, because the situation today is unique.'

'You're referring to what? Global warming?' Ezra conjectured.

'Boof,' Carl Buchannan exclaimed, dismissing the idea. 'That's a technical issue.'

'Is that what it is?' Ezra said.

'Rising oceans,' Carl said impatiently. 'A hell of an opportunity, wouldn't you say? Look, there are four methods of desalination.' He raised his fingers: 'One, multi-stage flash distillation; two, reverse osmosis; three, electrodialysis. Every one of them hideously expensive.'

'You said four,' Ezra objected. 'What's the fourth?'

'Carl doesn't know yet,' Klaus joined in, smiling, leaning back to let the waitress take away their plates of half-eaten food. 'Neither does anyone else. It's something *we* need to be the first to discover.'

The three men laughed. The waitress left, with their dessert orders. Ezra felt light-headed. He wondered what it was he was doing here, exactly, sat between these two men. The restless engineer in a hurry to move on, to get somewhere, and his energy convinced you that he would. The calm executive, who didn't need to say anything: anyone could tell, he would make happen what he desired, and so you wanted to desire the same thing.

Klaus turned to Ezra and said, 'Let me show you something. I mean, forget history. This is now.' He started moving glasses and cutlery around, clearing a space in front of him. 'This napkin is the island of Cyprus, okay? The tablecloth itself is the eastern Mediterranean. Over here,' Kuuzik said, using spoons and forks to draw a looping line of metal, 'is the north and eastern shoreline.' He picked up a knife and placed it across the napkin. 'This, Ezra, is the border: Greek Cyprus in the south, Turkish Cyprus in the north.'

'The Turks invaded in, what, the mid-Seventies?' Ezra guessed. 'A pseudo state ever since, right, recognised only by Turkey itself?'

'The whole island's chronically short of water,' Carl said, causing Ezra to wonder whether he and Klaus had rehearsed this show for him. 'What's the main industry? Okay, we can guess: tourism. Hundreds of hotels are constructed for tourists, who use much more water than locals. The Greeks implement recycling procedures. Desalination. Grey water systems. What do the Turks do?' Buchannan deferred to Kuuzik. 'Back to the map.'

While Buchannan was talking, Kuuzik had been doodling like a child with a magnet pen and one of those drawing boards that contain iron filings: trails of pepper across the white tablecloth now denoted the borders of countries in the Middle East. Ezra felt an urge to take a pen from the pocket of his jacket draped over the chair behind him, to pick up the challenge and further desecrate the fine linen by writing in the names of countries. Israel, Lebanon and Syria were delineated in their entirety.

'Go ahead, Ezra,' said Kuuzik, reading his mind. Ezra found himself being offered a black marker pen. Kuuzik was smiling at him. 'What's your geography like?'

Jordan, Iraq and Turkey had only partial borders shown, the bulk of their terrain dissolving north and eastward into the tablecloth's abstraction. Ezra wrote their names, giddy with the liberating glee of a timid boy doing something he shouldn't, but knowing he was protected by the leader of the group. He saw the indelible

262

black lines fray at their edges as the ink was absorbed into the thirsty white linen – which would have to be thrown away. Would its value be added to the bill? Or would Klaus be expected to cover such a cost in his tip? Or would the matter not be referred to in any way by either party?

'In eastern Turkey, as you know, Ezra, in Kurdish areas, massive dams have been built. There's one on the Euphrates,' Klaus said, 'reducing its flow as it goes into Syria.' He trickled the route of the great river with salt, which sparkled in the restaurant's glassy brightness. 'Another on the Tigris, which flows into Iraq. Now, there are big issues here about rights and responsibilities, about political control over your own dissident population, and your neighbours. But leave all that for the moment. The point is that Turkey is water rich.

'Let's go back to Cyprus.' As Klaus spoke he reached over to an adjacent table, from which diners had just left, and picked up a small, empty, transparent plastic bag that had held a hand-cleaning flannel. 'The Turks decide to move water from mainland Turkey to their enclave on the island, which has an annual shortfall of what, Carl?'

'About fifteen million cubic metres.'

Ezra made a whistling inhalation.

'A lot, yes,' Klaus nodded. 'Their efforts make for a humorous story, Ezra.' Kuuzik poured water from their jug into the bag he'd just pilfered. 'They used huge plastic containers, holding ten, twenty thousand cubic metres each. People got very excited as the first of these were towed across the sea. "Turkish water bags will serve Malta, Libya, Egypt." Unfortunately,' Klaus said, taking a lighter from his pocket, and holding it to his own water bag, 'they started melting in the sun.' His bag was breached, with a sickly smell of burning plastic. Water dribbled on to the tablecloth.

'The fresh water was lost in the salt water of the Mediterranean. So then the serious project began: a pipeline, Ezra, eighty kilometres long. Annual capacity, what, seventy-five, a hundred million cubic metres? More than enough for the whole island – yes, the Turks can give water to the Greeks. Let there be peace in Cyprus.

This is a good thing, no? A wonderful thing. But let's look at the map again.'

Klaus laid one knife vertically from the southern coast of Turkey down to the northern tip of Cyprus. 'Construction of the pipeline's nearly ready to begin. And look.' He took another knife, and laid it from the Cyprus napkin at a south-eastern incline towards a pepper shore. 'Now here is a surprise: we're almost halfway to Israel,' said Klaus.

Every object on the table, Ezra observed, was necessary, and appropriate, to Klaus's model. Each remaining knife, spoon, plate had its own preordained role to play: every prop Klaus needed was at hand, and nothing was left unused. Some people were like that, weren't they? They don't need to exert will: life adapts itself to their requirements.

Over iced passion-fruit parfait, with raspberries and a red wine and basil sauce, Klaus Kuuzik said, 'Whether the pipeline will work out, we can't be sure: supplying water to northern Cyprus was a political plan, which failed to take into account economic realities. Supplying Israel with water is an economic scheme, which fails to take into account political realities. Neither idea is based on ethical principles, needless to say.'

Ezra sipped the plummy pale-red Californian dessert wine Klaus had ordered, coating his tongue with its alcohol sweetness.

'In the long term, pipes and tankers will move water around the region,' said Klaus. 'DeutscheWasser will be a prime supplier. Sure. But perhaps what *we* can do, Ezra, with Isis Water, is to begin the flow now, today, with our bottles.' Klaus paused, though his gaze remained unwavering. It felt to Ezra as though Klaus was trying to communicate how vital Ezra was to what they might begin. 'To provide drinking water, let us say,' he resumed, 'so that no child in the occupied territories need ever go thirsty. This aim. For example. You see?'

'I'm not,' Ezra hesitated, '*entirely* sure I do.'

'Here is a great cancer,' Kuuzik said, pointing at that region of the tablecloth. 'With secondary tumours, you might say, spreading from it. What if we can do something to redress the injustice?'

'A water bottle,' said Buchannan. 'A hand grenade filled with life.'

Ezra stared at the Canadian, manipulating a toothpick with his fingers.

'I can see you're sceptical, Ezra,' Kuuzik said. 'You're right, you should be.'

Pepin realised his expression had given him away, but there wasn't much he could do about that. Now that he was aware of it he reckoned he'd probably been frowning, wrinkling his nose and chewing the inside of his cheek all at once. 'No, no,' he said. 'I mean, you're crusaders, right? You really are.'

'Without swords,' Klaus said, laughing. 'Of course,' he continued, 'we're civilised men. We believe in democratisation and human rights. In reform of the United Nations. In UN armies involved in peacekeeping operations. Of course.'

'Christ was nothing if not a pacifist,' said Buchannan.

'The practicalities need to be worked out,' Kuuzik resumed. 'That's what our team will be working on from now on. For the moment we're talking without walls. But this is certain: we can do something, Ezra.'

Coffee arrived, black espressos in tiny white china mugs and saucers that looked like they'd been filched from a child's tea set. Kuuzik stirred his sugar and said, 'Islamism – you know what it is? Yes, of course it's nihilistic, it's utopian. "You love life, we love death." But you know what it really is? It's history itself, the force of history, grunting, "Do not think you can leave me behind." But it's history's last murderous breath. It cannot compete with the gifts our future offers, so long as they are shared openly. You know, Ezra, Robert Browning wrote something like, "The present is the instant in which the future crumbles into the past."'

Buchannan shook his head. 'The view of a pessimist. What would an optimist say?'

'May I?' Ezra interjected. 'How about this: The present is the point at which the past is devoured by the future.'

To which the other two men raised their coffee mugs with their huge fingers, and saluted him.

*   *   *

265

After they'd got back to the office, Ezra Pepin's stewed brain and body stumbled through the afternoon like a car sliding along an icy road. He wasn't in control, but kept telling himself that he shouldn't fight it, but keep the wheels pointing into the skid.

He'd been copy-typing at his computer for several minutes without being aware that he was doing so. Perusing the screen, Ezra couldn't find a single mistake. From which moment error entered, and now he watched his fingers become clumsy senseless tools, hitting the wrong keys, repeating letters, missing others out. A deep fatigue dragged at him. He felt as if all the aged cells of his body were spongey with alcohol. At the same time his skull felt desiccated, his brain in urgent need of fluid. He managed to stumble to the toilets and slump in a cubicle for a dreamless half-hour.

Ezra left a message on the answerphone at home to say he'd work late, and not bother coming home before going out again, he reminded Sheena, to meet Minty Carlyle at the Phoenix. He'd grab a burger from Pepper's before the film.

They saw the coach pull into the parking bay outside the Taylorian Institute, on the other side of St Giles.

'Come on,' said Blaise.

Akhmed scurried after her, through the traffic. Spilling out of the coach were kids a year or two younger than themselves. Girls who'd begun to spurt into adolescence, huddling close to one another, as if intuiting signs of hidden threat in the vicinity; boys comparatively diminutive and juvenile, horsing around. Blaise and Akhmed followed them at a short distance, up the steps, across the courtyard of the Ashmolean. There was a slight breeze. A flagpole cable squealed with tension.

The trick was to look like they were just catching up with their party; stick too close and a teacher might question them. Once inside the foyer of the museum, the group received its orders, and Blaise drifted away.

Akhmed followed. When she slowed down, so did he, and

when she paused in front of the headless Aphrodite, he stood beside her. She moved on, and stopped again. A Roman woman minus lower arms and also her nose, like a leper. There was a torso of a boy, *Eros Soranzo* the sign said; he had no head, or arms, or even genitals. The goddess Athena was missing an arm. The statues stood solid and upright, torsos proud. Blaise imagined them as sculptures of disabled people in ancient Greece.

A large statue of Artemis had no head or arms, but the pleats of her stone robe hung from the nipples of perfect breasts. The torso of an Amazon warrior lacked an arm, hacked off in combat.

'Why don't they make copies of the missing bits?' Akhmed said. 'And stick them on? So we can see what they're meant to look like.'

'They're not missing,' Blaise said. Each statue proclaimed, Yes, look at me. I'm fine as I am. I made Emperor, said one. I was a god, said another. We function. We thrive, without an arm. A leg or two.

Akhmed padded after her through the dim chambers of ancient Egypt.

'I like these,' he said at Blaise's shoulder, as she studied a glass cabinet full of clay and wooden models of servants. Shawabtis: deposited in the tombs of the wealthy dead, to do their menial labour for them in the next world. 'If I should die suddenly,' Akhmed said. 'You never know. You can bury some of these with me.'

Blaise didn't seem to hear him.

'You'll have to be quick about it,' he said. 'When one of our lot dies, we get them buried as soon as possible.'

'Isn't it incredible, all this?' Blaise pondered, gesturing around the room, and beyond. 'The plunder, of the British Empire.'

Akhmed made a dismissive snort through his nose. 'Egypt wasn't in the Empire.' He shook his head. 'Never.'

'You know what I mean,' Blaise said. Akhmed claimed to do badly at school, but he seemed to retain every useless item of information he'd ever been given.

267

'See, the thing is, Blaise,' he said, 'really, you want to get your facts right first.'

She changed the subject. 'Have you got your family organised?' she said. 'All mine are coming.'

'I told you I have, didn't I?' Akhmed said. 'Mum's already making special trips over to Cowley Road for spices and stuff.'

Blaise wandered up a wide staircase. As long as you had a pencil and sketchbook in your hand, no one bothered you. Akhmed trailed behind her into English Delftware: cabinet after cabinet of odd crockery.

'Like a charity shop, isn't it, all this junk?' Akhmed said, scratching his neck. In Russian Art he asked, 'Can't we go to the café yet?'

Blaise turned round. 'If I want someone to bug me,' she said, 'I've already got a younger brother.'

Akhmed frowned, and bent his head to the floor.

'Look, why don't you just go round on your own for a bit?' Blaise suggested. 'We'll meet later.'

Akhmed nodded with his head away to one side. 'See them things,' he said, indicating a squat white box by the wall. 'They're humidifiers. They take out the oxygen.' He paused. 'Dehumidifiers, maybe. That's why people feel sleepy in museums.' He yawned, to demonstrate his point.

'What about the invigilators?' Blaise asked. 'How come they're all wide awake?' She'd said it for the sake of argument, and suspected she was on shaky ground: the woman in the corner of this room had one elbow propped on a small table and leaned her head on her hand. She looked like she might drop off at any moment. The white box droned in a sinister way.

'They're old,' Akhmed said. 'They don't need to sleep as much as we do.'

'I'll meet you in the Chinese room,' Blaise said. 'By the big wooden Buddha.'

'All right,' Akhmed agreed, with a sigh. 'Half an hour?'

'Make it an hour,' Blaise said, and walked out of the room. She strolled through the galleries of European paintings. Akhmed was right: the invigilators were old. The women were silver-haired and matronly. Each sat alone in her allotted gallery. The men appeared genial, avuncular, sitting vacant, unoccupied. They all looked like people left behind. Forgotten. Of course, Blaise figured: they're widows, and widowers.

Perhaps, like her, they appreciated the emptiness. She walked straight through rooms that other visitors occupied to tarry in vacant ones, sitting on a bench if there was one and pretending to gaze at whatever was in front of her, sketchbook on her lap. It was the hushed ambience of the museum Blaise liked. The echo of a door closing somewhere far off. A lock being turned, with a lingering finality. The footsteps of a class of schoolchildren, pattering across the wooden floors of interconnecting galleries. Silence. Voices carried from distant rooms, the museum's sepulchral ghosts.

Today she'd been thinking of going to the squat, but then Akhmed had collared her at break and said, 'You're planning one of your expeditions, aren't you? I can tell.' She certainly wasn't going to take him there, her secret place. She was too slow thinking, that was the trouble. She just said, 'Yeh, okay, come with me. I'm going to the Ashmolean.'

Really, though, she wasn't sorry she hadn't gone. She'd dropped in a couple of days ago. Zack acted like first he was happy to see her, then he wasn't, then he was again. He was awkward. Reluctant, Blaise thought, to obey his own instincts. Akhmed wasn't, really: he'd kiss her again if she'd let him.

A family of Austrians or Germans flushed Blaise out of Dutch and Flemish Still-Lifes on the third floor. As she descended the stairs she felt a particular painting pull her towards it. Her favourite in the museum. It was in the large gallery, Italian Renaissance Art, and Blaise placed herself before it. It was a portrait by someone called Tiziano Vecellio, who the sign said was known as Titian. Whether to his friends, or his patrons, or just in England – the weird way we called Firenze Florence, or Roma Rome – it didn't say. The three-quarter-length portrait was of a man called Giacomo Doria, who was a Genoese merchant. He was dressed in black, a robe of some kind, and stood – the painting was only of his upper half – in front and to one side of a marble pillar, against a dim brown background. There was a crest, his family or guild or whatever, in the top left-hand corner of the painting.

Giacomo Doria seemed to be holding something in his right hand, but if so it was very dark, indistinguishable from his cloak – it might have been material gathered in his fingers. His left hand hung by his thumb from his belt, with a languid arrogance. He had a long black beard, a sharp nose, dark eyes. He looked more like an Afghan than an Italian, Blaise thought; a mujahedin. His black hair was thinning at the front – Titian had scratched scribbles of paint across the dome of his head – but he didn't look old. Maybe into his thirties, she estimated. Or was his black hair dyed?

It was a strange picture. She didn't think he was a handsome man, yet he was impressive. It was his eyes that worried her. They looked at whoever stood before them unblinking, as they had done for centuries. The longer Blaise looked into them, the more she saw. There was suspicion in those eyes – of the artist, perhaps – aggression, even paranoia. As she gazed back at them it became apparent to Blaise that they revealed someone slightly unhinged. She wondered whether Titian had been a little afraid of this man he was being paid to paint, and painted his fear. What was he afraid of? She peered into the man's eyes. Giacomo Doria was practically alive, his breathing calm and measured, two feet in front of her. He stared back at her; he was watching Blaise. He knew her; her weaknesses, her secrets.

Titian's fear, Blaise surmised, was of the man's mental instability. An insanity of . . . what? Ambition, maybe. Power? A disturbance. Giacomo Doria's eyes were those of a bird of prey. The painting revealed a ruthlessness that was neither heralded nor proclaimed. It was subtly, clearly evident.

The sign said that Titian died in 1576, so Giacomo had been dead for some 400 years. But Blaise would not have been surprised if he stepped out of the painting. And if his first words were to command Blaise to do his bidding, there was little doubt that she would obey.

When a voice addressed her, it was as if she was physically struck with it.

'There you are.'

Blaise flinched.

'I was waiting ages. Where were you? I've been looking all over.'

Blaise turned slowly to look at him.

'I thought you'd gone without me,' Akhmed said.

Respiro was about the family of a free-spirited, insane woman in a fishing community on the island of Lampedusa. It was shot with bleached-out colours in a sun-blasted summer. There was an incredible image of scores of swimmers treading water together, shot from below, so that the human community looked like a single organism, its limbs rippling like fronds. Otherwise, the film failed to engage Ezra, and as if the filmmakers had bleached the screen the better to accommodate those dreaming spectators who wished to transpose their own images upon it, his mind kept drifting to summers of his own childhood.

Ezra's parents laboured years for him to come along and then they devoted themselves to his happiness, barely noticing that no more children followed him into their home. His father was an engineer who'd forged a career out of calibrating machinery for the manufacture of metal boxes, containers, bins. His mother a primary-school teacher. They possessed undoubted fondness for each other, but a capacity for affection seemed to find its fullest expression in their collaboration as parents. They doted on him.

Ezra was oddly tall: his parents were both short – still was, in Clive Pepin's case; even shorter now, the old man. By the time he reached double figures Ezra, a stringy boy, was already up around their height, so that, he fancied, their little trio resembled a circus family when, each summer, they embarked on camping holidays in Devon and Cornwall.

'Into the rain,' Dad joked as they headed west. 'Wipers ahoy.'

'Get away with you,' Mum admonished. 'The forecast is bright. It's your dad that's gloomy, Ezra.'

His father winked at Ezra in the rearview mirror. The film on the screen dissolved. The soundtrack faded. He pictured now the three of them playing cricket on a beach. On a hundred windy beaches. Pacing out a wicket on the hard sand, planting three stumps securely, resting the bails in their shallow cradles. A single stump at the other end for the bowler, his father, aiming a tennis ball underarm.

Ezra was in bat. He always was: when his parents' turns came his mother, an incompetent athlete, swung too early or too late at his deliveries; he clean bowled her every time. And his father threw up catches. So that Ezra would promptly return to the crease, and his father bowled kindly and his mother was positioned mid-wicket: she covered the whole on side, father the offside. What was left unmanned was the area behind the wicket, and any sensible choreographer of their straitened man-power – they rarely collaborated with a strange family – would have decreed that if the ball passed behind the wicket, play be automatically suspended, with the batsman obliged to fetch the ball he'd missed.

Not the Pepins. So indulged was the boy, and so selfishly accepting of his indulgence, that not only did he claim runs off byes, he also slyly nicked the ball behind: Ezra totted up countless runs while his willing mother chased after a tennis ball scurrying off along the windblown beach.

Peroni beers were half-price in the Phoenix bar to bearers of tickets to the Italian movie, and Ezra guzzled straight from the chilled bottle, as he listened to Minty. The alcohol from lunch had gradually dissipated from his body in the hours since, but left him with a tremendous thirst.

'I was halfway through a library book last week,' Minty was telling him. 'A volume of poetry by a Welsh woman published in the seventies, when it occurred to me I'd read it before. I looked on my bookshelves, and sure enough, sport, there it was. I had my own copy. A first edition.' She laughed at herself. 'My own damn copy!'

'Minty,' Ezra said, shaking his head, just managing to stop himself from saying, Poor Minty. 'You must have read more than you can cope with.'

'Probably,' she smiled. 'My brain's full up.'

'It's not good for us to live too much in our heads,' he said.

'That's a bit strange coming from you, Ez,' Minty responded, raising her eyebrows. 'Isn't that where intellectuals like us are supposed to live?'

'And for what?' Ezra demanded. 'For our own happiness? For the good of mankind?'

He wanted to tell her what he wasn't yet allowed to; about the scheme being dreamed up at Isis Water. About how a man such as himself could have an impact. For good this time.

The café window had a multi-coloured phoenix painted on the glass. To one side of the bar there was a box full of back issues of *Sight and Sound*. One or two students, waiting for a date or without one, read copies. Minty lit a Camel. She inhaled, then lifted her neck slowly, and blew a plume of smoke into the air above her. When she lowered her head and looked at Ezra, he sensed a wistfulness in her eyes that was at odds with the aggressive tone of voice in which words emerged from her tight mouth. 'You think we should act on our impulses?' she asked.

'I suppose I do,' Ezra pondered. 'But what's important is not the impulse, the spontaneity, but the reason. To act on a well-thought-out plan, that's the thing.'

Minty smiled at him, with what may have been approval but was more likely irony. She exhaled again, but before she could say anything Ezra said, getting to his feet, 'You ready for another glass of wine? I'm getting a fresh beer.'

Ezra's bicycle ferried his unbalanced body in an unstraight line home. The lights were out, the house silent. Ezra closed doors and ascended stairs with the exaggerated stealth of a drunk. Removed his clothes item by awkward item; performed ablutions in an echo chamber of an ensuite bathroom. He climbed into bed in slow motion.

Sheena was turned away to her side of the bed, her body curled into itself. The inertness of his wife asleep never failed to unsettle Ezra: he always needed to confirm her breath; her ribs' slight rise and fall. Then he was able to lie back, gaze at the ceiling. Close his eyes.

It was only now that for the first time that day Ezra acknowledged, lying beside Sheena, that he'd again failed to tell Klaus Kuuzik of his family's plan to go to Brazil, even though their flight was scheduled for little more than a month away, and the letting agency had a family lined up to rent the house. On the brink of sleep his concentration focused through the fug of booze and tiredness. What was he thinking of? What was he hoping for? Such a prospect Klaus had held before him. Sheena sometimes inveighed against environmental despoliation with words along the lines of, 'What I hate about these people is they believe, they ask us to believe, that technology will solve the problems caused by technology.'

Wasn't it the same with trade? Maybe it really was possible to solve problems of inequality and injustice. Missionary for noble capitalism: a strange role indeed. But Ezra couldn't fill it, could he? Because powerful evangelist as he was, a man who might well change the world, Klaus Kuuzik could not be allowed to threaten the architecture of one family's hard-won harmony. Ezra knew that he could not take Sheena's decisions for her, not without the risk of losing everything most precious. With which irreconcilable anxiety he slid into sleep.

Ezra Pepin was woken in the darkness, by what he didn't know at first. He lay with his senses alert: ah, yes, it was a sound. A sound coming from Sheena. What is it? Is she ill? It's not a cough. It's a shudder. Is she retching? Yes, she's trying to be sick. Or trying not to be sick. No. Wait.

A glance, and the luminous dials of the alarm clock told Ezra it was one-twenty-five. He raised himself up on his elbow, and leaned over Sheena. 'What is it, darling?' he whispered, touching her shoulder. 'What's the matter? Are you all right?'

With each sob, Sheena's upper body stuttered and shook beneath the cotton sheet, as if the plaintive motor of her unhappiness was trying to start up into a full-blown wail. Ezra waited, let her cry the worst of it out, letting her know he was there with one hand on her shoulder and the other on her thigh, through the sheet. The sides of her ribs juddered against his chest. Her bottom rocked into his groin. He felt his prick engorging. An image leapt to mind of him and Sheena in Tantric union, with her sobbing providing the single erotic movement.

Ezra shifted away. He felt under Sheena's pillow and found a couple of half-used tissues, which he offered her. Sheena took them, wiped her eyes, blew her nose. Her sobbing slowed to an occasional pathetic catch of breath. She sniffed, and swallowed.

'What's wrong, darling?' Ezra asked.

'Blaise,' Sheena said.

'What happened?'

Sheena felt round to the wall and switched her reading light on. She turned over to face her husband. Her eyes were livid and swollen from crying. They gave her a certain simian look; they reminded him of the monkeys at Cotswold Wildlife Park.

'We had a fight,' Sheena said. 'It was unbearable, Ezra, the things she said.'

Speaking brought back the sobbing. Ezra stroked her arm. 'There, there,' he soothed.

'There was no reasoning with her,' Sheena said.

'It's okay, darling,' Ezra comforted her.

'Oh, Ezra,' Sheena sniffled. 'She came in here as I was getting ready for bed. Cool as a cucumber, said . . .' Sheena broke off as she started sobbing again, but managed to resume, talking and crying together. 'She looked at me calm as you like and said, "By the way, you ought to know, Mum, I'm not going to Brazil. You can't force me."'

'That was it?' Ezra asked.

'She said she wouldn't go to Brazil unless we took everything we owned and gave it to shanty-town dwellers when we got there.'

Ezra bit his lip to keep himself from pointing out quite how much Blaise was her mother's daughter.

'I don't understand,' Sheena muttered. 'We were best friends.'

'I know, darling.'

'We've always been best friends, Blaise and me.' In a trembling voice, Sheena said, 'She called me a hypocrite, Ezra. But in that light-hearted way of hers. "Oh, Mummy, don't be a tedious hypocrite." '

'That's not so bad, is it?' Ezra asked.

'Yes, but then I lost it.' Sheena's facial muscles made a great effort. 'I yelled. I said things.' She sniffed. 'I shouldn't have.'

Sheena began crying again, and Ezra opened his shoulders, inviting her to sink into his embrace. A part of him went out to his partner, to her maternal pain. A small part too went out of their bedroom door and spooled along the corridor towards Blaise; though that could wait for later. And a large part of him, he had to admit, just felt dumbly content, a hulk of a man comforting his crying wife in the early hours of the night while the rest of the world was sleeping. It was a duty a man was happy to fulfil.

So that it was only slowly, as Sheena sobbed against his chest, that the significance of what she'd said sank in. My God. Of course: they couldn't go now. And as it did, Ezra felt the relief wash his brain, as if there were a chemical peculiar to that emotion whose entire supply had just been released, with enough left over to lighten his blood and warm his heart. Of course they couldn't *force* Blaise to go. So they'd remain in Oxford. He'd stay at Isis Water. And he'd not had a thing to do with it. It was all between Sheena and Blaise. He could not be blamed.

Sheena had almost cried herself out. Ezra found more tissues and she blew her nose; took deep breaths. Ezra was wondering how to phrase his next line. We don't have to go to Brazil? We can go another time? It doesn't matter, darling? We'll review it in a couple of years?

When, however, Sheena spoke first, it was as if in response to whatever precise formulation Ezra would come up with; it was in response to his intention.

'Don't worry, Ezra,' she said bravely. 'Don't you worry, sweetheart. We're going, and that's the end of it. Blaise says she doesn't want to come with us. Well, fine. If she really wants to stay behind, we'll just have to let her.'

Part Three

14

Picnic on Port Meadow

Into August

How many articles, essays, books had been written, Ezra Pepin wondered, about children and their rooms? The modern phenomenon of growing up with your own self-enclosed space. In the days following the row between mother and daughter all his children, it seemed to Ezra, and not just Blaise, retreated into their separate bedrooms.

Sheena had installed a broadband connection, a necessary service for prospective tenants, according to the lettings agency, and she also let Hector have an old word processor that had been replaced by an upgrade at Home Holidays: glued to the chair in front of it, Hector became an eleven-year-old screenager eavesdropping on newsgroups; sweeping cyberspace for threats to his safety; lurking in chat rooms for precocious conspiracy theorists. He'd be hacking within months, Ezra suspected; MI6 would swoop on their house and make Hector's nightmares come true.

Louie, too, disappeared inside his citadel: beneath the single high bunk bed the boy had a wooden fort, manned by plastic knights in armour. Louie orchestrated extravagant sieges of the fort, by time-crossed armies who marched across the Tartar steppe of the floorboards: battalions comprising Vikings and cowboys, footballers, Snow White, Buzz Lightyear and a troll. They travelled in jeeps, on horseback, by train. And their infantry were augmented by rhinos and dinosaurs. Robots and dragons. Paying homage to both the mercenary tradition and an older custom of terrifying enemies with fearsome beasts, post-modern regiments besieged the solemn paladins.

The boys emerged at intervals, reentering the congregation of family life. Blaise, however, remained in a sulky quarantine. She asked for food to be left outside her door. They heard her quietly speaking in there sometimes, but whether this was into her mobile, or murmuring to herself like an anchoress, her parents couldn't tell. She developed a cat burglar's ability to make herself invisible, slipping in and out of the house without being seen: people heard the front door close behind her, or her bedroom door click shut on her return. Occasionally Blaise did her holiday homework in the living-room, but spoke to no one. Sitting at the table, chewing a biro, with her earphones on, Blaise nodded her head. Agreeing with the beat of the music. All of a sudden she'd close her books and return upstairs.

Was it a good or a bad thing his daughter had her own room? Ezra wondered. Did such space allow her to develop herself, or condemn her to cultivate her own loneliness? Possibly, he thought, she was leaving the arena for her parents to sort out the problem; the boys too, all three of them tactfully intuiting that Ezra and Sheena required the communal areas downstairs for necessary adult negotiation.

Most of the conversations they had, in those ensuing days, took place in the evenings, outside, as had the earlier duologues in which the two of them had planned their adventure. They'd talked it up and now, Ezra reckoned, they had to talk it down. But it wouldn't be easy.

'She can carry on at Cherwell and do her GCSEs there,' Sheena decided.

'What, and stay here on her own?'

'Of course not. We can hardly rent this place out with Blaise in it, can we?'

' "To let: modern five-bedroom house," ' said Ezra. ' "Close to city centre. Comes with off-street parking and its own resident teenager. One thousand pounds per calendar month." '

'Don't be stupid, Ezra,' said Sheena. 'We'll be asking twice that.'

They took less care with the accoutrements, as if playing a sequel to their earlier performance but with shabby props. One evening at the beginning of August neither of them remembered to put the white wine in the fridge, and drank it warm. While Ezra no longer relished a single cigarette: he'd no sooner put one out than start rolling another, with tobacco-reeking fingers.

'So where's she going to stay?' he asked.

'With friends.'

'Any friends in particular? I mean, I haven't noticed many hanging out here recently.'

'Oh, come on, Ezra, teenagers don't like their mates seeing inside their houses. Of course she has friends.'

'There's Akhmed.'

'Yes. Well.'

'You want to come back and find our daughter behind a veil?'

'Oh, Ezra, that is so ridiculous.'

'Maybe it is, maybe it isn't. I don't know. I just don't see it's such a good idea to leave –'

'A headstrong young woman.'

'Our little girl, Sheena.'

'Look!' Sheena got up out of her garden chair. 'You don't seem willing to acknowledge how difficult it is to have my daughter treat me the way Blaise has.'

'We can't abandon her.'

'Of course not, but don't you see?' Sheena stepped towards and loomed over Ezra; her hands danced, adding emphasis to what she said; they seemed to want to grab her husband by the scruff of the neck and shake him. 'Don't you see? The whole point is it would be good for her. It's what she needs. Outside our smothering embrace, our poor girl can grow up.'

Sheena turned away and stepped to the edge of the decking. Looking out across the lawn and into the clear night, where stars were just beginning to become apparent in the still-blue sky, Sheena said in a quiet voice, 'It'd be the best thing we could do for her.'

And although the words that Sheena spoke then and in those days expressed her determination to see their plan through, there was already some note in her voice of defeat, a certain undertone, that acknowledged Blaise's refusal to accompany them as a desertion that had breached their voyage below the waterline; a tone which promised eventual acceptance that the trip could not reasonably be made.

Or was that, Ezra conceded, lighting another rollie, simply wishful thinking?

On Friday 8 August, Ezra put the boys to bed and came downstairs. He could hear murmured voices coming from the sitting-room. Sheena and Blaise sat close together and facing one another on the big white sofa, their arms and legs entwined like lovers, looking into each other's eyes as they confided who knew what? Ezra observed them from the doorway. He saw a dropped gaze, a stroking hand, a head-tilted tolerant smile: the nuanced choreography of mutual contrition, of Blaise's apology, of Sheena's forgiveness. Reconciliation. The sight delighted and unnerved him. It was as if they'd formed a single, twin-headed female creature, communicating with itself.

Sheena spotted him and said, 'Ez, come here.'

He sat on the coffee table, knees touching their sofa, as both Sheena and Blaise, holding some arm or leg of the other, turned bovine smiles at him, inviting him through glazed eyes to salute the manner of their repentance.

'Ez, guess what,' said Sheena.

'What?'

'Blaise says Akhmed's parents have invited us to join them at a picnic on Sunday.'

'Really?' he asked Blaise.

'On Port Meadow,' she nodded.

The two women gazed at Ezra. He sensed that they were looking for their reflection, in the mirror of his response to them. 'Well,' he said. 'That's very nice. Who's going to cook? I mean, what should we take?'

'They say we can bring dessert, Daddy,' Blaise said, smiling sweetly.

Ezra returned upstairs. He retreated into his room, too, during those days, partly to give Sheena time and space to come to what he saw as the only rational conclusion on her own, and partly to contemplate what Klaus Kuuzik and Carl Buchannan had discussed with him.

Sheena had presented the Brazilian escapade as a way for Ezra, on the verge of turning forty, on the brink of middle age, to reclaim his potential. The plan, having briefly seduced him, was then impossible to back out of. And here was a new boss who'd appeared in the company, perceived Ezra's worth and plucked him from the ranks of middle management, with the prospect of extraordinary deeds.

Now Ezra began to tidy his desk. To put back in their boxes the research material he'd been processing the past days, as if boxing it back up would stir his resolve or intention in the intricate negotiations to come; could add its measure to the minutely shifting, subterranean forces at work in the marriage of a man and a woman.

If all went well, Ezra thought, he'd put away these papers for good: in a year or two he'd carry them down to the back of the car and take them to the dump, and shed once and for all his fake academic persona, the pretence of what he neither wanted to nor could become. What a clarifying trip that'll be, to Redbridge waste-disposal site. He reconstructed a couple of flat-pack cardboard boxes, and began to stuff them with papers.

A whisper. 'Dad.'

Ezra jumped.

'Blaise. I didn't hear you.'

She was standing in the doorway, dressed in her Snoopy pyjamas. She came in and knelt beside Ezra's desk chair, leaning on the thin armrest. He put his hand on her back, and stroked it.

'Dad?'

'What?'

Blaise rested her head on his thigh. He stroked her hair. Then she lifted her head. 'Do you and Mum talk about everything?'

Blaise had brushed her teeth. Her breath smelled of strawberries.

'Yes. I mean, no, of course not everything.'

Her eyes flickered. 'Do you tell each other what you do?'

'What do you mean? Do you mean are we honest?'

'I suppose.'

His daughter was studying him now. He'd better tell the truth. But that was okay, there was no reason not to. 'Yes,' Ezra said. 'We'd never do anything to hurt each other, or you children.'

Blaise gave no indication as to whether or not she believed him. She nodded at the folders on his desk. 'What are you doing?' she asked.

'Tidying my papers.'

Blaise gazed at the manuscript, typed years ago into Ezra's first computer, an Amstrad. The edges of each sheet of paper were serrated, torn from the roll that fed through the integrated printer. 'Tell me the story of that girl, Daddy,' she said.

'Which girl?'

'You know, who was going to be scarified.'

Ezra smiled. 'Really?'

Blaise looked up at him with a babyishly pleading expression. 'Please, Daddy.'

Yes, Ezra realised: this was the outlet for his work. It wasn't anthropology, never should have been; he was a simple storyteller, a teller of tales to his children and his friends. This was the only homage he could pay the people whose lives he'd ruined.

'The Achia,' he said, 'removed all the hair from their body. Did I tell you that? It was something they did for each other: using splinters of bamboo, women shaved their husbands' beard. Men cut their wives' hair. Friends plucked each other's eyebrows and lashes, with tweezers made of flexible twigs.

'After I began handing out small mirrors, this mutual grooming gradually ceased. The first time the Indians saw their reflections, they were astonished. For half an hour or more they stared at themselves, holding the mirror sometimes at arm's length, sometimes right under their nose. But as they became used to them, so they began to use the mirrors to pluck and shave their own hair.

'One slight young girl, aged eleven or twelve, Yorugi, possessed a mirror I'd given to her.'

'Yorugi,' Blaise repeated. 'That's the one, Daddy.'

'Even though she rarely looked in the mirror, Yorugi always checked that she had it with her. I asked her why the mirror was so important.

' "One day I will be a woman," she said.

' "Then you will want the mirror?"

' "I will be old," she said. "I will become real."

' "You are not real now?"

' "Now," she laughed, "I am a child."

'Some weeks after this there was a commotion. Yorugi's mother was weeping. Her father called across the village to Yorugi's godparents – loud enough to broadcast the news – "My little girl's blood falls! My daughter's blood is here!"

'Now, I was sure no outsider had witnessed an Achia girl's initiation. I hoped they'd allow me to. I squatted silently outside my hut, and observed. Yorugi had gone.'

'Where was she?' Blaise asked.

'I didn't know. Her parents disappeared too, and her godparents started looking for her, in various huts around. They did this in a theatrical manner, as if playing hide and seek with a toddler. They came into my hut, ignoring me, and said, loudly, "No, she is not here. Yorugi is not here."

'I noticed various young men, meanwhile, slipping out of the camp. Eventually the godparents retreated inside Yorugi's family's empty hut, at which point the girl herself came in from the forest.'

'She'd been watching,' Blaise nodded, sagely.

'Presumably. Yorugi went straight to her hut where, as far as I could tell, her godparents gave her a massage, before leaving her unfed and alone.

287

'The next morning Yorugi's godfather soaked kymata vine shavings in water, which turned white and creamy in texture. Her godmother and other women joined him outside Yorugi's hut: the girl came out and they washed her, soaping and rinsing her from head to foot with the purifying shavings and liquid.

'Yorugi was led to a new hut the women had made. Her godmother cut off the girl's hair. Two cords made from nettle fibre were knotted under her knees: these were supposed to help her legs grow fat.'

'Why did she want to be fat?' Blaise asked.

'The Achia were horrified by thinness. How could a thin woman walk through the forest with a basket on her back, a child in her sling? The thighs and calves of an Achia woman had to be round and strong to be beautiful.

'The other helpers, meanwhile, now washed each other – having become unclean through their contact with the girl. When they'd finished, young men, those who had disappeared the day before, returned to the village, and now they too were washed. I wondered who these various young men were: I thought I understood by then the family relations of all the Achia in this village. When the bathing was over I asked one of them, Wekoni, Kabuchi's brother, whose own male initiation I had witnessed.

'"All the lovers of Yorugi are in danger," he explained.

'I thought of the slight, young girl experiencing her menarche, and of the eight youths who had been washed.'

'Eight?' Blaise demanded, with an expression of distaste. 'Wow,' she said. 'Gross.'

'"All of you are her lovers?" I asked.

'"We were all in danger," he confirmed. "Now we are safe."

'That afternoon Yorugi was painted, by her aunt, with a black paint made from beeswax, resin and powdered charcoal. The woman warmed the paste to liquefy it, and applied it to Yorugi's skin with a polished wooden blade. It made a shiny line that would not fade for days, even if she washed in the river. Her face was decorated with horizontal stripes on her forehead, and vertical ones on her nose, cheeks and chin. Then her torso was painted with six rows of vertical marks, from her neck to her pubis. The same was done to Yorugi's arms, and back. The effect was striking. Later, I spotted Yorugi at dusk, studying herself in her small mirror.

'That evening Yorugi's godfather gave everyone involved in her initiation some gruel made of pindo flour and corn and honey, and the girl herself had some – her first food for two days.

'Fatigued from concentration, not knowing what would happen from one moment to the next, I slept deeply that night. When I awoke and peered out of my hut, I saw the village was empty except for Yorugi's parents, and Yorugi herself, still in her seclusion hut.'

'Everyone else had gone?' Blaise asked.

'Yes. I went over and asked Yorugi's father, who looked extremely unhappy, what was happening. "I am sad, White One," he said. "My girl is scared. She will not be cut." I ascertained that Yorugi was to have been scarified with a stone by her godfather.'

'Like boys,' Blaise said.

'Not exactly,' Ezra said. 'Yes, boys had their first initiation at puberty, but those cuts were little more than a few scratches. The boys entered a time of freedom then, of sex with prepubertal girls. After they were done with youth, and were ready for marriage and a family, they would be cut again, deeply. Girls were given deep cuts at puberty, because for them it was now time for marriage and children.'

'So much sex, Daddy,' Blaise frowned.

'For them it was normal,' Ezra explained. 'It wasn't as sad as it sounds.'

'I didn't say it was sad,' Blaise said. Gazing at the carpet, she chewed her hair.

Ezra looked at his manuscript. Yes, he thought, let his memory be the one repository of this experience. It really has to be burned. '"My girl refuses to be cut," Yorugi's father said. "Our law is broken. My daughter lacks courage." He gazed morosely into the distance. "What shall I do, White One?" he asked.'

Ezra stopped talking. He sat immobile in his chair.

After some time, Blaise asked, 'What is it, Daddy? Are you going to finish?'

289

Ezra barely heard her. *What shall I do, White One?* He was back in the forest. 'What?' he murmured. 'Oh. Blaise.'

'What's the matter?'

Ezra shook his head. 'Nothing,' he said. 'You see,' he resumed, 'none of the villagers had ever asked me such a question before. No Indian had once enquired where I came from, from what tribe or family, still less sought my opinion or my advice on any matter. I had been intrigued by, and then grown used to, the Achia's utter lack of curiosity, which I understood as being bound up with their discretion and tact towards each other.

' "What shall I do, White One?" Yorugi's father asked. Shocked, and not wishing to interfere, I mumbled something noncommittal and slipped away. It was only much later that I understood he had asked me this question, had pleaded with me to help cure the disruption, because he sensed that I, with my mirrors and everything else I'd brought, was the cause of it.'

Blaise felt confused. Her father had told the story she'd wanted him to, but then instead of finishing it with the drama of the girl who refused to be cut, he'd carried on, and made it a completely different story. About himself. She had a dead leg, Blaise realised as she pulled herself up. 'Well, thanks, Daddy,' she managed.

'Sleep well,' Ezra muttered, as she leaned down to kiss him goodnight. She left the room. I just told her, Ezra reflected. I just told Blaise, if she could or wanted to hear it. It was all there: why it is I could never go back.

The Pepins and the Azams sat and knelt on tartan rugs, on the raised escarpment of pockmarked pasture that fringed the southern end of Port Meadow. Beneath the high bright sun, the Meadow was sprinkled with people. Optimists threw kites in the air and ran away, and the kites nosed up into the still haze sniffing for a stray current or gust. Bicycles glided along the track to Burgess Field, the smoothness of their movement hard to reconcile with the frantic insect pedalling of riders' thin legs. Couples, small groups, strolled slowly, as if consciously arranging and rearranging themselves into pleasing congregations for those gazing, like Ezra Pepin, from far away.

Out on the Meadow a lad marched in a horizontal line, directly towards the river. Suddenly he broke into a mad spasm, a dancing fit, a Bacchic frenzy, ducking and twisting and swerving.

Gesturing in his direction, Ezra said, 'I wonder what that chap's got playing on *his* Walkman.'

'The boy is sick,' said Abdul Azam. 'That what it is.'

Without taking his eyes off the spectacle, Akhmed's brother, Ishtiaq, said, 'A wasp is pestering him. Maybe he's allergic.'

The young man abruptly altered his tactics, breaking into a run and sprinting towards the river.

They'd met at noon, the Pepins bicycling over, although Blaise had left the house earlier and gone to the Azams: as her family arrived she was helping the sisters – introduced by Abdul as Zenab and Taslima – to lay the rugs with paper plates, plastic utensils and cups, and metal takeaway tubs, whose lids they removed under the instruction of Mrs Azam, who was herself, like her husband, seated on a low folding chair. With each object the girls lifted from the cardboard boxes they'd hauled over from the car park Mrs Azam gesticulated crossly, pointing to where things should be placed exactly, which serving spoons a particular dish required, and other precise points of picnic etiquette. Blaise responded to these peppery exhortations as if she understood them, which Ezra presumed she could not. It seemed important to her to try to second guess and obey Akhmed's mother.

'A wonderful idea, this,' said Sheena.

'Yes, it is,' said Abdul. 'Wonderful. Thank you. Taslima: chairs for Mr and Mrs Pepin.'

'No, it's for us to thank you,' Ezra said.

'My wife,' said Abdul. 'She is pleased to meet your wife.'

Sheena approached Mrs Azam. 'Hello,' she said. 'Sheena Pepin.' Her arm at her side, Ezra observed, was tense with readiness to offer itself for a handshake at the merest twitch of invitation, but Sheena was loath to raise it unilaterally; to impose upon Mrs Azam a method of greeting that may for all she knew have been alien, over-intimate, false for such a meeting.

Mrs Azam nodded her head at Sheena, though with her eyes averted, and muttered various sounds which might – in contrast to her loud and specific Bengali of moments before – have been embarrassed stabs at English. At English vowel sounds, at least.

'Akhmed you know,' Abdul drawled. 'This one my eldest son, Ishtiaq. Then Yusuf, he is not here. Ishtiaq he is just graduated from Liverpool University. Very good degree. Chemistry. He is clever one, Ezra, this boy.'

Akhmed sat on the ground beside his father, his shoulders hunched, while Ishtiaq stood grinning at Ezra. One would have thought it was the younger brother being embarrassed by their father's boasting.

'I haven't actually got the result yet,' Ishtiaq said, smiling.

'Nearly as clever as sister,' Abdul continued. 'Zenab study economics in Manchester, Ezra. She has her mother's brains. And Taslima taking *five* A levels. Of course,' he said, smiling his amusement at Ezra, 'they are all more clever than their father. Everybody more clever than Abdul.'

Ishtiaq turned to Peanut Louie. 'I'm glad someone thought to bring a football,' he said. 'Wanna kick?'

Louie, who'd been staring at one or other of the Azams, now looked down at the ground.

'Come on, Lou,' Hector said. 'He's not really shy,' he explained to Ishtiaq. 'Are you? Only for a minute.'

Ezra watched the three of them trot some yards away, and begin to pass Louie's blue plastic ball between them. Hector was indifferent, if not hostile, to football, as to every sport except swimming. You could see, as he scuffed the ball to Ishtiaq, his ineffectual ungainliness. He was only playing for Louie's sake, and once he judged that his brother was comfortable with this friendly stranger he'd surely slip back here to the main party. Such thoughtfulness, Ezra reckoned: that was something worth boasting about, wasn't it, Abdul?

Louie was wearing his favourite mauve buttoned shirt with

flowers printed on the back. Ezra recalled buying it for Blaise ten years earlier: an early example of chic clothing in infants' size. When Hector inherited it, a couple of years later, young men were briefly wearing such feminine shirts. The style then drifted back out of fashion, but this summer, Ezra had noticed, it had come right back in, with identical cut and design on sale in high street stores, retro cool, his children's chronology synchronous with fashion's ebb and flow.

'My wife prepare all this,' Abdul told Ezra, gesturing towards the feast being made manifest before them. The girls were removing the last of the lids from pots that contained hot food. Spicy aromas rose into the still air. 'Nothing from restaurant, Ezra,' Abdul emphasised.

The Azam boys both wore white shirts and dark trousers. The girls plain but bright shalwar-kameezes. All four children, Ezra observed, were the same height and slim build as their father and each bore the same delicate features, in contrast to their mother, whose coarser physiognomy marked her as someone from a different tribe altogether to the children she and her husband had engendered. As if the sly paternal DNA had outsmarted the mother's rougher genes.

Ezra and Sheena sat on folding chairs, the Pepin boys knelt on the rug beside the men. They were given a plate each, cutlery, napkin. The sisters, assisted by Blaise, carried each dish around.

'What a feast!' Sheena exclaimed in Mrs Azam's direction. Zenab translated, and her mother shook her head in modest agreement.

'What are these?' Sheena asked, taking a cylindrical pastry.

'Masala dosa,' Zenab explained. 'The bhaji's hot. They're nice with that coconut chutney.'

'These are potato samosa tartlets,' said Taslima.

'This is bhel puri, Mum,' Blaise told Sheena. 'It's made with tamarind and jaggery.'

'Jaggery?' Sheena asked, but before her enquiry could be answered, Abdul said, 'Mrs Pepin! Please! You have nothing to drink.

Akhmed, can't you see your sisters busy with food? Serve people, please.'

Akhmed rose and stepped over to a large cooler box, from which he extracted two unlabelled plastic bottles. Anticipating him, Blaise plucked a stack of transparent cups from a box, and chucked them loose as she moved from one person to another. Akhmed followed her with an opened bottle in each hand, saying little louder than a whisper, 'Lemon or ginger?'

There were many dishes, portions of which accumulated upon each person's plate. Under the hot sun they ate the tasty food in silence, except for exclamations of delight from Sheena Pepin as another pungent sensation impressed itself upon her tongue. Samosas and pakoras. Aloor dum, masala onion drops, green peas kachori.

The dishes were too spicy for Louie's palate. He ate nothing but plain parathas: rolling one up, he held each end and nibbled enthusiastically along it. He looked like he was playing a harmonica, consuming it as he played.

The men sat on and around one tartan rug, the women another, brushing off inquisitive wasps. Blaise knelt, like Zenab and Taslima, which looked odd to Ezra: he was sure she customarily sat cross-legged on the ground. She sat closer to Mrs Azam than to Sheena.

There was a restlessness about Mrs Azam as she ate. Her head was bent and her gaze encompassed little more than her plate, but within that limited circumference her eyes darted, and her lips moved. It could almost be mistaken for greed, but it looked to Ezra as if she were plucking up courage to say something, presumably to Sheena; her first sentence ever in English, perhaps, a vital item of information, or sentiment, that she just had to communicate. About their children. Or about the meal. But still she was greedy, gathering morsels with nervous fingers. Until gradually her agitation eased; tranquillised by food, Mrs Azam relapsed in her folding chair into the still silence of an idol.

Abdul Azam, on the other hand, ate without haste, regally chewing as slowly as he spoke.

'Nice place here, Port Meadow, Ezra,' he said. 'I don't come here. Abdul too busy working. It's like that.'

'It's true,' Ishtiaq confirmed, in case Ezra might not have believed his father. 'Dad never does anything like this.'

'We're honoured,' said Ezra.

'No, no,' Abdul said. 'Is our honour.'

'It's common pasture,' said Ezra. 'Never been ploughed. The Thames rises and floods the Meadow every year.'

'Like the Nile,' Abdul nodded.

'Wasn't it the Egyptians,' Ezra said, 'who used three calendars? A political one, another for festivals, and a third based on the rise and fall of the River Nile for farming.'

'And now we all agree to accept one calendar, of scientists,' Abdul smiled. 'Who are so clever, that astronomy is not accurate enough for them. That what it is. Earth does not spin around the sun precisely enough: they discover that planets had been losing two seconds every century.'

This amused Abdul enormously. He actually broke into a guffaw. 'Two seconds every hundred years,' he repeated. 'So now they measure time not by stars but atoms, Ezra. How they do this Abdul cannot explain. My son Ishtiaq would have to explain such things.'

Abdul paused, as if inviting Ishtiaq to tell Ezra exactly how atomic time was calculated. Ezra turned to Ishtiaq, who was frowning, perhaps gathering his thoughts. But before he could speak, his father resumed.

'In an actual fact time, Ezra, is measured by atom vibrations. In each atom many, many electrons moving, trembling, around nucleus like tiny planets around the sun. Do you know,' he asked, turning abruptly to Hector, sitting on the rug, 'how many electrons you can find in a speck of dust?'

Hector looked from Abdul to his father – who raised his eyebrows – to the ground, to the sky and back to Abdul, then shook his head.

'One thousand billion billion,' Abdul said, emphasising each word, and he chuckled again, with a pleasure infectious enough to make others smile. 'Latest atomic clocks,' he drawled proudly, as if he had something to do with making them, 'they lose one second in a thousand years.' He looked from face to face among the men and boys around the rug, nodding his delicate head. 'One second in a thousand years.' And then he stopped nodding, and instead started shaking his head, obliged to remind himself that he was being tempted to take for achievement what was only folly.

It was around then, or a little later, that it occurred to Ezra that for Abdul this picnic was a kind of farewell party; that he was treating all the Pepins to a grand send-off to Brazil. What else would it be? Or had Blaise told him, through Akhmed, that she was staying behind? He didn't appear to be disconcerted by her playing the role of daughter-in-law.

Conversation on the other rug, meanwhile, continued between Sheena and – when they were not obeying their mother's orders to replenish people's plates – Zenab and Taslima. The three of them spoke with a gathering intensity, their bodies adjusting to enable their heads to move gradually closer together. Mrs Azam presided, and Blaise sat close to her, saying not a word, occasionally stealing glances in Akhmed's direction which he, rarely looking up, caught only one or two of. But when he did, he let slip a furtive smile of sly triumph. And Blaise, Ezra reckoned, seemed happier, more genial, here today, than she had in weeks. What was going on?

Throughout the rest of that day, after they'd returned from the picnic, Ezra found his mind consistently slipping from whatever business it was preoccupied with to the same recurring notion. Lolling in the swimming pool with Louie, mowing the small lawn with the electric mower later that afternoon, and on, right up until he lay in bed waiting for Sheena to join him, Ezra Pepin was bothered by this simple reproach: I, we, have given our daughter freedom of thought and deed, ever since she attained the age of reason, and suppose it's not what she wanted? Not at all?

Sheena turned off the light and came out of the bathroom. She got into bed and after checking her alarm clock, then taking a sip of water from her glass, she nestled against Ezra, with her head on his chest, feeling his arm curl around her neck and shoulder.

'What were you talking about at the picnic?' Ezra asked. 'With Akhmed's sisters?'

'I was telling them about the São Paulo landless squatters project.'

'You were?' Ezra said, unable to stop the smile that lifted his lips. 'Did they join up?'

'They were very interested, actually, you old cynic, Ezra Pepin. Zenab and Taslima might well get involved in the solidarity campaign.'

'Really?'

'I wouldn't be surprised.'

They lay with one white cotton sheet covering their naked bodies, perspiring in the stifling night. It was the kind of heat that made everyone cranky; reaching the end of the day, Ezra congratulated himself on the effort he'd expended on remaining congenial.

'I've been thinking,' Sheena said.

'What about?' Ezra asked. He waited patiently through the long pause that followed, his wife's breathing felt through his own ribs.

'I rang the lettings agency.'

Ezra understood this meant something momentous. He didn't want to jump to conclusions, though. 'You did?'

There was another fraught pause. 'We'll stay,' she said.

Ezra felt a gulp of anxiety thrust up into his throat, as if Sheena had just issued a dreadful challenge rather than make the declaration he most desired.

'Are you sure?' he asked.

'While Blaise does her GCSEs,' she said. 'We'll review it in two, three years' time. Can you live with that, Ez? I was thinking, you could leave that job anyway.'

'Oh, no.'

'You could even go on a trip on your own to your tribe if you want. If that's what your heart is set on.'

Ezra squeezed Sheena's shoulder, and shifted his body away from hers so that they lay on their sides facing each other.

'I can live with it, darling,' he said. 'Can you?'

'Of course,' Sheena said. 'The whole idea of it was for you and the children, after all. I mean, my life here is fine.'

'You know, I do believe you're right,' Ezra said. 'I think it's very wise,' he added, trusting that these words, aided by the loving expression on his face, would vindicate Sheena's sacrifice, on his or whoever's behalf she thought she was making it. He kissed her. 'You're not worried about losing our daughter to purdah, though, are you?'

Sheena frowned and smiled at the same time. 'She'll do what she does. I can accept that. Freedom of choice means what it sounds like, doesn't it?'

Ezra kissed Sheena again, pressing his lips to hers. At the same time he inched across the mattress to snuggle closer to her. He felt his erection make contact with her thigh, and assumed she must be aware of it too. He withdrew from their kiss, and gazed at her.

'Ez,' Sheena said. 'I'm really tired. Not sure why. Maybe my period's on its way?'

'That's okay,' Ezra said. He kissed her again. 'You all right?' he asked.

'Yes,' she said.

'Sleep well,' he said, and rolled over. His phallus pressed beneath his body weight against the mattress. It was a pleasant enough sensation, and Ezra assumed he'd drift off to sleep with a hard-on sustained by erotic reverie. But within moments his brain was steering his mind back over the course of the picnic earlier that day. Snippets of dialogue, gestures, pauses, joined one to another and reeled through his mind's eye, snagging at certain moments that had bothered him even at the time but been easily suppressed. Discrepancies of communication which could have been swept under a barrier of language or culture returned to Ezra, and he suddenly realised, with a stab of annoyed admiration, that the Azams had not organised the outing at all. They hadn't invited the Pepins. They thought Ezra and Sheena had organised it, and invited them.

'Thank you.'

'No, thank you.'

'It's so kind of you.'

'No, it's so kind of you.'

What a comedy. What playthings they were. No, it was Blaise who'd engineered the occasion. She'd arranged the entire picnic – without much help from Akhmed, who, Ezra suspected, was wary of the enterprise – but told each family the other was inviting them. She'd brought them all together.

Which was quite an achievement for a girl just turned fourteen, Ezra considered; an accomplishment, indeed, of which he wouldn't mind boasting to Abdul Azam.

15

A Visitor to the House

Saturday 16 August

Ezra Pepin stood with Hector, and Simon and Jack Carlyle, on the shadowed platform of Havant Station. Looking out along the tracks in the direction from which their train might one day come, Ezra saw no movement. Trees stood unnaturally still, as if listening, in the warm air. A cool, unexpected breeze shivered along the platform. People who were sitting on the broken benches trembled. Others stood beside their luggage, primed for disappointment, prepared to bear it with fortitude.

'Mum said we should have gone via London,' said Hector. 'Up to Paddington. Across to Clapham Junction. Out of London from there.'

'Yeh,' Jack agreed, sagely.

'Your mother, Hector,' Ezra said, 'is a leading authority on the British rail network.'

It was the Saturday following the Sunday picnic on Port Meadow, and Ezra had allowed Hector to persuade him that there existed a computer games shop in Guildford selling a unique selection of imported software that he and Jack needed desperately to visit.

'Isn't that exactly the kind of junk you buy on the internet?' Ezra had asked. 'What do you need to go to an actual shop for?' It was an absurd demand, and he agreed to it. He also insisted, and at the same time regretted, that he'd have to accompany the pre-teen boys on such a trip. Simon had done the same. 'There's no point in us both going. Let me,' Ezra suggested, in the hope, the expectation, that Simon would demur and insist that he be the one to fulfil this tedious paternal obligation; after some to and fro polite negotiation Ezra would reluctantly allow Simon's will to prevail. Ezra could do with the day for work while Simon had nothing better to do with his time, and might even enjoy the expedition.

Instead, Simon said, 'Look, old chap, why don't we both go? We each thought we were going to go anyway, we'd each set the day aside. Ed's rehearsing. Minty's enjoying birthday indulgences, shopping for books and shoes; having a facial at that new place on Beaumont Street.'

At Oxford Station the woman at the ticket counter directed them via London. 'Couldn't we travel across country?' Simon wondered. The woman consulted her oracle and printed out an ambitious itinerary of four changes – three with changeovers allowing less than five minutes' slack in total, the fourth with a wait of almost an hour – that if successful would shave eleven minutes off the London time.

The journey down had worked. More than that, Ezra had to admit: it was an exhilaration. The men and their sons leaped from their carriages at Reading, Basingstoke and Bedhampton, scanned around for guards or information screens, then dashed for a connecting train already girding itself for departure from a distant platform. The two men fancied they were sharing elemental skills, passing on to their sons some aptitude necessary to the modern world, as they hunted through the jungle of railway stations, skittish trains, scrambled timetables.

They'd reached Guildford and taken a taxi to the shop, where the boys holed up for a spendthrift hour while the men strolled around before coming back to collect them.

On the return journey their precarious path gave way beneath them. The first train was late leaving Guildford, and was held up along the way. They spent an unexplained interval just outside one station, with a view of two large derelict brick warehouses. Half the roof slates had fallen in. The old warehouses looked like they had been abandoned for a century, superseded by flimsier sheet-metal sheds and Portakabins near by, but been spared demolition. English railway stations seemed to require these ruins.

The train took off again and hurtled along, desperate to get back on schedule. Then it slowed down, and crawled through the countryside. From tired fields black cows observed the train pass. The travellers missed their connection at Havant, where they waited for the next appropriate arrival, which was itself now running late. A voice issued from loudspeakers: 'The twelve thirteen South West train service for Southampton Central has been delayed by fifteen minutes.' The voice was computerised and female. 'Please accept my apologies for the late running of this train.'

Jack turned to Hector and said, 'My Mum said we'd be going by London, too.'

'Have you got your mobile?' Hector asked. He'd removed his glasses and was wiping them with a corner of his T-shirt.

''Course.'

'Why don't you text her, tell her what they've done?'

'Will you two boys stop, already?' Ezra demanded. 'Here,' he said, giving Hector a pound coin. 'Go and find a chocolate machine. Get us all a bar or two of something.'

Hector stared at the coin with an expression of puzzled contempt, then the boys left their bags of newly acquired computer accessories in their fathers' uncertain care and slouched off in search of sugar. Ezra's attention shifted to Simon beside him, chewing his lips with agitation. Ezra followed Simon's gaze, to two or three men in suits kicking their heels, fidgeting with mobiles, parading their self-important frustration.

As if Ezra had then asked him what was up, Simon said, 'Oh, why not just let them take over?'

'Who?' Ezra asked. 'What?'

'Women. Let them have it all, if that's what they want.' Simon's veinous face twitched. 'I don't know about you, Ezra, but whenever I see men working ostentatiously hard – when you know there's no national emergency, and today's Saturday for God's sake – it amuses me. They look like overgrown boys acting out adolescent games, fantasies, of how one should behave as a grown man. It's ludicrous.'

'You think slackers like you, Simon, are the real men of our epoch?'

'Go ahead. Laugh, Ezra,' Simon scowled. 'Don't you notice how one profession after another reports more women joining their ranks than men? Vets. Solicitors. Dentists.'

'Architects.'

'Indeed. It's not funny, it's just inevitable. I wonder how long the numbers will keep rising. I mean, obviously middle-class women have joined middle-class men in all their spheres of employment. What next? Do working-class women rise through the educational ranks, and middle-class men trickle down to join their proletariat brethren?'

'Sounds possible, Simon,' Ezra agreed.

'The point is,' Simon explained, 'that the gender engineered by evolution for reproduction tends also, in general, to be the more efficient one. It happens to be during our time that reproduction is brought under some semblance of control. We're the first to live with the consequences.'

Ezra kept quiet. Simon appeared to have nothing to add. Ezra thought of Blaise. He and Sheena had told the children that the trip to Brazil was postponed. Hector was relieved. Louie greeted the announcement with indifference, as if he'd never taken it altogether seriously in the first place. Only Blaise was disappointed, to judge from her immediate reaction, jaw dropping, eyes narrowing. But she collected herself, recalling that this was, after all, proof that her parents had changed direction purely to accommodate her wishes. Perhaps her initial annoyance, Ezra thought, arose simply because the victory had been too easily won.

That week Akhmed had seemed to be at the Pepins' house every day. On Monday Ezra came home from work to be greeted by the sight of the boy watching TV on his own. Ezra said hello, tried to engage him in conversation. Akhmed said little.

'What's the news?'

'Nothing much.'

'Iraq?'

A shake of the head. Giving nothing away; of his thought or opinion. Two days later, Akhmed got into a digital portrait Sheena took with Blaise's DV camera for a family trailer she wanted to email to one of her sisters. She set it up outside the front door, the camera perched on a car bonnet, with everyone facing the setting sun. Akhmed's small eyes were screwed tight, Sheena had a hand over hers, Hector's were hidden in the shade of the peak of his baseball cap and Louie's by his wide-brimmed sun hat. Ezra, just home from work, shielded his eyes with his briefcase; it looked as if there might be something heavy and precious inside, and Ezra was resting it atop his head. Only Blaise's brown eyes were open and clear before the low evening sun, gazing serenely at each future viewer of the image.

'Akhmed,' Ezra asked Sheena later. 'Is he stupid? Is that it?'

'Of course not.'

'Is that why he doesn't say anything?'

The night before, Friday, Ezra was getting changed after work when he saw Blaise outside in the garden. Sitting in a deckchair on their small lawn, wearing her gold bikini, she had her eyes closed. Standing behind her, Akhmed was rubbing suntan oil into her shoulders. Ezra stood at the window, peering out. The early evening sun was growing less harsh than it had been. Akhmed took longer than he needed to. He was using the suncream as oil with which to massage Blaise's skin. Ezra almost convinced himself that the image was lascivious, hinting at sexual precosity. In the end, though, he had to admit that there was something sad about it.

'Ezra, will you shush? The boy's shy. A little boring, even. If Blaise likes him, trust her.'

Ezra wasn't sure he did. Simon Carlyle was right, the world was hers for the taking. And whatever she wanted to do with her life he'd surely accept. Except to retreat from it. To efface herself.

'This is a platform announcement. The twelve-thirteen South West train service for Southampton Central is running thirty minutes late. Please accept my apologies for the late running of this train.'

Other trains arrived, from each direction: with their tinted windows they entered the station, came to a smoothly sinister halt, then pulled out again.

When the Southampton train finally approached, the passengers waiting on the platform shuffled forward with a certain trembling, sullen anxiety, as if worried that the driver might, in his unapologetic haste to make up lost time, not actually bring the train to a complete halt but only slow it right down and then begin to pick up speed. They attacked the doors and clambered aboard as quickly as they could. The train then sat in the station without moving.

'We won't get home in time to try out all this stuff,' Jack moaned. 'And it's Mum's birthday,' he added, grabbing at less selfish grievance.

'We're meant to be taking her to the Old Parsonage for tea,' Simon explained.

'I hope she has a nap this afternoon,' Ezra said. 'You too. All of us. The thing tonight won't get going till eleven or twelve.'

'Good God,' said Simon.

'At the earliest.'

Presently a message was broadcast on the train. 'This is your buffet car attendant speaking. We have unfortunately run out of change. Will anyone please come to the buffet car, at the front end of the train, with the correct change.'

'Does he mean,' Simon asked, 'that those intending to come to the buffet car should only come if they have loose change?'

'How do we know if it's the correct amount?' Hector asked.

'Or is he imploring anyone on the train with change to bring it to him?' asked Ezra. 'Perhaps buy something they don't necessarily want. I'm not hungry or thirsty, are you?' Ezra leaned into the aisle so that he could scrabble in his jeans pocket.

'I could do with a drink,' Simon suggested, hauling himself to his feet. 'One of those mini wine bottles. How about you, boys? Coke or something?'

Staying to guard the computer treasure, Ezra watched the others stagger along the rolling aisle. He wondered whether they'd get caught in a stampede of helpful passengers, rushing to assist the buffet car attendant, with his lack of change and his outrageously priced goods – about which Simon would surely come back complaining. Every item was twice the price it was in the shops. Ezra was too mean and too organised, usually, to buy food or drink aboard a train – even now that he could easily afford to, he would still rather prepare sandwiches and a flask for a long journey. The caterers needed more than half as many customers as would have bought if items had been sold at half the price. Accountants must have carried out cost analysis and consumer surveys, made calculations, and reckoned exorbitant prices promised optimum profit.

It mystified Ezra, this sort of financial process, if he were honest. An understanding of the basic mechanisms at work eluded him, despite the fact that he had this week taken part in meetings to brainstorm the Middle East water-bottle project. In addition to himself and Carl Buchannan, and the accountant Alan Blozenfeld, Thomas Kohler had joined them from Germany. 'My can-do man,' Klaus Kuuzik called him. A freelance advertising executive, Sarah Carney, had been hired on a two-year contract. And Professor Hisham Abu Ghassan, at St Antony's, was being employed as a consultant. Klaus Kuuzik had assembled his primary team.

'Suppose, for the sake of simplicity,' Klaus had addressed them at their first gathering in the boardroom at 10 a.m. that Tuesday morning. 'Suppose we say it costs us ten pence to produce a bottle of water. In the UK and elsewhere in Europe our customers pay one pound a bottle. In the Middle East the average child might be able to afford one pence. Now, suppose we assume for the moment that we can subsidise this sale – of course with the plant built in Turkey our unit costs will be lower than here – what is the best way to penetrate the market, without Isis Water being seen as nothing more than the cheapest rubbish on offer?'

306

All day they discussed a campaign. It was agreed they needed to make the product hip, desirable, emblematic. The best way to do that, Ezra said, was when cultural icons were seen to drink it. Who were they? Singers, of course. Athletes. Footballers.

The leaders of Hamas, said Professor Abu Ghassan. The martyrs of the Al-Aksa Brigade. The exiles of Hezbollah.

Arafat? Sarah Carney asked.

Bin Laden, Abu Ghassan said, frowning.

If such figures could be photographed with bottles of Isis Water, the product would be identified with the liberation struggle. They discussed the difficulties of providing free water to chosen groups; the hazards of faking such photographs, digitally planting bottles into preexisting images and using these in a brazen poster campaign. Would Palestinians, Klaus wondered, possess sufficient irony to see through the superficial deceit?

'Of course,' said Abu Ghassan. 'Irony was invented by Arabs.'

They went on to speculate as to whether or not bottles should be sold not in the whole of Israel but only in the West Bank and Gaza, then the refugee camps of Lebanon, before spreading out to Jordan, Syria, Egypt and beyond.

The value of a massive teaser campaign was agreed upon, making the brand as visible as possible before a single bottle appeared for sale, except for 'pirated' supplies manifesting in critical locations.

'If my demeanour is becoming gloomy,' Alan Blozenfeld said, 'it's because the more successful this venture is, the worse off we'll be. If we lose five pence per unit, the more units we sell the more money we lose.'

'Surely you are joking, Alan,' said Thomas Kohler. 'We shall be increasing returns to scale. The more we give away, the more dominant our position in the larger network, and the more we stand to make from the pennies we take from each transaction.'

They agreed to virtually give away the product as a loss-leader. It was a standard branding technique: Isis Water bottles would establish and uphold the image of the DeutscheWasser brand – whose other, more profitable lines, in municipal supply and in the vast market that technology promised in the haulage of water from region to region, would benefit from the association.

Buy Isis Water: support justice in the Middle East. Support justice in the Middle East: buy Isis Water. They were going to use the means of capitalism to achieve its opposite, they were not making profit but spending profit from here over there. Thomas Kohler was a fixer. Of course he wasn't in on the real reasons behind the project. Maybe none of the others were, either. Only Carl Buchannan and himself. If Ezra found himself musing on the future provision of water and waste-water contracts in the region, and whether they weren't the smokescreen disguising a philanthropic vision but might really be the reason for the project, then he dismissed such speculation as the product of a mind raddled with exactly the kind of cynicism that Klaus and Carl and Ezra himself were attempting to overcome.

Simon drank two glasses of wine for each of Ezra's small bottles of beer. Ezra observed a gradual loose swelling beneath Simon's skin, the wine seeping into the red flesh.

The boys played some game together on Jack's hand-held console, smirking and squeaking and nudging each other like two companionable robots.

'Jack's bloody glad you've put off this Brazil thing,' Simon said. 'As we all are, naturally.'

The last time the Carlyles came over for supper, two weeks earlier, Ezra had asked Blaise if she wanted to join them.

'No.'

'I mean, say if Ed came, too.'

'Ed? You don't have any *idea* how boring he is, Daddy.'

'You used to get on so well.'

'He's a musician,' she said. 'He's obsessive. Worse than ever.'

'Simon,' Ezra asked now. 'Tell me. Do you worry about Ed's future ever?'

'Ed? Not really. We're kind of assuming already he'll be an organ scholar somewhere. King's, maybe. Oxford, even. It's what he seems to want, consistently. Until he finds some damn fool to support him so he can compose, that is.' This last thought seemed to amuse Simon, and his swollen face chuckled to itself as if he'd made a rather witty remark.

The guard strode, his back straight, along the carriage. Ezra wondered whether the man walked with a sailor's roll on dry land. He gazed out of the window, at the cooling towers of Didcot power station and the bland brick commuter estates of the satellite town, which seemed to have spawned more of themselves since he and his group had passed by this morning. He wondered how long it would be, how many more generations of his progeny, before they covered the surface of England.

When you're a mother walking into Summertown with a three-year-old child, Sheena admitted, you didn't need to be a mind-reader to know when to let your hand fall loose at your side, so that little fingers would reach and find it there, and grasp your fingers tight. At the Co-op Louie took the pound coin she gave him and liberated one of the daisy chain of shopping trolleys. She lifted him inside: he'd never liked those folding shelves in the front of big trolleys that provide a baby seat. Louie preferred to sit inside the trolley itself, to have Sheena pass goods to him and let him stack them up around his body.

By the time they reached the checkout the trolley was so full the boy looked part of the bounty, a cut-price orphan for sale, but it was now that he came into his own. With great self-importance Louie lifted each item from trolley to counter's black rolling belt.

'Training him young, aren't you?' remarked the woman behind Sheena.

'There's a job going here bagging up, love,' said the checkout assistant. Sheena nodded modestly. She took no credit: Louie's behaviour tickled her as much as it did them and she watched too as the tiny boy heaved tins of beans and tomatoes, and bags of vegetables, on to the counter.

At much the same moment during that hot afternoon, Blaise was lying on her front on a rug on the lawn. She had on her gold bikini

309

thong. She thought she'd dozed off, and was dreaming the tired wasp droning around her. Whenever it stopped buzzing, she knew that meant the wasp was on or inside the can of Red Bull that stood within reach of her right arm. By now it was too warm to drink anyway. Blaise realised she probably wasn't asleep when she heard, through the open windows of the house, the front doorbell ring. Unless, of course, the sound of it had woken her. Still, she had no desire to move. Her cheeks felt slack and itchy on the woollen tartan, and her limbs felt heavy on the earth, as if the earth had got so hot it was slowly rising through the universe, and lifting her with it.

The doorbell rang again. Go away, Blaise murmured, opening her eyes. Sheena and Louie were shopping; Ezra and Hector on a train. Akhmed was at a family gathering. Whoever it was, she was sure it wouldn't be for her. She was staring at a group of flowers with bright-orange petals. White butterflies hovered around them. She wondered whether one of the students in the house next door, whose shadow she'd seen at the window, was still watching her. Blaise closed her eyes and with a droopy effort heaved herself up, clutching a small towel to her bare chest, and stumbled inside.

As Blaise pulled on the T-shirt she'd left on the kitchen table, the bell rang a third time. 'Can't you see I'm coming?' she snapped, marching through to the hall. She opened the door. A man she didn't recognise was jogging on the spot. He wore a pair of shorts and nothing else, apart from socks and trainers.

'Good afternoon. I am so,' he said. He was breathing heavily. 'Sorry to disturb you. Is your father in, by any chance?'

Blaise shook her head. The man was younger than Daddy, she thought, maybe. A little. He was lean and muscular. She wondered how long he'd been running, to be so out of breath.

'You are expecting?' the man asked, gulping air. 'Him back soon?'

Blaise looked at her watch. Surely he and Hec should have been home by now? 'Yes,' she said.

'It doesn't matter,' the man said. 'I thought I would drop in to ask Ezra something. While I was running.'

Blaise nodded. The fact that he had said her father's name relieved an unease she'd not been fully aware of feeling.

'I have run all the way from,' the man said. 'Cumnor. Over.' He turned and gestured towards the distance behind him. 'Wytham Woods. Across the Meadow. And I must run back.'

It struck Blaise as the man said the last word, pronouncing it beck, that it sounded like a clue, which her brain had fortuitously detected.

'But I would appreciate a refill of my water bottle, if you don't mind,' he said.

Blaise took the bottle from the man. She didn't know whether she should leave him there. She didn't want to. 'Come in,' she said, and led the way to the kitchen. The man followed. Blaise realised that she only had a bikini bottom on beneath her T-shirt, and she imagined the man was watching her legs. The thought pleased her. In the kitchen she fetched the filter-water jug from the fridge, and filled the man's water bottle over the sink.

'If you don't mind,' the man said, 'I would like also a glass of water.'

He stood close beside her. Blaise reached for a large glass that stood upside down at the far end of the draining rack. She had the odd feeling that the man stretched with her, so as to remain in close proximity, then returned as she did to their previous position. The sun poured through the windowpanes; the kitchen was hot as a greenhouse. She filled the glass, and handed it to him. He lifted it to his lips, and began to drink, greedily. His tanned body was covered in sweat, and she could see tiny beads of perspiration emerging on his skin: he was still sweating. The smell was strong and remarkably sweet. He finished half the glass and paused, even more breathless than before, and stood there beside her, gulping air. He had short brown hair cropped close to his head, and there were droplets of sweat sitting on top of it. Blaise curled her tongue inside her mouth. She wanted to reach up and run her hand, run both hands, over and through his hair. He raised the glass again and drank. She watched his throat pulsate, his Adam's apple rise and fall. She imagined the water falling through his almost hairless

311

chest, his hard stomach. As if in sympathy with him, Blaise realised that she too was breathless. She wondered if his sweat would taste as sweet as it smelled; she could sense her tongue's desire for it.

The man drained the glass, lowered it to the draining board. He took a deep breath, let out a long, slow exhalation. Blaise became aware all of a sudden of how much heat was emanating from him. That was why it was so hot in here. She wanted to edge closer to him; to be drawn inside his body heat. He didn't move. She looked up at his face, to find him looking at her, with deep blue eyes that wondered, Is that really what you're thinking?

Blaise met his gaze long enough to feel a flush of shame that was warm and pleasant. She lowered her gaze.

'Thank you so much,' the man said. 'I had better be on my way now.' He strolled back through the house. Now Blaise followed him. She didn't want him to go. But if he was going, then what she wanted, she thought, was to keep following close behind him.

'I have a good run in front of me,' he said. He turned on the threshold, and Blaise met his gaze as he said, 'You are so kind.' He smiled, turned and jogged away. His bare back rippled. His feet were slightly pigeon-toed. He rose easily off the soft tarmac.

'You never left a message,' Blaise murmured, after his departing figure.

16

Party

Saturday 16 August

'What are these?' Simon asked, of the yellow pills Ezra had passed back from the driver's seat. 'Ecstasy?'

'No.'

'Oh.'

Alarm in the syllable Simon uttered made Ezra waver. 'But almost,' he said. 'Kind of. A chemical variant for sure. But smooth.'

'Smooth?'

'And mild. Much milder.'

'You hear these stories.'

'I know,' Sheena, sitting beside Simon in the back, agreed. 'That's why I'm not taking any.'

'Hey,' said Minty, over her shoulder. 'I thought it was because you're going to be driving back.'

'Oh, that's right,' Sheena admitted. 'And yes, I did say I might take a small amount of something later. If I feel like it.'

The chances of which, Ezra reckoned, were about one in ten thousand. They were driving through the dark, across country. It was eleven o'clock at night and there was still, to their left, a long horizontal vestige of daylight along the far horizon.

313

'It really doesn't make sense, does it?' Sheena, leaning forward, demanded of Minty, who had taken over in the passenger seat ten minutes earlier, Ezra pulling over to allow the two women to swap places.

'*When the tree and the barn and the big bird meet,*' Minty read by the light from the glove compartment. '*There turn left.* Of course, it might make sense in daylight.'

'But everyone's going to be driving at night,' Ezra protested.

'Could the organisers be, perhaps, a little dumb?' Minty conjectured.

Roger Slocock had forwarded Ezra an email attachment whose printout was confusing them on this, the night of Minty's fortieth birthday. The directions were more like clues in a treasure hunt.

'We have to think laterally,' Ezra advised.

'What's actually *in* this?' Simon wondered, in the back.

'Let's hope the clue's in this town,' said Sheena.

'It doesn't say anything about a town,' said Minty.

'We also have to be patient,' Ezra added. 'Distances appear further at night. Periods of time seem longer.'

'Wait a minute,' said Minty. 'Slow down. What's that?'

In the middle of the main street of the small town, in among the shops on the ground floors of old brick houses, was one with the iron profile of a predatory bird jutting out like a ship's figurehead over the doorway.

'*Falcon Insurance Services,*' Minty read out. 'And look across the street: *The Antiques Barn.*'

'Why don't the directions just say, *The Antiques Barn*?' Sheena objected.

'There's a tree,' Ezra confirmed.

'Take a left,' Minty ordered. 'Just here.'

'What's it going to do to me?' Simon asked.

'*In the valley of death, look for the sign of salvation. There turn right,*' Minty read.

'A cemetery?' Ezra proposed.

'That's just what I was thinking, sport,' said Minty. 'You know, this is rather fun.'

'I guess the idea is,' said Ezra, 'that if you make it difficult to find, then only those who really want it will be there.'

'I really want it,' said Minty. 'I hope you do, too.'

'Oh, he does, don't worry,' Sheena said.

'It's been a long time,' Ezra concurred with a sigh. 'Losing it on the dance floor.'

Midnight found them three clues further on and driving in an undeniable circle in the deserted middle of nowhere, a three-mile loop, whose growing familiarity mocked them, until they found themselves behind a convoy of five or six other cars being driven with the hesitant irritation of people as lost as they were. But then, as if they were drops of water joining together and with surface tension flowing, the lead car took an abrupt right into the circle, through a gap in a fence beside chained metal gates, and the other cars followed, the stream of them spiralling down a lane into an old industrial estate. Within a minute they'd reached a wide quad of rusting, sagging, empty, single-storey warehouses around a car park already half-filled with cars. And one ancient four-storey concrete building, from whose many windows light of varied and altering hue pulsated.

Ezra turned off the car engine. A throbbing beat besieged them.

'Good God,' Simon said, and swallowed his pill.

'Let's explore,' Ezra suggested, after they'd gone inside, 'and meet back here in, what, half an hour?'

He set off alone, but Minty followed, and he let her hold on to his hand, allowed her to be led by him through the building. Beyond the lobby, the ground floor was a single vast space, sparsely dotted with dancing bodies. At its centre was a slightly raised dais with a horseshoe of decks, behind them two DJs, each wearing headphones. One could imagine that the booming beat that blasted the room did not exist, the room was actually silent, and in the silence each of the DJs was listening to something else through his headphones, because one DJ was bouncing up and down, nodding at the few people around the room and pounding his fist in the air above his head, as if trying to communicate a message – perhaps of martial victory – coming in on his radio. While the other was bent over the decks like a scientist, performing some delicate experiment with needle and vinyl.

Upstairs, the layout was different on each floor. Ezra and Minty wandered through labyrinths of tunnels and rooms and open areas. As they entered each one Minty felt herself infused with a strange conviction: that here she'd find treasure. When it wasn't there Minty suffered only fleeting disappointment, because by the time they entered the next section of the maze she found the same suffusion of hope rising from her belly, spreading through her body.

Ezra turned to Minty, saw her expression of anxious delight. 'You're coming up,' he whispered in her ear.

As they wandered around the building it carried on filling with people, of varied age, colour, dress. Two youths in tracksuits, a girl in fluorescent leggings, a middle-aged man in a suit. Where they'd all come from, Minty couldn't imagine. It was a miracle she and her group had found this place; that so many other people had also succeeded in deciphering those beautiful directions seemed incredible. Impossible. A woman in an antique dress, a girl in a tie-dye T-shirt, a shaven-headed boy in jeans. Some wore masks, others had faces painted like tigers. Tattoos, jewellery. Angel wings. Outfits of glowing wire; luminous tops. There were elves, aliens.

Minty followed Ezra. He seemed to be strolling at a perfect speed, not too fast, not too slow, pausing just as she realised she'd like to stop too, to look around her; and then anticipating by a fraction her wish to move on again, leading her forward.

Away from the main dance floor, the music was made up of sounds that evoked railways, factories, ships. Metallic rap and reverberation. Motors. Alarms. Along one corridor, with pipes and cables above their heads, were submarine drips, radar signals,

316

sonar echoes in tip-tapping, percussive rhythms. Minty heard the music go into slow motion. The beats stretched out. The music pondered itself, and altered its rhythmic texture, as they moved through rooms, alcoves, hallways.

'Whatever this is,' Ezra told her, 'it's making time slow down.'

'What is?' Minty asked.

'This pill,' Ezra said. 'Come on. We'd better find the others.'

Sheena and Simon weren't where they'd agreed to meet. Ezra embarked on forays around the building looking for them. Sometimes Minty stayed at the meeting point; sometimes anxiety made her insist on going with him. The building was full of people lost; looking for friends, a drink, a tap, a toilet. Others seemed rooted to the spot: they didn't know where they were any more, waited for someone to rescue them.

When Minty saw Sheena at last back at the meeting point near the front door she was so pleased to see her friend that she moved forward to embrace her, but before she could do so Sheena had addressed Ezra: 'Where the hell have you been?'

'We've been looking –' he began, but she cut him off by turning to address Minty.

'Simon's sick. He's out in the car.'

The night was still warm. Simon lay on the back seat of the Saab, his knees bent. 'I'm fine,' he muttered, eyes closed. 'Just let me die in peace.'

Minty knelt on the driver's seat. She stretched her arm over and put the palm of her hand to Simon's forehead. Then she got out of the car and walked away from it, lighting a cigarette.

Ezra followed her.

'If we have to leave,' Minty said, 'I'll cry all the way home.' She stopped and looked imploringly at Ezra. 'Please don't let him ruin this, Ezra. Please.' She looked up at the sky as she took another drag, as if tilting her head were the only way to keep her unhappiness at the prospect of departure from spilling out and overwhelming her.

Sheena joined them. 'What's in those pills, for God's sake?' she demanded.

'I don't know,' Ezra snapped back.

'I beg your pardon?'

Ezra sighed. 'They call them creativity pills,' he said. 'I got them from someone at work. They flood the synaptic pathways with, I don't know, dopamine. Serotonin. Other stuff maybe. The marketing guys rate this one highly.'

'Ezra.'

'Musicians use it. What its exact name is,' he shrugged, 'the precise ingredients, no, I can't tell you.'

This, thought Sheena, was the problem. You couldn't get a better example than this. Ezra had distributed samples of some unknown, illegal chemical, to their friends who never took drugs, in some place in the back of beyond. It was the kind of thing irresponsible teenagers did, and he was thirty-nine years old, the father of three children. Her children. She was struck with force and clarity by the sudden understanding that Ezra would never grow up. She'd always assumed he would, because people did, eventually. But no, her husband would grow old, and die, without ever reaching maturity.

'Well,' she said, shaking her head. 'Come on, then. We'd better get going. Minty, you can sit with Simon's head on your lap, okay?'

'No,' said Ezra. 'Simon's just come up. He's a little nauseous, it's normal. He'll recover. Give him an hour or two.'

'Are you joking?' Sheena asked. There was a groan from the car. 'What if he's allergic to what he took?' She turned to Minty. 'Are you serious?'

'This is Minty's birthday party,' Ezra persisted. 'It's her first and last experience of all this. Don't you see?'

Sheena's mouth formed a sardonic smile. 'Of all what?' she asked, and then glanced back at the party building. 'That horrific noise? Those sick-looking people? Did you see the puddles and the broken glass in the toilets? The sordidness?' Sheena looked at Minty, who gazed vacantly back at her, and shook her head. 'I'll drive him home, then. You two make your own way, whenever.

However.' She turned, still shaking her head, and walked to the car.

Ezra and Minty returned to the main room on the ground floor and danced. The DJs were different now, a man and a woman who poured thudding beats down from their dais. The music inhabited not just time but space as well, beats spilled on to the dance floor and pounded about in long curlicues, figures of eight, quadrangular successions. Minty danced in their slipstream. She forgot about Simon, and Sheena. The past dissolved, the future, too.

Spasms of rhythm, judders, stutters. It occurred to Ezra, watching her, that Minty danced as if she was blind. She'd never been into dancing, she admitted: it made her feel awkward. At teenage parties Minty was the pretty girl who stood in the kitchen, smoking, drinking, wisecracking with the boys, attracting them and putting them off at the same time. But this music invited her to move. The beat became a vehicle and she climbed aboard, and her body did what it did. People danced between bodies, spraying hot faces with a cool mist, or handing out bottles of Isis Water.

Hours passed in the world outside. Minty became a better dancer in front of Ezra's eyes: her movement had an element of surprised delight about it; the music was in her head and in her limbs, her shoulders, her abdomen. It was ages since he'd been with someone their first time. Eventually, he thought he saw her flagging, and felt it himself, and he led her off the dance floor and upstairs. A hot, sweet aroma drew them to a room where a bearded man was doling out chai.

There were benches made of metal girders and they sat down.

'Are you having a good time?' Ezra asked, knowing full well how rhetorical the question was.

'How could I not know about this?' she asked. 'When it was all around. How could you not tell me?'

'I just tag along with Roger and his crowd, really,' Ezra said. 'London, mostly. You have a light?'

319

They lit cigarettes. Minty's hand trembled. 'Even this fag tastes great,' Minty exclaimed. 'And this sweet tea. And if anyone had told me this music was stupendous . . .'

Ezra smiled. 'A lot of music is on nice candy.'

'How often do you do this?'

'Three, four times a year.'

Minty shook her head. 'Does Sheena not like it?'

Ezra took a drag, drew it in, exhaled. 'She always thought it was, I don't know, undignified. I remember her asking me, a while back, if I wasn't getting too old for this kind of thing. She said, "Do you want to die on the dance floor, Ezra?" '

They both laughed. 'I said that no, I supposed I didn't, but then again I couldn't think of a better place to go. Which didn't impress her.'

They took another, red, pill each, and smoked, and drank chai, squeezed against each other on the metal bench. Other people smiled back at them: they knew, somehow, that Minty could feel the chemical dispersing, breaking down and multiplying in a microscopic way, and flowing through her bloodstream. Was it that apparent? Her muscles relaxed, her skin prickled. Zones of her body tingled with a warm pleasure.

When he'd put his cigarette out, Ezra ushered Minty to sit on the floor in front of him, between his knees, and with his eyes closed he massaged her neck and shoulders. It was one of the things you did for someone at a party, you could do it for a friend that you were with or for a stranger, man or woman, with no ulterior motive. It was a matter of etiquette. He liked that, the way that behaviour informally became a custom.

Once Ezra felt he'd done enough, had pressed out all the knots he could find, had loosened Minty's stringy muscles until he was sure she was relaxed before him, he brought his hands to rest on her shoulders. Electronic sounds, rising in tone, like a series of questions: they were underlaid by a rhythmically unpredictable percussion, which had the urgency of something underground approaching. Ezra let himself be infused by the music, and by this feeling it induced of continual anticipation. When he opened his eyes, it was to a roomful of otherworldly beings. The light glowed, colours distinguished themselves from one another as if colour was living matter. The room shone with the sense of imminent arrival. It occurred to Ezra that if he was lucky, if he just sat here still and open and aware, he might be graced by revelation. Some understanding was about to be given to him.

Ezra realised that Minty had laid her hands on his on her shoulders, and she let them lie there a moment before leaning forward and twisting round, putting her hands on his knees now for leverage, and kneeling up high in front of him.

What with Minty's long legs and the metal girder resting on old car batteries, low to the ground, Ezra's face and hers were at the same height. Minty gazed at Ezra. First meeting, then trying to avoid, her eyes, he lowered his own gaze a few inches. It struck him that Minty's lips were full, and soft, and hungry. They parted, and moved towards him. Her lips melted into his. They kissed for a long time. Ezra was astonished by how good a kisser Minty was: both reticent and avaricious, holding back – neither giving nor taking everything – but what she did give Minty gave with a tender greed.

It occurred to Ezra after a while that this snog was so sumptuous, there was so much feeling in his lips, they might carry on all night. But then he realised Minty had drawn back. Disappointed, he opened his eyes: she stood up, and pulled him after her, and now it was her turn to lead him, on a journey up stairs, along corridors, and Ezra let himself be led.

Minty settled on a stairway that climbed in thickening darkness beyond them to a locked door. She stood on the step above him and they renewed their kiss. This time her fingers fluttered around Ezra's head, like insects. It was like having daddy-long-legs crawling across his face, through his hair; it was just what he might have feared from the irritating manner of Minty's hesitant yet intimate half-hug embraces. Her tongue, though, now engaged with his, and it seemed to discover a direct connection to his penis, which throbbed with pleasure and need.

Ezra took hold of Minty's wrists. He didn't want her spidery fingers on him. He wanted to get to flesh. Her body, her belly, her vagina. He stepped up, pushing between her legs, and as he did so he slid his hands up her skirt, raising it, and grasped her buttocks and lifted her up. He fumbled her panties loose. She undid his trousers. Her legs, Minty's fine, long legs, wrapped themselves around his waist; she lowered herself on to him. He rammed her against the wall.

Slim though she was, Minty was heavy enough to make it hard work for Ezra to both carry her and screw her; he pressed her against the wall but each time he retreated her weight came with him, and he thrust back at her with relief as the wall took the bulk of her weight again. The pounding beat of the music pummelled up the stairs like the fanfare of some prowling, growling beast. Their bodies submitted to the beat, and the beat was eaten up by time; it was impossible to tell how long they were there. Ezra realised at length that Minty was weeping and moaning. He couldn't work out why she was pretending. No woman had ever sobbed while having sex with him, and Ezra couldn't understand it, until it occurred to him that he was hurting her, thumping her back against the wall. He realised more or less simultaneously that his knees and his arms were burning, with an insupportable pain. He stood still for a while, Minty pressed back against the wall. Ezra leaned forward against her, breathing hard. Then he shuffled back and sat down, Minty astride him. He had to sit forward, on the outside edge of the step.

'You haven't come?' she whispered.

'I don't seem to need to,' Ezra told her. 'Quite happy, though.' They chuckled against each other.

'Oh, darling,' said Minty, her voice sticky in his ear. She started to ruffle his hair with her fingers and plant kisses across his head, which, rather than dearousing him, as he expected it to, sent a tingle of annoyance to his phallus that caused it to engorge even more.

'Okay,' he said, taking hold of her hands, 'that's okay. Why don't we just hold each other?'

Minty rested her head on his shoulder. He offered her water, which she declined with the slightest single shake. He drank some. Ezra felt himself detumescing, finally, and Minty slid off him. 'I'd better find a toilet,' she said, and she descended the stairs.

By the time the others got back to Oxford Simon had been resurrected from the back seat, clambered clumsily over into the front, and been yacking for twenty minutes without pause. Sheena's annoyance with Ezra, and with Minty, had shifted to her passenger, and she was glad to reach Bainton Road and drop him off outside the Carlyles' house.

'Now you're sure you're okay?' she asked.

'Honestly, I feel inexplicably light-hearted,' Simon beamed. 'Are you positive you won't come in? You are the most wonderful company, Sheena Pepin. I mean, we're having an enthralling conversation; seems such a pity to cut it short.'

It wasn't yet two o'clock. Sheena parked the car, let herself into the house. All was quiet. The kitchen was clean and tidy: Blaise had cleared up. Had she done it on her own, or organised the boys to help her? The latter, surely.

Simon was fine. Ezra and Minty were welcome to that cacophonous squalor – how could they call that a party? – let her have her birthday fling. Sheena would retrieve a few hours' sleep from the night: a far preferable alternative. Barefoot on the carpets, she looked in on the children. Their bedroom doors were open, the light on on the landing. Louise had already kicked the duvet off his bed. In his pyjama shorts he lay on the bare mattress, legs tucked up to his stomach, spine curved protectively around himself. Dreaming, in exile, of the womb.

Hector lay still, barely breathing, a slight frown on his face. Sheena held her own breath, fearful of waking him: he looked like he was floating an inch below the surface of sleep, apt to rise at any moment. Her beloved boy. Would Hec find a woman to hold him, Sheena wondered, to protect him from the anxiety that gnawed at him?

Reaching Blaise's room, Sheena trod softly over to her

323

daughter's bed. Blaise lay on her side. Her lips were parted; she looked so young, prepubertal; the duvet on her body gently rose, and fell, but her head was still as death on the pillow. She looked exhausted and alone.

This planet, thought Sheena, undressing in her bathroom, is so heavily populated. And the more people there are, the more loneliness there is in this world, because that's the human condition. None more so than a mother's, her children sleeping. Separate. Which must be why a mother learns, if she's willing, this self-sufficiency of the heart. Because to train your children to validate your existence with their love is to inflict an unpardonable burden upon them. It is, Sheena believed, the one thing you should not do.

Ezra knew how important it was not to think, and he took Minty back down to the main dance floor. They swallowed a blue pill each, and danced. Ezra absolved himself of responsibility: Minty could try and think if she wanted to, she could try and focus her feelings on Ezra or any other thing she might wish to, but if she was dancing then the dance, he hoped, would engulf her.

The room was packed: hundreds of people jigged and tripped and cavorted. Ezra and Minty wove a way through until they found a space that they could claim, and then they joined the flailing dance. If they rested, or closed their eyes, geometric shapes formed themselves in their vision, liquid fractals that melted and reformed and changed colour with the rhythms of the music. So they opened their eyes and danced again. Around them wild-eyed dervishes danced.

The light that Ezra had kept sensing through the night was there all the time now: it made what he saw shine with more light than there was. A party, Ezra decided, is illumination. That's what it is. Of what? Of nothing. Nothing else. A light that illuminates itself.

The lighting in the room, meanwhile, was dimmed, and then turned off. It was entirely dark, except for bulbs at the DJs' consoles, and the music darkened, sinister and compulsive, lifting the partygoers out of time's reach and into some other dimension.

Outside, though, the day was breaking. Dawn lightened the dance floor with an uncanny, gradual tact. What had been an occult, nocturnal conglomeration of individual experience altered with the lambent light into a communal responsibility to lift this party to the highest level it could reach and carry it to a conclusion. From being lost in the discovery of her body's response to music, Minty found herself gradually joining the crowd around her; a newcomer coming in.

DJs built a great ladder of music, and the dancers climbed on to a shimmering, silent plateau. Ezra and Minty were lost in an exhausted cacophony of whistles, shrieks, handclaps and howls. They embraced each other in the middle of the crowd.

'I'm so happy, Ezra,' Minty told him. 'I never imagined I could have this.'

'It's phenomenal, isn't it?' he replied.

'I love you so much, darling,' she said.

They cadged a lift off a couple who drove south-west and dropped them outside Southam, at a petrol station that was open. A young Asian man stood behind the counter.

'Can we get a taxi round here?' Ezra asked him, while Minty coaxed coffees from the cheap machine, and chose chocolate bars.

'At this time on a Sunday morning?' the man replied.

'Well, do you know anyone who'd like to earn fifty quid by driving us to Oxford?'

The young man stared at Ezra.

'Maybe a friend, or there's someone you know?'

'I'll do it,' he said. 'Plus the cost of the petrol, yeh? I'll call my uncle to take over here.'

'I feel like someone's washed my brain,' Minty said in the back of the Honda ferrying them home. 'Debugged it. Got rid of cookies and worms.' She closed her eyes. 'My hard drive's clean.'

Ezra murmured agreement. 'Scooped out,' he said. He sat back comfortably, glad of the leg room. Their driver had put on Pakistani pop music as they drove through the countryside towards Banbury. Minty leaned against Ezra. He had his arm around her, she rested a hand against his chest.

After a while, Minty asked, 'What are you thinking about, darling?'

'Blaise,' Ezra answered without hesitation. A single word, one harmless syllable. It burrowed into Minty's mind. All these years he'd thought of Sheena. Now he was thinking of her clone daughter. Even if Minty were to abide, what next? Would Blaise conceive with her callow boyfriend, give birth to a troublesome daughter just to land her poor father with another angry woman to kowtow to; to steer his destiny around?

'I was thinking,' Ezra said, 'about the loss of ideals. It just struck me, maybe Blaise is my conscience.'

'You? Are you crazy? Sheena's the one she's –'

'I'm glad if she is.'

'Oh, Ezra,' Minty said, leaning closer against him. 'You fool.'

'What were *you* thinking about?' he asked.

'You. Me. Us. The others.'

'Sure,' Ezra said. 'There's that.'

They cruised towards home, past the green hedgerows and the yellow fields. To Ezra's relief the driver was content to drive at a relaxed pace.

'There's all that,' Ezra agreed. 'But you know? This question of culpability? I mean, children look at the world and they demand of their parents, "What did you do?" We say, "Well, we did this and we did that. We marched now and then. We gave what we could. We've given you what we thought you needed." But is it enough? Suppose it never can be?'

The car glided past Upper Heyford, Steeple Aston, where the road widened and opened up. Ezra sat back and gazed at green fields under the blue sky. The truth of what had happened began to seep into his consciousness. He'd had sex with his and Sheena's friend Minty. What on earth was he going to do? He must be out of his mind. Minty clung to him. He closed his eyes. The car's wheels spun and glided across the surface of the earth, and with a little luck they wouldn't be home yet for at least another fifteen, even twenty minutes.

17

Urban Rain

Tuesday 19 August

Tuesday of that week had been designated Bring Your Daughter to Work Day at Isis Water. Employees struggled to overcome their children's reluctance and their own embarrassment at this transatlantic innovation; they found it hard to square with their aloofly charismatic German boss, until they saw three athletic-looking girls striding beside him under a thick grey sky towards the company building, each one as tall as their father. The youthful Amazons, dressed in short summer skirts and tops in muted greys and blues, ambled, loose-limbed, across the sandstone plaza, and everything became clear. Any man would want to show them off.

Up close, as seventeen-year-old Erika, fifteen-year-old Petra and fourteen-year-old Marianne introduced themselves in faultless Canadian-accented English to other daughters dragged in for the morning, as they ferried documents, took messages, stood in the photocopying queue, it was evident that the girls were scentless, spotlessly pretty consumers of healthy food, plunderers of exercise and guiltless denizens of sleep.

Ezra Pepin had prevaricated over inviting his daughter to participate. He didn't imagine that Blaise would want to come to his office. In the end he'd only raised it the evening before, asking

Blaise in an offhand way whether if she didn't have anything better to do she'd like to come into work with him the next morning.

'You want me to get a holiday job?' Blaise frowned.

'Maybe,' Ezra said. 'But that's not what this is about, honey.'

He started explaining it – with the rest of the family, seated around the supper table, listening in – and then he admitted that actually he had no idea what it was about himself, at which they all laughed, and Blaise said, 'Sure, Daddy. Could be fun.'

And now here she was, running errands for Chrissie Barwell, whom Ezra had co-opted to help him co-ordinate the setting up of a huge bottling plant with the Izmit office. Shortly before 11 a.m. Petra Kuuzik buzzed each of the members of her father's Special Operations Team, and invited them, plus any daughters in attendance, to coffee and cake in the CEO's office.

Erika and Marianne brandished trays of French patisseries. *Mousse cassis. Lunette framboise.* 'We just collected them from Maison Blanc,' they explained. Marianne bent down to Carl Buchannan's four-year-old twins: they concentrated on the *éclairs au chocolat* and the *tartes chocolat morello* before them as if the choice they had now to make were the most important of their lives.

'There's no need to feel guilty,' Klaus Kuuzik addressed the group. 'There are cakes like these being handed out right the way through the company.' In an aside to the nearest person to him, Thomas Kohler, he stage whispered, 'Not as good as these ones, of course.'

Klaus introduced his tall daughters to Ezra, Ezra introduced his daughter to his boss. Blaise was wearing a faded, flowery summer dress of Sheena's that fitted her perfectly. He noticed that she was blushing slightly. It made her look even prettier.

So her guess had been correct, Blaise thought: the runner she'd given water to, this man, was indeed her dad's boss. She'd been sure he wasn't one of her father's colleagues, or a junior member of what he called his team: the man had power, a natural authority. Blaise had sensed that about him, and she was right. It looked like Mr Kuuzik wasn't going to refer to their previous meeting. She wasn't sure why not, really, but she was relieved that he didn't. No, she was more than relieved. It made her feel they shared a secret. She wondered whether it was the same one.

'You must be very proud of your father,' Klaus said.

'Um, yes,' Blaise managed dutifully, staring at the carpet. Almost heroically, Ezra thought, considering the novelty of the concept. She frowned, and glanced up briefly. 'Why?' she asked.

Klaus looked at Ezra, smiling, and back to Blaise. 'Has he not told you of our project, and his part in it?'

Blaise turned to her father, with a quizzical look that turned into one of suspicion, to defend herself against whatever riddle Kuuzik was offering.

'He is clearly too modest, even in his own home,' Klaus said, laughing and shaking his head. 'Come with me, my dear,' he said, 'let me show you.' He took Blaise's bare arm and ushered her towards a screen on the wall on the other side of the room. Ezra stayed where he was, but the Kuuzik girls followed in a little herd: they put Ezra in mind of some presidential female bodyguard, wary of this other girl inveigling herself into their leader's confidence. Young chaperones. Ezra was as impressed as everyone else by the German girls. In comparison with his own daughter's pulchritude, however, he thought their gymnastic build made them appear maladroit in the confines of normal life, blown beyond the optimum scale, so that as they shuffled across the room after Klaus and Blaise he found he felt almost sorry for them.

Standing before the vast screen, Klaus called up a Peters projection map of the world, rotated so that Israel was at its centre: he was obviously outlining the project to Blaise, bending towards her and then back towards the map, pointing now at England, now across to the Red Sea. Presumably he was giving her, Ezra regretted, the line about increased trade making the world a better place, and not the truth about using company profit to do good. Ezra feared that Blaise's motionless posture, her forbidding hunch, meant that she resented Kuuzik's presumption, his pedagogical zeal. But then she laid a hand on his arm, and then she herself pointed up towards Turkey, and Klaus nodded and spoke. Then

Blaise opened wide her arms, and shook her head worriedly, and Klaus laughed and said something more.

At the end of elevenses, as they were all leaving, Ezra felt Klaus tug his sleeve and heard him whisper, 'We take lunch today, you and me, yes? At Al-Salam. It's time we discussed your salary.'

And so an hour later the two men watched from the third floor mezzanine their own girls and several others walk away across the great vestibule below them.

'Your daughter, she is a beautiful girl,' Klaus said.

'You think so?' Ezra said. 'It's nice of you to say so, Klaus. Yours, too, I must say. All of them.'

The two men soon followed the girls from the building, and crossed the grey square to Park End Street. There was no blue in any part of the sky.

'They say an Atlantic depression is encroaching,' Klaus said. 'Still, if anybody needs rain, we do. If God doesn't give us water, we have nothing to sell.'

They ordered food. A green Perrier bottle of sparkling mineral water was delivered to their table.

'Isn't it odd?' Kuuzik said as he poured, bubbles effervescing in the tall glasses. 'They import this stuff across the Channel, when we're practically over the road.'

'It's curious,' Ezra agreed.

'Everything will change with your new bottles. We shall be very unpopular with the rest of the industry.' Klaus laughed, raised his glass and saluted Ezra. 'We should be prepared for this. Bottoms up.'

'Chin-chin.'

'Ezra,' Klaus said. 'First we discuss money. Blozenfeld told me what your salary is. It is an insult. Don't you agree?'

Ezra paused. He wasn't sure how to answer this question. 'Can I ask you something, Klaus? Why aren't we discussing this in the office?'

'I don't concern myself with salaries,' Kuuzik replied. 'For the rest of the workforce I gladly leave it to Alan and Personnel. But for our special project, I thought I should handle the issue. Let it be clear, between each one of you and me.'

The two men nibbled on the raw vegetables that were offered as appetisers: red pepper, green chillies, olives, tomato, cucumber.

Ezra gave a tense shrug. 'Let's negotiate,' he said.

'I propose to increase your salary times four,' Kuuzik said.'

The bubbles in the fizzy water ballooned in Ezra's mouth. 'I accept,' he said.

Klaus stared at him. 'Where did you learn to negotiate?' he asked.

'Okay. Let me think. I accept, as long as this won't affect my supply of free water.'

'Ha!' Klaus exclaimed. 'That bizarre and corrupt English practice is something I should already have put a stop to.'

Their starters arrived: moutabale, grilled aubergine with sesame seed oil, lemon juice and garlic, for Kuuzik. Ezra bit into his Lebanese cream cheese. It melted in his mouth.

'What we should really discuss is the launch of the project, of course,' Klaus said. 'Did you have a chance to consider it further?'

'I did, Klaus, and I don't think this first launch should be anywhere near the Middle East, whatever Hisham says. It would be contentious from both the Arabs' and the financiers' points of view. I mean, who's the launch for? The money people, right?'

'Exactly. Closer to home, then. Oxford?'

'Paris or London. But make the launch an exotic party. With all the magic of Arabia. A kitsch extravaganza. Great music, the best belly dancing, but also snake charmers, fire eaters, fireworks. Give the shareholders, your people from Berlin, the journalists, a fantastic carnival. Convey to them that we're investing in an exciting part of the world, not one of the most intractably depressed.'

'That's very good, Ezra. I like this direction.'

They spoke more of the launch until the main course arrived.

'Tell me this, Ezra,' Kuuzik said. 'Why do the Americans want the British as their closest allies?'

Before Ezra could formulate his answer, Klaus added, 'I mean, I know we're all Americans now. Sure. *Ich bin ein Angelino*. But you know what I mean.'

332

'The special relationship is based on our shared language.' Ezra munched the minced meat and crushed wheat.

'No, no,' Klaus said, disappointed. 'I mean underneath everything. Behind the façade. Afterwards.'

'Afterwards?'

'You're meant to teach them, right? That's what they expect.'

'Teach them what?' Ezra asked, his attention distracted by the taste of sesame sauce.

'Well, how to relinquish Empire, I suppose. With grace. With dignity and humour. Even the creation of Empire pales beside the British achievement of letting it go.' He passed Ezra the yoghurt. 'And let me try some of those grilled vegetables.'

'There may just be a few Indians, to begin with, who'd disagree with you, Klaus.'

'Of course, sure,' Kuuzik shrugged, as if to acknowledge that there are always people who disagree with the person who happens to be right. 'But still, it was the most dignified, the least destructive relinquishing of Empire in history.'

'You think the Chinese are ready to take over?'

'Not in our working lifetime, maybe. Soon after, though, no?'

As they enjoyed their dessert, Kuuzik eating cream cheese pastries, Ezra licking honey off his fingers from a succulent baklava, Klaus observed the brown stain at the end of the index and middle fingers of Ezra's left hand.

'Surely you are not a smoker?' he said. 'I am so surprised.'

'The occasional rollie,' Ezra said, to which evasion the nicotine stains gave the immediate lie.

'This is not personal, my friend,' Klaus said. 'But when I see someone smoking a cigarette, all I think is, This person is stupid. There is no justification I have heard that would alter my impression.'

'I only smoke after meals now,' Ezra said. 'I'm down to twelve meals a day,' he joked, but Klaus didn't laugh, and back at his desk that afternoon Ezra gathered the small plastic pouch of tobacco, the Rizlas and the disposable lighter, and he dropped them in a bin, just moments before taking the second

333

call of the day from Minty, the click of whose lighter he heard, followed by the exhalation of smoke away from the phone, before the sound of her voice.

'Ezra, darling, please don't make me do this,' she beseeched him.

'You have to let it go,' he told her. 'You know that.'

'I can't live without being with you, Ezra. If I can't be with you, I have to see you. If I can't even see you I have to hear your voice. Otherwise . . . I can't be held accountable.'

'Minty,' he soothed. 'Dear Minty. We can't do it.'

'I'm sorry, darling,' she stuttered. 'I'm a fool. I can't help it.'

The day before, Monday, he'd met her at lunchtime in the side bar of the Lamb and Flag. Minty came in off the cobbled lane and found him, and her eyes were shining. How much more attractive Sheena was, Ezra thought, how much more his kind of woman than their skinny friend with her smoky nervousness, her unpredictable intimacy, her lurching enthusiasm, as she sat down fast beside him.

Minty ordered a gin and tonic and lit a cigarette. 'To hell with resolutions, sport,' she grinned in a carefree way that told him all he didn't want to know. 'I'll repent of all sin when I'm fifty. Sixty, maybe. Who cares but God?' She moved to kiss him.

'Not here,' Ezra hissed. He wanted to add, And not anywhere else, either. But he might as well have let her, really, for she sat so close beside him, one hand clutching his, her perfume sickening him, that they could not have been mistaken for anything other than what they were: lovers. Middle-aged adulterers keeping a lunchtime rendezvous, no less tawdry now than at any time in any pub like this fifty, a hundred years ago.

Ezra's distaste for the situation, and for the woman with whom he shared it, was increased by the fact that Minty's unwelcome proximity, her perspiring grasp, her perfume lodging in his nasal membrane, her jostling breath, were arousing him. He could feel a furious hard-on fill and throb between his crossed legs, beneath the table, an erection entirely separate from his will and his intention; separate from himself.

His unwanted arousal further complicated what Ezra knew he had to do, which was already going to be difficult for someone soft-hearted – as witness his indisciplined child-rearing, he conceded – but it had to be done. With his rebellious body standing in the way.

'Minty,' he said, freeing his hand from hers. 'You know how fond I am of you. We know how fond we are of each other. But what happened at the weekend we have to keep as a secret moment, a special birthday memory between us, don't we? We both put our families first. Neither of us wants either Simon or Sheena hurt. The children, God forbid.'

Ezra took a nervous sip of ginger beer, and began to roll a cigarette; he was surprised to discover his fingers were trembling. He racked his brains trying to remember the rest of the speech he'd prepared – he knew that wasn't all of it – as he watched his insolent fingers struggle to roll the thin paper over the screw of tobacco. The concentration necessary to this task had a welcome side-effect; blood returned to his fingers. When, finally, he accomplished a smooth, narrow cigarette, had licked and sealed it, lit it, exhaled, and removed a wisp of tobacco from his lower lip, only then did Ezra look at Minty: he suspected at once that she had probably spent every waking moment since their farewell on Woodstock Road, in the back of the temporary taxi at 11 a.m. the day before, in an empathogenic glow of fantasies of transformation. Of her, of their, lives. It struck Ezra then that although he'd had no inkling, the truth was that not only had Minty been in love with him for years, but the fact that they would eventually consummate this longing, and that he would one day – this day – realise, had been working its way backwards, bleeding somehow retrospectively into his consciousness. So that, if he were honest, he did know; he had known all along. That she loved him, was waiting for him, and when the moment came he would seize and surrender to it.

Minty sat limp and immobile beside him. She looked as if she was gazing through the open doorway to the bar beyond, stunned by some outrageous spectacle among the drab customers there. She'd shut down, unable to cope immediately with the mental and emotional blow he'd just delivered.

Ezra understood that this was not to proceed as he'd hoped. That Minty was not going to respond with a similar noble speech of her own. Outside the pub they were not going to hug each other, embrace their mutual commitment to friendship, family and sly memories. A forlorn hope: she had been hoping for something quite else.

The remainder of his speech was necessary, right now. It was more or less ready. He'd imagined when he composed it that morning, after suggesting lunch during Minty's third phone call, that it might be hard for him to deliver because he'd be choked up himself with sympathy for his broken-hearted friend. It was to Ezra Pepin's surprise, then, when it came to him that he should jettison the speech: there was only one reasonable course of action open to him. The cruelty of it gave him a cool tremor of pleasure. After his words if he were to spout them there would be no clarity here: no, Minty would argue, weep, beseech.

Ezra reckoned he had a brief moment more, while Minty remained in this petrified state, for action. Grabbing his tobacco, papers and lighter from the table, he got up and walked out of the pub.

And the remarkable thing was that that evening, while Louie was in the bath, Ezra sat on the toilet to pee and Sheena turned from where she was kneeling, bubble bath foam on her hands, and said, 'Oh, what were you doing with Minty at lunchtime?'

'Minty?' Ezra asked, standing and pulling his trousers up to cover the sudden lurch of his stomach.

'Yes, Luigi came into work and said he saw you.'

'Luigi?'

'Remember they all met at Jill's barbecue the other week?'

'Oh, right,' Ezra said. He lowered the toilet lid and sat back down. 'It was to do with work,' he began.

'Minty?'

'A report needs writing, but not in the usual bland style? They want it poeticised, romanticised, to appeal to some Balkan clients. You know how poor Minty's so dissatisfied, what with the failure of her poetry.'

336

'Failure, yes,' Sheena concurred. 'Dissatisfaction, I didn't think so. I thought she was perfectly happily growing into the role of a north Oxford lady of leisure.'

'You may be right, Sheena. Because I thought I might do her a favour, I offered her a stab at it, for a decent fee, because getting paid for something you do is an important basis for self-esteem –'

'I so agree.'

'And she turned it down.'

Sheena twisted round to face him. 'You are kidding.'

'Didn't say as much. She said she had no practice at such work, and she didn't want to screw up, specially for a friend. For me. Which may have a modicum of truth.'

'More likely she considered it beneath her.'

Ezra frowned. 'You think?'

'It offended her artistic integrity.'

'Well,' Ezra pondered. It was breathtaking how easy this mendacity was proving to be; it took little effort. 'That does make a certain sort of sense.'

'Yes, it does.'

Sheena turned back to the bath, to Louie and his animals and bubbles, her spine stiff with indignation on behalf of her husband, no less than pride at her own insight. Then she turned back towards Ezra. 'That was very nice of you, Ez,' she said, with complete sincerity, shaking her head and then nodding. 'That was very thoughtful of you. It really was.'

Ezra leaned forward off the toilet seat and knelt on the floor beside Sheena. Winking at Louie, he dabbed some foam on Sheena's nose and some on his own, rubbed noses together – which made Louie chuckle with delight – and then he kissed her, overcome with relief and love for Sheena, his unsuspecting, innocent wife. During their marriage, out in the wide world around them the divorce rate, as everyone knew, had doubled; half of all children experienced their parents' divorce before the age of sixteen. Ezra felt, as he kissed Sheena, suddenly ageless; could feel himself both young and old with her and she with him, imagined their old age the reward for loyalty, the compensation for occasional incommunication, their children long gone, their libidos spent and habits worn and rubbed together, companionable as two trees growing old and gnarled and intertwined.

Ezra broke from Sheena, leaned into the bath, dabbed foam on Peanut Louie's eager nose and on his own, and bent towards their laughing boy.

And now here he was in the office the next day with Minty weeping into the phone. 'But how can you be so strong, darling?' she sobbed. 'So heartless, and brave and strong?'

'We have to be, Minty,' he said, slowly, appraising every word before releasing it. He considered telling her she was probably suffering from a chemical comedown, the Tuesday blues, but refrained. He was lucky he never seemed to get them himself. 'We both have to be strong,' he said. 'You know we do.' He should be patient with her, and calm. He wanted to yell down the line, though he couldn't think what to shout.

Ezra looked outside. The day was still growing dim, a slow fade towards a premature night. A depression from the Bay of Biscay was apparently moving east north east. All the lights in the office were already on, which made it seem even darker than it was, at three o'clock on a summer afternoon.

'But I want you, Ezra,' Minty croaked, trying hard to breathe seductively between her sobs.

Through the triple glazing Ezra thought he heard a low growl of thunder, though perhaps it was something in the building. A flatulent rumble through the heating ducts. Large equipment being shifted somewhere downstairs. It was hard to make out clearly, when you were on the phone; when you had someone crying in your ear.

It was 5 p.m. Ezra couldn't wait to get home, to share the news of his salary increase with Sheena. The two of them may have maintained a principled disregard for wealth and its trappings – a shared intuitive recoil from acquaintances' displays of extravagance – but this was different, an unsought gift, and recognition, if

338

of a particular, limited kind, of Ezra's value in the world. That value would be expressed in practicalities: they'd no longer need to worry about the mortgage, the children's university education, a new car. His salary would purchase, and thereby prove, its own meaning.

Ezra noted with curiosity, however, that he also wanted to put off telling Sheena. Until he'd shared this news with her neither it nor, it felt, his actual future would become entirely real. He wanted to hold it off a moment longer, to remain on this anticipatory brink of real life.

At the end of Hythe Bridge Street, instead of following the road round towards Worcester College Ezra strolled up George Street. Past the Old Fire Station, the cinema, the themed pubs, the theatre. When he reached Cornmarket he stopped and stood there, on the corner outside Debenhams. People swarmed past him, countless people moving fast, criss-crossing, making the constant subtle adjustments of migrating birds. People flocking. The resentment of morning's sleepy trudge and rush to work had gone, this was the tired relief of citizens returned to liberty, keen to get home before the storm. The spectacle was immensely soothing.

All over the centre of the city people were leaving: beneath a purple-black sky, this exodus, this flocking home, flight paths criss-crossing, people fleeing in outward radiation. Ezra Pepin stood on the corner opposite Waterstone's, not once jostled, awestruck by the crowd. By the faces of countless men and women. The energy, the willpower, invested in every trajectory, each journey from waking to sleeping upon which each individual was embarked that day. By the thought that, flip forward a hundred years, they would all be gone, each and every one, replaced in their entirety by a different cast. Another parade of bodies, of extraordinary will, of animate being made purposeful.

It was dusk near as damn it in the gloom. Ezra realised, walking along St John's Street, that he was stooping beneath the low black cloud that had spread across the sky above him. Other people were running, scampering away. They stopped: out of breath, they trembled with keys, then vanished, falling through the front doors of houses. Ezra ambled. Lights had been switched on, yet curtains not yet drawn, not while there was still a smudgy light outside, as if to do so would be to cause affront to the dying day.

Before the rain fell, Ezra sensed an extraordinary thing. In Wellington Square he jumped the low wall of the garden and cut straight over the tree-encircled lawn, grass already brown and worn where workers from the university offices would take their lunchtime sandwiches, students sprawl, winos slumber. It was empty now, and treading across the grass Ezra sensed a pull from the earth below him. Not gravity so much as a yearning. A thirst, exerting a pressure that he could feel. Waves, corrugations in the air between the earth and the gloomy sky, that shook the pressure loose.

As he entered Little Clarendon Street great single drops, globules, of water splattered on the ground, bursting into dark splodges on the grey pavement. A pattering percussion, the tuning up, the developing orchestration of a storm. Streetlights came on: were they responding autonomously to the unsummery murk, or to the initiative of a city council engineer?

As Ezra walked along Walton Street the huge cloud above ripped itself open. Rain plunged down. The weight of heavy water falling on his hair, his head, his shoulders, was staggering; it would be enough, he thought, to pummel a frail person to the ground. It was monstrous and vivifying. A man a few yards ahead had his umbrella dented by the force of the water and got as drenched as Ezra, who didn't bother to stop himself laughing in the downpour. The man didn't look back but promptly scurried off, resentful of the storm and this stranger's laughter both.

A few cars with their headlights on crawled through the cinematic rain, and everything – people, cars, buildings – looked as they might have looked fifty years ago. Shimmering reflections in windows and puddles. Shiny metal. An illusion of spick and span clean. The odd person stooped over, hooded, fifties stoics in their sopping clothes, doing what needed to be done with neither false heroics nor self-indulgence.

Ezra ducked into a doorway across from the cinema. He knew full well as he did so it was that of The Raj Cuisine.

'Come in, Ezra. Come in,' Abdul drawled. 'You are wet. Please. This way.' He barked something in Bengali at the younger of two waiters, who doubled in his bow-tie as a magician and produced from nowhere a paper tablecloth which he folded and laid on a seat at the table in the corner. Ezra removed his drenched jacket.

'You will have something to warm,' Abdul suggested. 'A whisky?'

'What a lovely idea. Thank you.'

Ezra hadn't been to the Raj Cuisine in years but he felt like he'd stepped back in time because, incredibly, it hadn't been altered. The same red plush upholstery, the same flock wallpaper, nicotined ceiling, large framed paintings – garish copies of Mogul miniatures of elephants, semi-clothed girls, mustachioed warriors with jewel-encrusted turbans. There were only eight tables, plus the one at which he was sitting at the back, spread with copies of two or three of that day's newspapers, where people who came to collect takeaways sat unless the restaurant was full.

Beside the table was a tiny corner bar, behind whose counter Abdul stood. He appeared taller in there. Perhaps there was a platform.

'After *they* leave,' Abdul said, nodding towards the one table occupied at this early hour, 'we might as well close restaurant. Nobody out in storm like this, Ezra.'

The four young men tucked into their curries and lagers. Ezra fancied he could tell, it being apparent in the particular knowing over-emphasis of almost everything any of them said, that they'd chosen this restaurant on account of its retro ambience. It was ironic to come here – not to mention cheap – and a relief from the demandingly imaginative fusions on offer elsewhere.

'Thank you,' said Ezra, lifting the whisky that Abdul had one of his waiters bring around to him on a small tray, even though if he and Ezra had reached towards each other he could have passed it easily over. Ezra took a long sip and felt the liquor slide burning

341

down his throat. 'A most welcome remedy to rain,' he said, nodding his head with appreciation in the most anodyne way; like one of those dogs who used to nod on a car windowsill. You didn't see them any more. Not in Oxford, anyway. Maybe they were still nodding out of car windows in the country town he came from.

'Will you have some food?' Abdul asked. 'Even without your wife?'

'No thanks, Abdul. I was just passing when I got caught by the downpour. I thought it would be nicer to say hello to you than to stand under the cinema awning.' Ezra sipped his drink.

'So, Ezra, I hear the trip, big trip to South America, is off.' As Abdul spoke he fidgeted with glasses and bottles around him, a fridge on the floor behind, with implements unseen beneath the counter. On the surface was a single spike, on which the students' order was skewered. Ezra could remember observing it during busy evenings, he and Sheena trying to work out the dextrous logic by which Abdul and his waiters took the orders on and off the spike. 'I hear,' Abdul added, 'from my son.'

There was reproach in the words. *I should have heard from you, my friend. My fellow patriarch.* But he was here now.

'Well, we've postponed it, yes,' Ezra agreed gravely. 'It wasn't the right time, for all sorts of reasons.'

'Of course,' Abdul said. 'The women they don't want to go. That how it is.'

'The women? You mean Sheena?'

'Abdul here five years building business. Then I am ready, I send for my wife. My wife not want to leave village, Ezra. With two children in Bangladesh. She didn't want to.'

'It must have been a frightening prospect for her,' Ezra said.

'It like this.' Abdul grinned. 'Abdul have to put foot down.' Ezra pictured him doing so, with his childsize foot, beside his large rustic wife. 'I order her to come, I tell her family, she must come or I divorce her. It's like that.'

Ezra tried hard to think of something to say. 'I can't imagine that particular threat cutting much ice with my wife,' he managed.

'Thing iz, Ezra,' Abdul intoned. 'Thing iz, man not in command.'

'No, but actually, you see,' Ezra said hurriedly, angry with Abdul for not listening to him; for just grinning as he spoke. It was very simple: why, he'd put his foot down too, he'd just done it in such a way that Sheena didn't realise he had. Wasn't that actually more powerful, in a way? He'd needed neither brute force nor the weight of tradition, but rather an understanding of the subtleties of human relationships. 'Forget what I just said. It was the other way round. I was the one.'

'I am sorry you could not go to Brazil, Ezra,' Abdul continued blithely. 'It's good for man to build new life. New place.'

Ezra wished his trousers were not quite so sopping. They stuck to his skin. He feared the damp would have seeped by now through the paper tablecloth beneath his backside to the upholstery below. 'Don't be sorry for me, Abdul, I can assure you that –'

'Sometimes I think it much easier, being Muslim. Even you don't need to believe all what imam say. In our house, Ezra, we have Qur'an, Bible and Torah.'

'Really?' Ezra tried to remember whether they had a copy of even one of these books at home in Blenheim Orchard. Did the Pepins actually own a bible?

'For the children.'

Ezra sipped the last of his whisky. 'Your children are a credit to you. It was good to meet them the other day.'

'Most of them, yes. Akhmed I don't know. What he do at school? He like anything? Abdul don't know. The boy doesn't tell his father.'

'I know what you mean.'

'Sometime I think he's simple.'

'Surely not.'

'The others are too clever.' Abdul smiled, all the while fiddling with cutlery, more beer bottles for the students, a bottle of wine for a couple who had come rushing in out of the rain. Like his waiter, this constant activity while he spoke gave Abdul the air of an illusionist, speaking to distract his audience from the cups and balls, the white rabbit, about to be conjured up.

343

'You know my dream?' Abdul asked. 'I tell you, Ezra. Ten years ago I buy building for restaurant in Banbury. It need complete renovation, that cost money. To get money, I need to use Raj Cuisine as security. And if new restaurant fails, I lose everything. You see?'

Ezra looked around the single-room restaurant. Was that why he'd never changed things here?

'This place always make a bit of money,' Abdul said, reading his mind. 'Enough to see children through college. How I can take risk? You know, I don't have one day off in twenty . . .' Abdul gazed at the brown ceiling. 'Twenty-six years. This what my dream: when children all gone, Abdul will be free. That what I'm saying. Then I can take chance, let someone run Raj Cuisine. I go to Banbury. Make new restaurant, Ezra. Menus, lighting, recipes: everything new.'

Abdul's face suddenly changed: it took Ezra a second to realise that he'd stopped grinning that facetious grin of his, because although the smile was gone and he was looking at Ezra with a serious expression, his eyes for the first time were open and clear.

'Abdul make best Indian restaurant,' he said, 'in *whole* of Oxfordshire.'

18

By the River

Through the last days of August, to Friday 5 September

Ezra Pepin called an ABC taxi for the mile and a half journey from the Raj Cuisine to Blenheim Orchard. As soon as he got through the front door of the house he removed his shoes. He began to undo his trouser belt, when a gentle voice reproached him.

'You're late, Daddy.'

Ezra looked up to find Hector sitting halfway up the stairs. He looked down again, unbuttoned his damp trousers, which flopped round his ankles. He stepped out of them. 'I missed supper?' He took off his jacket, and carried his damp suit and sodden leather shoes as far as the boy. 'I hope you made sure no one threw my portion away, old fellow,' he said.

'I don't think it got as far as you having a portion, Daddy.'

Ezra tossed his wet clothes up on to the landing above them, and sat on the soft blue carpet. 'Don't I depend on you to look out for me? You know we have to,' he said. 'We have to look out for each other, Hector, with these loopy women of ours.'

'Sorry, Daddy.'

'No, no, I'm joshing. Did you have a good day today? What did you do?'

'I read mostly.'

'Best thing to do in rainy weather. What did you read?'

'Lots,' Hector said vaguely, casting his mind back then suddenly brightening. 'I read *Kidnapped* again. I haven't read it in *years*.'

'The Highlands.'

'Daddy, don't you think Robert Louis Stevenson is about the best in . . . I don't know . . . the world?'

'Incontrovertibly,' Ezra agreed. He waited for reasons, or which book in particular Hector might consider to be supreme, but the boy's emphatic declaration, and his father's accord, seemed to settle it. 'Well, I'd better get some clothes on.'

Sheena appeared in the hallway below them. 'There you are, Ez. Thanks for the call.' She stared at him a moment. 'Where's your suit? Have you been gambling?'

Ezra wondered whether it was his imagination, or had Sheena become funnier recently? 'It got wet.'

'You were out in this? Are you mad?'

'I got caught.'

'Well, remove those sopping socks and come and listen to this.' As Ezra descended the stairs, Sheena advanced to the telephone answering machine. She pushed *Play*. The machine, a female, informed them, *You have one message. First message*, followed by a real woman's voice, sounding thin and distant.

'What a long time it is since I thought of suicide. I used to all the time, once, when I was younger.'

Ezra, in his white shirt and red tie, his black briefs and wet socks, felt himself tremble, trying, as he anticipated Minty's message coming right out with it, to suppress the tension.

'I suppose it's something you grow out of, isn't it? You just become . . . I don't know, accommodated to yourself. To your life. An accommodation. But now such thoughts have returned. Isn't that awful?' There was a pause. 'I should be seeing someone . . .'

The voice trailed away. Ezra wondered how anyone could be so stupid: Minty cracking up. How could it not have occurred to him? 'What the hell's all that about?' he asked, keeping his voice as steady as he could.

'Search me,' Sheena shrugged.

'When did she leave it?'

'Half an hour ago. While we were eating.'

'Did you call her back, darling?'

'No. I thought maybe you might know something about it.'

'Me?' Ezra frowned. 'Why me?'

'To do with that work you offered her?'

'Oh. Right. Of course. Though unlikely. Sheena, she's not on medication, is she? Prozac or something? That she might have run out or taken too much of?'

'How would I know?'

'You're more likely to than I am. Women talk, right? Maybe you should call her, darling.'

'Oh, come on, Ez, don't pull that gender crap on me.'

'I just thought because she's more your friend, isn't she?'

'You two,' Sheena mocked, 'are the ones who party together now. Who go out dancing.'

'What shall we do?' Ezra asked. 'Shall we just leave it?'

'Might be best.' Sheena pushed *Play* again, and then *Delete*.

'She'll probably ring tomorrow to apologise,' Ezra said.

'If she even remembers leaving the message. Wait. Have you been drinking whisky?'

'Wait. Have you been eating food?'

'There's a plate for you in the fridge.'

'Come and talk to me while I eat?'

Sheena looked at her watch. 'Louie,' she said. Ezra looked through to the sitting-room. His younger son was in a state of deep hypnosis, staring at his video of *Mulan* for approximately the fifty-seventh time. 'You can have ten more minutes, sweets,' she called. 'Then it's straight to bed.'

Ezra put the plate of lasagne in the microwave. He found the bowl of green salad, and poured on some more dressing.

'Ugh, I don't know how you can eat it like that,' Sheena grimaced. 'Swimming in oil.'

'Guess what happened today,' Ezra said. 'Well, you won't guess, but I'll give you a clue: I got a raise.'

'What do you want me to guess?' Sheena asked. She pulled the cork from the opened wine bottle on the table with her fingers, and poured herself as well as Ezra a fresh glass of Rioja.

'How much,' he said. 'It's a new job, though. I mean, the same kind of work, but much more interesting.'

The microwave pinged. Ezra brought his plate to the table, took a bite, and murmured his appreciation.

'I didn't make it, Ez,' Sheena pointed out. 'M & S. Look, you know I don't like riddles.'

'Well, okay, I'll tell you: from now on we receive four times my old salary.'

Sheena stared blankly at her husband for some little while, as if waiting for him to say, Only kidding! Funny, eh? He added nothing. 'But that's ridiculous,' she said eventually.

'Crazy, isn't it?' Ezra munched his salad.

'Why would someone pay you such a vast amount of money?' she asked. 'What for?'

'It's the chap I tried to tell you about before,' Ezra said, while thinking that Sheena didn't need to find it quite so baffling that he might be thought worthy of a high-flyer's wage. 'The new Chief Executive. He's put together a small team for a major development –'

'But Ezra,' Sheena interrupted. Her expression suggested puzzlement and frustration both. 'We had it all worked out. Home Holidays is doing so well you could soon give up your job entirely. But I mean, I don't know, I won't be able to take *that* much money out of the company. We were budgeting for you to leave Isis Water when I'm bringing home *half* that.'

'I know,' Ezra nodded. He took another forkful of mince and pasta and béchamel sauce, and followed it with lettuce, cucumber, avocado. 'It's marvellous, isn't it?'

'What's "marvellous" about it?' Sheena asked. 'And please try and keep your mouth closed when you're eating. For God's sake.'

Ezra swallowed his food. 'We can pay off the mortgage,' he said. 'Move to a bigger house if we want. Chalfont Road, maybe. With our combined salaries. We can do what we want, darling.'

'That's true, I suppose. We can send Blaise to the High School in time for her GCSEs.'

'Well, wait a minute.'

'And Hector can go to St Edward's.'

'Hang on.'

'If we're really going to have all this money. I mean, let's not pretend that Cherwell's not a lot rougher than Hector would like.'

'Sheena, I'm not sure.'

'Of what?'

'We'd need to talk. I thought we both wanted our children, I mean, it's the principle.'

'But that's precisely . . .' Sheena grimaced. 'What *do* we want, Ezra? That's what you really need to give a little thought to. What *do* you want?'

'Well,' he said. 'I'd like you to come to the launch of this new project. A huge party, it should be a lot of fun.'

'Oh no. Not more of that corporate hospitality. I told you after the last time I really didn't want to –'

'This is different, darling,' Ezra interrupted. 'On September the 6th at the –'

'The 6th? Well, that settles it. Jill and I are presenting our new site to the good people of Cheltenham. We've got our own launch.' Sheena replenished their glasses. 'We're having to work hard to get them excited, actually. It's a bit worrying. They're the first town yet that hasn't responded eagerly.'

Ezra polished off the last blob of lasagne on his plate, and filled his mouth with red wine.

'I'd better take Louie upstairs,' said Sheena. Her chair scraped on the terracotta tiles. She went through to the sitting-room, and negotiated with their youngest son beside the television, working her way towards shutdown. She managed to mute the TV without provoking outrage.

Blaise came into the kitchen from the hallway. 'Dad,' she said, louder than she needed to unless she intended Sheena to hear, too. 'I'll come with you to your launch if you'd like me to.'

Time during those next couple of weeks seemed to lose its sense of flow; was composed instead of disconnected acts. Work was frantic, because on top of the project itself Ezra was involved in organising the launch. Sending out invitations, writing speeches. Conferring with a PR company creating an AV presentation, and with a professional entertainments organiser. So many Arab performers were to be brought over from Paris the company might as well have chartered a plane and flown everyone from England across the Channel, for a party in the heart of Barbès.

Minty left no more messages at the Pepins' home, but she fractured Ezra's working days with repetitive versions of the same forlorn conversation. He was sympathetic, sensible, and kept her at bay. At home, meanwhile, there was an entirely new kind of tension in the house, a brooding realignment of territory and interest. Sheena paid Blaise to childmind Louie full-time through the school holidays; Ezra wasn't sure whether his wife was working more hours than ever at Home Holidays as an expression of her unreasonable resentment at his salary increase or because, as odd asides and irritations suggested, the business wasn't going as well as it had. Perhaps the idea of Home Holidays had reached the crest of its commercial wave.

'We have to compete with other eco alternatives *and* cheap air fares,' Sheena complained. 'Is that fair? And what's worse is that people seem to be using us to have a summer holiday at home, but then taking a long-haul vacation in the winter.'

Sheena was more than happy to work, convinced that Cheltenham's resistance was a blip. The thing was to press on, to have the company grow organically. It was almost time, she suspected, to think in terms of a European expansion; the trouble with that was it would be beyond Jill's expectations or, indeed, abilities. But not hers. Oh, no. Sheena was convinced that what had stretched her so far was only the beginning of what she was capable of.

Did Jill realise this, at some level? There was a new tension in the cramped office, too, though maybe Luigi was the cause. He continued his camp flattery of Jill, but there was also, Sheena sensed, an authentic sexual hunger coming from him. It was aimed in her direction. As if she gave out without wishing to the scent of her own uncomplicated desire, and certain men picked up on it.

Blaise and Akhmed took Louie on expeditions. Swimming in the lido at Hinksey, playing football in University Parks. Louie looked like a tiny chaperone to a teenage couple, as if only because of his presence they never held hands. Blaise was beginning to tell herself that she wouldn't need to say anything: Akhmed surely accepted now that nothing more would happen; he seemed content with friendship, didn't he? Sometimes Hector hung out with them, too. After the pulverising storm, the heatwave returned, as if climatic dissent had spent itself in one riotous night, a bold but fruitless interruption to the long hot summer of 2003. One afternoon Akhmed and Hector spent hours trying to fly a huge kite on the Meadow.

'It took about twenty goes to get it to stay in the air,' Hector told his parents at supper that evening. 'But once we did, we let all the string out, and there must have been some proper wind up there. We both had to hold the spool. When Akhmed let go I got lifted into the air.' If he made it sound like too much fun they might miss the point. 'It was dangerous, Dad,' he said, frowning. 'I mean, I wasn't scared, but one time I got carried about thirty feet.'

Most days, though, Hector read and mooched about the house, the summer holiday like a long, tedious weekend.

'Are you not seeing Jack today?' Ezra asked him in the kitchen, before setting off for work, on the Monday before the launch.

'He might come round. I'm not going over there, Daddy.' Hector studied his jam-covered toast, before taking a bite from it. 'His mum's weird,' he muttered between munches.

'Minty? What do you mean, weird?'

Hector swallowed. 'She stares at me.'

'Stares?'

'As if she's looking for something.'

Ezra studied his son. It was undeniable: Hector had inherited his brown eyes, the shape of his nose, his mouth.

'Yes,' Hector said. 'Just like that, Daddy. Jack says it must be the menopause.'

351

Ezra lifted his briefcase. 'I doubt that, Hector.'

Blaise stomped blearily down the stairs.

'Blaise knows what I mean,' Hector said. 'She saw Minty in Summertown.'

Ezra rested one hand on the kitchen table. 'She spoke to you?' he asked.

Blaise stumped around the kitchen to the fridge. It looked like she'd forgotten how to walk smoothly, and might require the first part of the morning to retrain her limbs. 'Yes,' she said.

Ezra swallowed. 'What did she say?' he asked.

Blaise carried a milk carton to the sideboard. 'Nothing.'

'What did you talk about?'

She opened the cupboard where the bowls were kept. 'Nothing.'

Ezra looked outside. There was obviously something. What did Blaise know? It struck Ezra how brown the grass on the lawn had become this dry summer. He'd not noticed before. He shook his head. 'See you later,' he said, and made for the door.

Later that same morning Ezra was called into Klaus Kuuzik's office. He brought the CEO up to date on preparations for the launch, and made to leave.

'Oh, Ezra,' Klaus said. 'I almost forgot. I received a letter. You might be interested. Have a look.'

Klaus passed over a white envelope. There was no stamp. Ezra discerned nothing from the neat, slow handwriting spelling out Kuuzik's name and that of the company. He withdrew a single sheet of white paper. He unfolded it and saw the signed name at the end of the typed letter: Blaise Pepin. The surname eerily resembled the way he wrote his. A childish imitation. Genetic recapitulation. Ezra looked up, aghast, at Klaus, who smiled and, nodding benevolently towards the letter trembling in Ezra's hand, said, 'Yes. Read it.'

The words on the page jumped and floated in Ezra's nervous vision. Letters disassociated themselves from those around them, embarrassment causing him to suffer from some novel dyslexic condition. He told himself that Klaus and he were friends and

352

colleagues as well as chief and indian. Klaus had, moreover, three daughters himself: whatever was in this letter he might understand. Ezra closed his eyes, took a deep breath, opened them, and read.

Dear Mr Kuuzik,

Thank you very much for showing me Isis Water's plans in the Middle East (not to mention the delicious pastries.)

I do not understand why you want to expand your company's interests into that region. You must know about the problems in Palestine. These problems won't be solved by global capitalism. They will only be solved by a just political settlement.

I understand that money must flow. But not why every business has to grow. If capitalism depends on eternal growth, then where will it end? It will eat up everything.

I suppose I should talk to my father, but we do not really discuss his work at home.

With great respect, Mr Kuuzik, I ask you: please don't sell your water in Palestine. Remain in Europe.

Yours sincerely,
Blaise Pepin

Ezra scrutinised his daughter's letter to his boss, trying to process its content; hoping to decipher its meaning. Was she oblivious to her father's position? Did she simply want him to look stupid, was that the point? Was she determined just like her mother to embarrass her family while making crass political statements? And at such a young age! So precocious!

'Look, Klaus, I'm sorry,' Ezra began, still staring at the letter. 'I just had no idea, I mean, I don't know what she –'

'Please,' Kuuzik interrupted. 'Don't apologise, my friend. I think it is so excellent, this letter.'

'You do?'

'This idealism, that is also independent. She shares our hopes, but from her own perspective. I think it is really impressive, Ezra. Maybe soon we can take her into our confidence, no? Let her know the real thinking behind the project. You know, my own daughters

353

I believe are good girls; they take what we feed them. Your Blaise.'
Kuuzik shook his head. 'She thinks for herself. You should be very
proud of her, my friend.'

With which words Ezra decided that he probably was.

That afternoon Ezra slipped out of work a little early. He cycled
not north but south, under the railway bridge and along Botley
Road and then right into Abbey Road. At the end he pushed the
bike over the bridge across the stream and on along the path beside
the slow-moving Thames. The hot air hummed with midges. The
ring-road droned in the background. The river on his left looked as
if deep beneath the surface a great effort was required to move its
turgid load towards the sea. To his right passed the new estate
beside the railway line, and then the Cripley Meadow allotments.

Ahead of him Ezra could hear the shrieks and splashes of kids
leaping into the basin of water by Medley Bridge. He paused and
peered at them through his sunglasses until he was sure that none
of his nor the Carlyles' children were there, or any others he
recognised.

Ezra dragged his bike into the trees on Fiddler's Island. He lay
the bike down and walked through to a patch of grass beside Castle
Mill stream. Minty wasn't here yet. Fortunately, there was no one
else here, either, so far as he could see. He hoped that when they'd
agreed to meet on the telephone just now, she was picturing the
same spot as him. He'd gritted his teeth to tough it out, gambling
that Minty remained sane and scared enough not to jeopardise
their marriages. Today, though, when she admitted she honestly
didn't know whether she could hold it together for another day if
they didn't see each other, some hunch, or cowardice, made him
weaken.

Dragonflies seemed to skate across an invisible plane some
inches above the stream. Ezra gazed out across the Meadow. There
were no kites in the sky, only birds: swallows veered and swerved
as if scanning the ground below. Searching desperately for something. Like widow birds, seeking evidence of hidden graves. Swerving and veering without pause. Ezra laughed at himself: most

likely the swallows had no interest in the land below them. No attachment whatsoever; no, they were swooping on insects in the gulleys and currents of the invisible sky. He had wanted to bring them in his mind down to earth, when they lived self-contained up in the air.

Minty surprised him. 'Didn't you see me? I was waving.' She knelt down, out of breath, and embraced him, burying her head in his neck; he could sense that she was smelling him, inhaling his aroma. After what seemed like minutes, Ezra gently prised her off him.

'How do you do it, Ezra?' she asked, with what looked like adoration and anger cohabiting dangerously in her limpid eyes.

'I have no choice,' he replied. 'And neither do you.'

Minty lit herself a cigarette. 'Can't we just see each other?' she said. 'Meet in some civilised friends' apartment.' She gave that worldly, throaty chuckle of hers. How misleading it was, Ezra thought. She looked at him, smiled with her mouth closed, raised her eyebrows. 'Like French adulterers.'

Suddenly, as if a fuse had been lit to his libido, Ezra felt himself rise from disinterest to readiness in a second. 'What would it do to Simon if he found out?' he asked.

Minty blew smoke into the air. 'Frankly, sport, I suspect he'd be delighted.'

Ezra folded his legs to cover up his erection. Surely it wasn't Minty, surely it was her eagerness transmitting its chemical message to his reptilian nerves. But good God, he wanted it. Right now. He must get rid of her, make her leave first, then retreat into the trees, to shoot his spunk at the undergrowth before riding home.

'Well, I think Sheena would be devastated,' he said. 'But the adults, I grant you, could cope and recover. It's for the children, Minty, that we have to draw a line under this madness.' He watched his hand reach out to her arm and squeeze it, his disingenuous hand, pretending a friendly gesture, in reality blind and hungry for contact with her flesh. It slid down her arm to her hand. His fingers encircled hers: he could feel the passage of his arousal advancing towards fulfilment.

Minty gazed out across the flat plain. 'What about when the children have left home, darling?' she asked.

'What about it?' Ezra laughed.

'If we agree,' Minty said, turning to face him. 'Ezra: if we resolve to postpone our own happiness until all our children have grown up, I think I could live with that. But could you?'

They were looking into each other's eyes. The tears Minty seemed to have brought with her had spilled, her mascara run. How weird it was. After fifteen years of marriage, he was still attracted to his wife, and they seldom had sex. Here was their friend he'd never considered himself attracted to, and Ezra wanted urgently to fuck her.

But what on this earth was Minty talking about? After the children have left home? Did she have any idea what she was proposing? Louie was three years old. Was she saying that if they pledged themselves to each other now, she would cause no trouble for the next fifteen years? A man could fall in love with a woman who would say such a thing. But they'd be in their mid-fifties then, and who knew what other ructions and calamities might occur in the meantime?

'Oh, Minty, you fine undeserving fool,' Ezra said, taking her hand. 'Yes, I could,' he told her. 'But one thing might make it easier.'

'What thing?' Minty asked eagerly.

'Do you think if we made love now, we could lay the ghost? Put it to sleep for these years ahead? For me, anyway, it might be possible. I mean, I don't know –'

'Oh, yes,' Minty said, and she pushed against him. Ezra let himself fall on the grass behind, and Minty was kissing him, lying across his chest. Her body was identifiably lighter than Sheena's. Ezra rolled her over and soon entered her, and humped her as he had two weeks before, at the party, though this time, without the drugs, Ezra came, and came soon, groaning with ecstatic regret. While Minty didn't come at all. She came nowhere near, but lay there beneath Ezra's spent weight, a mosquito hovering within earshot, wondering, as she looked up at the green-black leaves of

356

the still branches above her, why she allowed herself this brutal, this unfathomable, deception.

At home Ezra showered and changed into white cotton trousers and a blue linen shirt. Sheena prepared supper. *Rogue Male* spread face down across his chest Hector lay on the sofa, exhausted; as if Summertown library were a fiendish organisation, dispersing these bromides across the locality, lulling the population for some insidious invasion. Luckily there was someone in the house capable of defending the family: Louie challenged his father to a wrestle on the carpet, where despite giving away a hundred and forty pounds he grappled him into a hotly disputed submission.

When Blaise entered the room Ezra recovered to tell her, 'There's a letter for you, over there.'

'What's it say?' Blaise asked, as she opened the envelope that was on the mantelpiece.

'Read it.'

After a split second's perusal, Blaise said, 'I can't.'

'Are you blind?'

'It's written in turquoise ink. It's illegible.'

'I'm sure it's perfectly legible.'

'Can't you read it, Daddy?'

'Give it here.'

Sheena came through from the kitchen to the sitting-room area, carrying a bowl of crisps, as Ezra read aloud.

'My dear Blaise,

Thank you so very much for your frank and charming letter. I appreciate your comments more than I can say at this moment in time. I would only ask you to trust us – me and your father and the rest of our team – when I say that we are involved in a project to make this world a better place. And if we did not believe this, we would not do it.

I look forward to renewing our acquaintance.

Yours sincerely,

Klaus Kuuzik.'

357

Ezra finished reading the letter and lowered it to his lap. Before he was able to say that actually he was, he had to admit, impressed that the busiest person he had ever met had found the time . . .

'You see, Ezra?' said Sheena, announcing a declarative question. 'You see? You tell me there's this incredible man running your company now, but this is why I won't have any more to do with your work? Because he sounds like just the same patronising company stooge as all the rest. You see?'

Ezra shook his head. How he wished he could tell his family all about the project, and the real motives behind it. In time, he told himself. Be patient.

'I don't know what you're talking about, Mum,' Blaise said, reaching forward to retrieve the letter from her father. 'It's polite. It's friendly. Obviously Dad's told you about my letter. What did you expect? A complete shift in company policy because of a letter from a fourteen-year-old?'

'Mum's talking about the tone of the letter,' Hector said.

Blaise looked at her brother sadly. 'When what's being said is sailing over your head,' she said, 'it might be better to lie low, don't you think?'

'There's no need to be rude to your brother,' Sheena admonished her.

'Enough!' Ezra declared, pulling himself to his feet. 'Supper!'

'Enough?' Sheena asked, addressing anyone and everyone. 'There's plenty more. As much as anybody wants, as long as they're living in this house.'

An hour or two later Louie and Hector slumped off to bed at more or less the same time. Sheena put on a DVD of a favourite old movie, *Matador*. Ezra went up to his spare-room study. The time had come to evacuate the clutter from his life. By Christmas they'd be in production at the Turkish plant and shipping bottles to Tel Aviv, and maybe even direct to Gaza. This weekend would be the launch for investors and brokers. Sober greedy lies and tacky razzamatazz. In a year or so the family could move to a bigger house, and he'd have his own room at last, but it wouldn't bear a trace of his academic past: he'd use it for peace in which to think more deeply than was possible at work. He'd use it to listen to all the music he never seemed to listen to any more. To start collecting the books of photography he'd always wanted to. Maybe he'd even write again? But stories this time, knowing what they were.

On Friday afternoon Ezra left work. The Isis Water building was in a chaos of costume fitters and racks of clothes. He met Blaise at Oxford Station, where they caught the sixteen-fifteen to Paddington. He needed to be at the hotel a day early to join those overseeing preparations for the launch. Blaise could have followed her father on Saturday, but she was keen to take advantage of this stay in four-star luxury. And when Ezra asked if she planned to go shopping on Saturday Blaise surprised him by saying she'd just as soon watch the financial presentation in the afternoon, if that was possible; if that were permissible. She reckoned she'd find it interesting. Was she dropping hints, he wondered – to herself as much as to him – that she might be interested in a similar career to his? Well, and why not?

Between Didcot and Reading the railway line ran through the wide, sweeping Thames valley, green and gracious in this unending English summer. Blaise had heeled off her trainers and sat with her feet tucked under her buttocks in the seat opposite Ezra, who gazed out of the window, when there was a file open on his laptop awaiting last-minute suggestions for pepping up Alan Blozenfeld's speech. Looking out at the bending river only made him dream of idling downstream in a rowing boat.

'Daddy.'

Ezra turned to Blaise.

'Daddy, tell me the story? Of the warrior who died?'

'You want another story?'

'Yes.'

'His name was Pakani.'

Blaise shrugged.

'Okay,' Ezra said. 'I know the one. Well, when someone died, everybody else gathered their belongings, and the whole tribe would leave at first light, to set up a new camp some way distant. They hoped that the spirit of the deceased – all dead spirits sleep during the day – wouldn't be able to find them.

'Now Pakani, husband of Tikangi, father of Bekoni and Kabuchi, was a great hunter, the best in the tribe, but one day he made a mistake: even though I'd been with the group for a year by then, and lived as they did, I'd been unable to give up my boots, for fear of snakes. I was often naked.'

Blaise grimaced. Ezra ignored her.

'But never barefoot. And my caution was vindicated by Pakani's misfortune: the great hunter stepped on a venomous snake, was bitten, and fell sick. His companions carried him back to the camp and the women applied a compress derived from a certain plant. Though this medicine might be important, it wasn't crucial: everyone knew that whether Pakani recovered or declined was already decided. His destiny was preordained.

'Tikangi nursed her husband: she covered him with ashes; she stuck vultures' feathers on him; she spooned water and honey into his mouth. To no avail. Pakani died. The whole group mourned. Tikangi, his wife, grieved loudly, joined by her daughters Bekoni and Kabuchi. That night, however, one man was particularly distraught: Chimuni, the chief of the group, was also Pakani's brother, and now with a voice of thunder he sang his lament.

'"My brother has gone. He is here. He must be avenged."

'No one in the camp could sleep. Chimuni's voice was stentorian and spellbinding. "The snake has killed the great hunter. My brother is dead. Who will avenge him? I will avenge him."

'Pakani had been the victim of a terrible injustice, and his dead spirit was certainly still there, hovering just beyond the light of the fires, waiting for the debt that was owed him. Tomorrow the group would leave this place, but that might not be enough. Pakani, after all, was a great tracker when alive, and surely would remain so in death. His people mourned him, but they wished he would leave them, and go to the Invisible Forest.

'Pakani would not leave. Because he suffered the agony of solitude. To have lost the companionship of his fellows is the

360

greatest injustice that could befall him. But it is also the avenue of redress.

'"The hunter is gone," Chimuni sang. "My brother is gone. I shall avenge him."'

'Revenge against the snake,' Blaise assumed.

'The dead man desires one thing: a companion, to go with him on his voyage to the home of the spirits. If he is given one, he will leave the living. But who will it be? Someone he loved, of course, who made him laugh with happiness. One of his children will be killed, almost always a girl – a boy is a future provider. This is the hunter's vengeance, with which he will be honoured. He will carry his daughter off crouching on his shoulder, just as he carried her so often when he was alive. On the voyage into eternal oblivion she will be her father's faithful companion.

'Chimuni was burdened with the pain of his brother's death and with the responsibility of avenging him. Pakani had two daughters: Kabuchi, still a baby, whose birth I had witnessed less than a year earlier, and Bekoni, who was now eight years old, a spirited, happy, friendly girl.

'"The snake has bitten the hunter," Chimuni sang. "I shall kill the daughter of Pakani and Tikangi. I shall kill Bekoni. I shall take up my bow."'

'How did Bekoni feel?' Blaise wondered. 'Lying there in her family's hut, hearing herself named as the one to be killed? That's so horrible. Sacrificed in revenge for her father's death?'

'I know,' Ezra agreed. 'She lay awake, trembling in the night, keeping herself from dropping off; listening, watching Chimuni across the campfires. Midway through the night Tikangi, her mother, emerged from the hut, stoked the fire just outside it and sat there, singing softly to herself. It was a barely audible dirge, but I was able to decipher that her mourning for her dead husband was joined by grief for Bekoni, who in Tikangi's mind was as good as dead.

'Chimuni stopped singing. Tikangi ceased her lamentation. The village was silent and still. Perhaps everyone apart from me fell asleep during those next few hours, I don't know. At dawn I saw Chimuni cross the clearing with his heavy bow, enter the hut, and strike the prone figure of Bekoni, breaking her neck. The girl was dead, killed in revenge for the accidental death of her father. They were both buried that morning, Pakani laid first in the grave, his body curled up and bound in a foetal position, Bekoni draped over his shoulder. And so she went with him into the Invisible Forest.'

Ezra looked at his daughter, then out of the window. What a terrifying story it was. He wondered whether Blaise, when she requested it, had remembered its content.

'You didn't do anything?' Blaise asked.

Ezra turned back to her. 'Do anything?'

'To stop him.'

'What could I do, Blaise? I was from outside their culture. I had no right to intervene.' Ezra laughed bitterly to himself. 'Not that I hadn't already interfered enough. More than enough.'

'But to save the girl's life.'

Ezra gazed at Blaise without saying anything. How curious. His great sin, which he'd found hard to admit to himself, and never had to anyone else, was that he'd interfered too much in the Achia's way of life. And here was his daughter castigating him for not interfering enough. Maybe she was right, maybe he should have. It wouldn't have saved the girl, they would merely have killed him, too – he'd never have met Sheena; his children would not have been born; he would be extinct – but maybe he should have tried anyway. That, he supposed, would have been the heroic choice.

'After the burial,' he said, deciding to add a coda to the story, to leave his listener with a different temper, 'the Indians packed their belongings in a matter of minutes. And in a festive mood they set off, to walk for some miles and set up camp in a new place further upriver, forgetting the dead left behind them with every footstep.'

Suburbia, patches of rubbed grass, industrial sheds, scrubby hedges. Ezra stared out at the unlovely landscape. He turned back from the window to find Blaise studying him. He winked at her, but she didn't respond, though she remained peering intently at him. Or through him.

In an attempt to shift his discomfort, Ezra asked, 'How's Akhmed, honey?'

Blaise blinked. She still gazed in his direction, but he was able to watch subtle shifts and tremors around her eyes and mouth, as if clouds of thought were passing by beneath the surface.

'He's just a friend,' she said. Blaise's expression took on a certain petulance, as if she'd been accused of doing something wrong. 'He's sweet, Daddy,' she shrugged. 'Okay? I mean, he liked me too much. He was never *serious*.'

'I didn't realise,' Ezra said, blandly, suppressing an exultant bubble in his stomach.

'We weren't really a couple, you know.'

'No?'

'And they think they're so special,' Blaise said.

'They do? Who?'

'Oh, the children of immigrants.'

'What do you mean, *special*?'

'You know. That they're obliged to interpret the culture to their parents. On behalf of them. When in fact all children do this, don't they –'

'Do they?'

'All children do this for their poor parents drifting out of date, out of reach of the times they live in. Just when you want your parents to explain the world, you realise you're beginning to explain it to them.' She gazed out of the window.

'Surely not.' Ezra tried to work out whether such moments had already arisen between himself and Blaise. What she'd said made no sense, until he thought of himself and his father. When he was more or less the same age as Blaise was now. Explicating the plots of films. Telling him the names of famous singers, sportsmen, young politicians.

Blaise found herself recalling the moment a week before, when she'd met Minty Carlyle coming out of the Animal Sanctuary shop in Summertown. They'd said hello, Minty had asked whether Blaise was browsing, Blaise had said she was after a card for her grandad's birthday. It struck her that Minty was peering at her with open hostility; she suspected that Minty didn't like her. It was a relief when she'd grown out of having to call her Auntie Minty – a strange fad in their families' friendship, which seemed, now she thought about it in relation to Louie, to have long passed by. Blaise was glad, too, that Jill was her godmother, while Minty was Hec's.

Minty had stared at her with that dislike evident in her narrowed eyes, and said, 'I only hope you appreciate your father, that's all. I could forgive anything, I could accept anything, if only you did.' And then, instead of waiting for any kind of reply – thank God – she'd walked off along South Parade.

Suddenly Blaise heard her father clear his throat. 'I don't want to talk about Akhmed,' she said hurriedly. 'Will you tell me something?'

'What, darling?'

'What was my childhood like?'

'Don't you know?'

'What was I like as a child?'

'My goodness, darling, your childhood is barely over!'

'Of course it's over, Daddy. Please: think.'

Ezra duly pondered. 'A person changes a great deal,' he said. 'As a parent one shares a house with a succession of people. You were no different.'

'Which was your favourite person? The best time with me?'

'Now.'

'Daddy!' Blaise's right foot jerked forward, automatically as if her knee had been tapped to check her reflex, and kicked her father on the shin.

'Ow!' Ezra winced.

'Apart from now,' Blaise insisted.

Ezra sighed, put his laptop on the empty seat beside him, and turned back to his daughter. 'When you were very little,' he said. 'Trying to crawl. It was so frustrating for you not to be able to move around of your own volition. Well, you did move: you rolled. You'd be sitting up, and you'd look at where you wanted to go, lie

364

back and roll over a couple of times. Then sit up again, only to find you'd rolled in the wrong direction: instead of moving towards Mummy on the sofa, you'd rolled in a diagonal to the bookcase. So you'd fall on your back and try again. You were so determined. You looked like a spy in a James Bond film, ducking under laser beams.'

Blaise smiled, and Ezra continued, 'When finally you did get yourself into the correct crawling posture, on all fours, you'd aim straight ahead, only to set off backwards. You could only find reverse gear.

'Of course, you cracked it soon enough, darling, and that was when you entered this period I'll never forget: when you scuttled around the house picking up every damn thing you could lay your hands on – every sharp, or poisonous, or small and swallowable object we owned. You'd pick it up, study it, discard it, and then grab something else. As if you were making an inventory of all our possessions, like some demented little old landlady.'

'But you liked that?'

'It was hell, Blaise. We couldn't take our eyes off you for a second. You fiddled with electrical appliances, dragged heavy furniture on top of yourself. You had bruises and bumps on your head the whole time, you looked like a tiny pugilist. You created havoc. It drove Mum crazy. Me, too, but I found it so impressive, this drive to development. To ownership of the world. Nothing was going to stop you. You were unstoppable. Not that we wanted to. Our first child. It was thrilling, actually.'

It was only when he'd finished that Ezra was able to perceive the effect his recollection had been having on Blaise, and now he saw her face once again tremble. As if he'd hurt her, had reduced her somehow, with the memory. She squeezed her eyes shut. Her lips closed over her teeth to keep them still. She fought back a need to weep as if to reveal it to her father, or simply in a public place, would be a terrible humiliation. Unable to keep down whatever it was that was rising, Blaise bowed her head. Ezra waited some moments, then stepped across to the empty seat beside her and put his arm around Blaise's shoulders. She hid her head against his chest and let go. Her breath sobbing out of her lungs as Ezra held her against him smelled of milk, and then of satsumas, and then a little later of tobacco, faintly, as he hugged his daughter to him, in what he suspected was not simply comfort, but also an apology, for the dazed parental wonder Ezra only wished he could offer her always.

19

Hotel Corridor

Ezra Pepin stood beneath the platform at the front of the Adelphi Suite as it gradually filled. Guests had been observed coming into the Waldorf Hilton, and were physically screened when they entered the inner lobby. At the door of the conference room they showed their invitations again, to Isis Water staff, and were pointed, or in some cases escorted, to their seats among the two hundred or so stackable but comfortable chrome and blue-cushioned chairs. The majority of invitees were men, most middle-aged, who on this hot summer Saturday wore drab suit and tie. In convivial packs they sauntered forward. Many shared a habit of checking the seat before they sat down. Then they rustled papers, or leaned towards each other and conversed in low, discreet voices.

Chrissie Barwell whispered in Ezra's ear that all the speakers were here, backstage, and he nodded. He allowed himself for a moment a little self-congratulation: he really was a damn good organiser. He knew what he had to do himself, and he knew what could be delegated; that was the skill, and he happened to have it.

The people who should be here are here, Ezra thought. The technicalities are in hand, the presentation will begin on time and proceed in due order, these guests are about to be impressed. They'll make the decision to invest. And after that . . . looking out

367

across the grey and balding heads, Ezra spotted his daughter entering at the back. A prickle of embarrassment crawled up his back. He realised at once that he'd made a terrible mistake allowing, encouraging, Blaise to attend. He'd duped himself.

'I'll be right back,' Ezra told Chrissie. He walked along the front of the platform. Blaise was seating herself in the centre of a row towards the back. Ezra strode up the aisle beside the wall, alarmed by the sight of his girl dressed in her bright eclectic teenage garb, slouching into this room full of middle-aged and older men, as out of place a person as you could imagine, the sight of her practically screaming, 'I am innocence, I am truth, I am imminent disruption.' Wasn't her letter to Klaus Kuuzik merely a foretaste? Hadn't her mother risen to her feet at the back of countless meetings to protest at colonialism and hypocrisy?

Hold on, Ezra told himself. He slowed down; perhaps he was over-reacting. It was hardly Blaise's fault that this invited audience were so conservative in their manner of dress. And anyway, there's someone in a polo shirt and slacks; another in a casual skirt. Don't be ridiculous, man. What are you going to do? Haul her out?

Ezra advanced no further along the back wall: he asked the security guard in that corner to make sure he or one of his colleagues stood close to that girl near the back, ready to whisk her away, in the unlikely event that she acted out of order.

And then Ezra returned to the front, and resumed his overseeing role for the presentation, by a succession of speakers, of Oxford Isis Water's first audacious venture abroad. Klaus Kuuzik introduced the project. Thomas Kohler gave a reassuring description of the hard credentials of the private security firm, run and staffed solely by ex-SAS men, with whom Isis Water were going to work in close partnership. Professor Abu Ghassan explained why in his opinion, contrary to received wisdom, now was the perfect time for penetration of the Middle East market: to engage Arab custom and loyalty before a settlement was reached, not after, when all the magpies would come swooping.

Between each speaker brief films were screened. About the company. About Israel and Palestine and future markets beyond.

About the world shortage of water, an increasing challenge that presented unprecedented opportunity for resourceful companies: huge profit would be made from the shunting of water south from northern and western regions.

Ezra glanced intermittently in Blaise's direction; there was nothing about her attentive presence to suggest disruption, he reckoned. And he was right. Blaise gazed forward, though she hadn't really seen much since Klaus Kuuzik had stepped back from the front of the stage. With her mouth closed, she was tapping her teeth with her tongue. She imagined her teeth to be the keys of a piano, and she ticked out a tune upon them.

Sarah Carney corroborated Hisham's insights with an outline of strategies the company, along with advertisers Jacobsen and Brown, intended to employ. Carl Buchannan outlined the logistics of diverting, bottling and shipping Turkish water.

Alan Blozenfeld spoke in numbers, of investment criteria, interest rates, projected returns, illustrating his speech with diagrams and graphs. Klaus Kuuzik returned to the stage to wrap up proceedings with a declaration of his excitement at the courage no less than the lucrative reward this venture promised.

Klaus made a joke that prompted a particular kind of laughter, common in such large gatherings: it told of relief, but had also a knowing, rehearsed quality. Blaise Pepin may have been the only person who didn't even smile. She was certain that Klaus could see her; that although his gaze ranged around the conference room it kept returning to her, and if she betrayed herself by acknowledging his eye with a smile Blaise feared that she would then blush crimson. Other people around the hall would notice; heads would turn. So she sat immobile, inexpressive.

Blaise hardly heard Kuuzik emphasise Isis Water's belief that water was a commodity of value only when supply was renewable. 'Let us bear in mind always,' he said, 'that we do not inherit the earth from our parents; we borrow it from our children.' He finished by staking his future as Chief Executive of Isis Water, indeed his reputation in the industry, on the belief that initial loss would turn to trading profit within five years. Which, Ezra reckoned, was a flourish of pure bravado – was he gambling that no one's memory would last that long? Or perhaps the higher the level of power, the less promises meant. And then Klaus reminded everyone present of their invitation to the party that evening, at which their celebration could find full expression.

The company had booked two entire residential floors for senior employees and guests, in addition to further rooms dispersed throughout the five storeys of the hotel. At half-past seven Ezra rose from a nap in his room on the second floor. He showered, brushed his teeth, rolled his armpits with aloe vera anti-perspirant deodorant, and pressed a spray of Sienna on to his neck and wrists. He dressed in his rented galabeya, which he'd chosen from the costumiers' brochure, passed around the office, prompting merriment and ribald teasing, for days. Ezra's choice was a black cotton kaftan, embroidered with a row of four white circular swirls which rose up the centre of the gown from its hem. At the chest the column split into two rows that ran up to the collar, then tracked around each shoulder to meet at the back of the neck.

Ezra liked the elegant simplicity of the design, and he'd taken only a moment to select it from the brochure a fortnight earlier. Now, standing in front of the full-length mirror in his hotel bedroom, he wondered how it was possible that the brochure – even though it had featured the galabeya worn by a model, a swarthy, mustachioed Arab – failed to show what here was painfully apparent: the white-embroidered line looked like a zip up the middle of the gown, undone near the top. Elegant? It looked absurd. Risible.

For a moment Ezra stared at his preposterous reflection, wondering whether he had time to unpick the white embroidery, or if there was some other way out of this mess. Then it struck him that actually he could not have chosen a more appropriate costume if he'd tried. This was a fancy-dress party, wasn't it? What he was wearing was a conversation piece, an ice-breaker that would save him a great deal of effort with the guests it would be his duty, as a senior employee, to mingle with.

370

It was in this jaunty mood that Ezra closed his door behind him and put the keycard into the galabeya's one pocket, along with a few name cards and a handkerchief that were the only objects he needed to carry with him. No keys, no money, weighing him down, ruining the fall of his gown. He knocked on Blaise's door.

'Coming,' she called. 'Just a sec.'

Hotel corridors are invariably gloomy. Lit by weak electric light, regardless of the time or the weather outside. Ezra heard laughter sing out of an open doorway, a door click shut and footsteps recede briefly, out of sight along the curving corridor.

The door opened. Blaise stepped back into bright light. She was wearing a veil. For a moment of confusion Ezra's brain told him this was something to do with Akhmed, and his fears that she would be swallowed up in a repressive subculture.

Blaise lowered the veil: in front of Ezra Pepin stood not his daughter but someone else. A gorgeous creature, her pretty face made up to draw all stray attention to itself. Eyes defined, blue and sad and sparkling. Glossy lips lustrous with promise and hunger.

Ezra's gaze rose to the top of Blaise's head, to a gold Egyptian headpiece, red and blue painted hieroglyphics around each side, at its front a cobra in a striking position. From each of Blaise's pierced ears three coins hung on little chains suspended from stars. Around her lovely neck was a silver pendant necklace.

'It's the Eye of Horus,' Blaise told her father.

She wore a bra covered with tiny jewelled beads. Burgundy, green. Gold, purple. There were silver coins along the bottom edge of the bra, and more coins which hung underneath and formed a triangular drape. Around her lissom belly, following its curve of a womanly girl, of a girl pretending to be a woman, was a thin belt of small coins.

Over Blaise's hands stretched long latticed and beaded gloves which ran from a single loop over each middle finger up her arms, to just above the elbow. Ezra took it all in. A turquoise beaded belt rested on her hips, from which fell a long skirt, on top of it a semi-transparent scarf of chiffon or nylon or something, covered with coins and various coloured beads, down to a hem that was ruffled

371

and trimmed with another row of gold coins. At one of her feet was an anklet with silver bells. Blaise stood barefoot, only three or four inches shorter than her father.

Ezra had swallowed the sight of his daughter in a single tilting gulp. His blood, he feared, was draining into the maroon carpet. Blaise had not merely grown up, she'd been transformed in a single evolutionary spurt into someone else. This lurid gypsy who stood before him would now reveal that she had been sheltering in their house with them all these years, masquerading as a commoner child. She was a fugitive princess from some fairy-tale realm.

'What do you think?' she asked, and even her voice was changed, more deep and sultry than it had been two hours before. 'Is this okay, Daddy?' Her mouth was very slightly open, and he could see the tip of her tongue as she ran it along between her lips. Less seductive gesture than the novel taste of lipstick.

There was no blood left in his brain. Ezra could not calculate what he thought. Whether any thoughts he might have had were more fearful, angry, incestuous, philosophical, happy or sorrowful in their astonishment. 'It's fine,' he mustered. 'You look wonderful, darling.' He noticed for the first time a smudge of magenta lipstick beyond the corner of one side of her lips, the slightest trace of her inexperience. 'Wait,' he said. He felt for his white handkerchief, leaned forward, and carefully wiped off the glossy smear. Ezra leaned back. 'Quite wonderful.' He held out his arm. 'Shall we?'

The Palm Court had been transformed into an Arabian nightclub, with round tables and chairs filling most of the floor, except for a space for dancing between them and the stage. Along the sides of the room were curtained alcoves. Inside were low upholstered benches and cushions, in deep reds, greens, blues. They and the wall-hangings were decorated with the interlace, the intricate curlicues, of Arabic design. Ezra paused to study them.

'Look,' he said. 'Can you imagine how long it took people to make these? This divine geometry. I could gaze at them for hours.'

'Come on, Dad,' Blaise said, tugging his sleeve.

Coaches had arrived from Oxford filled with a hundred and fifty employees of the company who ranked in between menial staff and senior management, all costumed in fancy dress: Ezra and Blaise jostled towards their table between merchants in flannel suit and fez; pious women in black purdah, modest men in djellaba; Ali Baba lads, Salome girls, Cleopatra, a number of Yasser Arafats in kaffiyeh headdress and scarf, Bedouin, two Lawrences of Arabia, Roman centurions, a disciple or two, Moses with a plastic clay tablet . . . It was a time-spanning epic of a film set milling with extras from Isis Water who bustled and thronged in and out of intimate circles.

Being led to the tables, by Moroccan, Algerian, Tunisian waiters dressed in impeccable black-and-white service attire, were the guests and executives. Ezra and Blaise found themselves at a table with the President of the Qatar International Bank and his wife on one side; on the other a journalist from *The Economist* and a budding music producer whose small label imported CDs from North Africa and Egypt.

'Isis Water,' he explained to the bank president and the journalist, 'are sponsoring our research into music in the West Bank and Gaza, with the promise of recording contracts for young artists.'

Ezra was able to speak of this venture from Isis Water's point of view – as did colleagues of similar plans at other tables; of how the company was dedicated to enriching the lives of their customers in ways beyond the supply of water. To investing in the spiritual as well as the material well-being of the community.

The bank president's wife said, 'That is such a fine idea, because music transcends boundaries like no other human activity. Just last year I saw Daniel Barenboim's West-Eastern Divan Orchestra when they performed in Chicago. Have you heard them, my dear?' she asked, turning to Blaise. 'Most of the musicians are your age, and drawn from all over the Middle East. Arab and Israeli.'

'See, what we're looking for is the exact same thing,' the young producer said. 'But from the street.'

On the stage, entertainments commenced, while at the tables falafel, fried tomatoes and mutabbal were served. Artichoke hearts with coriander, pickled green olives. Fallahi, yoghurt and jarjeer salads. Chicken Fatteh, roasted leg of lamb, artichoke musaqa'a. Lebanese wine – Château Musar, Hochar – was poured.

A magic show took place. A flautist made a snake rise out of a box. Tumblers back-flipped and cartwheeled on to each other's shoulders, creating pyramids and ziggurats. A contortionist lay on her stomach, then lifted her legs behind her, and kept lifting them until she could scratch her nose with a toe.

While the audience ate sweets with tiny cups of cardamom-scented coffee, a dozen musicians came out and sat on one or other side of the stage and began to tune their instruments. Ouds and drone rebabas, according to the programme on the table. A harp and a gourd-shaped kind of lute. Drum and tambourine. Something like an oboe, another like a flute, and a zurna, a Turkish horn.

They played for a troupe of belly dancers in bright, glittering costumes. They danced with cane and sword, with veils and finger cymbals. During the third or fourth number they made a gesture towards the audience, waving their hands with forefingers outstretched. To Ezra's horror, Blaise rose from her seat beside him and in a few steps crossed the dance area, climbed steps and joined them on stage.

What was she doing? Did she think they really wanted some amateur to share their spotlight? Her naivety was inexhaustible. Couldn't Blaise have waited just a brief moment, to see if anyone else, anyone older and wiser, was dumb enough to respond to their pretended invitation? To Ezra's surprise, the dance troupe greeted Blaise with a clapping welcome, which allowed the rest of the audience to applaud their fellow member for her pluck. Though also for her dancing. Because, unless he was rotten with partiality, it was clear to Ezra that his fourteen-year-old daughter was not simply a good sport, remarkably self-confident, and extremely pretty, she was also the best belly dancer up on that stage. All six of the troupe were game, they were doing their best, performing little hip shakes and shimmies they must have practised a million times, and all Blaise did was to get up there and undulate her body in response to the music.

But she was the one your eyes wanted to watch. Even the bored musicians perked up. And she smiled at them, as if they were playing something special for her, and so they did, the music lifting with a little fillip, an audible spring in its step.

Leaving their leader and Blaise on the stage, the rest of the troupe descended to the dance floor, beckoning to the audience to join them. Extroverts stepped forward; guests in dinner jackets and dresses, employees in fancy dress.

Ezra Pepin, however, remained gazing at his daughter, who was working less hard than the woman striving beside her, who might have been dancing her entire life and would never have the poise, the delicacy, the power of this girl who'd started dancing to this music for the first time five minutes earlier.

Or maybe not, Ezra acknowledged. Maybe Blaise had been taking belly-dance classes at school or out of school for the last year or two or three. When it came down to it there was a lot about what Blaise did and how she spent her time of which he was ignorant. And if that were so for her physical existence, how much more so for her interior world? The private realm of his offspring, of his flesh and blood, of which he knew next to nothing, Ezra mused, watching Blaise dance beside the troupe leader with a radiant smile upon her lovely young face. And wasn't that inevitable, of course, but still so odd, how he and Sheena mated and gave birth to a child with a mix of their genes, and from the very beginning she inhabited, she owned, her own inviolate autonomy? The secret world of our own children. We provide for them, try not to hurt them, give them our love. And guidance? Sure. Even me, thought Ezra, even me; at least, I stand full square in the centre of civilisation, demonstrating to our children that there's a space here for them too whenever they wish to claim it. It was easy to be cynical or take it for granted. But this was important, he figured, whatever anyone said. There was a space for each individual whose shape they would have to define for themselves. Blaise, Hector and Peanut Louie Pepin.

*   *   *

375

Blaise was joined by Chrissie Barwell, and Merry Sever from Sales, who practically adopted her for the evening like older sisters: they danced a while, then took her to their table near the back of the room. On the way, Blaise waved to her father with a kind of 'I'm okay' reassurance. He also saw her stop at Klaus Kuuzik's table. Klaus rose gallantly to his feet, and they conversed with ease before Blaise moved on to rejoin the women.

Ezra danced with the short wife of the Jordanian ambassador. They shook and shivered in a disco jive, with the occasional vague nod to Arabic moves. He was relieved that the dancing was informal, since he'd never been taught the waltz, polka, Charleston. How nice it would be, though, to get hold of a woman, he thought, as he shimmied with the plump wife of the MD of Goldberg Green; to hold her sweaty hand, place your other hand on her back and glide together. There was the rave, of course, where you sought oblivion in company with indispensable others, each person's energy feeding the atmosphere. The uncomfortable hybrid here – with all sorts of winks and twinkles from carousers trying hard to convince themselves and their partners that they were dancing together, and having a great time doing it – Ezra could only manage for limited periods. After he'd kissed the bony hand of the wife of the President of DeutscheWasser, this chivalric Englishman, he made for the bar. He'd been standing there a while when he realised that Lawrence of Arabia hovered at his shoulder. Ezra turned.

'I'm a dreamer,' Lawrence said.

It took a moment to recognise Roger Slocock, his red hair hidden beneath the turban. 'Hi, Rodge,' Ezra said.

'I'm a dreamer of the day, Ejra. I'm a dangerous man.'

'Hit the sauce early, eh? Take it easy, now.'

'I may act out my dream with open eyes, Ej, to make it possible.'

'You're gibbering, old son.'

'I'm in character, Ejra,' he explained. 'How often can we say that?' Roger grinned, glassy-eyed with this insight. 'Nice costume,' he muttered, and stumbled away.

Ezra stood and observed the scene. A little giddy from dancing.

Perspiring some of the alcohol that had given lightness to his feet. One of the most pleasant aspects of dancing was taking a break from it. All he needed was a cigarette.

Through the crowd he noticed Klaus Kuuzik, sitting at the side in one of the alcoves, lounging on the cushions like some Ottoman pasha, conversing with another man. Klaus was listening to the man with a tender concentration; then he responded, leaning towards his interlocutor with that peculiar intimacy which, Ezra knew, meant the other man would be oblivious to everything else that was happening in the room. He recognised that intensity, and envied the other man for experiencing it this moment while he, Ezra, merely observed. Then Klaus became distracted by someone else who had approached him from the other side. A woman. Her gloved hand touched Klaus's shoulder, in a gesture of gauche familiarity that Ezra wanted very much not to see, and keep seeing. The first man smoked from one of the hookahs with flavoured tobacco that had been laid on. Klaus spoke now with the woman who'd approached him, looking up, inviting her to join them. She moved forward into Ezra's line of vision: Blaise reached towards Klaus, he took her hand, and she sat down beside him.

'What a beautiful daughter you've got, Ez.'

Ezra turned. 'Thanks for looking after her, Chrissie,' he said, raising his glass.

'You're joking: it's a pleasure. So composed and grown-up. I can't believe she's fourteen. When I think what I was like then. And it wasn't much more than ten years ago.'

'You're saying my kid's precocious?'

'Sophisticated.'

'I tell you,' Ezra said, 'it seems to me like she's shifted generations tonight. Which must mean I have, too. And her mother.' Ezra laughed, and mimed a train engine bumping a carriage along tracks. 'Blaise has just *shunted* us along.'

'What I always tell you, Ez. Middle-youth is the new black.'

'Chin-chin.'

'Cheers.'

Ezra circulated, was introduced to odd people, made

introductions himself. Blaise appeared and dragged him back to the dance floor. The musicians had been replaced by a DJ playing Middle Eastern pop. Blaise wiggled her hips and Ezra copied her as best he could. In response to her uninhibited gyration, he let himself go. He swung his shoulders, pumped his arms, and she took the moves and elaborated upon them, improved them; in then copying her, Ezra felt the improvement, and smiled, and realised that his delight was genuine. Maybe the galabeya helped: beneath the outline of the cloak itself, his body and limbs knew gratitude at the lack of restriction. My daughter, Ezra acknowledged, is teaching me to dance at the disco. So this is why people pretend it's fun – because it is!

Time must have streamed by in the world beyond the Palm Court. Around midnight the first guests started leaving. Ezra was seeing the President of the Bank of Qatar and his wife out when he noticed Blaise taking hold of Klaus Kuuzik's hand and urging, pulling, him towards the dance floor.

Ezra accompanied his guests to the lobby of the hotel. After they'd left, he fell into conversation with some of the Oxford crowd, who were gathering, in their fancy dress, for the first of the coaches home. The English men and women, in their costumes for desert bedouin and ladies of a palace harem, sat and stood around in various states of tired dishevelment: already returned to the quotidian from their flight on a magic carpet.

When he returned to the banquet room, Ezra decided on a final brandy. Standing at the bar, he inhaled its fumy threat, knocked it back in one punitive gulp, then strolled one last time around the room. Carl Buchannan nodded to him. Gideon Juffkin said, 'Wiggy, Ez. Wiggy.' Jim Gould squeezed his shoulder. Ezra felt like a Steadicam shot, and imagined the reverse shot back at him, dreamy, tipsy, a middle-aged fool entering his prime.

Blaise was no longer on the sparsely populated dance floor. Neither was Klaus. Ezra continued to dawdle, but the camera gradually took on a definite quality beyond simple recording: that of scrutiny. Ezra's eye was a hunter's. He tried not to admit it to himself, but he was actively searching now. He looked in the alcoves along one wall. Perhaps they'd each gone to the loo. They'd reappear at any moment. Ezra walked slowly back down the other side of the room: they weren't there, either. Neither of them, the pair of them. There was nowhere left to look. He stood, clenching his diaphragm, suppressing the insects that were breeding in his stomach. Inebriated inanities floated into his ears from the mouths of those departing past him.

'What a bash, eh?'

'It was a riot.'

'A mash.'

'Hey, that dancer!'

'The kid in the gloves.'

Ezra walked slowly up the many stairs, to the second floor. He knocked on Blaise's door. There was no reply.

'Blaise?' He knocked again, loud enough to surely wake her. Nothing.

In his room, Ezra sat on the end of his bed. What in God's name was he supposed to do? He tried to invoke an authority outside himself that might issue guidance. None appeared. It was his, Ezra Pepin's, problem, and no one was going to help him. Somewhere in the hotel – in his room, presumably – Klaus Kuuzik, the man who'd single-handedly launched Ezra's life on its true path, was having sex with his fourteen-year-old daughter.

Ezra put his head in his hands. Was Blaise a virgin? Of course she was. And Kuuzik, the miserable, hypocritical bastard, was screwing her. Only wait. Scanning back over the evening Ezra forced himself to acknowledge that not once, or even twice, but three times he'd seen with his own eyes Blaise approach Kuuzik. If anything, she had seduced him.

It occurred to Ezra that he had no idea whether Kuuzik was married still. Was his wife alive? Had she been in the banquet room? Did the three daughters reside with their father? Did they even live in England? Perhaps they had been on that day at work on a fleeting visit from some other country. Ezra didn't know. In all the friendly conversations of these last months, Kuuzik had given little of himself away.

If Ezra was trembling with rage, or maybe fear, as he stood in the middle of his hotel room, these, he understood, were atavistic emotions growling in the primitive depths of his being. They were directed at Klaus Kuuzik. Was it possible to imagine a girl of fourteen seducing a man of forty? Of course not. She was testing, teasing, feeling her way with her new body, into the murky waters of sexuality. She'd gone so far without thinking, without thought, following her immature instincts, not knowing where it would lead. Any man who found himself being clumsily flirted with by such a girl understood what was going on, and what his responsibility was. Because that was what had happened, wasn't it, Blaise discovered herself in a hotel room with an aroused man, and though she must have realised she'd gone much further than she wanted, it was too late. He took advantage of her. It was rape.

But Klaus? Impossible. Whatever the temptation of a gorgeous girl, even if she'd offered herself with such seductive generosity, how could he possibly screw his, Ezra's, daughter? Could Klaus not see what a betrayal, a dishonour, was being inflicted? What was Ezra supposed to do in response? Act as if nothing had happened? Seek out Kuuzik's fourteen-year-old daughter, Marianne, and fuck her? Perhaps that was what was going to happen next: Kuuzik would offer his girl to him. Not humiliation after all, but an archaic male bonding that took place amongst the financial elite, sacrificing their daughters' maidenhood for their own powerful futures, as the royal houses of Europe had once done, and certain tribes still did.

Oh, nothing had changed. Everything had changed.

Do something, man. Let it be.

Go there. Stay here.

The options banged against each other inside Ezra's skull. He was confounded. Exhausted. He barely noticed he'd lain down; maybe he was already falling asleep, and swooned backwards.

Ezra awoke with a jolt. The room was bright. Between his skin and gallabea he was covered with a prickly, sour sweat. He sat up. His head throbbed, one heartbeat after another drumming against his cranium. His watch said 3.47 a.m.

The gloomy corridor was too bright for that hour of the night. The lift descended in its own good time.

The Palm Court had been cleared already. The tables and chairs, the alcoves with all their cushions and drapes, the temporary bar, even the stage. And the floor must have been washed. Because two young men, Albanians possibly, one in jeans and T-shirt, the other wearing a tracksuit, seemed to be sweeping the wooden floor for mines. Guiding large circular polishers in front of them, swooshing them to and fro across the smooth floor with a calm, mechanical patience.

At Reception Ezra asked for the number of Klaus Kuuzik's room. When the night receptionist hesitated, Ezra told him that he had important financial information for Mr Kuuzik from Beijing. The man was confused sufficiently to glance around and then write the room number on a piece of paper, as in a film scene in which bugs were everywhere, before folding and handing it over.

Walking away from the desk, Ezra wondered whether the time difference accorded with his story. Then he stopped walking, and stood still in the middle of the empty lobby. It occurred to him that just because they'd left the banquet room together, it didn't mean they'd gone straight to Klaus's room. Perhaps they'd not gone deeper into the hotel at all. No, they'd gone outside, and were even now wandering the streets of Soho, talking. Why, Ezra realised, berating himself for his depraved suspicion: that made much more sense.

'Let's get out of here,' Klaus might have suggested to the girl whose idealism had so impressed him. 'Let's go somewhere we can talk, just the two of us.'

'Yes,' Blaise would have said, to the first important adult who'd taken her seriously. Flattered and proud. They'd ambled through the summer night, that's what they'd done. Looking at the dreams and the realities of life from each other's point of view. Stopped in some seedy all-night café for a coffee, and who knows, even emptied their hearts. That made sense, it really did. The high-flying philanthropist, the teenage girl: they'd recognised a lonely innocence in each other. Wasn't that a romantic thing for two distinctive people to have done?

Ezra stepped outside the front of the hotel himself, and breathed in the cool air. Dawn was breaking, trying to bring colour as much as light to the grey stones and streets, though with less success so far. A street-cleaning vehicle, its green shell faint, as if the colour had been chemically desaturated, was whirring along the Aldwych. The effortful sound of its small engine whining past, and gradually receding, served only to accentuate the silence of the great city at that early hour of the day.

Ezra went back inside the hotel, and walked through the lobby to the lift. The one in which he'd descended was still on the ground floor, doors open, awaiting his return. Inside, he pushed 4. The doors closed. The lift rose slowly. It had its own maroon carpet. The lift eased to a smug halt. The doors seemed to wait a measured moment. The length of an intake of breath. Then they slid open. Ezra stepped out on to the fourth floor. After another pause, the doors closed behind him. He noted from the numbers on the sign on the wall in front of him which way to go to get to Klaus Kuuzik's room, and he walked along the dimly lit, maroon carpeted corridor. It curved before him. Ezra walked easily, tired and calm. There was no hurry any more. Not because the things that were so important hours, minutes, before no longer mattered, but rather because he, and his position in unravelling events, had altered: something told Ezra in his weariness that he was no longer outside but now, perhaps for the first time in he didn't know how long, in sync, in tune with the ordained order of reality unfolding before his footsteps.

He found Kuuzik's room. Some twenty yards away was an alcove. There was an unmarked door, presumably to one of the walk-in cupboards where the maids kept their linen, towels, bathroom accoutrements. Ezra stood in the alcove. Within a minute he heard a door open, and peered around the corner. Blaise backed out of Kuuzik's room. She smiled and then leaned back in, over the threshold of the room, her torso disappearing from view for a moment. Then she re-emerged, and turned, and walked towards Ezra. He stepped backwards, pressing his body against the cupboard door.

Blaise strolled by. Ezra watched her amble barefoot away along the corridor. She was carrying some items of her costume: the Egyptian cobra headpiece, the long crocheted gloves, the silver necklace; they dangled from her left hand. She was swinging them slightly, and her tread lifted a little, as if she was humming a tune to herself; her head was shaking, minutely, from side to side as well. Her sun-bleached brown hair was no longer piled high on her head, but fell around her bare shoulders. She vanished around the curving corridor. Ezra closed his eyes. His neck tipped, unable suddenly to support the weight of his head, which dropped towards his chest. He slid down the wall, until he rested on his haunches. There he slumped, breathing awkwardly, dead weight gradually spreading out and working down to the floor just as surely as if he'd been put there by a pair of fists. Though his mind worked on; wondering how on earth he was going to tell Sheena.

Ezra threw clothes and possessions into his travelling case. At Reception he left money and a note in an envelope for Blaise, telling her he'd gone home early, and for her to follow him back to Oxford with Chrissie Barwell. He left a note for Chrissie asking her to take care of Blaise.

The first train on a Sunday morning didn't leave Paddington until three minutes past eight. Ezra took a taxi to Marble Arch and waited less than five minutes before an Oxford Tube coach pulled up. He climbed in his galabeya to the upper deck. Outside, the sky seemed to be a uniform block of grey cloud, so low the top of the coach almost touched it. Along the motorway to Oxford Ezra gazed out at the colourless landscape, a single word, *unforgivable*, repeating itself inside his brain, ricocheting in slow motion around his skull.

He took a taxi home from the station. It was seven-thirty. The house was still. The sound of people talking came from the sitting-room. Ezra left his bag in the hall. Louie sat cross-legged on the sand-coloured carpet, too close to the big television, watching *CBeebies*. He hung on every word of the pair of presenters, who shared a similar perky manner. Manic depressives employed during their up periods on children's TV.

Ezra said hello. Louie ignored him. Ezra walked over and knelt down and kissed the top of his son's head. Louie stared at the screen, mesmerised. The remote was in his lap, the first tool the child had mastered.

The kitchen was a mess. Sheena had filled the dishwasher before going to bed – its orange *On* light still glowed in the dim light – but she'd not tidied away condiments, unsullied cutlery, empty wine bottle. Ezra did so while the kettle boiled, then he carried two mugs of tea upstairs.

Sheena slept with her mouth slackly open. She looked puffy and exhausted in the half-light, as if sleep were tiring her. Her black hair trailed across the pillow. Two or three white hairs showed themselves unapologetically. Ezra placed a mug on the table beside Sheena. It seemed wrong to wake her. He walked round to his side of the bed, removed his shoes, and sat on top of the covering sheet. He leaned back against his pillows and drank his tea, waiting patiently, feeling exhausted but too grim, too empty, for sleep. There was no need for sleep. There was no point. Sheena would wake soon enough.

It was the sound that woke her. Sleep was a weight. Sheena had to make a real effort, from a prone position, to lift it off her. She pushed, and supported herself on her elbows.

'What are you doing here?' her drowsy voice demanded. She twisted around. Her eyes were scrunched up against the threadbare light. 'What time is it?'

Ezra made no reply.

'What's the matter?' Sheena asked. 'Why are you sobbing? What's happened?' She blinked. 'Is Blaise here?'

'No.'

'Is she all right?' Sheena said, raising herself clumsily up.

'Yes,' he muttered. 'I mean, she's not hurt. She's not dead or injured.'

'Good,' Sheena said. 'Christ, Ezra. Don't do that to me.'

He shook his head.

'Are you all right?'

'Of course not!' he spluttered. When was the last time he'd cried in front of her? Of anyone? From amidst the sobs he stole a single deep breath. 'I mean, yes, I'm fine.'

'Oh, God, Ezra,' Sheena exclaimed. He turned to her. 'When did you make this tea?' she asked. 'It's got a white film on top of it. No. Wait. Just stop there. I can't do anything without a cup of tea. I'll be back in a minute. You can tell me everything.'

Sheena got out of bed and shivered. 'It's cold,' she said, as she went into the bathroom. Ezra heard her pee. The loo flushed, taps ran. She emerged tying herself in her white bathrobe, picked up the mug of cold tea, and left the room.

They each sat upright, facing ahead, holding hot mugs of tea, and Ezra described the evening. He recounted the moment Blaise opened the door of her hotel room, when there stood a lifesize doll before him, the marionette of a ripe young woman. He knew he was about to deliver the confession that would condemn him, and, abject, condemnation was what he wanted. Yet something, some vestige of self-preserving instinct, restrained him, curtailed his need for punishment.

Ezra outlined the events of the party, which was marked like staging posts by the three separate occasions when Blaise approached Klaus Kuuzik. He recounted their disappearance from the ballroom, his search, and he told Sheena in as much detail as he could remember the thoughts that raged through his mind as he tried to work out whether or not to storm Kuuzik's room, so that Sheena might, despite her propensity for deciding right and wrong with precipitous clarity, appreciate the extent of the dilemma he faced. Even if he had done the wrong thing, or failed to do the right thing, as he now understood was the case, at least Sheena might agree that although it was a mistake, it was one that anyone could have made.

Ezra stared straight ahead as he spoke, in a dull monotone, the mode of delivery expressing its form, solemn and penitent. Sheena gazed at her tea as she listened. Eventually Ezra described making his way to Kuuzik's room, seeing Blaise emerge, and hiding in the alcove to watch her walk away along the corridor. He finished, and waited, for the verdict.

'Are you sure?' Sheena asked, at length.

'Sure? Sure what?'

'That they had sex?'

Oh yes, Ezra was sure. He recalled Blaise's hair falling on her shoulders; the way her necklace and gloves swung from her fingers; how her body swayed to the tune in her mind. He recalled her head slowly shaking from side to side, and could imagine all too well the smile that was on her face, hidden from him. Lasting at most half a dozen seconds, the glimpse had given him as full a picture as a father could possibly need of a girl sauntering, along her own path, towards a newfound freedom.

But no, he had no proof. And it was better, he suspected, not to be sure. 'No,' Ezra said. 'I'm not one hundred per cent certain. Not really.'

'So you're not even sure,' Sheena said. 'How did she look? From what you saw. Did she look unhappy?'

The cobra headpiece swinging from her left hand. Her tread rising and falling. Ezra wondered what tune it was that played in her head. 'No, Sheena. I suppose actually she didn't. She looked happy.'

'Right,' Sheena said. 'I see. Now this guy, Klaus, you've been telling me for months what a great guy he is, right? I didn't really believe you, Ez, and I certainly don't now. But I mean, what exactly is the big deal here?'

Ezra gazed at the tea going cold in the mug in his hands. He hadn't drunk a drop of it. 'I beg your pardon?' he said.

'Who are you crying for?'

Ezra winced. 'What do you mean? Are you not listening? Our daughter, of course.'

Sheena laughed. 'Sweetheart,' she said. 'This is a moment in our lives, you and me, don't you think, for quiet celebration? It sounds like Blaise chose who she wanted to have. What better way to lose her virginity? In a hotel room with an older man. Maybe he even gave her an orgasm. Her first time. That would be something, wouldn't it?'

'Would it?'

'Well, would you rather she lose it, I don't know.' Sheena paused, then made a dismissive sound, as if dislodging something from her throat. 'Outside in the dark, with some cruel skinny youth.'

'That's hardly the point.'

'Some drunken, painful, thirty-second fumble,' Sheena spat. 'In the middle of nowhere.' Her tone suggested that what she described might be her own bitter memory.

'Wait a minute,' Ezra said. This was not going the way he'd imagined. 'You're not taking . . .' He was unprepared for this. He didn't know what he was supposed to say. 'Wait.' Ezra took a deep breath. 'She is under-age. That's the point. This was statutory rape, Sheena.'

'Yes,' Sheena agreed. She frowned. 'That's true.' Her countenance opened. 'And if Blaise comes home and tells us she was raped, we'll do whatever we need to, we'll do everything we can, Ezra, to get your man locked up. And I mean: everything. But from what you've told me, it was, I don't know, it was the *opposite* of rape.'

'But, Sheena . . .' Ezra stuttered. His brain felt like it had been jolted, as if he'd looked up and found himself in some kind of mental traffic accident. The shock felt familiar: he recalled the dislocation he'd experienced when, after some months with the Achia, he first began to comprehend the extent of the differences between their way of thinking – their morality, their cosmology – and his own. Or rather that of the culture he was from. And he was struck by how asinine had been his presumptions of common humanity; how profoundly alien these human beings were.

'But, Sheena,' Ezra said. 'Don't you see? This is our daughter we're talking about.'

Sheena sighed, as if simply impatient to move on, now that she'd been woken so early, to her shower, and getting dressed for a new day. 'Yes?'

'Well, what was Kuuzik thinking of? I mean, I'm one of his senior employees. A trusted colleague.'

'Does he know she's fourteen?'

'Yes, of course he . . .' Ezra tried to recall conversations. An introduction. 'I don't know, though. I'm really not sure.'

'Maybe he genuinely assumed she was sixteen.' Sheena put her empty mug on the bedside table, and got up, gathering her hair as she did so.

'But don't you see?' Ezra demanded. 'How can I look him in the eye?'

Sheena stepped over to her dresser. She took a hair grip and clipped it into her hair. She reached for another, then stopped. Her hand hovered in mid-air for a moment. Sheena turned back to face her husband. 'Oh, I do see,' she said, staring at Ezra. Her left hand still held a hank of hair behind her head. 'Yes. Oh, I'm sorry. Of course. I'm so stupid.'

'Look, Sheena —'

'It's not about Blaise. It's about you.'

'No,' Ezra said, loudly.

'Ez, sweetheart, I can see the problem. My God, of course. I'm sorry. How can you show your face?'

'This is about Blaise, Sheena!'

'There's no need to yell. I understand. You're right. You should have stopped it. Interrupted. Yes! I'm sorry.' Sheena shook her head. 'You should have broken the bloody door down.'

'Sheena, we're talking about molestation, interference —'

'He would have respected that, I don't doubt.' Sheena emitted a brief snort of laughter. 'I haven't even met the man, yet I don't doubt that. Isn't that weird?'

Ezra hurled the tepid contents of the full mug he'd been holding. The brown liquid streamed towards his wife. Most of it struck her around the chest and soaked into her white bathrobe. The rest splashed across the duvet, on the carpet; some drops up into her

388

face. 'It's not about me,' Ezra said. 'Or him. Who gives a fuck about him?'

Sheena gaped at Ezra, open-mouthed. Drops of cold tea dripped from her hair, her chin. 'Did you just throw that at me?' she asked.

'Our daughter,' Ezra said. 'Are you some kind of monster? Don't you care about Blaise?'

Sheena turned to her dresser. She seemed to be looking for something, as if the next lines of her script were secreted there. Having scanned them, she turned back, her eyes bright. 'You weak bastard,' she said. 'You come back here blubbing. What do you want me to say? Well, I'm saying it. Yes, you should have intervened.'

'But not for Blaise?' Ezra could feel his voice creaking, and sensed that he was close to tears again. He closed his eyes and shook his head. He was unable to look at Sheena, to accept how little he knew her. 'You heartless . . .'

Sheena pulled a tissue from the pocket of her dressing-gown, and wiped her face. 'Yes, for Blaise, then, if you like,' she said, in a tired voice. 'I don't care. You have it however you like. For Blaise. Yes. That's fine.'

How was it possible, Ezra wondered, to live so long so close to someone, and know them so little?

'It's like you held back, last night, in that hotel, the same way you do with me. You know something, Ezra? You want to know? I'll tell you. You've never once in all these years given me a good fuck. Do you realise that? Not once.'

'Is that right?' Ezra asked. He smiled a thin-lipped smile at her. 'That's all you've ever needed.'

'A man who won't hold back. Who doesn't think I'll break up, I'll fall apart, if he lets himself go. Who can do it and just keep doing it until I've had enough. Is that so much to ask? A man without caution.' Sheena began to pace the area between her dresser and the bed as she spoke. 'A man unafraid of what he does.' She alternated between looking intently at Ezra and peering wildly around her, as if not wanting to look at him, resenting it when she did, but then unable to fix on anything else.

'So why don't you get some other man to do what you want.'

It seemed like what Ezra said had shocked Sheena, because it made her suddenly focus on him. 'Are you serious?' she asked. She emitted a brief, theatrical kind of laugh, dismissive of any innocence he might attempt to pretend to. 'You can't seriously expect me to believe you don't know.'

Maybe it was the colour draining from his face, an open target. Maybe it was the drops of cold tea still in her hair. Maybe she believed Ezra and maybe she didn't, but now Sheena let him have it: the time it began, when Hector was small and she realised it was something she couldn't bear to live the rest of her life without; the names of strangers Ezra had never met; the discovery that she could have it without it interfering with her family. Ezra remained kneeling on the bed, his head bowed. It was difficult for Sheena to conclude. A way eventually occurred to her.

'You should try it,' she said.

However often afterwards Ezra reconsidered that moment, he would never accept that he decided to say anything. He simply heard his own voice, and Sheena heard it too. 'Ask Minty,' he suggested in a hoarse whisper.

When she struck him, her open palm on the side of his head, it felt to Ezra like the most generous gift. Sheena gave him permission to defend himself. Ezra sprang off the bed and grabbed her wrists, twisting and squeezing them tight to her body then half-picking her up and dragging her into the bathroom. Sheena struggled, but Ezra was surprised by how much stronger than her he was. The restriction upon his limbs imposed by the gallabea was a greater obstacle than Sheena's resistance. He pulled her into the shower cubicle and dropped her there, and turned on the cold water, and stood at the threshold, pushing Sheena back when she tried to escape. She was crying, but the water would wash away her tears. Finally, Ezra left her there, and walked back to the bedroom, pulling the wet gown over his head. He sat on the end of the bed, naked, breathing hard. Well, here we are, he reckoned. This is where we are. He looked up, and saw Louie standing in the doorway. Ezra got up, and walked towards him, but the boy turned and ran off along the corridor.

Ezra closed the door. Here we are, he thought. This is who we are.

20

The Raj Cuisine

September 2004

The following summer, the unsettled weather was a dire contrast to the heatwave of 2003. Showers and depressed temperatures in June gave way to strong winds and heavy rain in July. August was a month of cold and thunder. Only in September did a weak sun manage to divulge a little warmth into the shortening days. One Sunday evening in a house on Bainton Road, Minty Carlyle carried a lemon meringue pie she'd made through to the dining-room where Simon was telling a story, which had already taken up most of the meal, to the guests he'd invited: Simon and Ian and Dan's new tennis partner and his wife.

'Actually, we're not married,' the woman had said, as Simon attempted to effect introductions when they arrived. 'We're partners.'

'Of course,' Simon had said. 'We're all partners now. Business partners, tennis partners, therapy partners. Marriage may be over, but we can't stop partnering.'

They'd chuckled in the hallway, as Simon took their coats, though it wasn't funny, but even so Simon, encouraged, hung the man's coat on an imaginary nail on the wall and turned away: the coat fainted to the floor, Simon hammed a dramatic double take, and the men broke up with laughter.

'He does that at the tennis court,' the man told the woman, with apparent admiration. 'Hangs his tracksuit top on a nonexistent hook. Cracks me up every time.'

'Did I tell you, Minty?' Simon asked. 'Bill's a bloody good player. A lot better than Ezra, actually.' He turned to their guests. 'Always thought he was a better player than the rest of us. Bloody annoying.'

'When we all know you were,' the man said, jabbing his finger towards Simon's chest, and the two of them chuckled again.

Simon told more of the story. Minty cut the lemon meringue. The woman asked, 'So what happened to the parents? How did they . . . ?'

'Oh, they separated within, what, days, Minty?' Simon replied. 'Hours.'

'The children live with the mother?' the woman asked.

'The older boy, Hector, lives with his father, actually. Yes, yes, a bit odd.'

'I mean, parents separating is one thing,' the woman said. 'It happens. But the children? That's really breaking up a family.'

'It's what Hector chose, apparently. He's a quirky little chap,' Simon said. 'Broke Sheena's heart, I'm told.'

'They still live here?' the man asked.

Simon shook his head. 'Sold the house round the corner in Blenheim Orchard. Sheena bought a bigger one on Chalfont Road. Threw herself into the business. Very successful. Full-time nanny for Louie, who's starting at the Squirrel soon. Blaise is a day girl at the High School. She's a remarkable woman, Sheena. Isn't she, Minty? There was something about her in today's paper, actually. Did you see it? I'll find it for you.'

Simon dashed into the sitting-room. Minty served portions of the pie to her guests. 'Cream or custard?' she offered. What were their names again? Joan or June, and he was Bob, wasn't he? Or did Simon call him Bert? How they'd enjoyed the story, and were willing to slurp every last drop that Simon could milk from it. The man shook his head sadly at each salacious exaggeration of Blaise's adventure that Simon provided; he took off his glasses and rubbed his eyes and said, 'How can you tell nowadays? Look at them. How can you tell how old they are?' The woman seemed more intent on perceiving the story as a detective mystery, one that with sufficient concentration she might solve.

Simon returned with the business section of the Sunday paper, opened and folded. 'There you go,' he said, handing the newspaper to the woman. 'Not a very good picture of Sheena, I'm afraid. She looks a lot younger than that in real life. A brief article but it gives you an idea of how well she's doing, right? Franchising their idea here, there and everywhere.'

The woman nodded, and passed the newspaper to her husband. 'And the father?' she asked. 'Ezra. Where's he, Simon?'

'He moved back into his father's house in Dorset.'

'Wiltshire,' Minty corrected him.

'Exactly. Moved back in with his old man. Who promptly died, earlier this year. Or maybe the end of last. Yes, leaving Ezra with the house. What he does there I have no idea. Not a lot, right?'

This question was lobbed in Minty's general direction. She chose to ignore it. The man, Bill or Bob, slung the paper on to the window seat behind him. 'What's wrong with the man having custody?' he asked no one in particular, though Minty heard a trace of petulance in his voice that suggested echoes of other conversations that might have taken place between him and his partner. Maybe he'd had an earlier marriage.

The woman turned to Minty and said, 'Men. When they could wriggle out of paying childcare they forgot their kids. Now they're forced to pay up, they want to see them all the time.'

'All I'm saying is,' the man said, 'if you have to have single parents, men can do it just as well as women. That's all I'm saying. But what intrigues me,' he added, 'is the question of how pre-meditated it was. A girl of that age? It's worrying. Don't forget our Ruby is just turned twelve. I mean, did she plan it?'

'That's the sort of question you'd have to ask her,' Simon said.

'Who's to say you'd get a straight answer?' June or Jane said.

'Teenage girls are furiously manipulative. She might well not have known herself.'

'That,' Simon said. He swallowed a mouthful of pie. 'Is a very good point. Equally: was it premeditated on Kuuzik's part? What happened has got out, round the company; people were there, after all, and even if Ezra slipped quietly out of the hotel, people still asked why he left early. There have been, apparently.' Simon forked and then fed himself another slice of the lemon meringue. He chewed, and swallowed half a mouthful, and said, 'Rumours.'

Simon paused, and ate again, leaving the last word of his sentence dangling like a worm for Rob and Jean, with their greedy faces, to ogle. How Simon was relishing this, telling these strangers the lurid domestic saga of their supposed best friends; he liked this role, Minty reckoned, even more than that of a buffoon.

'Rumours?' the man asked. 'Of what?'

'That he'd done it before.'

'Kuuzik? With girls?' asked the woman. 'Really?'

'That's the hearsay, apparently. The reason that his company have shifted him from continent to continent. I've not heard of any proof. But who knows?'

'The ones who get away with it,' the woman said, and then she seemed to mime a spasm of panic. 'It makes me shudder,' she told Minty.

'If the Pepins had pressed charges,' Simon continued, 'something might have come out. Maybe he was on police files in Germany.'

'Or Canada,' the woman said, nodding intelligently.

'But the girl, Simon,' said the man. 'She sounds like she was smart enough. She must have known what an impossible position seducing his boss would put her father in. What was she thinking?'

Simon sat back, frowning, easing into a sort of professorial posture, as if this were the moment he'd been waiting for, when he would deliver the words they might really find it worth listening hard to. 'I rather lean towards the idea,' he said, 'of the child as the nemesis of her parent. Because Ezra, her father, was a terribly conflicted chap, you see. He did this job he hated. He was a failed academic. He didn't really know how to give his wife what she wanted. Sheena was, I'm quite sure still is, an extraordinary woman. She pretty much cut ties with her old friends, apart from her business partner, Jill, who keeps us informed. We hardly ever see her, do we, darling? I mean it's sad, but understandable.'

Minty said nothing. She had seen Sheena, just the day before, walking home from town. Minty had come up from behind, and slowed her pace so as not to catch them up. Sheena and Blaise strolled ahead of her along the wide pavement on St Giles, shopping bags swinging, arm in arm in girlish concord.

'You'd want to start afresh,' the woman said.

'Quite,' Simon nodded. 'Remind me to tell you about the protest over there at Frenchay Glade, used to be called the Wasteland, that she got me involved in. Anyway, Ezra, he wasn't really there, somehow, do you know what I mean?'

They ate their dessert, the Carlyles and their guests. The woman picked at hers, breaking off tiny morsels with the corner of her fork, occasionally depositing one on her tongue, but leaving even more pie on her plate than her hostess did. Minty found that it irked her.

'I wonder,' the woman said. 'I'm thinking, assuming we've pieced it together correctly, that there were hours between them leaving the party and Ezra watching her come out of Kuuzik's hotel room. Maybe they did walk around a while. Or talk in his room. Maybe Blaise was hoping all this time that her father would stop her. It was a kind of challenge. To see how much he loved her.'

'I suspect that's exactly what Ezra thinks,' Simon affirmed. 'And must blame himself for. Why did he keep putting off going to Kuuzik's room, through those hours of the night?'

Each of the guests refused Minty's offer of a cigarette, though both insisted they didn't mind if she smoked. Minty put the lighter and unopened pack together on the table beside her place.

'A man could blame himself for the rest of his life,' the man said.

'That would be plain silly,' said the woman.

'But listen,' the man said. 'It just occurred to me. How about, if the girl had a political intention? The project in the Middle East. It was cancelled, was it?'

'Not at all,' Simon said. 'Are you joking, Bill? I'm surprised it doesn't ring any bells. Now that everything's shifting there. DeutscheWasser just got some huge subsidised water contract as part of this European initiative.'

Minty removed the plates from the table, took orders, and returned with a pot of coffee and one of camomile tea. Hers, she'd decided, was a non-speaking part in this odd little play. She would fulfil the obligations of a bit-part player, let Simon act his leading role, performed with such careful relish. He'd told the story a number of times over this past year, but she didn't think he'd had such eager listeners as these two, helping him string it out to fill the entire evening. Avid strangers who would soon go home. She could be patient, and see the evening through.

'Do you mind if I ask,' the man said. 'I mean, okay, it's a bad business. But why exactly did they split up? Was it her? She kicked him out? Or did they both realise at the same time their relationship was untenable, or what?'

'I believe it was mutual, Bill,' Simon frowned. 'What happened with Blaise and Kuuzik was the event, the object, that breached their marriage.'

They sipped their coffees and herbal teas in silence. Minty restrained herself. For the first time that evening she wanted suddenly, forcefully, to join in. Because they didn't split, for Christ's sake, it was so lazy to say that. 'They broke up,' we say. 'It's sad. They separated. What a shame.' Respectful of the mystery of other people's relationships we spout this decorous crap, because we're too lazy to nail the truth. Ezra left her. They didn't split. He couldn't and wouldn't take it any more, the accommodation he'd made with this woman. For fourteen years. The thing with Blaise was both final straw and revelation: Sheena had no heart. Yes, Ezra had failed to protect their child: a grievous error that had been confessed and might be forgiven. He'd have to live with it. Sheena, however, didn't *want* to protect her daughter, was happy to let Blaise bring, at fourteen, calamity upon herself. Wasn't that a kind of horror? How could Ezra share his life with her any longer?

'Excuse me,' Minty said, grasping her cigarettes and lighter as she rose. 'I'll just be a moment.'

As she walked through the kitchen towards the back door Minty heard Jenny ask, 'And the children, Simon. Those two poor boys. How do they . . . ?'

Minty lit her cigarette and wandered out on to the lawn. The middle of September, and the evening air was cool enough to make her tremble. She held one bare arm across her midriff, clutching the elbow of her other arm.

It must be about ten-thirty by now, Minty reckoned. Soon they'll go, Bill and Jenny, and with any luck Simon will have spent in this evening's performance whatever satisfaction he wished to obtain from having known the Pepins, and will let it rest.

She sucked smoke deep into her lungs and held it there, daring it, urging it, to hurt her. Just last week she'd told Ezra on the phone he had only to say the word and she'd join him, move down there to the cottage, taking Jack with her. Jack and Hector could see out what remained of their childhood with a twin brother, almost, which might make up for being semi-estranged from their own, what with Ed and his scholarship, on which he'd left last week.

What was Ezra doing? Odd jobs, he'd told her, and she could hear the smile in his voice. And he was writing again, he'd added, although he wouldn't tell her what. Ezra, though, would not commit himself, and the days succeeded one another, and she seemed to live and breathe through them. She recalled the party Ezra took her to last year, on her fortieth birthday. It was the happiest day of her life. Really? Happier than your first son's birth? Yes, almost. Kissing Ezra, at last. Admit it. She remembered sitting on a metal girder and asking Ezra why he'd never just done it, gone back there to that village in the rainforest, for however many months it might take to do the research with which he could complete his unfinished thesis. And Ezra saying, 'No, Minty. I can't, don't you see? They'll be gone. Altered. Dead, probably. The day I left I knew I could never go back. Because I was the first contact. Me. I gave them mirrors, tools, the idea of another way of living. I was the virus.'

398

'But it would have happened eventually,' she'd protested, and he'd only laughed; at the inanity of her remark, presumably.

And suddenly Minty Carlyle, standing on the lawn outside her house on Bainton Road, smoking a cigarette while her husband entertained their guests inside, at once Minty understood, with a brittle clarity, that Ezra Pepin neither loved her nor would ever invite her to live with him. She looked up at the dark sky above her, imagined somewhere beyond the clotted clouds a ripe moon, and as if it was from the moon that revelation had fallen she called out to it, 'Yes, all right, you fool, you bloody, bloody fool. But miracles happen here on this earth, don't they?'

Abdul Azam stood in his tiny kiosk in the Raj Cuisine, its eight tables full this evening with a mixture of customers. Young and old. Couples, students, professionals. One of his waiters spiked the carbon of their orders on the counter, en route to the kitchen with the top copy. In his own good time, at his own reliable pace, Abdul poured the drinks that had been asked for, wrote prices beside the dishes requested. He was the eye and the mind, the still point surrounded by urgent provision and convivial din, at the centre of his restaurant.

Abdul's youngest son, Akhmed, had just left. Abdul had sent him home to get a decent night's sleep for school tomorrow, had had to order the boy out of the door, and that was a good sign, one of many lately. It was Akhmed himself who'd volunteered to help cover while Jamal, Abdul's number-one waiter, was back in Bangladesh. Akhmed said he wanted to see with his own eyes what it was exactly his father did; how the business was run, from day to day, and from moment to moment. Abdul's elder sons had never shown the slightest interest, nor his daughters come to that – for which Abdul was grateful. He wanted more for his children than to run a small restaurant, putting on a smile so often for the customers that after twenty, thirty, years you couldn't get it off again, it was there for ever, it was you, you were good old Abdul at the Raj Cuisine, and everybody came to see you.

No, he didn't want that for his sons, that's not why he came to this godforsaken country. That's not why he entered his house after midnight seven days a week, while all his family were sleeping, and got up a few hours later to slip out of the house each morning to go back and clean up the restaurant – why pay other people to do what you could do yourself? – maybe, if he was lucky, being sleepily greeted by the first child up as they blinked their way to the bathroom.

Except that actually that wasn't entirely true, was it? Be honest, Abdul Azam, he told himself. Your children have inherited your capacity for labour. Ishtiaq was often up before you, off on his paper round, and Zenab was in the kitchen setting the bread to rise for her mother, and Yusuf, my goodness, would be beetling across town on his bicycle for prayers at the mosque before school!

Akhmed was the lazy one. He never lifted a finger without being told to, not even for himself, it was a miracle he could be roused to carry his own weight from one room to another. He hadn't even bothered to retain the Bangla he was born with: from the day he started school he spoke English even at home, despite his mother's incomprehension, and nothing Abdul did or threatened to do would budge the little slouchabout. If he forbade him from speaking English, Akhmed merely shrugged and clamped his mouth tight shut.

'Thing is, Akhmed,' Abdul had told him this evening, as the boy was finally ready to leave. 'Thing is this: if you don't want to work hard, don't bother. That what I'm saying. Don't waste my time.'

'No, Dad,' Akhmed replied. 'I won't.'

'I just don't want to waste our time. It's like that.'

The fact was, the business with that no-good English girl by whom the boy was smitten seemed to have given Akhmed a good shake. Having his heart broken bucked him up, made him realise it was no good relying on others, because you had no say in where they might lead you. If you wanted to make something of your life, you had to do it yourself.

What was odd, though, was just how pleased Abdul found himself by his son involving himself all of a sudden, of his own free will, in the business. It wasn't what Abdul thought he wanted, but now that it was happening it gladdened his heart, actually, it really did. He must beware, Abdul told himself, of building false hope on such flimsy foundations. Akhmed may be the least academic of the children – he'd barely got good enough GCSEs to stay on at Cherwell – but still he might change his mind once he'd taken A levels. He was only sixteen – which in this country, at this time, was still young, still fresh and unformed.

The others – his niece Yasmin included, his brother's child they'd brought up with their own – had all gone to university, and maybe after all it didn't matter if the last one were to choose not to. Abdul had made sure they had the opportunity: that was it.

He'd done it through hard work, pure and simple. Anyone of his intelligence and ability could have done it, but he actually had and that was what counted. He was fifty-four years old now, he'd brought up three sons and two daughters and a niece and was seeing them through college to careers and marriages of their own. And if they were more English than Bangladeshi, well, that was the future, and he hoped – he had decided – for good things from it. If they went to the mosque even less often than he did – except for Yusuf, who went much more – well, that was their choice, too, and not a bad one, despite their mother's disappointment.

'Enough blood,' he'd argued with Yusuf just a week or so ago. 'Tell them, your friends, to work. That all what I'm saying.'

And the girls, well, it was incredible what different lives from their mother's lay ahead. Abdul thought back to the young man that he was when he first came to England, the assumptions he brought with him, and he shook his head with incredulity.

And all this was due to his, Abdul Azam's, hard work, that was the only secret. It was like that. No secret at all, really, but to earn the fruits of a life's work took, well, a lifetime.

The reason why work mattered – and he must remember to tell Akhmed this tomorrow – was because it was work that paved the road to the future. It was that simple. That was what it was. The clever people who came to the restaurant were right. There was no Allah who created the world, no God waiting to judge mankind when the last days came. The world is here. There is nothing behind it or above it, no absolute to transcend to. There is only nature around us and ourselves, living our lives together. What is, is, and becomes, and will one day die. And if you didn't work hard, applying every second, every brain cell, every muscle at your mortal disposal, you laid no path forwards. In fact, you slipped back, because the future would carry on without you. You would slip into the past while you were still alive, and then you might as well be dead.

And now, Abdul thought, here was Akhmed eager to learn. It warmed Abdul Azam's heart. Perhaps, he thought, this means that soon I'll be able to renovate the Banbury restaurant, even a little ahead of schedule. The time is coming. I've waited all these years.

Some of the tables had emptied over the last half an hour, but here came a late-night influx. It was almost eleven, and the final screenings of the night were ending over at the Phoenix cinema. In came a group of students, one or two couples, eager to discuss what they'd seen as they ate their kormas and tikka masalas, their bhajis and peshwaris and pilau rice.

And look, here was a single customer. Sometimes they came in, men or very occasionally women who'd watched a film alone. But this one in particular, he came to the restaurant at least once a week. Film Fan, Abdul called him. A tall, earnest young man with round glasses and a thatch of unbrushed hair that once he sat down, always at the takeaway table next to Abdul, you wanted to pat. To reassure him.

Abdul had spotted Film Fan as soon as he entered, and while the young man waited, politely, inside the door, Abdul poured a cold Singha beer. He leaned over his counter, stretched, and placed the glass on the takeaway table just as Sanna escorted Film Fan over. When he reached the table, the young man saw the cool beer waiting for him, and he felt welcomed. He looked at Abdul and he grinned in gratitude, his mouth forming a slightly lopsided shape. That made Abdul smile.

Film Fan took a slow sip of beer, put the glass back down on its mat, and then he began to tell Abdul – who continued pouring other people's drinks and writing prices on bills – about the film he'd seen. Some nonsense concerning a motorbike.

'It's about Che Guevara when he was young,' Film Fan said. He took off his glasses, and wiped them on his shirt. 'It's about the growth of conscience, I suppose,' he said, rubbing his eyes. 'It's really very good, Abdul,' he said, putting his glasses back on. He took another sip of beer, and nodded.

Film Fan would go on to tell Abdul the story, in due course. Also which country it was made in, the names of the actors, and of the director, and how the film compared to his or her earlier work. Abdul had learned a little about the movies from Film Fan, even though he had never in his life stepped inside a cinema. They all came to Abdul, and he listened – though if they asked for advice he was prepared to pass some on. It was only fair. It was a two-way thing. He had so many very clever customers, did Abdul Azam.

Acknowledgements

To The Gregor von Rezzori and Beatrice Monti della Corte Retreat for Writers and Botanists, for a residency in the autumn of 2003, and to Ledig House International Writers' Colony, for a residency in the spring of 2004, boundless gratitude. *Grazie mille*, Beatrice. Ben, Dorothy and Josie: thank you so much.

Amongst the many books that lie behind this one, I should like to record its special debt to *Chronicle of the Guayaki Indians* by Pierre Clastres, translated by Paul Auster.

Thank you Jan Jones, John Banville, Toby Pragasam, Ali Rojob and Dildar Rojob, for information and ideas. Sean Hand for sound advice. The *Oxford Times*, Christopher Gray's columns in particular. Tom Sherry, Co-ordinator and Tutor in English and Creative writing at Ruskin College, Oxford, for employment as well as the example of a tireless, inspiring teacher. Victoria Hobbs and Sara Fisher, at A.M. Heath. Sarah-Jane Forder, and all at Bloomsbury, including Chiki Sarkar, Arzu Tahsin, Mary Morris and Mary Tomlinson; especially, as always, Alexandra Pringle. And Hania, for being here.

A NOTE ON THE AUTHOR

Tim Pears is the author of four previous novels: *In the Place of Fallen Leaves* (which won the Hawthornden Prize and the Ruth Hadden Memorial Award), *In a Land of Plenty*, *A Revolution of the Sun* and *Wake Up*. *In a Land of Plenty* was made into a ten-part BBC TV series. Tim Pears also received the Lannan Award in the USA. He lives in Oxford with his wife and children.

A NOTE ON THE TYPE

The text of this book is set in Linotype Sabon, named after the type founder, Jacques Sabon. It was designed by Jan Tschichold and jointly developed by Linotype, Monotype and Stempel, in response to a need for a typeface to be available in identical form for mechanical hot metal composition and hand composition using foundry type.

Tschichold based his design for Sabon roman on a font engraved by Garamond, and Sabon italic on a font by Granjon. It was first used in 1966 and has proved an enduring modern classic.